"You were married to Daniel O'Toole, despite what he chose to call himself during your marriage."

Revulsion closed Charlotte's throat as it always did when she was forced to confront the fact that she had lived with a terrorist. That she had loved that same terrorist with a passion and intensity she sometimes suspected she would never be able to recapture with another man. She spoke coldly, the only way she could keep her emotions at a safe distance.

"Yes, I was married to O'Toole, but that doesn't mean anything, however much you try to twist facts. O'Toole wanted to hide out for a couple of years, so he invented a character called Riordan Gray and moved to Iowa, where he acted his way through a completely phony life. I was just the unlucky woman in Des Moines who got dragged into playing a supporting role in his performance."

"You're wrong," Rick told her. "I have it from a reliable source that Daniel O'Toole was deeply in love with you. That he bitterly regrets leaving you."

The words hit her like a blow and she responded with disdain. "In case this insight hasn't occurred to you, Mr. Villier, it isn't flattering to know that a murdering son of a bitch is in love with you. Besides, I'd take the information from your informer with a huge grain of salt. Who was your so-called reliable source?"

"Daniel O'Toole," he said.

JASMINE CRESSWELL

DEAD RINGER

MIRA®

ISBN 1-55166-712-6

DEAD RINGER

Visit us at www.mirabooks.com

Printed in U.S.A.

For Jane Jefferson
In celebration of a remarkable life
on her ninetieth birthday

Prologue

At 10:30 p.m. on Christmas night, Charlotte Gray and her husband, Dan, arrived home from her parents' house in West Des Moines. They'd spent the previous eight hours celebrating the holiday with the usual happy-go-lucky crowd of Leone relatives. Her three older brothers had been there, too, along with her sisters-in-law and a cluster of young nieces and nephews. Miscellaneous cousins, part of the sprawling Leone clan scattered across the suburbs of Des Moines, had dropped in to sample Eleanor Leone's famous cookies and to exchange Christmas greetings.

Charlotte and Dan had overdosed on eggnog, played with her nephew Billy's cool new train set and threatened dire punishments for any adult who flipped the hidden switch on Singing Barney's back, thus subjecting everyone to the horrors of yet another squeaky rendition of the "I Love You" song. In the car on the way home, Dan laughingly told Charlotte that there was nothing like a stuffed dinosaur singing about universal love and brotherhood to make him feel homicidal.

Later, she would wonder if he'd been serious.

At 10:33—it took them only a couple of minutes to race upstairs and tear each other's clothes off—Charlotte and Dan tumbled on top of their king-size bed and made passionate love. Then, for good measure, they started over more slowly and made love again. They'd been married less than seven months and they were both still hungry for each other's bodies. Even so, their lovemaking on this special night seemed extraordinary to Charlotte in its tenderness and intensity.

Shortly after midnight, Dan remembered that garbage pickup was scheduled for the early hours of the morning. Charlotte, sated with sex and already half-asleep, groaned and suggested they should forget about garbage until next week. Dan snuggled up against her, then sighed and said that he'd better take care of it. He reminded her that their garbage cans were overflowing with discarded Christmas wrapping and the debris of holiday cooking.

Dropping a kiss on Charlotte's forehead, and pointing out that he was earning major brownie points by freezing his ass off in the cause of trash control, Dan pulled on a pair of jeans, and muttered something rude about Christmas cookies when he couldn't fasten the snap. Then he tugged on the new sweater she'd given him with the polar bear on the front, and trekked downstairs. He looked good in the sweater, Charlotte thought. The dark color brought out the blue in his eyes, and complemented his light brown hair.

Drifting off to sleep almost before Dan left the room, she heard the garage door go up and the clang of garbage cans being dragged across the concrete floor.

Those were the last sounds she ever heard from her husband. Setting the dark green cans tidily on the frozen grass that separated the sidewalk from the road, Riordan Michael Gray, affectionately known as Dan, disappeared into the snowy night, never to be seen again.

One

When Charlotte finally realized Dan hadn't returned to their bed it was 4:00 a.m. on the morning after Christmas. Alarmed, but not yet panicked, she ran downstairs to check on his whereabouts, and discovered the garage door was closed again. Puzzled, she wondered if Dan had decided to tackle some other minor chore and then fallen asleep in his favorite couch-potato chair.

But Dan wasn't in their tiny den, or the living room. Their home was part of a new town house complex, and it was modestly sized with no nooks and crannies. It took very few minutes of searching to reveal that Dan was nowhere in the house or the attached garage, and that his down jacket was missing from its hook by the back door, along with his snowboots. Checking the den for the second time, Charlotte quelled a surge of rising dread. Where could Dan be? Her husband wasn't an athlete, but he wasn't prone to pratfalls, either, although she supposed it was possible he'd encountered a patch of black ice and slipped on the frozen sidewalk.

Refusing to give way to the fear nipping at her heels, she dragged on a ski jacket over a pair of sweats and ventured outside, teeth chattering in the frigid night air of Iowa in winter.

When she could find no trace of her husband in the area that fronted their town house, terror washed over her in a giant wave. My God, where was Dan? Something dreadful must have happened to him while she lay sleeping. Had he suffered a heart attack? Been mugged and left for dead? Stomach heaving, she pushed that awful thought away and started to run up and down the sidewalk, screaming his name, peering behind bushes, expecting to find his limp body beneath every parked car.

She hadn't realized—hadn't cared—how much noise she was making until her neighbors, Alan and Lisa, came out of their town house and tried to lead her back inside. Frantic to find Dan, Charlotte refused their offers of help, pulling away from them and sobbing out Dan's name. In the end, Alan and Lisa had to forcibly restrain her and carry her into their house.

Alan dialed 911 while Charlotte wept onto Lisa's shoulder, rambling incoherently about kidnappers and carjackers and drive-by shootings. Lisa and Alan were sympathetic, or at least not openly skeptical, but the police officers who responded to the emergency call soon pointed out to Charlotte that there was no evidence—none—that her husband had been kidnapped. Or carjacked. Or shot. Or brutalized in any way. Until she started crying out for her husband, nobody had reported hearing any suspicious sounds. No gunshots, no squealing tires, no screams for help had disturbed the peaceful night. The garbage cans still stood neatly on the sidewalk. The icy winter grass betrayed no hint of a struggle. There was no dropped item of clothing.

There was, in fact, no evidence that any crime of any sort had been committed.

Slowly, with a growing sense of incredulity, it dawned on Charlotte that the police believed Dan had grown tired of their marriage and had voluntarily walked away. That he'd gotten up from their bed and literally walked to freedom, deliberately disappearing into the darkness, not even bothering to take his wallet and credit cards with him.

Only the fact that both their cars, her blue Saturn and Dan's new silver Toyota, were parked safely in the garage, provided some slight contradiction of the police theory that Dan had chosen to leave home entirely of his own free will. She did manage to get one of the cops to concede that it was strange her husband had walked into falling snow, with a temperature ten degrees below freezing, when there were two perfectly good cars available for him to use. That, however, was as much of a mystery as the cops were prepared to allow.

The officers promised to put out a state-wide alert for hospitals to be on the look-out for an unidentified male with concussion or memory loss or any other inability to identify himself. Charlotte had the impression that the cops dutifully took down her description of Dan more to pacify her than for any other reason: white male, brown hair worn rather long, grayish-blue eyes, exactly six feet tall, average build. No distinguishing features except a tattoo of a rose on his butt with the name *Julie* written underneath.

The first time she'd seen that tattoo, Dan had grinned and told her no man should be held accountable for acts of sheer folly committed when he was seventeen. And that was all Charlotte had ever known about *Julie*. The niggling thought flashed across her mind that Dan had been awfully good at using humor to turn away questions, but she banished it almost before she had time to register what she was thinking.

At one surreal point in her conversation with the police, Charlotte even grasped the incredible fact that they were considering the possibility that she might have killed Dan herself and disposed of the body in some snow-covered cornfield outside of town. Fortunately both car engines were cold, and there wasn't a spot of blood in the house, or any sign of a struggle. Otherwise Charlotte wondered if she might not have greeted the dawn from the vantage point of a police interrogation room.

As soon as the cops satisfied themselves that she probably hadn't murdered her husband, they left, telling her they'd be in touch once they'd checked the local hospitals. A day later they kept their promise and called to let her know that no unidentified male matching Dan's description had been treated in any hospital in the state of Iowa over the preceding twenty-four hours.

If not for the fact that her father was a successful building contractor, a fixture in the local community for more than thirty-five years, Charlotte suspected that would have been the end of any police interest in Dan's disappearance. The cops would have filed a Missing Person's report and turned their attention to more urgent business, at least until the next time an unidentified dead body turned up. But Chuck Leone was a councilman and just a bit too important to ignore, so the police handed the case over to a couple of detectives, and promised Chuck that they would come out to interview his daughter in depth if seventy-two hours passed and there was no word from Dan.

Charlotte's parents tried to persuade her to come and stay with them while they waited for news, but she was adamant in her refusal. Even though each hour passed without producing any trace of her missing husband, she still expected to pick up the phone at any minute and hear kidnappers delivering a ransom demand. She couldn't understand why nobody seemed to concede how important it was for her to stay close to home, right by the phone, so that she could rescue Dan from whatever disaster must have befallen him.

In response to her frantic plea, her father agreed that when the ransom demand came through, he would help her to raise the necessary money. Despite the fog of misery that blurred her grasp of other people's emotions, Charlotte realized that her father didn't believe he would ever have to make good on his promise.

Her family and friends weren't quite as obvious as the police in voicing their skepticism, but as day faded into night and back to day again, they tried to probe gently to discover if there were any stresses in her marriage, any hidden reason why Dan might choose to walk away from a relationship that had seemed so superficially perfect.

Charlotte could barely wrap her mind around the questions, let alone provide answers. She knew with every fiber of her being that she and Dan had loved each other and that they'd been blissfully happy in their life together. Therefore, Charlotte knew he couldn't have left the marriage voluntarily. Therefore it followed logically that he must be a prisoner somewhere. From her perspective it was quite simple. She and Dan were madly in love, which meant Dan had been forced to leave home against his will. He was being held in a basement dungeon, unable to communicate with her. There was absolutely no other way to explain his absence.

Since Charlotte refused to leave her house, her parents, protective as always of their youngest child and only daughter, quietly instituted a system whereby they made sure she was never alone. She told her brothers that she didn't need baby-sitting but, insofar as she could feel anything beyond terror over Dan's disappearance, she was grateful that they didn't listen, and that at least one member of her exuberant, interfering, loving family was always on hand, doing their best to keep her from flying apart at the seams. It was good to know that in a world gone mad, her family was the same solid anchor it had always been.

Another night passed in a blur of sleepless torment. When the seventy-two hour mark had come and gone, a detective called to make an appointment to come out to interview her with his partner. Charlotte waited for the cops to arrive, trying not to jump out of her skin in the process.

Her mother, Eleanor, had failed to persuade Charlotte to eat any breakfast, but she hadn't given up hope and kept popping into the living room to offer bagels, or cornflakes, or scrambled eggs. Charlotte had finally agreed to drink something, simply to put her mom out of her misery. Now Eleanor was puttering around the small kitchen, trying to maintain the illusion that preparing a pot of Charlotte's favorite Constant Comment tea would somehow set the world magically to rights.

Her father, Chuck, wasn't quite as good at pretending. He sat in the leather armchair—Dan's chair—unable to disguise the fact that he hadn't a clue what to do or say next to comfort her. His hands, gnarled and arthritic from years of work on building sites, rested awkwardly in his lap. He'd always been a man who found deeds easier than words, and for the past few days, words seemed to have deserted him completely.

A knock at the front door made them both jump. Chuck, relieved to have a chore, sprang up and returned to the living room, bringing two middle-aged men with him. The men introduced themselves as Detective Rob Wexler and Detective Sergeant Hank Diebold.

What kind of a name was Hank? Charlotte thought wildly. Nobody was called Hank anymore. After introducing himself, Hank didn't seem to have much to say, even though he was presumably the senior officer. He retreated to a corner of the living room and watched the proceedings in a silence Charlotte found nerve-racking. But then, for the past three days, she'd found almost everything nerve-racking. Having spent the first thirty years of her life as the beloved daughter of two good people who'd stayed happily married to each other for forty-one years, she wasn't well-prepared for marrying a husband who up and vanished six months after the wedding.

Detective Rob Wexler was short and overweight

with a bristling mustache. He reminded Charlotte of Hercule Poirot, and she wanted to laugh with Dan about how old-fashioned the guy's handlebar mustache and slicked-down hair looked.

Except that Dan wasn't available to share the joke. Charlotte fought a fresh wave of panic—panic that curdled into a feeling of nausea, an unwelcome counterpart to the headache that had been throbbing and pounding at her temples ever since she woke up and found that her husband had slipped away into the ether.

"We're sorry to bother you, Mrs. Gray." Detective Wexler didn't manage to inject much sincerity into his disclaimer. "I know how upset you must be by what's happened."

"I'm upset that nobody seems to be making any serious effort to find my husband." Charlotte tried to stop pacing and found that she couldn't. It was as if her legs functioned on some nonstop motion command from a part of her brain that refused to switch off. "I know what everyone at police headquarters thinks, but there's no reason why Dan would have left home voluntarily. We weren't unhappy together. We didn't have a fight. I don't understand why nobody except me believes he's been kidnapped, or…or worse."

She was at the point where she was baffled enough to consider anything, up to and including the possibility that Dan had been abducted by aliens. Being sucked up into an intergalactic spaceship seemed a lot more credible than the alternative, which was that Dan had *chosen* to leave her. He loved her, she loved him. She would never, ever believe that he'd walked out on her.

"Aside from the fact that there was no evidence of a struggle, your husband isn't the sort of victim who gets kidnapped, Mrs. Gray. Nowadays, in this country, kidnapping is usually a sexual crime, not a way for criminals to raise money. And kidnappers go after kids, not adult men."

"You're talking generalities, Detective. This is a specific case. I'm Dan's wife, and I'm telling you he had no reason to leave home. None. Therefore, he must have been the victim of some sort of foul play, whatever your statistics say about missing persons. The FBI needs to start a nationwide hunt for my husband right away. Time isn't on our side and I want Dan home again." She fought to prevent the catch in her voice turning into tears.

"The FBI is a tad busy these days." Detective Wexler spoke with the sort of false patience people employ for talking to the mentally challenged. "We need to be sure your husband's been kidnapped before we ask them to take a team away from the hunt for Al Qaeda terrorists." He turned to a fresh page in his notebook. "Since you *are* the person who knows Dan best, Mrs. Gray, perhaps you could give us some details about his background. Some leads for us to follow as to where you believe he might have gone."

Charlotte bit her lip to prevent herself from yelling that since she'd just explained that Dan hadn't gone anywhere of his own free will, what the hell did it matter about his background. They weren't going to find him attending his high school reunion, or hanging out with one of his stepsiblings. Why did officialdom find the concept of unwilling departure so hard to accept?

Her mother came in at that moment, carrying a tray of refreshments, and Charlotte poured herself some tea. She didn't take a cookie, though. Even the sight of food made her stomach spew acid. She always felt cold these days, and she wrapped her hands around the warmth of the pottery mug, using the interruption to get her emotions back under some sort of control.

"Dan was born in California," she said, when everyone had thanked Eleanor and helped themselves to drinks. "His parents were divorced soon after he was born, and his father died a few years later."

"Do you know how his father died?"

"Yes, he died in Vietnam. He was an air force fighter pilot and one of the last combat deaths of the war. Dan always said how much he missed growing up without his dad."

"Still, your husband must have been proud of his father."

"He was. Although I guess he resented the fact that he lost his dad fighting in a war nobody understood and not many people supported." Charlotte showed the detective the silver-framed photo of Dan's father that stood in a place of honor on the mantelpiece over the fireplace.

Wexler walked across the room to show his colleague the photo. Hank Diebold studied it carefully, but remained silent. "Does your husband look like his father?" Wexler asked, returning the photo to the mantel.

Charlotte reflected for a moment. "They had the same basic coloring, and they both have regular features. Yes, I guess there's some similarity. But you can see for yourself." She gestured to their wedding photo standing on a small side table, although she couldn't bear to turn and look herself. "That's my favorite picture of Dan."

The detectives both studied the photo in silence, and Eleanor spoke for the first time since helping everyone to tea. "As you can see, our son-in-law was…is…a really nice-looking young man," she said. "Not movie-star handsome, but nice-looking. Although I wouldn't say that Dan had any very noticeable features. Nothing like a wide mouth, or bushy eyebrows, if you know what I mean. His features are very regular, don't you think, Detective?"

Wexler murmured a polite agreement that Dan was good-looking and, setting the wedding photo back on the side table, asked Charlotte if her mother-in-law had remarried. Charlotte explained that Dan's mother had remarried several times and had two children in addition to Dan, each with different husbands.

"Her latest husband is a sheep farmer in New Zealand," Charlotte added. "Dan's mother emigrated to New Zealand about ten years ago, I believe, taking both of her other children with her. They're quite a bit younger than Dan and were still high school age when his mother left the States."

Wexler swallowed a bite of Christmas cookie before responding. "So I'm guessing your husband isn't very close to his family. Have you alerted your mother-in-law to the fact that her son is missing?"

"I sent her an e-mail," Charlotte said. "She hasn't responded yet. Unfortunately, based on my past experience, she sometimes doesn't check her e-mail for four or five days at a stretch."

"Was there some reason you didn't choose to phone your mother-in-law with the news?"

"I'm not sure of her phone number." Charlotte was embarrassed by the admission. "I always kept in touch with Dan's mother by e-mail, not by phone. Dan used to call her occasionally—in fact, he called her on Christmas Eve—but I never made a note of the number, and directory assistance couldn't find the listing even though I told them it was an emergency."

"I see." Wexler managed to make it sound as if he didn't see at all. "Your husband probably had his mother's number written down somewhere. It's hard to remember all those codes you have to dial to reach a foreign country. Have you looked for your husband's address book since he left?"

There it was again. Since Dan *left*. Charlotte gritted her teeth at the detective's turn of phrase, but managed to answer calmly enough. "Dan's address book was the first place I checked. I searched his computer, too. He kept a lot of his records there, rather than on paper." She shrugged, not quite managing to make the gesture casual. "The number isn't anywhere I can find. Dan must have known it by heart." In fact, the phone numbers that were in Dan's address book had all been for friends and business acquaintances in the Des Moines area. Recent numbers for recent friends, with no links to the past.

"I see." Wexler brushed cookie crumbs from his mustache. "How about your mother-in-law's mailing address? Did you find that?"

"No. But I know their sheep station is somewhere

near Canterbury, which is one of the biggest towns in the South Island.''

"How about your mother-in-law's new married name? Do you at least know that?"

"It's Mary Oliver. Her current husband is Walter Oliver, but I've never really spoken to him."

Wexler sent her a speculative look. "Haven't you met your husband's parents, Mrs. Gray? Didn't your mother-in-law come over from New Zealand for the wedding?"

"No." Charlotte felt her cheeks flame. Why was she suddenly feeling so defensive, for heaven's sake? New Zealand was eleven thousand miles away, and Wexler himself had suggested that Dan wasn't likely to be close to his family. Why would he be, after a childhood of constantly changing stepfathers, and homes that rarely lasted more than a year or two in the same location?

"Dan's mother made a video, apologizing for not coming to the wedding and sending us her very best wishes. I guess since she's been married so many times, weddings aren't a big deal for her. Besides, she and her husband were in the middle of a major renovation of their house and the timing didn't work for them." Charlotte felt compelled to justify her mother-in-law's absence although, truth be told, she'd been hurt by Mary's refusal to attend the wedding. Not for her own sake, but for Dan's.

There had been two hundred and thirty guests at their wedding, two hundred friends and relatives from her side of the family, and thirty friends of Dan's. None of Dan's guests had been relatives, not even a distant cousin, and all his friends had been of recent vintage, part of a circle of acquaintances that had been formed since Dan established his business here in Des Moines.

It was understandable, of course, that her husband wouldn't have kept friends from his early childhood since he'd moved around so much as a kid. But he'd spent four years at Berkeley, and another three years at Yale Law School, and his guest list hadn't included friends from college, or from law school. Except for his best man. Dan had chosen Greg, his roommate from Berkeley, to be his best man, but Greg had canceled at the last minute because of a broken leg, and Dan had been forced to ask Travis—one of Charlotte's favorite cousins and the man who'd introduced them—to pinch hit. Greg had called several times since the wedding and always talked about making a visit to Des Moines so that he could meet the woman his best buddy had married, but somehow the visit had never materialized. So Charlotte had never met a single person who'd known Dan for more than two years, and nobody who'd ever met him before he took up residence in Iowa....

Charlotte didn't like the direction her thoughts were taking, and she was almost relieved when Detective Wexler changed the subject. "Where did your husband work, Mrs. Gray? Was he having any problems at his place of business, as far as you know? Any financial difficulties that might have been weighing on his mind? Any disputes with his bosses?"

"Dan is self-employed," Charlotte said. "He owns a mini-chain of five coffee bars, called Panini, and I'm sure he didn't have any business problems. The opposite, in fact. He was talking about expanding the business and opening new restaurants in another part of the state, maybe in Cedar Falls or one of the other university towns.''

Wexler scribbled a note. He seemed to be taking a lot of them, which had to be a good thing, Charlotte supposed. ''Did you have money of your own, or your family's, invested in your husband's coffee bars, Mrs. Gray?''

''No. Dan had more assets and a higher income than I did when we got married. And he never asked my parents for a penny.'' She wasn't going to allow this weasly little snot of a detective to imply that Dan had married her in order to get access to her parents' money.

''That's true,'' Chuck interjected. ''Dan had been living in Des Moines for over a year before Charlotte met him, and all five coffee bars were already open and doing well long before the two of them decided to marry.''

''Do you know what your husband did before he came to Des Moines, Mrs. Gray? Has he always worked in the restaurant business?''

''No. As a matter of fact, Dan used to be a lawyer. Until a couple of years ago, he was employed as a full-time lobbyist for a consortium of international coffee growers in Washington, D.C.''

Wexler scratched his head. ''That's quite a career change. Lawyer and lobbyist to coffee-shop owner.''

''Yes, it is, but it's easy to explain how it came about.'' Charlotte was anxious to make Wexler understand just how reasonable her husband's abrupt career change had been. ''One day Dan counted up the hours he'd worked during the preceding week and realized that, if he included cocktail parties and re- ceptions, he'd put in ninety hours, plus he hadn't had a day off in almost a month. He resigned from his job the next day, and moved to Iowa a month later.''

"Does he have family in Iowa? Cousins? Uncles? Grandparents? Is that why he chose to set up shop here?''

"No. He just wanted to come to a midwestern town where nobody cared much about Washington politics, or international tariff negotiations, or being seen by the right people at the right parties. Des Moines is a pretty good place to live if you want to maintain a reasonable balance between working hard and having time for the rest of your life.''

Hank Diebold finally spoke, coming out of his cor- ner to return his empty mug to the tea tray. "Have you been in touch with Dan's employees since he left town, Mrs. Gray?''

"No, but my father has. Dad?''

Chuck nodded. "When you're running a family business, things can go to pot damn fast without somebody in charge. So I notified each of the man- agers that Dan was missing, the victim of foul play, and that they should carry on as best they could until we heard from him. If they had problems they couldn't solve, I asked them to call me.''

"And have they called?''

Chuck nodded. "Just once. One of the managers called with a personnel issue—an assistant manager with a drinking problem. It's messy, but nothing that the manager couldn't handle once he'd talked it over with me.''

"Do you agree with your daughter that your son-in-law's business is doing well, Mr. Leone?'' Wexler made a vague flapping gesture, although Charlotte had the impression he wasn't usually a vague sort of man. ''You're an experienced entrepreneur, so you might spot problems that your daughter wouldn't notice.''

Chuck got up and walked over to the window, as if he preferred not to look at his wife and daughter while he answered. ''I asked each of the managers how business had been in the run-up to the holidays, and all five said it had been great. Receipts were up fifty percent over the same time period last year. That was one piece of good news at least, because with the fall-off in the economy since 9/11, I'd been ready to hear there was trouble brewing.''

''So there should be plenty of money in the Panini bank accounts?''

''Yes, there sure should. But we still have to solve the problem of how we're going to meet the next payroll if Dan doesn't come back pretty damn quick. Fortunately, because of the holidays, Dan paid all his employees through January 2nd, plus he already gave them their holiday bonuses. That means we have another few days before we have to worry about how we're going to meet the next payroll.'' He sent his daughter an apologetic glance. ''I should have warned you, sweetie, but I hoped Dan would come back and we wouldn't have to bother ourselves about this.''

Charlotte was ashamed to realize that she hadn't given a moment's thought to such mundane issues as meeting payroll for Dan's employees. Thank goodness her father was more on the ball. As a contractor employing upward of two hundred tradespeople, and subcontracting many more, he had instantly realized the problems that loomed ahead of them.

"Dan has his corporate account for Panini at the same bank we use for our regular checking account," she said to her father. "Can we get permission to write the payroll checks even though Dan isn't here?"

"We can write them," Chuck said dryly. "Trouble is, nobody can sign them. I already put in a call to my lawyer, to ask for advice. With the holidays, though, I've had a hell of a time finding anyone to take my calls. Nobody seems to go into the office between Christmas and New Year. Guess that's no surprise."

"Dan uses Whitaker, Crane and Elmsford as his lawyers," Charlotte said. "And he deals personally with Brody Elmsford, the junior partner. Brody's a good friend of Dan's. We should call him."

Her father nodded. "If you like, I could put in a call to Brody while you're finishing up with the detectives here. I've met Brody a few times and he's a good man. If I can manage to reach him, he'll give us sound advice."

"Tell him we have to find some way to access Panini funds so that we can cut the paychecks for everyone. Call him at home if he isn't in the office. Tell them it's an emergency." Charlotte tried not to sound as panicked as she felt. She silently calculated how much money she would need to meet the next payroll and nearly choked when she came up with a figure in excess of eighty thousand dollars. And that wasn't counting government payroll taxes. No way she could provide that sort of money from her personal funds. She and Dan had less than a thousand bucks in their checking account, and the mortgage payment was due in a week. They had about six thousand or so invested in the stock market, plus the equity in their house, and that was the grand total of their assets, apart from Dan's business. Fortunately they didn't have any credit card debt, but even if she scraped a home equity loan from a sympathetic bank officer on the basis of their good credit record, it was obvious she lacked the resources to meet payroll, even for one pay period.

Her father should have reminded her earlier about the problems of paying Dan's employees, Charlotte thought, then immediately felt guilty for blaming other people for her own problems. Panini was Dan's company and she should have been on top of the payroll issues yesterday, instead of sitting around waiting for her father to do her thinking for her.

Charlotte realized she was flexing and unflexing her hands and tucked them under the flaps of her sweater as she answered another long string of questions from Detective Wexler, most of them totally irrelevant queries about how she'd met Dan, and how long they'd dated before she'd married him.

By the time she was through answering, Wexler's attitude was so carefully noncommittal that she began to feel as if there was something suspicious about the fact that she'd met Dan at a party thrown by her cousin, Travis, and that they'd been married a mere five months later. Good grief, she had been thirty years old, and Dan had been thirty-five. Definitely old enough to know that their relationship was something special and that they wanted to spend the rest of their lives together. She'd dated more than enough frogs to recognize her prince when she found him.

Her father returned to the living room and Charlotte knew right away that something was wrong. "What is it, Dad? Did you reach Brody?"

"Yes, I reached him." Chuck's voice was gruff.

"What did he say?" Charlotte had the unnerving sensation that the top of her head was about to blow off. "Dad, tell me!"

"He said that Dan came in to meet with him two days before Christmas." Her father and mother exchanged glances, one of those secret married glances that outsiders couldn't interpret. Her father drew in a visibly unsteady breath. "Apparently when Dan arrived at Brody's office, he had already prepared a document signing his business over to you. Dan's trained as a lawyer, so I guess he knew what he had to say to make everything legal. He just wanted Brody to double-check that he'd covered all the bases, and then he got the documents notarized right there and then. The handover of Panini's ownership was effective the moment he signed those papers."

Charlotte was stupefied. "Two days before Christmas?" she said. "Dan signed Panini over to me two days *before* Christmas?"

Chuck nodded curtly. "Naturally, Brody Elmsford assumed you were aware of what was going on. In fact, Dan specifically told him that this was the first step in a mutually-agreed-upon divorce proceeding. Dan's given you full power of attorney, so you'll be able to access Panini's bank accounts. There's not going to be any problem with payroll." Her father's voice roughened with barely suppressed anger. "At least the bastard didn't walk out on his employees."

"But I don't understand." The air rushed out of Charlotte's lungs in a painful whoosh, so that she was panting as she spoke. "What did Brody mean about a divorce proceeding? And why would Dan do something as strange as handing Panini over to me? It's his business, not mine. I'm an architect, for heaven's sake. Dan knows I have no interest in the restaurant business. Why would he sign it over to me? That's crazy!"

Chuck exchanged another glance with his wife, this one easily identified as embarrassed and miserable. "I'm sorry, Charlie, but I guess handing the business over to you was Dan's way of compensating you for ending the marriage."

"Ending the marriage?" Like a Furbie toy, she seemed capable of nothing except parroting back her father's words. *"Compensating me?"* Like she had to be paid for sexual and housekeeping services rendered!

Chuck took her hands into his, patting them with awkward affection. "Sweetie, I'm real sorry, but I have to say this news from the lawyers changes everything. It looks like the police have been right all along and Dan wasn't abducted. Based on the arrangements he made with his lawyer, we have to accept Dan knew several days before Christmas that he was going to be leaving town. He walked out on you, Charlotte. The bastard left you."

Two

Try as she might, Charlotte's exhausted brain couldn't find any way to assimilate the information that Dan had left her without a single warning word. That he was planning to *divorce* her, for Christ's sake! She and Dan loved each other. He couldn't possibly have left of his own free will. She felt like a car engine trying to respond to a driver who was simultaneously pressing the brakes and the accelerator. Since there was no way to make sense of such contradictions, the engine had no choice but to blow up.

The surge of conflicting emotions built to such an incredible level of rage and betrayal that Charlotte turned and walked out of the room before she said or did something unforgivable. How could she possibly accept that Dan had been making preparations to leave her in the week before Christmas? There had to be a mistake, there *had* to be! If she hadn't known Brody so well, she would have found it easier to believe the lawyer was lying than that Dan had hired him to execute documents turning his business assets over to her as the first step in a divorce proceeding.

She walked into her bedroom and stared blindly at the king-size bed, seeing Dan as he had been that last night, his eyes blazing with passion, his hands gentle with love. The cops might suspect that her short-lived marriage had been on the rocks and that the stresses of the holiday season had culminated in an explosive argument, but she knew the truth. If Dan had been planning to leave, why had he held her in his arms and whispered how much he loved her and what a miracle it was that he'd found her? Was she really supposed to believe that Dan had spent the afternoon helping Billy build a village for his train set and playing peekaboo with baby Emma, while secretly planning to take out the trash and walk away from their life together? How could she weave such an extraordinary fact into the fabric of her marriage and come up with any pattern that made sense?

She couldn't. So instead of trying to understand the incomprehensible, Charlotte stood at the window and stared out at the skeletal branches of the oak tree in her neighbor's yard, and at the snow sleeting down in a dank, icy curtain, her brain empty of any thoughts at all.

Her mother came and put her arm around Charlotte's shoulders, murmuring something that was supposed to be comforting, but Charlotte seemed to have lost the capacity to grasp meaning, and Eleanor's words carried no more reassurance than the droning of a bee. She knew her mother meant to be kind, though, so Charlotte didn't move away, just stood in a frozen block while the words *divorce proceeding* thrummed inside her head.

She was vaguely aware of her father talking to the detectives, and the sound of heavy masculine feet climbing the stairs. She had no interest in why they were coming upstairs, and didn't attempt to listen to what they were discussing.

Her father came into the bedroom and asked her something. Something about searching the den, and checking Dan's hairbrush. He clearly expected her to reply, so she mumbled that he should do whatever seemed best.

Charlotte returned to her thoughts. If Dan truly had told the lawyer he was initiating a divorce proceeding, then their life together had been a meaningless charade. If he had been so desperately unhappy in their marriage, she had to wonder if she understood anything at all about their marriage. Not to mention how little she understood love, or trust, or what the hell she'd been doing with her life for the past year. In fact, Charlotte decided, if Dan had truly wanted a divorce, she could no longer trust her own judgment about anything. Every detail of her life was changed in shape and configuration as a result of being viewed through a new lens.

Her father disappeared downstairs with one of the detectives. The other went into the bathroom.

"Come on, honey," her mother said, giving her a squeeze. "There's no point in standing around up here, Charlotte. Come down to the kitchen and help me put all those teacups into the dishwasher. Better to have busy hands while you take all this in. I've always found that housework is a good way to take your mind off your problems."

Charlotte obediently followed her mother down to the kitchen, although the idea of washing cups as a substitute for worrying about Dan would have been laughable in other circumstances. She found a tin with a picture of Santa and stored the leftover cookies, then stood at the sink rinsing mugs, letting her mother's chatter pour over her until the detectives came to take their leave. They hadn't stayed long. Or perhaps they had. Charlotte wasn't sure. Her concept of time was as blurred as everything else right now. Anyway, the detectives eventually came into the kitchen and said goodbye and promised they would be in touch.

To say what? Charlotte thought wildly. That they'd found her husband shacked up in a motel with his latest bimbo? That Dan had sent a message saying he hoped she would find ownership of five coffee bars adequate *compensation* for six months of marriage and a lifetime of broken promises?

Her father returned from escorting the detectives to the front door and sat beside her at the kitchen table, covering her hands with his. His palms were leathery, and his many calluses scratched against her knuckles. Honest evidence of honest hard work. For some reason, that made her want to cry. She didn't cry, though. Crying, Charlotte was vaguely aware, was a luxury that she couldn't afford to indulge in because once she started to weep, she would never stop.

Her father spoke gruffly, which was always his way when he was moved. "It was nothing you did, Charlotte, honey. You were everything a wife should be. It was Dan who deceived you. He deceived all of us. God almighty, I was really wrong about that guy."

Did it make a difference if your heart was breaking over a man who wasn't worthy of it? From Charlotte's perspective, it sure didn't feel like it. "I understand, Dad." She didn't understand, of course. She didn't understand anything anymore.

"I can't bear to see you looking like this," her mother said softly, stroking a lock of hair out of Charlotte's eyes. "Come home with us, baby. Let us take care of you for a while."

She wasn't a baby. She was an adult woman, even if she did seem to have the judgment powers of a two-year-old where men and marriage were concerned. Charlotte felt a stabbing pain in her side, and a sudden, intense desire to be alone. The pain was almost welcome in contrast to her previous suffocating numbness. Wasn't the final and darkest circle of hell supposed to be a pit so cold and drained of feeling that even hellfire couldn't burn? Pain, she reflected, was actually better than that terrible numbness.

Charlotte took a short, unsteady breath. "No, thanks, Mom. I'd prefer to stay here. Really. This is my home, and I have to learn to cope with...with my new situation."

Her parents tried to change her mind, but it was a relief to have a plan of action, even if the plan involved nothing more than being left alone to wallow in her misery, and Charlotte was adamant in her refusal. Eventually, with great reluctance, her parents put on their coats and gloves and scarves and drove home, leaving her to the echoing silence of the house she had once shared with Dan.

Three

Later, when Charlotte looked back, she could never recall the next three weeks with any clarity. She was vaguely aware that Des Moines suffered two bouts of unusually severe weather, with a snowstorm, followed by a period of intense cold, crowned by an ice storm that left fifty thousand residents without electricity. The bitter, dreary weather coincided so perfectly with her bitter, dreary feelings that the weather and her feelings merged to become one and the same. Snow and ice and cold outside. Snow and ice and cold inside her heart.

The inclement weather put a halt to almost all building projects, which was fortunate, since Charlotte's powers of concentration had vanished along with her husband. Right now, she suspected that drawing up plans for a kiddie tree house would stretch her skills to the limit. Working on plans for her father's new middle-income housing development in the suburb of Clive was beyond her, although nobody in the office was cruel enough—brave enough?—to confront her with the evidence of her multiple screwups and missed deadlines.

The police made no move to contact her for a week. Then Detective Wexler called and asked permission to come and remove Dan's laptop. He wanted one of the police experts to examine the hard drive, he explained. He also asked for permission to search Dan's office, which was located adjacent to the original Panini restaurant. Charlotte gave her permission, without feeling more than a faint burst of curiosity as to why the cops were suddenly showing signs of interest in Dan's disappearance.

In the last week of January, her state of zombielike calm was finally pierced when Sergeant Hank Diebold telephoned and told her that he would like to make an appointment to meet with her as soon as possible. He had some important news to share with her about her husband.

"You've found Dan?" Charlotte hadn't realized the extent of her despair until she felt the flicker of a tiny flame of hope. Perhaps, after all, it would turn out that Dan had been suffering from some extraordinary brain fever. Perhaps now the fever was cured, or at least being treated, he would come home to her as soon as the hospital released him.

"No, we haven't found your husband, Mrs. Gray. I'm sorry. But we do have some information we'd like to share with you."

The flicker of hope sputtered and died, but Charlotte agreed to speak with the detective later that afternoon, since there was nothing urgent enough to keep her at the office. She went into work each day so that she could pretend her life still had some shape and purpose, and to prevent her family hovering over her with an outpouring of love and concern that had become more onerous as each day passed with no word from Dan. Her career as an architect, which had once seemed so fascinating, now seemed almost intolerably trivial.

Of all the things she didn't understand about the end of her marriage, Charlotte understood Dan's silence least of all. Okay, so he had made up his mind to divorce her, which was mind-blowing in itself. Weren't couples supposed to be unhappy, or constantly fighting, or sexually incompatible before they decided on a divorce? But why had he walked out without a word of explanation? And having left, couldn't he at least pick up the phone or write an e-mail to tell her what had gone wrong? The worry about Dan's silence was only compounded by the fact that his mother had never responded to Charlotte's increasingly frantic messages. And her most recent note had bounced back with a notice that the e-mail address Charlotte had used was no longer valid. The only conclusion Charlotte could reach was that Dan's mother had disappeared along with Dan. Charlotte could think of plenty of explanations as to why that might happen, but she didn't like any of them.

Unlike Sergeant Diebold's previous visit, this time Rob Wexler of the shiny hair and bristling mustache didn't accompany him. Instead Diebold arrived in the company of a tall, lean African American, a man well into middle-age, who moved with the smooth, economical motions of the very fit.

"This is Deputy Director Tremayne Washington," Diebold said, indicating his companion. "He's from the FBI's Counter Terrorism Center and he'll explain to you what we've discovered about your...husband."

There was a definite hesitation in Diebold's voice

before he said the word *husband,* but Charlotte wasn't given many moments to mull over the significance of that tiny pause. The FBI guy was extending his ID for her inspection and she examined it intently. Not that she would have had a clue if it was fake, but at least scrutinizing the shield gave her another few seconds to pretend that she wasn't scared out of her mind about what she was going to hear.

They were going to tell her Dan had gotten a quickie divorce in Vegas, Charlotte decided. No, they'd have told her that over the phone. Maybe he was a bigamist married to six other women. Or maybe he'd undergone a sex change operation and become a woman. Or—

Hank Diebold interrupted her increasingly hysterical train of thought. "May we sit down, Mrs. Gray?"

"Yes, of course. I should have asked if you would like some coffee. Or something cold? A soda?"

"Nothing, thanks." Diebold and Washington both sat down and Charlotte followed suit. Diebold actually looked sympathetic, which seemed an especially bad sign. In fact, nothing about this interview suggested that Diebold or Washington had good news to pass on to her.

"Mrs. Gray, I'll get straight to the point." Tremayne Washington had a deep baritone voice, commanding in its richness. "I expect you recall that when Sergeant Diebold was here a couple of weeks ago, he and his partner asked for your permission to take hairs from your husband's brush or comb, to see if they could find any strands with follicles attached. They informed you that they wanted to run DNA comparison tests for identification purposes."

Stomach heavy with dread, Charlotte murmured an acknowledgment although she had only the vaguest recollection of any such conversation taking place. She'd been in a state that was close to mental fugue for a couple of hours after hearing that Dan had planned to divorce her.

"After their interview with you on December 28, the police here in Des Moines became a little suspicious of the sudden way in which your husband left town without any warning to anyone," Washington said.

"They did?" Charlotte glanced up, her attention caught. "I had the impression the police totally dismissed my fear that Dan had been involved in some sort of terrible accident."

Embarrassment flashed briefly across Washington's features. "The police didn't suspect that harm had come to your husband, Mrs. Gray. They did suspect, though, that he might have been engaged in some form of criminal enterprise. Criminals have more reason than law-abiding folks to quit town without warning, and we found it strange that nobody seemed to know anything about your husband's past."

"Dan wasn't a criminal," Charlotte said hotly. "I lived with him. I know what sort of a man he was, and he didn't have a criminal bone in his body." Her defense of Dan was instinctive. It was also ridiculous, she realized. Far from knowing what sort of a man her husband had been, it was blindingly obvious that she had no clue as to what had really made him tick. Nor could she deny the obvious truth that she'd never met a single person who had known Dan for longer than a couple of years.

Neither man responded immediately, but she felt their reactions. It was as if after weeks of isolation from the world, she could suddenly sense other people's emotions with piercing clarity. She read pity coming from Hank Diebold, and barely controlled impatience coming from Tremayne Washington. Neither reaction was reassuring.

"I think you may know less about your husband's motivations and habits than you believe," Washington said. "The truth is, your husband is a world-class master of deception." He spoke mildly, as if he saw no need for forcefulness when he was utterly confident of his facts. "Let me tell you what *we* have discovered, Mrs. Gray."

"Yes, please do." She gave her words a sarcastic edge, which seemed to be her only defense against sounding pathetic and victimized.

"Detective Rob Wexler managed to lift a clear fingerprint from your husband's hairbrush and the police department here ran an immediate check through the FBI's fingerprint database. That check produced a solid match. However, the match was so shocking, the police wondered if there could be a mistake. So the police requested and received permission to expedite confirmation of your husband's identity through DNA testing at the FBI labs, using the hair follicle they retrieved with your permission from your husband's brush."

Washington was clearly choosing his words with some care. He's covering his ass, Charlotte thought dazedly. He's about to make a criminal case against Dan, and he wants to make sure I agree the evidence they've used was collected legally. She had to swallow two or three times before she could speak. "Are you here to tell me that Dan—" She swallowed again. "That Dan's DNA is on file? That he has a criminal record?"

Washington's expression became even more grim. "More than that, Mrs. Gray. The truth is, I'm here today to ask for your help." He leaned forward, betraying his first hint of urgency. "We have a lot of questions for you, Mrs. Gray, and I hope you'll agree to cooperate with us. Sergeant Diebold is confident, based on his previous interview, that you had no knowledge of your husband's true identity, or his past activities. We've conducted a preliminary background check, and you seem to be a model citizen. We would normally need a much more in-depth security review before telling you what I'm about to reveal, but in view of the urgency of the situation, and in view of your family's three-generation history here in the Des Moines area, we've received permission from the director himself to tell you the truth. I would like your word, however, that nothing I'm about to tell you will be repeated outside the walls of this room."

"But I have to tell my family," Charlotte protested. "I can't keep secrets about Dan from my family. They need to know whatever I know." She was shivering, but she didn't feel cold. In fact, for the first time in weeks, she felt feverishly hot and sweaty.

"No," Agent Washington said flatly. "You are not to discuss what I tell you with anyone. Not your mother, or your father, or any of your brothers, and certainly not with any of your friends or cousins. Do I have your word?"

She hesitated. "Well, yes, I guess so."

"No qualifiers, Mrs. Gray. Yes or no, straight up."

"Yes." Charlotte had no intention of keeping her word. She had to lie to Tremayne Washington, she reasoned, because it was obvious he wouldn't tell her anything unless she did. But this was her husband they were discussing, and nobody from the government had the right to tell her what she could and couldn't reveal to her family about him.

Deputy Director Washington struck her as anything but gullible, but he apparently decided to take her promise at face value. Perhaps he'd already made arrangements to throw her in jail if she broke her word, Charlotte thought, aware that she was teetering on a dangerous knife-edge between hysteria and unnatural calm.

"Sergeant Diebold and I have come here to tell you that we have a perfect match for the DNA samples we took from this house," Washington said without any more preamble. "We've established beyond any reasonable doubt that the man who married you under the name of Riordan Michael Gray is actually a much-wanted international terrorist and criminal whose place of birth is uncertain. He is known to various branches of law enforcement under the name of Daniel O'Toole."

Charlotte laughed, probably astonishing herself at least as much as the two men. It had been a rough few weeks, and her life no longer operated within the safe parameters that had nurtured and protected her for thirty years. But even so, despite everything, her world wasn't crazy enough for her to believe that Dan—her husband!—was a terrorist. Terrorists were religious fanatics who flew planes into buildings.

They weren't men who lived in suburban Des Moines and liked to watch Sunday afternoon football a whole lot more than they liked being dragged to church, let alone the local mosque.

The two law enforcement officials stared at her stony-faced, and waited for her laughter to stop. She gave a final hiccup and drew in a deep, steadying breath. "Look, Mr. Washington, I'm sure you believe what you're saying, but it's ridiculous. Nuts. Insane. Dan is no more a terrorist than I am."

"That's not a very convincing argument, Mrs. Gray. We've spent the past week seriously assessing the possibility that you were working with him."

"You suspect *me* of being a terrorist?" Charlotte sprang up from the sofa. "You can't be serious."

"Deadly serious. And there's no pun intended."

"Then I find your suspicions not only crazy, but offensive in the extreme."

"They weren't meant to be offensive," Washington said calmly. "Sit down, Mrs. Gray. I simply want you to understand that we haven't rushed to conclusions or taken anything at face value. When the DNA match identified your husband as Daniel O'Toole, it struck all of us as strange that he would actually have married you. Why? What possible purpose could he have in infiltrating a well-established family in America's heartland? It was logical to ask ourselves if you might be one of his coconspirators. However, we've assessed that possibility with great thoroughness and rejected it."

The fact that anyone would suspect her of being a terrorist was even more insane than suspecting Dan of the same thing, but this time Charlotte felt not the slightest desire to laugh. On the contrary, she felt an intense longing to close her eyes and wake up again in a new and more rational universe.

Dan, she thought achingly. Dan who had made love like an angel and was suspected by these people of having the soul of a devil.

She must have looked closer to passing out than she'd realized, because Hank Diebold stood up. "I'll get you a glass of water, Mrs. Gray. I'll be right back."

He came back and she took the glass from him with a tight murmur of thanks, the ice chinking against her teeth as she drank. The water was fresh, and her throat parched, but she didn't feel any better when she'd finished drinking, just a little less likely to faint. And right at this moment, she wasn't at all sure that being conscious was a blessing.

Charlotte set down the glass and reluctantly turned to look at the FBI agent. "If this Daniel O'Toole person is so dangerous, then why isn't he in prison?"

"We wish," Washington said simply. "Or better yet, we wish he were dead, so that he could save us all the trouble and expense of a trial. God knows, he's killed enough innocent civilians in pursuit of his cause that he deserves to be executed—"

"No," Charlotte said, holding up her hand in an instinctive gesture to ward off any more revelations. "No, there has to be some mistake." She sprang to her feet because she couldn't sit still and listen to these horrific statements anymore. The man she'd fallen in love with, the man with whom she'd shared all the thousand and one intimacies of married life, was accused of being a cold-blooded killer of innocent people. Law enforcement officials wished he was dead. Her skin felt dirty from the inside out.

She walked over to the window, looking out onto the familiar scene of barren yards, and snow-plowed roads, needing the sight of something mundane to re-orient herself. It was all very well for Agent Washington to suggest that Dan deserved to be executed. He was talking in the abstract, but she had to deal with memories that seemed to have infiltrated from a parallel universe. She had shared Dan's life for almost a year. She'd been his wife for more than six months and enjoyed almost every minute of the time they'd spent together. She'd gone willingly to his bed within a week of meeting him and found the sex exhilarating, wonderful, life-altering. How was it possible that she had sensed no core of darkness within him? How had she lain in the arms of a professional killer and felt nothing but love and passion? How was it possible that she had considered having a child with a man who was willing to murder children for the sake of his cause?

Nausea welled up, the vomit catching in her throat. The only way to control the sickness was by concentrating on the hope that the FBI had made a terrible mistake. They had screwed up with the DNA testing. Dan might be a lowlife who had walked out on their marriage with no warning, but she wouldn't—literally couldn't—believe that Dan had been the monster Agent Washington was portraying. Turning back to face the two silent, watchful men, she repeated her previous statement that there had to have been some error in the identification process.

"There's no mistake, Mrs. Gray." Washington's

mellifluous voice turned flat. "We've been looking for this man for more than three years. He's the brains behind the most extreme and violent breakaway faction of the IRA. He's not only killed dozens of innocent civilians, he's also run a counterfeiting scheme that has severely threatened the security of our national currency. O'Toole laundered millions of fake dollars through Eastern Europe, and in the process provided a chunk of the money that's kept the mainstream IRA army supplied with weapons. Until the tragedy of 9/11, O'Toole was number one on the FBI's Most Wanted list of international terrorists, and he topped similar lists in the U.K., as well as in Eire. Unfortunately, Daniel O'Toole is a master of disguise, so it's been extraordinarily hard to keep track of him. Law enforcement had lost sight of him for almost two years before he resurfaced here."

Hope flared again, a surprisingly sturdy companion that refused to die. "I have dozens of photos of Dan," she said. "Probably hundreds if you count all the wedding pictures. Why would a master of disguise who's on everybody's Most Wanted List allow himself to be photographed so repeatedly and so extensively."

"Because he doesn't care if he's photographed. O'Toole doesn't disguise himself by dyeing his hair a new color, and putting on wire-rimmed glasses," Hank Diebold said. "He's much more subtle and clever than that. He disguises himself by having plastic surgery, which fools computer programs designed to measure bone structures when making identifications. But then he takes the next step and does something even more important than changing his physical appearance: he changes every detail of his daily life.''

''I don't understand what you mean—''

''Most criminals, even the clever ones, disguise themselves by going from blond and fat to dark and thin, but they keep right on smoking a specific brand of cigars, or being fans of the same baseball team they've supported since they were little kids. O'Toole is way too smart for that sort of mistake. He changes his entire lifestyle. Since he spent the past couple of years being a restaurant owner married to a woman in suburban Iowa, you can be sure that by now he's a stevedore working on the Liverpool docks in England. Or he's a wallpaper hanger in San Francisco whose friends are all gay. Or he's providing casual labor on a ranch in Wyoming. We can't even begin to guess where he might have gone or what he might be doing. We only know that whatever environment this man selects, he can blend right in, which makes it nearly impossible to know if there are any constant character traits we should be on the lookout for, much less physical ones.''

Charlotte took another sip of water and wished it were vodka neat. Or poison. Was that what Dan had been doing during their marriage? Throwing himself enthusiastically into the role of yuppie suburban husband, complete with mindlessly devoted wife? ''If you know so little about O'Toole, how come you have his DNA profile on record? He must have been in custody once, so why did you let him go?''

''We didn't let him go, of course. He escaped.'' Washington looked as if he'd bitten into something sour.

"How was that possible? According to you, he was a known terrorist. Aren't terrorists kept under close guard?"

"Yes, when they're in prison. But O'Toole escaped from a hospital in Belfast where he was supposedly too badly wounded to pose a flight risk."

"Are you saying he was able to deceive an entire hospital staff about how badly injured he was?" Charlotte didn't bother to conceal her incredulity.

Washington lifted his shoulders in a gesture of weary resignation. "Seems incredible, I agree, but the doctors swore O'Toole was incapable of walking. That his lung had been pierced by a bullet, and that his life was hanging in the balance. Even so, there was a two-man police guard on duty 24-hours a day in the ICU, as much to prevent assassination by rival political factions as to prevent O'Toole having a miraculous recovery and walking out of the hospital."

"Is that what happened?" Charlotte asked. "He had a miracle cure?"

"There were no miracles," Washington said, his bitterness unmistakable. "Only human error."

"By the hospital?"

"Not really. It was more the police who screwed up. The doctors who certified that O'Toole was on death's door were later determined to be IRA sympathizers. They swore that they'd given their honest medical opinion regarding O'Toole's condition, but it's obvious they'd dramatically overstated the extent of O'Toole's injuries. He'd been in intensive care almost a week, supposedly suffering one near-fatal crisis after another. Then one of the police officers got called away—to confer with one of O'Toole's doctors, no less. That was apparently the signal O'Toole had been waiting for. He overcame the other cop left behind in his room, unlocked the shackles, which were only on one wrist for—quote—medical reasons, and made good his escape.''

Charlotte was almost afraid to ask. ''Did he...kill the guard?''

''No. Which is a bit of a surprise, I guess, because he certainly had killed people with his bare hands in the past. Anyway, despite letting O'Toole escape when they actually had him in custody, the police authorities in Belfast did do one thing right. They ordered a DNA test on their prisoner, and it was taken only a few hours before he escaped.'' A faint glow of approval flickered in Washington's dark brown eyes. ''We're damned lucky they ordered the swab, because it was anything but routine to take DNA samples back then. But the IRA has a long history of falsifying birth certificates and other official records, so the police in Eire and the U.K. have been aware for a long time that it's hard to know exactly who you're dealing with when it comes to terrorists. Luckily for us, they've been building a data base of DNA samples for a lot longer than we have over here.''

Washington didn't seem happy to admit that the FBI was outpaced by its international rivals in at least one area of law enforcement. ''Anyway, since 9/11, we're learning fast that when terrorists have enough aliases, and have traveled using enough different passports and nationalities, it gets to be almost impossible to determine exactly who it is you're dealing with. We don't know where Daniel O'Toole was born, or educated, or why he became such a fanatic supporter of the cause of a united Ireland. We do know he's used both Irish and Canadian passports, as well as British and American ones. Our best guess, in fact, is that O'Toole was actually born in the States. Another case of the expatriate being more fanatical than the native born citizen. However, among all the uncertainties, what we do know for sure is that the man who escaped from the hospital in Belfast, and the man who was living here in this house as your husband, is one and the same person.''

"Why was my…'' She couldn't say the word husband, Charlotte discovered. Which probably didn't matter much, since it was quite likely that Dan wasn't her husband and never had been. Who knew how many other women he might have "married'' during his various incarnations?

"Why was O'Toole imprisoned in Belfast?'' she asked. Dreading Washington's answer, she added, "What had he done, exactly?''

"He'd done plenty,'' Washington said grimly. "O'Toole was—is—the operational leader of the Armagh Army, which is the most violent and fanatical breakaway faction of the IRA, and that's saying something, as you might imagine. Six years ago, under O'Toole's direction, a band of about twenty Armagh Army 'soldiers' mounted an attack on the Craigavon Hotel, which is on the coast of Northern Ireland. Apparently, from what authorities were able to piece together after the event, O'Toole believed he was targeting a group of moderate political leaders. Like most of the terrorist organizations in Northern Ireland, the Armagh Army would like to wipe out any politicians who have a real chance of negotiating a lasting peace.''

"Had he made a mistake about the people he was targeting?'' Charlotte asked.

Washington nodded. ''O'Toole's information about who was meeting in the hotel was wrong. Disastrously wrong for the Armargh Army, as it turned out. We suspect that false intelligence was deliberately planted by the Red Hand Group, which is an organization of Protestant fanatics who are every bit as ruthless and brutal as the Armargh Army. So instead of wiping out a group of unarmed political moderates, the Armargh Army discovered they'd lobbed their grenades into a group of militant fanatics from the Red Hand Army who were primed and waiting for the attack. The Armargh Army soon found itself in a pitched battle, trapped and with no way to escape. More than a dozen people were killed, and another dozen injured, mostly Armargh Army soldiers. Fortunately—for once—none of the victims were innocent bystanders. The British authorities arrested everybody within sight, but since it was the Red Hand boys who'd set the trap, they managed to escape as the British troops moved in to put a stop to the battle. Still, the authorities in Northern Ireland were jubilant when they realized they'd captured Daniel O'Toole.''

If she allowed herself to register that they were talking about the man she'd lived with for the past six months, Charlotte knew she would throw up, or pass out. But if she focused on learning what she could about a stranger called Daniel O'Toole, she could just about absorb what she was hearing.

"How did the authorities in Northern Ireland know

they'd captured Daniel O'Toole?" she asked. "Presumably he didn't identify himself when they took him into custody?"

"Good question." Washington flashed her a glance that was equal parts surprise and approval. Considering that she'd been married to a terrorist without ever noticing anything wrong, he'd probably assumed she was dumber than a rock. A justifiable conclusion, Charlotte reflected wearily. At this moment, she *felt* dumber than a rock.

"O'Toole wasn't talking, which is what you might expect for a thirty-five-year old who'd been fighting for various radical IRA factions since he was fifteen. Besides, O'Toole was genuinely unconscious by the time law enforcement arrived on the scene. Unconscious and bleeding. We know that from doctors whose diagnoses are reliable. But one of the Armagh Army soldiers, a sixteen-year-old kid who had no experience with handling police interrogation, gave away O'Toole's identity. By mistake, of course, but law enforcement in Belfast was absolutely confident the ID was correct."

"And you're one hundred percent confident that there's a match between the DNA sample you took from Dan's hair follicle, and the DNA sample provided by the police in Belfast? I've heard lots of horror stories about problems with the FBI labs."

"Those problems have been fixed," Tremayne Washington said, tight-lipped. "We're one hundred percent positive that Riordan Gray and Daniel O'Toole are the same man. I'm very sorry, Mrs. Gray. There is no possibility of error."

"Don't call me Mrs. Gray. I can't bear it." She

drew in an unsteady breath. "I'm probably not legally married, quite apart from anything else."

"I understand how you feel."

"I'm sure you don't," she said bitterly. "Do you really understand how it feels to believe you're happily married to a good man, and then to wake up one morning and discover that you've been living with a monster?" Not to mention the fact that she had never once noticed anything wrong. Except for Dan's curious absence of old friends and family, but she'd never allowed herself to consciously register how strange that was. Charlotte couldn't fathom how her judgment could have been so seriously out of whack.

"It must be very hard for you," Hank Diebold conceded. "We are sorry, Ms. Leone. Just because we work in law enforcement, it doesn't mean we can't understand some of what you're going through."

"But you can do something to help us," Agent Washington said. "And that's one of the best ways to start on the path to recovery. Daniel O'Toole doesn't usually leave such large footprints for us to pick up on, and we've never before had a witness who knows him intimately. You do."

Charlotte shook her head. "I know nothing about Daniel O'Toole," she said. "Nothing. I knew a man called Riordan Michael Gray and, believe me, he didn't have anything in common with the terrorist you've just described to me."

"You're the closest we're ever likely to get to an eyewitness," Washington said. "There's even an argument to be made that O'Toole must have had some real feelings for you. To the best of our knowledge, he's never been married to anyone before."

That final snippet of information was one piece too much for Charlotte. The idea that she might have been used as a convenient cover by a man who threw grenades into hotel lobbies with complete indifference to the lives of innocent bystanders was bad enough. The thought that she might have been uniquely attractive to him was more than her system could tolerate.

She retched, and the room started to spin. She rushed for the bathroom and barely made it inside before she threw up. Her hopes, her dreams, her life, all headed down the toilet in a sour-smelling stream.

It was fortunate for Daniel O'Toole that he'd left with the Christmas garbage, Charlotte thought bleakly, or she would have saved the FBI the expense of a trial and killed him herself.

Four

Charlotte carried her morning cup of coffee out onto
the balcony of her Bayside condo and stood resting
her elbows against the balustrade, soaking up the heat.
This had been the ritual start to her day for the past
year, ever since she arrived in Tampa Bay. The sun
was beginning to disperse the early-morning mists
and light danced over the rippling waters of the Gulf
of Mexico in a dazzling pattern of gold and aqua. A
pelican dived into the trough of a wave in search of
food, and emerged triumphant a few seconds later
with a fish flapping in its beak.

A beautiful sight, if you could manage to ignore
the fact that the fish was dying in order for the bird
to live. Three years earlier, Charlotte realized such a
thought would never have occurred to her. A year
ago, it would have reduced her to tears. This morning,
she simply watched the scruffy brown pelican enjoy
his breakfast, her emotions disengaged. For the past
six months or so, her feelings seemed to have been
perpetually disengaged, except when she experienced
a brief moment of cynical amusement.

For almost a year after Dan's disappearance, Charlotte had submitted to weekly sessions with two FBI-approved therapists who specialized in grief counseling, first in Des Moines and later in Tampa Bay. She hadn't found the sessions too helpful, but that might have been because neither therapist had been told the real reasons for Charlotte's unhappiness. They knew only that Charlotte's husband had walked out on her without warning, since the FBI didn't want anyone to learn the truth about Dan, and Charlotte sure as hell felt no burning urge to defy the Bureau and reveal the sordid facts. She wasn't a masochist and had no desire to inform the world that she was an idiotic woman who'd fallen for a cute smile and great sex without stopping to uncover the rotten core beneath Dan's charming exterior.

To this day, nobody in her family had any idea who or what her so-called husband had really been. She called her parents every week, in what her therapists would no doubt consider a textbook case of contact-without-intimacy. She hadn't even informed them when the FBI brought her the news that, to the best of their knowledge and belief, Daniel O'Toole was dead, killed when a basement stash of volatile explosives blew up in a remote border town between Kosovo and Albania. The FBI made no attempt to explain what twisted path had led an Irish nationalist to an illegal munitions dump in the Balkans, and Charlotte had preferred not to inquire.

The news that O'Toole was dead had been the trigger for Charlotte's current state of emotional shutdown. The Tampa therapist—informed that Dan had died, but not how or where—had been far more worried by her emotional lassitude than he had been about her earlier state of simmering rage. Charlotte had taken care of that problem by the simple method of ending her sessions with the therapist. After the agony of the first few months following Dan's disappearance, she really liked the comfortable state of not-feeling that news of his death provoked. To hell with the therapist's fears about her repressed emotions turning inward and building up dangerous pressure. He should try living with constant, unremitting anguish for a few months. He would soon discover that not-feeling was a whole lot preferable to letting it all hang out. Besides, far from finding her present uptight and repressed attitude dysfunctional, Charlotte thought she was coping pretty damn well, all things considered. She had a challenging job, she earned a decent income, she paid her taxes, and she was polite to her fellow citizens. What more could anyone ask of her?

Tampa Bay's morning rush hour hadn't yet begun and she could barely hear the distant hum of traffic. The near silence added to the illusion of being alone with the ocean and at peace with the world. She breathed deeply and slowly, achieving a sensation of calm that she accepted without attempting to probe how deeply the calm was rooted. If superficial calm was the best she could achieve, she'd take superficial. She'd done almost a year of frantic, and calm was a whole lot better.

A light breeze stirred the ficus tree growing in a tub on her balcony, but the breeze wasn't strong enough to mess up her hair, which was scraped back from her face in a tight, practical twist, anchored with old-fashioned pins and copious amounts of hair spray.

Since arriving in Tampa, Charlotte had discovered a passion for neatness and order that included every detail of her personal appearance, as well as the pristine blandness of her sparsely furnished condo. The therapist claimed that Charlotte's newfound passion for organization was symptomatic of her need to control every detail of her life so that she could never again be surprised. Or worse, betrayed into suffering devastating loss.

Charlotte was sure the therapist was right, but couldn't see how that was a problem. So what if she liked being organized and in control? And why did she need to learn to trust again? Trust was for children and fools, not sensible adults. She didn't enjoy uncertainty, and she didn't want any extraneous people in her life. Wasn't that pretty much the ideal lifestyle for a woman who planned to dedicate the next decade or so to achieving big things with her career? To hell with personal growth and self-forgiveness. She'd take being in control of her life any day. No more surprises. That was her motto for living these days.

The temperature had already begun its steady climb toward the nineties, but at this early hour the humidity made the air soft rather than oppressive, and Charlotte's tailored linen slacks and crisp, square-necked blouse felt comfortably cool as she lingered over her final few sips of black coffee.

Charlotte quite liked the heat and humidity of Florida in summer. Ever since the disastrous end to her marriage, she despised cold and snow and winter, so the arrival of the sweltering months of July and August didn't bother her. Where other people wilted, she flourished. Her family was always urging her to take a break from the heat, but no amount of cajoling would ever persuade her to return to Iowa, not even in summer. Among the other things Dan had smashed to smithereens was Charlotte's easy connection to the town of her birth and her close ties to her exuberant extended family.

At first she'd grieved for the loss of intimate contact with so many people she loved but, with the news of O'Toole's death, she'd passed beyond grief and simply accepted the break with her family as one more penalty she had to pay for the crime of having been utterly and completely gullible in her willingness to fall for O'Toole's lies.

Charlotte swallowed the last of her coffee and, her morning ritual complete, walked back into the kitchen, rinsing her cup and stowing it in the dishwasher before picking up her purse and heading for the elevator. Six-thirty-five. Her morning routine was so formalized these days that she could be on time to the second with barely a glance at a clock.

She liked to get to the office early, before anyone else arrived. For the past several weeks she had been working diligently on her drawings for the new Bay Palms Regional Hospital and she was in the final stage of honing the details, a technical process that stretched her skills to the limit. Her skills, but not her patience. In the old days, she'd had a tendency to enjoy the creative part of her work and get bored by the nitty gritty details. No more. Now she had an endless supply of patience, at least where her drawings were concerned.

The bidding for the prestigious project was intensely competitive, with four of the best architectural firms in Tampa jockeying for the contract. Scott & Stravinsky, the firm she had worked for ever since arriving in Tampa Bay eighteen months ago, was considered to have the inside track since they'd collaborated with the hospital board on earlier renovations. Winning the bid was by no means guaranteed, however, and Charlotte was pulling out all the stops.

She intended to make sure her design won the bidding, at which point she expected to be rewarded with a partnership, even though the next youngest partner at Scott & Stravinsky was in his forties. To that end, she'd been putting in plenty of sixty-hour weeks to underscore her ambitions and her willingness to work hard. Today would be no exception to her usual twelve-hour day, even though her plans for the new hospital were virtually complete.

The big advantage of such an extended work week—aside from all she could achieve relative to the other associates—was that it left only a few hours to fill before bedtime. For the last couple of months her schedule had been so exhausting she'd achieved the bliss of actually sleeping for five or six hours straight when she finally fell into bed.

Who said the age of miracles was past, Charlotte reflected cynically.

The intercom rang just as she reached the tiled area that served as a mini entrance hall to her one-bedroom condo. She picked up the phone. "Yes?"

"Ms. Leone, this is Luis. There is a man waiting here who wants to talk with you."

"I'm not expecting anyone, Luis. Who is it, and what does he want?"

"His name is Hanseck. John Hanseck." Luis made

a valiant attempt at the name. "He say he is from the FBI. There is no problem. He jus' need your help."

The FBI *again*. She'd hoped she was finished with them when they gave her a final briefing three months after O'Toole's death. What could they possibly want now? Charlotte felt mild irritation, but nothing more than a tepid flash of curiosity about the reason for the visit. "Tell Mr. Hanseck I'm leaving for work. I'll stop in the lobby on my way down to the parking garage if he wants to talk to me for a couple of minutes. Thanks, Luis."

"You're welcome. I tell him." Luis hung up.

Charlotte got off the elevator at the ground floor level and saw a tall man leaning against the reception counter that fronted the mailbox area, chatting to the night doorman with unexpected friendliness. In her experience, FBI agents all walked around with steel rods up their asses, but this one seemed a little more relaxed than the general run. He was wearing the dress slacks, white shirt and conservative striped tie that seemed to be the FBI uniform and his brown hair had been cut into the regulation FBI crop, but his face had a bright pink tinge of mild sunburn, as if he'd broken away from his desk and found time to spend a few hours outdoors. A recent arrival from the north, Charlotte speculated, who was still excited by the gleaming white sands of the Gulf Coast beaches.

"Ms. Leone?" He crossed the lobby, taking off his sunglasses as he walked toward her with shield and accompanying identification extended. "My name is John Hanseck. I'm with the Tampa Bay office of the FBI."

Charlotte glanced at the shield and the ID. She'd

seen enough of these over the past eighteen months that she could recognize the real thing at twenty paces. She gave a brief nod of acknowledgment. "How can I help you, Mr. Hanseck?"

"I have some news for you. Some unexpected news." He gestured with his sunglasses to draw her to the corner of the lobby where they could speak more privately.

Charlotte accompanied him without making any comment, then waited. Gone were the days when she would burst in with a question the moment there was a pause in the conversation.

Agent Hanseck flicked an appreciative glance toward her. No fool, he recognized how silence could subtly shift the balance of power in any encounter. "I know you like to be at your desk by seven-fifteen, Ms. Leone. My predecessor, Andy Prentiss, left a note to that effect in your file, which is why I came here so early this morning."

Charlotte waited.

"Well, I'll cut right to the chase." John Hanseck's voice took on an authoritative note as he abandoned any further effort to engage her in an exchange of social niceties. "Information has surfaced that suggests your husband wasn't killed in the Balkans as we previously thought. To the best of our current knowledge, Ms. Leone, your husband is alive."

Something hot, sharp and excruciatingly painful sliced through Charlotte's heart before the ice reformed and left her whole again. "I have no husband, Mr. Hanseck. I assume I was probably never married in a legal sense. Even if I was, I'm now divorced. If you're referring to Daniel O'Toole, I'd like to make it crystal clear that I have no interest in the life, death, or whereabouts of that man.''

Charlotte turned to leave, and John Hanseck held out his arm, preventing her. ''Not so fast, Ms. Leone. I need to confirm that O'Toole has made no effort to contact you.''

''Absolutely none.'' She spoke coolly, the numbness safely back in place. O'Toole had been dead and now he was alive. Okay, she'd deal with it. Neither situation could impinge on her life in any significant way, as long as she didn't let it. She spoke swiftly, determined to squash this FBI agent before he became a real nuisance.

''For the record, let me make my position clear. Daniel O'Toole has not been in touch with me. He hasn't sent me any letters, or any e-mail messages. He hasn't phoned, nor has he attempted to meet with me. No strangers have passed on any notes supposedly originating with O'Toole. There have been no unusual or unexplained incidents in my life, or gifts delivered without an identifying card. Nothing.''

Agent Hanseck tilted his head. ''That seems pretty clear-cut. Still, in light of our new information, I did need to check. I'm sure you understand.''

''I understand that the FBI believes O'Toole had genuine feelings for me. I'm equally sure that you're mistaken—''

''He did marry you, Ms. Leone—''

''He simply needed somewhere to hang out for a couple of years while he regrouped. My family was large enough to provide excellent cover.''

''True, but he chose you and your family, not any one of a thousand other equally suitable families.''

"I'm aware of my misfortune, Mr. Hanseck. Trust me, I don't need your reminder."

"O'Toole has always enjoyed a reputation of being devastatingly successful with women—"

"Don't go any further with that one," Charlotte heard the weariness in her own voice. She was no longer emotional about O'Toole, merely tired of her inability to be rid of him. "If you and the Bureau are still worried in case I'm so infatuated that I'm protecting him, then you couldn't be more wrong. He's a terrorist, with people's blood on his hands. I have no feelings toward him other than a desperate regret that we ever met."

"Agent Prentiss, my predecessor, suspected that you were withholding information from us, but I don't share his views, Ms. Leone. I've studied all the files and I don't believe you've withheld information. There's no evidence that you ever had a clue about O'Toole's true identity and plenty of evidence that you felt badly betrayed by his departure."

Charlotte actually felt a glimmer of bitter amusement. Agent Hanseck was dead right in his assessment; she'd never had a clue. Clueless Charlotte at your service. She swallowed a sigh and tried one more time to convince this latest FBI worker bee that he was wasting his time.

"Since you're new to the Tampa Bay office, Mr. Hanseck, I'll repeat to you the promise I gave your predecessor when we first met. If I ever hear from O'Toole, or from anyone who claims to represent him, I will notify the FBI immediately. As of this moment, however, I can assure you that I've heard nothing from the man since he walked out of my house the day after Christmas, a year and a half ago. Therefore, I have no further information to provide to your agency that could possibly be relevant or of use. I've already been fully—some people might say excessively—debriefed on such general information as I have regarding O'Toole.''

John Hanseck glanced nervously toward Luis, apparently seeking reassurance that the night guard was more interested in packing up his belongings for the end of his shift than in straining to hear anything Charlotte had to say. Then he turned back to Charlotte.

''Don't go yet.'' Hanseck made his words sound more of a request than an order. ''I'd really appreciate it if you could take a few more minutes to talk to me. Can I buy you breakfast at the coffee bar down the road? They do a great café *latte* and their croissants are the best in town.''

When Dan disappeared, she'd sold Panini to its managers at a rock-bottom price. It had taken her another year to overcome her distaste for trendy coffee bars, but Charlotte could now enter such a place without having her stomach perform back flips and her skin break out in a sweat. Even so, she had no desire to spend any more time than she had to with an FBI agent, especially in a coffee bar. She resented having to adjust her mindset to accommodate the fact that O'Toole still breathed air on the same planet she did, and she would have preferred to spend the next hour alone.

Annoyed that she cared even marginally about O'Toole's continued existence, she spoke more curtly than she intended. ''Thanks for the offer, Mr. Hanseck, but I don't eat breakfast and, as I've mentioned, I'm really busy today—"

"I need to talk to you, Ms. Leone. We can do it in my office downtown or over a cup of coffee at the café. Your choice."

The not-so-subtle subtle threat didn't intimidate her, but Charlotte decided to accompany him to the coffee bar, anyway. Sometimes the quickest way to get rid of FBI bureaucrats was just to go along and let them scratch whatever bug was gnawing at them. "All right, I'll have a cup of coffee with you, Mr. Hanseck. But I have a meeting starting at nine, and I need to check some measurements on one of my drawings before then, so I can't give you more than fifteen minutes. And before you make another threat about taking me downtown to your office, let's have a reality check here. I know as well as you do that the FBI has no legal authority to question me. I've committed no crime, and I'm not a material witness to a crime. Any information I share with you is purely a gesture of goodwill on my part."

John Hanseck shot her a rueful grin. "You're right, and I'm sorry. Could we start over? I'm very grateful that you've agreed to talk to me, Ms. Leone, and I'll remember in the future that when your file says you're smart and not easily intimidated, it means what it says."

On another day, Charlotte would have been mildly amused that Agent Hanseck seemed to think he could flatter her into cooperation once he realized his attempts at coercion had failed. But in the wake of the news about O'Toole, there was a jagged edge to her emotions that prevented even mild amusement. John

Hanseck was like all the other agents assigned to her case: it was going to take him a while to understand that she wasn't being uncooperative, she simply had no information to share. New investigators always had a hard time grasping the simple fact that she knew less about the real Daniel O'Toole than they did.

She walked without speaking along the block and a half to the coffee bar, matching her stride to Agent Hanseck's. She wasn't silent because she felt any hostility toward the man, but because she didn't have anything specific to say, and her supply of small talk had vanished eighteen months ago, along with the Christmas garbage. O'Toole's possible resurrection from the dead wiped out whatever tiny store of conversational platitudes she'd managed to rebuild.

The restaurant smelled pleasantly of fresh baked bread, cinnamon and brewing coffee. The smell was uncomfortably evocative of the Panini restaurants, but Charlotte disciplined her thoughts to remain focused on the present, something that was still a little harder to do in a coffee bar than it was in most other places. She ordered a small regular coffee and didn't argue when John Hanseck insisted on paying for it, following him when he carried their tray over to a window seat. The glass was tinted against the sun and shaded by the fronds of an indoor plant suspended from the ceiling, but they had a clear view outside to the street, such as it was. Between the heat and the early hour, it was hardly a bustling scene of activity.

"Since we're both busy people, I'll cut the small talk and get right to the point," John Hanseck said. "I want you to know how and why we discovered that O'Toole is still alive."

"Do I need to know?" Charlotte sipped her coffee. "I certainly don't care."

"You need to know. That's why I'm here." Agent Hanseck spoke crisply. "Three months ago, the Bureau received information from the French police regarding an Algerian terrorist they had in custody. Their captive was a man named Hakim Belaziz, who was accused of master-minding an attack on six French monks in 1996. Hakim never confessed to the murder of the monks, but he did acknowledge that he'd recently sold a supply of weapons stolen from the Algerian military to a breakaway faction of the IRA. He identified that faction as the Armargh Army."

Charlotte experienced a moment of ironic amusement that a group of Islamic fanatics had somehow managed to convince themselves that they were advancing their cause by selling weapons to a bunch of Catholic fanatics.

She didn't think her face betrayed much of what she was feeling, but John Hanseck seemed to catch some hint of her mood. "You probably know from earlier conversations with the Bureau that many of these terrorist cells have links to each other," he said.

"Yes, I did know that. I've wondered from time to time why none of these zealots ever seem to notice that the only thing they have in common is hate."

"Most of them are too busy misreading the lessons of history to have time to notice something obvious like that," Hanseck said dryly. "Anyway, according to the French authorities, the Irish terrorists double-crossed the Algerians—"

"How did they manage that?"

"They paid for their weapons in counterfeit currency," Hanseck said. "No surprise, Hakim was pissed as hell to have been cheated. Angry enough, in fact, that he was persuaded to cooperate with the French authorities, at least to the extent that he set up another meeting with the man from the Armargh Army who'd passed the phony money. The French aren't telling us exactly what happened, but they didn't manage to make an arrest, so apparently something went wrong with their setup."

Charlotte shrugged. "Most likely the Algerian deliberately sabotaged it. However angry he was with the Irish terrorists, he was probably even angrier with the French police."

"That's possible. However, what's important to us right now is the fact that the French authorities did get blood samples from the three Armargh Army soldiers who turned up to negotiate with Belaziz." He paused for a moment. "One of those three blood samples provided a DNA match for Daniel O'Toole."

"I see." Charlotte stirred her coffee, although it was her usual black, without sugar. "How did the French police manage to get blood samples if they couldn't get close enough to make any arrests?"

"Bullet wounds," Hanseck said succinctly. "The French *Sûreté* hasn't passed on any details about who shot whom, but they're positive of their identification."

Charlotte looked out the window at a woman jogging with a baby in a stroller. "Do the French police know if O'Toole survived his wounds?"

"No. So it's possible he's dead, of course, although he was alive enough to escape from the trap the

French *Sûreté* had set. What we can be certain of in light of this new information is that O'Toole didn't die on the Kosovo border.''

Charlotte waited for a moment until she was sure she had everything together, then lifted her shoulders in a slight, dismissive shrug. ''I'm not sure why you've told me all this, Mr. Hanseck. I still have no new insights to contribute.''

''Quite apart from any help you might be able to give us, Ms. Leone, we want to warn you personally to be on a state of heightened alert.''

''Thank you, but I'm not planning any trips to Europe in the near future. I'm much too busy at work.''

''You don't have to go to Europe to be at risk. Part of the reason I'm here this morning is that we have intelligence that strongly suggests O'Toole has returned to the States after spending the past eighteen months in Europe.''

Charlotte controlled a little shiver of shock. ''He's come back to the States? That's…unexpected.''

''Yes. His arena of operation has always been Europe in the past. But we've collected some intelligence recently that suggests he's set up shop in Miami.''

''In Miami?'' The information was so surprising that Charlotte felt a twinge of genuine curiosity, a novel sensation these days. ''What in the world is O'Toole planning to do in Miami?''

''I wish to God we knew,'' Hanseck said. ''We've put together some fragments of information from a couple of different sources, and there seems to be a chance that he's plotting some terrorist act against a tourist resort here in the States. Heaven knows, there are plenty of those in Florida, so a Miami base of operations could make sense.''

Charlotte took a sip of coffee and managed to swallow it without gagging. If she ever allowed herself to consider the fact that she had been married to a man who planned the deaths of innocent people, including children, she would go mad. She couldn't allow herself to dwell on the knowledge that she had slept peacefully in the arms of a man who might at this very moment be plotting to blow up a kiddie theme park.

The sip of coffee was a mistake. She pushed her mug away, sickened by the smell, and avoided Hanseck's sympathetic gaze as she spoke. ''The Armargh Army has never targeted Americans before,'' she said.

''That's true, but we believe they've changed their tactics. They watched what happened in Afghanistan after September 11 and then asked themselves why they'd wasted thirty years blowing up buildings and murdering civilians in Northern Ireland. These are the hard core lads, remember, who feel furious and betrayed that the IRA has agreed to surrender their weapons and take part in serious political discussions with the British government. Why negotiate and make concessions when you can bomb your way to total victory? Provided the bomb's big enough and it goes off in the right place, there's no limit to what a terrorist attack can achieve.''

''The right place being America,'' Charlotte said.

Agent Hanseck nodded. ''Of course. The lads from Armargh believe they can achieve spectacular results with a single successful attack on the American homeland. And they're probably correct if their goal is to capture the attention of the American public.''

Successful meaning hundreds of dead bodies, Charlotte thought bleakly. She took a paper napkin and surreptitiously wiped the sweat from the palms of her hands. She didn't want Hanseck to know he was getting to her. An image of Dan stretched out on the rug, playing with her baby niece, flashed into Charlotte's mind and she quickly pushed it aside. No way she was going to walk down that mental path.

"Is O'Toole really irrational enough to think he can avoid capture?" she asked.

"Probably not." Hanseck spoke with unexpected ferocity. "But O'Toole is like every other crackpot terrorist I've ever dealt with—more than willing to be a martyr for the cause. Most terrorists find real life much too messy and complicated to deal with, so they're quite happy to die and move on to glory.''

And she would be more than willing to help O'Toole achieve glorious martyrdom if he ever came within killing range, Charlotte thought savagely. She disapproved of capital punishment, and she'd never so much as held a gun, but she'd be willing to make an exception in the case of Daniel O'Toole.

She drew in a steadying breath, alarmed by the anger rebuilding inside her after months of relative tranquility. She was relieved when she discovered that she could still speak with her usual cool control. She didn't plan to let her emotions start running riot again just because O'Toole might be alive. Damn him to hell, anyway.

"I'm horrified by what you've just told me," she said to John Hanseck. "I wish I could help, but I can't. O'Toole has no reason to contact me, and from a selfish point of view, I'll admit that I'd have preferred to believe he was dead.''

"We told you because we think O'Toole might be planning an imminent relocation to the Tampa Bay area, and we're not sure why he would make that move," Hanseck said quietly. "I can't tell you how or why we believe that, but we do.''

The same hot, sharp pain that she'd felt before sliced through Charlotte's heart and this time the ice didn't quite reform. A wound deep inside throbbed with the knowledge that O'Toole wasn't just breathing the air of the same planet as she was. God help her, he might even be breathing the air of the same town.

She pushed back her chair and stood up, unable to bear the burden of hearing any more news about Dan. "I'm late for work, Mr. Hanseck. I have to go. As I promised you before, in the extremely unlikely event that I am contacted by O'Toole, or any member of the Armargh Army, I'll let you know. You have my word.''

"Thank you. Here's my card. Call me, Ms. Leone. Call me if you have even the slightest reason to be suspicious. And a final word of warning. Do not, under any conceivable circumstances, agree to meet with anyone you don't know, in any location where there aren't plenty of other people around.''

She'd had the same warning from Agent Prentiss months ago, but it still had the power to chill. Charlotte nodded an acknowledgment, the extra cup of coffee turning to acid in her stomach. She took Hanseck's card, shoving it deep into the pocket of her slacks. Then she hurried out of the café, desperate to get to the sanctuary of her office.

Nothing had changed, she told herself. Nothing at all. She was going to put this conversation out of her mind and work on forgetting that it had ever happened. As far as she was concerned, Daniel O'Toole remained dead and buried. Buried somewhere dark and deep, where he could inflict no more pain.

She really, really wanted Daniel O'Toole to be dead.

Five

Exactly a week later, John Hanseck was waiting for Charlotte again as she left for work. This time he didn't bother using Luis as an intermediary. She went down to the parking garage and found him leaning against the side of her white Sebring coupe, reading a magazine. A magazine devoted to deep sea fishing, she noticed. If that was his recreation of choice, he must be in hog heaven now that he'd been transferred to the Tampa Bay area.

"Hi." He straightened as she approached and gave her a smile that was both warm and—she was astonished to notice—appreciative. It had been so long since she thought of herself as a woman that she'd forgotten what it was like to be on the receiving end of an admiring male glance. "I decided to wait for you down here so that your night watchman wouldn't start whispering to your neighbors that the FBI has you targeted as a suspect for some criminal activity."

"I appreciate your tact." And she did, Charlotte realized. She valued her anonymity and was grateful that Agent Hanseck seemed to understand that. "And before you ask, the answer is, no I haven't been contacted by Daniel O'Toole since we last spoke."

"That isn't why I came," Hanseck said. "Or not

the most important reason, anyway. I have a favor to ask. I'm hoping you'll have time to make a trip downtown to the FBI offices and listen to a couple of tape recordings that have come into our possession. We're optimistic that you'll be able to tell us whether one of the men speaking on the tapes is your husb—'' He broke off, catching his mistake. ''Whether one of the men on the recordings is Daniel O'Toole,'' he finished.

Charlotte didn't reply right away because she didn't trust herself to speak. She'd spent the past week convincing herself that she wasn't affected by the news that O'Toole was still alive. She'd even managed to focus on work sufficiently to make a decent job of her presentation to the hospital board. She must have held up okay, because one of the crustiest and most senior partners had taken her to lunch yesterday and told her that she'd done a fine job, and the project looked as if it was in the bag for their firm, thanks to her efforts. If the contract came through, Charlotte was pretty sure she'd get her partnership.

But despite the good news at work, and despite a determined effort to think about other things, she hadn't been able to forget what John Hanseck had told her. Self-deception could only be taken so far, and the news that O'Toole was alive couldn't be ignored. Of course it mattered whether her ex-husband was alive or dead. If O'Toole was dead, she was safe. He could never perpetrate some horrific act that would make her cringe to remember that she had once called this man her husband. But if he was alive, she had no protection against the fallout of his fanaticism. She hadn't turned on her TV for the entire week, or glanced at a newspaper, because she'd dreaded coming across a news report about some terrible act of wanton destruction perpetrated by "terrorist Daniel O'Toole."

"I'm willing to do whatever I can to help," Charlotte said, using her remote to click open the locks on her car door. "But I have meetings all morning with prospective clients, and they'd be difficult to cancel. When would you expect me to come?"

John Hanseck opened the car door for her. "I'll adjust my schedule to your convenience, but obviously the sooner the better. Today if you can possibly make it. My partner and I need to decide on a course of action, and our decision depends in part on whether or not you identify one of the speakers on these recordings as O'Toole."

"Are the FBI offices still in the Zach Street building?" Charlotte asked. "I went there once before to meet with Agent Prentiss, and it's not too far from where I work."

"Yes, that's where we are still. This is important, Charlotte, or I wouldn't have bothered you again. It's really urgent from our point of view. That's why I came here in person, instead of just making a phone call."

FBI agents were usually so formal that she felt a little shock of intimacy as he said her name. Charlotte mentally reviewed her schedule. Truth be told, now that the presentation to the hospital board was over, she had plenty of free time, and the sooner she did what Hanseck asked, the sooner she would be able to resume her policy of striking all thoughts of O'Toole from her mind.

"How about the early part of this afternoon, as soon as my client meetings are finished?" she suggested.

"That would be great. What do you call early afternoon? One? Two?"

"I can probably make it by one-thirty."

"Great. We'll be waiting." John Hanseck stepped back so that she could get into her car, touching the fishing magazine to his forehead in a farewell salute. "Thanks, Charlotte. I really appreciate your willingness to help out."

That use of her name again. He was certainly a lot more laid-back than his predecessor, Charlotte reflected. She was rather glad that if she was going to have to do something as uncomfortable as listen to clandestine recordings of O'Toole's voice, it was going to be in John Hanseck's company rather than with Deputy Director Tremayne Washington, or Agent Prentiss, or any of the other stiff-necked representatives the Bureau had turned loose on her over the past eighteen months.

Her brief moment of goodwill toward John Hanseck had more than dissipated by the time she actually got escorted into his office that same afternoon. Charlotte wished she could square it with her conscience to refuse to cooperate, but of course she couldn't. Instead she was confronting the possibility that in a few moments she might find herself listening to her exhusband's voice. She hoped to God that she wouldn't hear him plotting to kill people.

She was introduced to Hanseck's partner, Shirley Nicholson, a handsome woman in her early forties.

After the usual exchange of civilities, Charlotte was quickly ushered into a windowless, soundproof room to listen to the recordings.

A technician seated at a complex control board took off his headphones just long enough to shake hands and mutter that his name was Jim Chavez, before turning back to his keyboard. Nobody made any attempt to explain how or why they'd come into possession of the recordings she was about to audit. Shirley Nicholson simply got down to the task of explaining what the FBI wanted Charlotte to do.

"I believe my partner has already told you that we need to clarify the identity of a man whose voice we've captured on these recordings. Jim has set the system up for you to listen to the tapes through headphones, which should make it a little easier to concentrate. There are three men speaking on the first segment you'll hear, and two on the second, but there are only four separate speakers in total because one man is the same on each recording."

"I understand."

"It's the speaker who's the same on both recordings that we want you to concentrate on identifying," Shirley continued. "We believe that man might be Daniel O'Toole and we'd appreciate your opinion as to whether you agree. This identification, if you can make it, is for our information only, not part of an effort to collect evidence for a court proceeding, so we don't have to be neutral in explaining to you which voice we're interested in having you identify. On the other hand, we don't want to prejudice you to the point that you pin a name on someone you don't really recognize. We think one of these speakers might be O'Toole, but we're by no means certain. Don't let our opinions sway yours.''

"I understand," Charlotte said again. "I'll do my best to listen with an open mind."

Absolutely the only way she was going to get through this, she knew, was if she focused rigidly on the fact that she was trying to identify the voice of a dangerous international terrorist. She could not allow her thoughts to wander off into any back alleys about her intimate past relationship with that terrorist.

Jim finished keying instructions into the computer and handed her a set of earphones. "Okay, Ms. Leone, I'm going to play a recording of an actor reading Abraham Lincoln's Gettysburg address. Raise or lower your hand to let me know when the volume is just right for you. I have all the settings for playback adjusted for average or normal and you should be able to hear each individual word with perfect clarity. However, if you'd like more base, or more treble, let me know. Different people react better to a slightly different range of settings. It's very individual and we want to get it just right for you. Nod your head when you're ready for me to switch from Abe's speech to the actual recording."

Charlotte adjusted the ear phones to a comfortable position, blotting out extraneous sounds. "Okay, I'm ready for the test piece." That is, if you didn't count the fact that her heart was beating so hard and loud that she could hear it reverberating inside the head phones.

"Fourscore and seven years ago our fathers brought forth on this continent a new nation, con-

*ceived in liberty, and dedicated to the proposition that
all men are created equal…''*

But not according to O'Toole, Charlotte reflected
bitterly. As far as he's concerned, only his fellow fanatics are worth counting as equals. The rest of us are
just collateral damage on the way to a world reshaped
according to his rules.

*"…that this nation, under God, shall have a new
birth of freedom—and government of the people, by
the people, for the people, shall not perish from the
earth.''*

Charlotte was in no mood to reflect on the irony of
hearing such famous words right before she listened
to a conversation among a bunch of conspirators who
stood for everything Abraham Lincoln had fought to
oppose. She moved her hand in a sideways motion to
indicate that the volume was acceptable and that she
was ready to listen to the clandestine recordings.

Jim keyed in a command to the computer and the
words she was hearing changed instantly from sono-
rous clarity to crackling static. A voice spoke through
the static, the Irish brogue so thick that she could
barely understand what was being said.

Her ear took several seconds before it finally tuned
in to the accents and she began to pick up the drift
of the conversation. "Why can't we go out to dinner?
There's not a fuckin' bite to eat in this place.''

"Because we need to keep an extra low profile for
the next few days, you know that, Ryan.''

A second voice spoke, the brogue less pronounced,
and a subtle note of command in his words. "Padraig's been in custody for more than twelve hours.
We've no idea what information he might give up.''

"Padraig's trained. He's one of us. He won't betray us."

"Let's hope you're right. But in case you're not, we need to concentrate on packing up this place and moving out to a motel. We all have our prints and DNA on record. We have to be sure we don't leave any trace evidence for the American cops to find. Since September 11, they've been spendin' a bloody fortune to make sure that their computers can all speak to each other. That makes us easier to track."

"Fuckin' Padraig." The first voice spoke again. "Why wasn't he smart enough to keep away from the ponies?"

"Or at least why wasn't he smart enough to know that you can't pay off your bookie with homemade dollars." A third voice spoke, the brogue thick enough to cut with a butter knife.

"We'll order pizza." The second voice spoke again, the note of command still subtle, but definitely there.

"I'm sick to dyin' of pizza," the third speaker whined. "I want a meat pie. A nice steak and kidney pie, with a good thick gravy, like me mither used to make for our Sunday dinners."

"Are you goin' to be cookin' for us then, Sean? Because how else are you expectin' us to come up with a pie for your dinner? Americans don't sell kidneys for dog food, let alone for humans."

"Fuckin' Americans." Sean sounded more gloomy than angry. "What we need is a woman to cook for us."

The first speaker—Ryan?—gave a hearty guffaw of laughter. "You just need a woman, that's your trouble, Sean. It's been too long since you had a boink, and you're gettin' mean-spirited.''

"No, he's gettin' horny, and that's fuckin' worse.''

The conversation degenerated into an exchange of crude comments on Sean's sexual habits until the static became so thick that Charlotte could only make out the odd word here and there, and identifying individual speakers would have been impossible, even if she'd recognized any of the voices.

Which, to her enormous relief, she didn't.

She waited until the end of the recording, then took off the headphones.

"Did you recognize anyone?" John Hanseck asked eagerly.

She shook her head, still limp with relief. "None of those men sounded anything like Dan. My ex-husband didn't have any trace of an Irish accent.''

"For people who have the knack, accents are easy to fake.'' John Hanseck was pacing, no longer able to conceal his nervous tension. "Try to imagine the voices stripped of their accents.''

"That's easier said than done, Mr. Hanseck. Their brogues are thick, and the men were almost talking in dialect by the time they started to discuss Sean's sexual preferences. Not to mention the fact that there's a huge amount of static on the recording.''

"I know.'' Hanseck shook his head in visible frustration. "We tried to clean it up, but there are limits to what we can do without distorting the voices themselves. Jim's going to play the recording again, and this time, please do your best to listen to the quality of the voices themselves, not the accents.''

Charlotte closed her eyes in an effort to improve

her concentration. Imagining these voices without their accents was the equivalent of asking her to look at a two-hundred-and-fifty-pound football player and visualize him as a six-month-old baby without benefit of before and after pictures. But it was a little easier the second time around since she already knew what the men were going to say. As she listened, she became increasingly confident none of the speakers was Dan. Her relief climbed toward euphoria as she concluded that the timbre of all three voices was unfamiliar, quite apart from their thick brogues.

"Okay, what do you think?" Hanseck asked. "Any chance that one of those men is O'Toole?"

"No, I don't think so."

"Positively not?"

Charlotte hesitated. "I'm *almost* positive none of them is Dan."

"Define *almost*," Shirley snapped. She shook her head. "Sorry. I didn't mean to sound so aggressive. This identification is important because of what's being discussed on the second tape, and you're our best hope."

Charlotte drew in a shaky breath. "*Almost* means I'm ninety-nine percent sure Dan isn't one of the speakers, but not a hundred percent sure. The accent is so distorting it affects my ability to judge. Maybe I should listen to the other recording before I finally make up my mind?"

"Excellent idea," Shirley said, and John nodded his agreement.

"Signal when you're ready for me to roll," Jim said. "The quality of this recording is better, so that should help some."

Charlotte put on the headphones again and lifted her hand. "Okay. Now."

This recording had almost no background static, and the speakers were no longer discussing anything as run-of-the-mill as meat pies and women. There was no exchange of names before a man started speaking. This must be the fourth conspirator she'd been told about, Charlotte thought, because she hadn't heard him on the other recording.

"You're late." The newcomer had a high voice and no trace at all of an Irish accent.

"I had a tail to shake."

"You got rid of him?"

"Of course, or I wouldn't have risked coming back to the apartment, would I? I'm not stupid, like Padraig." The second man sounded bored at being asked such a superfluous question. Charlotte recognized him as one of the voices from the earlier recording. The voice that she was ninety-nine percent sure wasn't Dan. The voice that one percent of her thought might conceivably be her ex-husband.

The first man spoke again. "Has the Elf agreed to the date for the operation?"

"Yes. He warned me that security will be stepped up on the Fourth. I told him that if he does his part of the job properly, that isn't going to be a problem."

"It better hadn't be a problem. I don't want any fuck-ups with this operation. You've had over a year to plan it—"

"I've had less than three months. You're forgetting that I spent over a year cleaning up the mess that had been made of my operations in Kosovo."

"That's true." The admission was grudging. "But

since the disaster in Paris with the Algerians we can't use those fine Kosovo-manufactured dollars anymore. Nobody's taking our money these days without checking first to be sure it's the real thing.''

"Then it's lucky for us that you have enough of the stuff that comes straight from Uncle Sam's coffers to keep us in business. We appreciate your generosity to the cause. Although I'd like to remind you that I made a hell of a lot of money with the Kosovo operation. I'm supporting everyone in Miami on the profits we made before Paris.''

"We're grateful. Even if you did walk out on us.''

"I'm back, aren't I? I've been givin' loyal service....''

"Yeah, I guess I don't have any complaints.'' There was a moment's pause, then the newcomer continued. "Jesus, everything depends on this damn crazy Elf. Are you confident he knows his stuff?''

"He knows his stuff.''

"With these fucking tree huggers you can never be sure they won't spot a baby toad in the target zone and decide against pushing the trigger.'' The newcomer sounded disbelieving as well as disgusted.

"You've got no worries. This so-called Elf was part of the team that blew up half of Vail mountain to prove that skiing destroys the environment. He also set fire to the agricultural department at the University of Oregon. He may call himself an Elf, but I'm thinkin' he's ruthless enough to make you look like an old granny.''

The newcomer laughed and his voice took on a sudden deep brogue. "I wouldn't mind looking like my old granny. Have you forgotten that she personally planted the bomb that blew up the Haydon Shopping Mall in Belfast? And she was seventy-five years old when she did it.''

''No, I hadn't forgotten. How could I forget a grand battle like that?''

A battle? Charlotte thought, rigid with disbelief. This slug's belly referred to blowing up a shopping mall as a *grand battle?*

The newcomer spoke again. ''If your Elf does what he's promised, you should be in possession of the disk before the end of the month. Will you have it then?''

''Of course.'' This was the one-percent-chance-it-was-Dan speaking. ''And my team already knows exactly what they have to do. No worries there.''

''Care to share your proposed method of penetration with me?''

''No.''

The newcomer gave a short bark of laughter. ''Still the same suspicious bugger as always, aren't you, boyo?''

''I prefer to think of meself as a cautious man. And I never met you face-to-face until this operation. I have reason to watch what I say.''

''Since you're so cautious, I suppose there's no need for me to be asking if there's any way this Elf can trace you if there's a problem before the Fourth?''

''There's no way. Even if the Elf is caught and decides to talk, we're in the clear. He doesn't know anything about who we are and what our plans might be. He thinks I'm just another crazy environmentalist who wants everyone in the world to go back to living in caves and weaving cloth out of flax on hand looms. Stupid bugger.''

Jim stopped the recording, although Charlotte was fairly sure she'd heard the start of another exchange. Probably the FBI didn't want her to be in possession of any more classified information than was absolutely essential.

"Well?" Hanseck asked. "What do you think now you've heard that second recording?"

Charlotte was euphoric with the relief of being able to reply with perfect honesty that she hadn't recognized either of the two voices. "With the static gone, it's easier to hear the timbre of the men's voices, and neither one of them sounds anything like the man I knew as Riordan Gray," she said. "I'm willing to say that I'm a hundred percent sure he wasn't speaking on either of those recordings."

All three FBI agents exchanged glances that Charlotte couldn't interpret. Then Shirley Nicholson swiveled her chair around and gave Charlotte a polite smile. "We appreciate the time you've taken to help us out, Ms. Leone."

"I'm not sure how much help I've been...."

"We're glad to know that the woman who is most familiar with his voice doesn't think the man on the recording is O'Toole," John Hanseck said.

"We don't want to arrest any of the men you heard talking for another couple of weeks," Shirley Nicholson explained. "We want to give them just a little more rope to hang themselves and give us a chance to identify the Elf they're talking about on that second tape. But if you'd given a positive ID on O'Toole, we'd have had to move in and arrest him right away. He's too dangerous for us to leave on the loose if you'd actually provided a positive identification."

"If the speaker you heard wasn't O'Toole, it seems likely the intelligence we've received about his current whereabouts is false," John Hanseck added. "That means O'Toole may not be in the Tampa Bay area, which is good news for you, I expect."

Charlotte nodded. "Yes, it sure is. I'm glad I was able to help." She was relieved enough at the outcome of the session that she wasn't rushing to get out of the room. The mood swings she'd experienced over the last few days seemed to have broken her state of emotional paralysis, and she was so exhilarated that she hadn't been forced to listen to her ex-husband plotting mayhem and destruction that she felt a stir of something akin to excitement. As long as you weren't personally involved, there was something a little intoxicating about being in possession of secret information. For the first time, she understood what might draw men like Tremayne Washington and John Hanseck to serve with the Bureau.

"What in the world did those speakers mean when they talked about an *elf* having something planned for next week? An elf? That's kind of a weird name for a terrorist, isn't it?"

"It's not elf as in fairy. It's E.L.F.," Shirley Nicholson explained. "The initials stand for Earth Liberation Front."

Charlotte frowned. "From the way the two men were speaking, I'm guessing that's an environmental group. I've never heard of them."

"I'm not surprised," Shirley said. "They don't seem to have made much of a splash in the national media."

"But who are they?" Charlotte asked.

"Environmental terrorists," Shirley said bluntly. "In folklore, elves are magical creatures who accomplish great things at night while mortals are sleeping. So these nutcases call themselves elves because they creep out of the woodwork at night and do the dirty work that regular environmentalists aren't willing to tackle."

"What sort of things have they done?" Charlotte asked.

"They've blown up power plants and destroyed construction sites. They've attacked university research facilities and set fire to experimental farms because they don't approve of commercial agriculture. And don't mention genetic engineering when they're within earshot unless you really want to set them off."

"I can't say I'm all that happy to eat genetically modified food myself," Charlotte commented.

"No, me neither." Shirley's mouth twisted wryly. "The problem is, their goals may be okay, but their methods aren't. People have been killed while the elves are protesting about the destruction of Planet Earth. Of course, that doesn't seem to bother them too much."

"As long as they don't harm any puppies or snowdrops, the elves are happy," John Hanseck muttered. "Our boy on the tape was right about that. Kill off people, but save the innocent animals and plants, that's their motto. Jesus, I don't understand where some of these people get their priorities."

"I had no idea there was such an active and violent underground in the environmental movement," Charlotte said.

John shook his head. "Very few people do. These days Muslim fundamentalists are hogging most of the media attention, but this country is full of kooks and weirdos of every description, all trying to grab attention for their cause. And most of them don't mind if they take out a few hundred people in the course of making their point. Let's be sure we save the planet, even if half the planet has to starve to death, or be blown up, in order for us to achieve that. That's the way they think."

"Well, at least we'll able to stop this particular plot," Shirley Nicholson said, speaking briskly, as if she felt John Hanseck's remarks pushed the limits of acceptable Bureau neutrality. "It always makes us nervous in law enforcement when two extremist groups get together, as the E.L.F. people and the Armargh Army are planning to do on this occasion," she explained to Charlotte. "Pooling their resources means that they notice the flaws in each other's plans and their success rate goes way up. But this time, thank goodness, it looks like we're going to be able to scoop up most of the perpetrators and get them sentenced to some serious prison time."

"I hope you succeed," Charlotte said. "Those people I just heard certainly deserve to be in prison."

"You're right, and we'll get 'em. Don't worry." She flashed a quick smile. "Score one for the good guys."

"And I'll probably never hear that you succeeded," Charlotte said.

John gave a rueful nod of acknowledgment, followed by a resigned shrug. "That's the nature of our work. The press never hears about our successes, but man, they sure have a field day going after our failures.''

Shirley got to her feet, holding out her hand to Charlotte, her smile openly friendly. ''Well, here's to another top-secret success for the Bureau. We really appreciate you stopping by, Ms. Leone. We couldn't have done this without you. I'm sure I don't need to remind you that you signed a confidentiality statement and you're not allowed to repeat anything you heard here today. It would be disastrous if word got to the media about these recordings and you would face criminal prosecution for leaking any information. That includes to your family, of course.''

''I wouldn't dream of saying a word to anybody. I'm glad I could help.''

''I'll walk you back to the elevators,'' John said. ''It's a rabbit warren in here and it's easy to get lost.''

Shirley accompanied John and Charlotte all the way to the elevator banks, chatting about Tampa Bay and how much she enjoyed working in this office after three years assigned to the pressure cooker atmosphere of headquarters.

The elevator arrived. ''I'll come down with you,'' John said to Charlotte. He directed a pointed look toward his partner. ''Bye, Shirley. I'll catch up with you in a few minutes.''

The elevator doors closed and John turned toward Charlotte, giving her a wry grin. ''I need to have a few words with my partner about being more sensitive at picking up on undercurrents. She sure missed what was going on back there.''

Charlotte turned to him, puzzled. ''She did? What was going on? I must have missed it, too.''

John shook his head in mock despair. "I was sending out major vibes that she needed to get lost."

"You were? Why?"

"Because I'd planned to be witty and amusing all the way to the elevator and then, when you were completely dazzled by my charm, I was going to ask you to have dinner with me on Friday night."

Charlotte would have told John that she couldn't possibly consider having dinner with him, but she was so shocked by the reality of an FBI agent asking her out on a date that she was literally speechless. She swallowed, and tried to find both her voice and a polite way to refuse the invitation.

"Please don't say no," John said softly as the elevator doors opened and they walked out into the atrium of the building. "Last week I discovered a really great Italian restaurant a few blocks from here. It overlooks the water, and the chef is fabulous. He's from Sardinia, and his signature dish is fresh seafood with a wonderful light wine sauce. Trust me, the food is so good, it almost doesn't matter who you share it with. So come for the meal, if not for the company. Say yes, Charlotte. I know I'd enjoy it and I think you would, too."

Perhaps it was the momentary euphoria that followed on the realization that she hadn't been listening to Dan's voice. Perhaps it was the fact that John already knew the truth about her past, so there would be no probing questions, no need for evasion, no need to worry about phrasing everything so that it would reveal nothing, and yet not be entirely untruthful.

Why not go? Charlotte found herself thinking. John Hanseck was a civilized man, in a rock-solid profession, and he was only inviting her to share a meal, not commit to anything demanding or long-term. It had been eighteen months since Dan left her, more than enough to get over the shock. Did she really want to pay her ex-husband the homage of living for the rest of her life in a form of self-imposed isolation? Maybe it was time to take at least a small step back in the direction of leading a normal life.

Charlotte looked at John Hanseck and noticed for the first time—really noticed—that he was a good-looking man. He had laugh lines around his brown eyes, and an appealing strength in the line of his jaw. Not that laugh lines were any guarantee that a man wouldn't disappear with the Christmas garbage. Dan had had laugh lines, too.

No sooner had the thought formed than Charlotte rejected it. It was past time for her to stop judging everyone she met with a backward nod to Dan. The fact that she hadn't penetrated Dan's charming mask didn't mean her judgment was fatally flawed. She'd been manipulated by a master, and she'd fallen for his tricks. At some point, didn't she deserve forgiveness for the sin of being too trusting and too easy to deceive?

She looked at John without smiling. "All right," she said, and her breath hurt as it squeezed out of her constricted lungs. "I'll have dinner with you."

John didn't realize what an utterly amazing thing had just happened. How could he? He gave her a friendly smile. "Great. I'll look forward to it."

Thank goodness, he didn't reach out to touch her arm, or pat her shoulder, or make any other physical contact with her. Instead he swung around and started to walk back to the elevator, making it seem as if the invitation wasn't such a big deal after all.

He spoke over his shoulder. "I'll pick you up at seven-thirty and make the reservation for eight. Does that sound good for you?"

Charlotte nodded, scarcely able to credit what she'd just done. "Yes, that sounds fine." She had to swallow a couple of times before she could finish her reply. "I'll be ready at seven-thirty."

Six

Charlotte turned away from the mirror, her nose wrinkling in disgust. She looked as if she was playing dress-up with her mother's cast-offs, she thought, stripping off the blue chiffon dress and tossing it onto the pile of clothes already on her bed. She'd lost weight, quite a lot of it, since she last went shopping for play clothes, and everything in her wardrobe seemed dated, if not downright dowdy. Or maybe it was just that it had been a long time since she last really looked into her mirror, and she was shocked by the pale, uptight woman who stared back at her with eyes that were cold, assessing, and much too wary.

Charlotte stuck her hands on her hips and surveyed the pile of clothes on her bed. It was seven-twenty, and her indecision was getting ridiculous. Unless she planned to greet John Hanseck in her bra and panties, she was going to have to haul ass. There was nothing left hanging in her closet except a robe and a couple of ratty sweatpants, which narrowed her choices to the stuff strewn over her bed.

She bent down to search through the pile, and a cluster of slightly damp curls flopped onto her forehead. Gritting her teeth, she snatched a brush off the dresser, sweeping her hair off her shoulders and back into its usual severe twist. Why had she even considered wearing it loose when the humidity was so high? Besides, she never wore her hair loose these days.

She rummaged through the clothes on the bed and found the black silk slacks that had been her first choice of outfit twenty minutes earlier. She added a sleeveless fuchsia top that was only a little too big, and thrust her feet into a pair of high-heeled black sandals. Then she marched out of the bedroom without stopping for so much as another glance in the mirror. Enough already. This wasn't a real date, and it was insane—not to mention embarrassing—that her hands were shaking.

At seven-thirty she decided that John had stood her up. At seven-thirty-one she decided that he'd blown his chance, even if he did condescend to show up. At seven-thirty-two, her intercom buzzed and John announced that he was downstairs.

"I'll be right there. Don't bother to come up." Amazingly she sounded like a normal person, not like an insane woman whose panic was escalating rapidly toward full-scale hyperventilation. She picked up her purse and was halfway to the elevator before she remembered that she hadn't locked her front door. She came back, locked the door and practiced a friendly but not-too-friendly smile for when the elevator doors opened and she would be face to face with John.

She needn't have bothered. When the doors glided opened, her facial muscles froze and she could only stare at him like a wild animal caught in the glare of oncoming headlights. He was leaning against the wall opposite the elevator, waiting for her. He'd obviously come straight from the office, but he'd stripped off his jacket and tie and unfastened the top button of his shirt. All in all, he looked remarkably unlike an FBI agent.

He straightened and walked across the lobby to her side, his gaze openly admiring. "You look beautiful, Charlotte."

"Thanks." Her voice cracked a bit, but it was a relief to discover that she could speak at all.

"I came straight from the office. I'm sorry I'm late. We had so many crises this week, I gave up counting."

"There's no need to apologize, you're barely late. Anyway, you have the sort of job that has to come first."

John gave a quick grin. "Not all the time. Sometimes I'm just pushing papers around like any other bureaucrat."

She'd noticed before that John seemed to have a healthy attitude toward his job, one which suggested he took it seriously without having delusions of grandeur about how utterly irreplaceable he was. She liked his modesty.

"I've been looking forward to this all week," John said, escorting her to his car. "Café Oristano would be a great restaurant even if it was located in New York or San Francisco. In Tampa, it's a minor miracle."

He was right, Charlotte concluded three hours later as they finished their dessert, a fabulous Reine de Saba chocolate torte, baked without flour. The meal had been great, and the service quiet but attentive. Best of all, John had been a really pleasant dinner companion. He was well-informed, smart and had a slightly wacky sense of humor that made her smile. In fact, the evening had been filled with the sort of easygoing banter that only a couple of weeks earlier she'd imagined was lost to her forever. She was truly grateful to him for the gift of ordinary, everyday fun.

A warm breeze fluttered over her skin as they walked to the car, and the air felt thick in her lungs after the air-conditioning in the restaurant. She had the odd sensation that her body was coming alive again after being frozen into an eighteen-month state of suspended animation.

Despite her reawakening senses, she wasn't sure how to react when John put his arm beneath her elbow with a distinctly proprietary air. Fortunately he didn't attempt to get any closer and Charlotte was grateful for the reprieve. She had an uneasy suspicion that he would expect to kiss her good-night when they got back to her condo, and she had no idea how she was going to handle that. She'd once been a passionate woman with a lusty appetite for sex, but since Dan left, she'd lost the capacity to feel desire. For the past eighteen months, she'd preserved a nunlike state of chastity, never once tempted to break her self-imposed state of celibacy. Even now, although she'd enjoyed both the evening and John's company, she wasn't experiencing the smallest hint of sexual arousal.

John opened the car door on the passenger side. Before she could climb in, he tugged lightly on her arms and swung her around to face him. Then he bent down and kissed her gently but firmly on the mouth. His lips pressed against hers with commanding expertise. His tongue flicked lightly against her mouth.

She was so surprised that she sucked in a gasp of air and her lips parted. His tongue touched hers, but before she had time to react, John stepped back.

"Just so that you don't spend the whole drive back to your condo wondering whether or not to kiss me good-night," he said, smiling.

She managed to return his smile, although she was a little upset by the kiss. Not just because she hadn't been expecting it at that particular moment, but also because she had felt so little response. Not pleasure, and not even dismay that John had caught her unprepared. Just...nothing.

Charlotte got into the car, still slightly dazed, which was either pathetic or amusing depending on your point of view. Not many thirty-two-year-old women could be thrown into turmoil by a rather polite kiss. Apparently some significant parts of her hadn't joined in the general revival of her senses. She was suddenly impatient with her inhibited, uptight self. What the hell was she waiting for? Men didn't come in much more agreeable or better-looking packages than John Hanseck and, technically speaking, his kiss had been just fine. It was only her response—or lack thereof—that had been the problem.

She reassured herself with the thought that renewed sexual desire would probably come later. She shouldn't expect too much, too soon. A mere two weeks ago she couldn't have imagined going out to dinner with a man and having a good time. Maybe two weeks from now, once she was further into recovery, she'd be longing for John to kiss her. That was a cheering thought, and she told herself it could happen if she shook off her emotional shackles and allowed herself to step back into the land of the living.

John didn't follow up his kiss with any effort to turn their conversation in a more suggestive or intimate direction, a sensitivity for which she was deeply grateful. Instead he picked up where they had left off. They'd discovered during dinner that John had an Italian grandmother who came from the same part of Umbria as Charlotte's grandfather. Now they discovered that ten years ago the two of them had both been visiting distant cousins in Orvieto during the same week in August.

It probably wasn't all that amazing a coincidence in the grand scheme of things, but it was an intriguing link, and they had a lot of fun discussing the local fiesta they'd both attended and the copious amounts of Chianti they'd consumed as they danced in the town square beneath the stars. It amused them both to think that they might have passed within touching distance of each other all those years ago—that they might even be distantly related. They were still trying to discover if they shared any third or fourth cousins in Orvieto when John drew the car to a halt outside the entrance to her apartment building.

Charlotte was so grateful that the whole evening had passed off so much better than she could ever have expected that she felt a burst of bravado. She leaned over and pressed a swift kiss against John's cheek.

He caught her head, just lightly, and held her still, changing the kiss to something much deeper and more passionate than she had planned.

She caught a hint of his cologne as he leaned over

her. Something pleasant and unisex, of the sort produced by Calvin Klein. Maybe CK-Be? She realized it was more than a little bizarre to be analyzing John's cologne when he was passionately kissing her, but she didn't quite know what else to focus on. She didn't protest, she didn't even stiffen up when his tongue pushed against hers, but she would have felt no less emotion if she'd been kissing a Ken doll.

When John finally drew away from her, he was breathing hard, and there was a flush of color along his cheekbones. It occurred to her fleetingly how odd it was that two human beings could share the same experience and yet react to it so differently. Still, despite the ambivalent end, the evening had been about the most pleasant she'd spent in the last eighteen months, and she told him as much.

"I had a wonderful time, John. Thank you for suggesting this." She smiled at him warmly. "The restaurant was as good as you said and the company was pretty darn good, too."

He looked at her with undisguised appreciation, and just enough sexual heat to be flattering, even if she couldn't reciprocate. "From my point of view, the company wasn't just good, it was outstanding."

"I had fun," she said, which was more of a compliment than he probably realized.

"Would you like to try this again next week?" John asked. "I know a great place to go dancing in Ybor City." He paused for a moment. "That is, if you like to dance."

A million years ago, dancing had been one of her favorite activities, but Charlotte hesitated, not sure that she wanted to commit to something that would obviously be more of a real date than dinner at an Italian restaurant. "How come you know all these great places when you've only just arrived in town?" she asked, parrying for time.

He grinned. "Because I'm a hotshot investigator, remember? Besides, the first thing the Bureau recommends when you're assigned to a new location is to get to know the terrain."

"Especially the dance clubs and the restaurants?" she asked, smiling.

"Especially those," he said, returning her smile. "They're right at the top of the Bureau's search and find list." He reached out and took her hand. "Okay, Charlotte, what gives? I've spent enough time with you now to know when you're putting me off. Are you going to come dancing with me next Friday? Down Under is a great club." He carried her hand to his mouth and dropped a casual kiss onto her knuckles. "Say yes. It's much easier than inventing excuses for saying no."

"All right, I'll come." She felt a tiny burst of pleasure that she'd actually been able to screw up her courage to the point of saying yes, even if part of her was screaming out a warning to say no. "Thanks, John, I'd like to go out with you again. And if this club you're recommending is as good as the restaurant we went to tonight, it should be great."

"It will be," he said, escorting her to the smoked glass doors of her apartment building. "We're going to have a night to remember, you'll see." He waited while she swiped her key card through the lock and keyed in the entrance code. The buzzer sounded and he pushed the door open for her, waiting until she was safely inside and exchanging greetings with Luis before giving a quick wave and striding back to his car.

Getting dressed to go dancing with John turned out to be easy in comparison to her struggles of the previous week. Charlotte had spent a considerable amount of time over the past few days shopping for clothes and now was the owner of several new outfits. After her evening out with John, it had suddenly struck her as crazy that everything in her wardrobe was a minimum of two years out-of-date and at least a size too large. What had she been trying to prove all these months? That Daniel O'Toole remained such a dominating influence in her life that she could never again buy frivolous clothes when he wasn't here to admire them? That sure as hell wasn't the message she wanted to send to herself.

She slipped on a pair of new, honey-colored shantung silk slacks, together with the matching sleeveless top, then added a pair of long, fancy earrings made out of gold and topaz. The earrings had been given to her by her eldest brother a few years ago and were a perfect color complement to her outfit. She shook her head a couple of times and the earrings swayed seductively, but they looked way too nineties, she decided, so she discarded them in favor of a trio of simple gold bracelets. With the addition of a pair of high-heeled sandals and a spritz of Sunflowers perfume, she was done.

She checked her final appearance in the bedroom mirror, pleased with what she saw. The woman star-

ing back from the mirror was sleek, elegant and just
a little bit sexy.

She pouted at her reflection and gave a provocative
little wriggle of her hips, just to admire the way her
new pants shimmered in the light. *Eat your heart out,
Daniel O'Toole. See what you're missing? While
you're making crazy plans with your stupid elf, I'm
making plans for an evening out with a sexy FBI
agent. An agent who is planning to throw your ass in
jail, by the way.*

Charlotte angled her chin upward and gave a satisfied tug to the hem of her top, which barely
skimmed the waistband of her pants. Picking up a
snazzy new gold lame purse and tucking her driver's
license and a fifty-dollar bill alongside her lipstick
and tiny comb, she headed toward the kitchen in pursuit of a drink of ice water.

She'd made it out of the bedroom and into the living room before the significance of her own thoughts
struck home. She stopped dead in the middle of the
room, staring blankly into space, her heart pounding,
her mouth desert dry.

My God, what had she done? She had just made a
mental link between Daniel O'Toole and the man
she'd heard talking on the FBI tape, plotting mayhem
with the so-called elf. Her subconscious, it seemed,
had completely reversed the negative judgment she'd
offered to John Hanseck and Shirley Nicholson regarding the identity of the speaker on those clandestine tapes.

Heart pounding, hand clutched to her throat, Charlotte tried to assess which conclusion was correct.
Had Daniel O'Toole been speaking on those two

tapes or not? Had her subconscious thrown up a truth that her conscious mind wasn't willing to accept?

After a minute or two of frantic consideration, she decided that she was still confident of the opinion she'd given to the FBI agents. She didn't believe Daniel O'Toole had been speaking on either of the two recordings. Which left the puzzle of why her subconscious had produced that weird little snatch of interior monologue back in the bedroom. Charlotte could only conclude that she had experienced one of those odd glitches in brain chemistry—the type of misfiring signal that produces false memories more vivid than the real thing.

The intercom buzzed while she was still standing and staring into space. It required a physical effort before she could jolt her muscles into making the movements necessary for her to pick up the phone. "Yes?"

"It's John. Shall I come up, or are you ready?"

"I'm ready. I'll be right down."

John chuckled. "A miracle woman. Two dates, and ready on time for both of them. I think I'm in love."

Even if she hadn't just freaked out, she wouldn't have been able to think of anything to say in reply to that particular comment, which was way more than she was ready to handle, even as a joke. Charlotte mumbled that she would be right down and hung up the phone. By the time she reached the lobby, she had herself back together again and was able to greet John with a friendly smile. She decided not to mention her moment of doubt about the recordings. It would be crazy to request a second audit of the tapes just because she'd suffered a meaningless twitch of brain reflexes. What she needed to do right now was to stop obsessing about Daniel O'Toole and concentrate on having a good time.

John made that easy. He obviously had a flair for finding great places to go and have fun. The club in Ybor City had an interesting decor, a decent-size dance floor, and great special effects in terms of lighting and sound. The deejay was more than competent, and played an interesting range of music from disco, to early nineties rap and late-breaking chart-toppers.

Perhaps because she wasn't in the mood to spend much time talking, Charlotte threw herself into the dancing with an enthusiasm that bordered on the manic. John turned out to be really good, so much so that at one point when they were taking a break to drink cold sodas, she looked up at him, laughing.

"I think you're faking it," she said. "You can't possibly be a real FBI agent. I know for a fact that it's written in J. Edgar Hoover's handbook that federal agents aren't allowed to dance as well as you do."

"You're out-of-date," John said, grinning. "I believe you're referring to rule number twenty-two in the J. Edgar handbook. But those got thrown out years ago. Right around the same time it was discovered Mr. Hoover had spent most of his spare time wearing pink frilly dresses. Those pink frills kind of undercut the moral authority of his regulations, you know?"

"Yes, I guess they would have," Charlotte smiled at him, happy to be out of her condo, happy to be putting her past behind her, happy to be dancing like a single woman whose heart was whole and fancy-free.

Screw you, Daniel O'Toole, wherever you are. I can be happy without you. And why the hell was she thinking about her scumbag ex-husband when she was dancing with a man as charming and honorable as John Hanseck?

The deejay started to play a song from the seventies by the Village People and John put down his glass of Coke, laughing as he reached out to take her hand. "Hey, listen to that. They're playing my song."

Charlotte shot him a disbelieving look. "You like the Village People?"

"Sure, why not?" he said, leading her back onto the dance floor, where the lights were flashing in a dazzling, psychedelic display. "I'll let you into my dirty little secret. I don't just like disco music, I love it." He gave a wriggle of his hips and stomped his heel, managing to look sexy rather than ridiculous. "Hey, man, watch me go. I should have been born fifteen years earlier, then Travolta wouldn't have stood a chance."

She rolled her eyes. "Right, I'm sure his career would have been over once the casting director saw you."

"Wanna make a bet?" Hitching his thumbs into his shirt as if it were a jacket, John sashayed around the edge of the dance floor in an impressive imitation of Travolta in *Saturday Night Fever,* stopping every so often to spin her around, or pull her into his arms for a few seconds of close body contact. He was good enough to attract admiring attention, but it was clear he was dancing to please himself and her, not to show off for the crowd, and his enjoyment was contagious. Charlotte found herself partnering him with an abandon that would have seemed unimaginable a few weeks earlier. She felt lithe and agile, as if shedding her hang-ups about O'Toole had lifted a physical weight from her body. She danced with the pent-up energy stored from eighteen months of stifling self-control.

The deejay apparently shared John's enthusiasm for disco. He was on a roll and played an entire set of fast-paced hits from the seventies and early eighties. The crowd on the dance floor bobbed, swayed and heaved in a fractured, but communal rhythm, the strobe lights giving the scene a surreal luminescence. The air-conditioning was cranked so high that anybody sitting on the sidelines would have been forgiven for wondering if they'd miraculously been transported to the frozen tundra of the Arctic Circle, but since she'd been dancing so hard, Charlotte could feel her top starting to stick to her back as sweat pooled along her spine.

The music finally changed to something slow, a tune that Charlotte didn't recognize. John held out his arms and she flowed into them, caught up in the mood of the moment. "I'm so glad we came here tonight," she said to John.

His arms tightened, drawing her close. "So am I," he murmured, and she felt his fingers run lightly up her back and tangle in her hair. "I really enjoy spending time with you, Charlotte."

She wasn't sure whether to give him an answer that would push him away, or draw him closer. Fortunately she didn't have to decide because it was almost impossible to carry on a conversation. It was approaching midnight, and the dance floor was getting more and more crowded. Somebody bumped into John, toppling hard enough against him that he was pushed up against her. Knocked off balance, Charlotte took several clumsy steps backward before she regained control of herself.

"Sorry," John said, holding out a steadying hand. "Are you okay? Want to sit down?"

"No, I'm fine." She turned to apologize to the woman whose foot she'd trodden on. "Sorry. I hope I didn't hurt you?"

The woman shook her head. "I'll live. Jeez, it's a zoo in here tonight, isn't it?"

Charlotte turned back to John. As she turned, he crossed his eyes and clutched his throat with his hand in a dramatic gesture.

She laughed. "Stop it, John. There isn't room to fool around. Gross. You look like Jim Carey pretending he's eating dog food."

John didn't answer. Instead he lurched toward her, falling against her so hard that she completely lost her balance and followed him down onto the floor.

Charlotte wasn't hurt, apart from a bumped knee, and she quickly stood up, only to realize that John was still lying on the floor. She knelt down again, trying to protect him from people's feet, horrified to see that his eyes were closed and his breathing had become shallow and erratic. What in the world was wrong? Was he having a heart attack?

"John? What is it?" She put her ear to his chest but it was impossible to hear over the megavolume of the music. "Oh my God, John! Talk to me!"

An eddy of confusion was already rippling out from the spot where John was lying. A short, stocky man pushed through the encircling crowd that was growing denser by the moment. "I'm a doctor," he said, squatting down next to her. "Stand back," he ordered. "Give me some room, can't you?"

"What happened?" the doctor asked, unbuttoning John's shirt and pressing his ear against John's chest just as she had done. "Jesus, can somebody get the music turned down? I can't hear anything."

"I don't know what happened." Charlotte's mind was a blur where there should have been clarity. What was it about her? she thought wildly. What quality made her attract husbands who disappeared with the garbage, and FBI agents who collapsed for no reason? "He was fine a few minutes ago. We were dancing, and then he just…passed out."

"Did he take anything?" the doctor asked, reaching for John's pulse. "Ecstasy? Coke? PCP? Meth? If he did, now is the time to tell me."

Charlotte shook her head. "Absolutely not."

"Don't lie because you're afraid he'll be arrested."

"He didn't take anything, I'm sure. He's with law enforcement. He'd never do any illegal drugs."

Another man pushed his way through the thickening crowd. "Step aside, please. Make way. I'm the club manager. What's happened here?"

"This man looks as if he might have had a heart attack," the doctor said. "We need an ambulance."

"I already called," a woman said, gesturing to her cell phone. "They're on their way."

"Great." The manager quickly selected three strong-looking young men. "Could you carry him into my office? It's over to the right of the bar. It'll be quieter there. If you could come with me, miss,

"Yes, of course—"

Just as the three men picked up John's inert body, the music stopped and the lights went out, leaving the room in total darkness. Sounds of frightened laughter and a couple of muted screams echoed in the sudden silence. Charlotte shut her eyes, then opened them again, able to see a little better once her pupils had dilated to accommodate the darkness.

Before she could locate John, or the men carrying him, she felt herself grabbed from behind. A canned announcement advised everyone to stay where they were and wait for the emergency generators to kick in. Lights would come on in sixty seconds.

She twisted around, furious at whoever hoped to take advantage of the darkness to cop a cheap feel. "Get lost, creep."

A gloved hand clamped over her mouth and she was spun back into her original position. She started to struggle, anxious to break away, but she felt something hard and round sticking into the small of her back and a voice spoke into her ear. The voice was low-pitched, with a slight French accent, but it was crystal clear in its menace.

"I have a gun and I will use it. Start walking now. I will guide you."

Guide her? Like hell he would. Charlotte had once been a cautious woman. Back in the days when she had a husband, a home, and a family to lose, she would never have defied such an order. But her would-be kidnapper was out of luck. She no longer had anything to lose and he was about to discover he had chosen the wrong woman for his sick sexual games.

Steaming mad, she rammed her elbow backward into her attacker's ribs, simultaneously stamping down on his foot with her high-heeled sandal and biting the hand covering her mouth with all the force she could muster.

She hoped to catch him off guard, but her captor wasn't so easily vanquished. He must have been wearing shoes that tied over his instep because the heel of her shoe tangled in the laces and snapped instead of grinding into his foot and breaking his bones. He did give a grunt as her elbow pummeled into his gut, but his hold never loosened, much less broke. A leather glove protected his hand from her biting teeth and he never relaxed the pressure he was exerting on her mouth sufficiently for her to scream. Given the darkness, even screaming might not have been enough to attract attention to her plight.

What the hell had happened to the emergency lights? Why was it still dark?

"Walk, Charlotte. I am in a hurry."

He rolled the R when he said her name, giving it an exotic intonation. How did he know her name, anyway? Apparently he hadn't just randomly selected her as a victim. Had he been lying in wait? Stalking her?

She shivered, repulsed by the thought. She might not be able to break free of his hold, Charlotte decided, but she sure as hell wasn't going to cooperate by walking out of the door with him. If she struggled hard enough, the lights would probably come back on before he could make it to the door.

Her efforts to escape weren't helped by the rising tide of panic rippling through the room. Nobody was paying much attention to other people's problems and her silent struggles were invisible. Her captor was incredibly strong, and once he realized that she hadn't been intimidated by his gun, he changed his tactics. He simply swung her up into his arms and carried her. The second her hands were free, she reached up to scratch his face, but she didn't get his eyes, as she'd hoped, since he was wearing goggles. For some reason, that really freaked her out. Had he *known* she was going to scratch him, for God's sake, and come protected?

She screamed for help, trying desperately to attract attention now that her captor was using both of his hands to carry her and couldn't keep her mouth covered. Nobody responded, perhaps because it was difficult to be sure where sounds were coming from in the pitch-blackness. Besides, the continued darkness was obviously getting to people and her scream was simply one amongst several.

"Where are the emergency lights?" a man's voice boomed. "What the hell is going on here?"

The cry was taken up, the noise level rising along with the panic. But despite the eddies of movement as men and women pushed blindly in search of the exit—any exit—her captor somehow managed to circle the dance floor without bumping into anyone. How was he doing that? How could he move so fast and so successfully?

The answer came to her at once. He was wearing night vision goggles. That was what she had felt when she tried to scratch his eyes. Charlotte reached up again, trying to rip off the goggles and take away his advantage, but he jerked his head back, then abruptly stopped and stood her on her feet.

"I don't have time for this," he said. "The lights will come on again in twenty seconds." He swung out with his fist.

The rat bastard had punched her out! Charlotte felt a burst of excruciating pain that spread in a swift wave from her jaw to her teeth to the top of her head. Red stars exploded behind her eyes and she fell away into oblivion.

Seven

Brian Fitzpatrick paced the deck of his cousin's boat, the *Dream of Ireland*. Well, the boat was registered in his cousin's name, but Fitzpatrick had bought it and he paid the astronomical sums of money it cost to keep the damn tub afloat. A military man himself, Fitzpatrick had little love of the sea. Still, his cousin was a useful ally, and deep sea fishing was his thing, so Fitzpatrick was willing to pay for the boy's pleasures. And, as it happened, the boat was going to come in pretty damn useful over the next few days.

Fitzpatrick still thought of himself as a soldier, though he'd left the military years earlier. He had reached the rank of major in the United States Army before he was court-martialed by a bunch of pantywaist Pentagon officials who were too afraid of the media to stand up for what every real soldier in the field knew was right. Even now, eleven years after his trial, he still got mad as hell when he thought about pencil-pushers, safe behind their desks, deciding what was appropriate behavior for a soldier during battle.

The incident that precipitated Fitzpatrick's persecution occurred during the Gulf War, when he'd been part of a small reconnaissance party, moving toward the front lines where everyone knew—even the pen-cil-pushers at the Pentagon—that Saddam Hussein's elite guards were buried in foxholes, waiting to fire their goddamn shoulder-launched missiles and wipe out as many U.S. troops as they possibly could.

The situation on the ground in Saudi Arabia was nowhere near as comfortable and well-organized as the TV reporters in their fancy safari jackets made it appear, and on the day when all Fitzpatrick's troubles started, an unexpected attack of SCUD missiles the night before had made life more miserable than usual. To add to the woes of a sleepless night, Fitzpatrick had been ordered to spend the morning escorting the lieutenant-colonel of a British Special Forces unit, who was newly arrived at the American Forward Operations base.

To Fitzpatrick's chagrin, the British colonel had been treated by the top brass and the media as if he were a supreme expert on the status of Operation Desert Storm. All this attention simply because he had been decorated for his bravery during combat in the pathetic Falklands War ten years earlier. The colonel had already been interviewed for a nightly news segment with Dan Rather, as well as giving quotes to more print journalists than you could shake a stick at. And not just reporters for the British tabloids, either. *Time* and *Newsweek* had both sent reporters to do a personal profile, although nobody from the media had ever bothered to interview Major Fitzpatrick and ask his opinion of how the war was shaping up. Why were they interviewing Brits when there were plenty of red-blooded American experts to talk to?

The lieutenant-colonel, a prick in fancy uniform

named Gervaise Cavendish, was the son of a baron. He spoke as if he had a hot potato stuck in his mouth, and walked around the desert camp as if he was expecting to present arms to Queen Elizabeth at every goddamn corner. There were a quarter of a million U.S. troops on the ground in Saudi Arabia, and maybe two hundred Brits, so Fitzpatrick thought he should have been able to go about his business without running into any foreigners. Unfortunately he'd gotten shafted. For political reasons, the president and General Schwarzkopf wanted to remind everyone it was an international coalition fighting the Iraqis, not just the Americans. So Brian Fitzpatrick had gotten stuck with helping to create the illusion that the Brits were actually doing something useful. More useful that is, than strutting around looking as if they owned the goddamn sands of Arabia.

No doubt for reasons of personal aggrandizement, Gervaise Cavendish had requested the chance to take a personal tour of the area where every one expected the imminent battle to take place, and Fitzpatrick had been assigned to accompany him. They'd hand-picked their teams of half a dozen men each, and set off into the desert. This was at least two weeks before anyone realized that Saddam's supposedly elite guards were all starving to death, that the fighters were not only scared shitless, but were mostly armed with nothing more effective than worn-out French surplus small arms, half of which weren't operational because they were bunged up with sand.

Fitzpatrick and his men had split off from the Brits as each team explored slightly different desert areas, where piles of boulders looked as if they might be haphazard attempts to form a barricade. Fitzpatrick had been shocked—not surprised, and certainly not unprepared, dammit—when they came across a nest of Hussein's personal guards, buried like fucking vipers beneath a wall of sand, their bunker reinforced with what looked at first glance to be concrete, and turned out to be thin gray sheets of molded plastic.

Later, at his court martial, the prosecution had claimed that Major Brian Fitzpatrick lost his head in the face of unexpected enemy fire. That for all his military prowess and his success in war simulation games, he'd been goddamn fucking *scared* when he actually found himself in the midst of a real battle. They claimed that he'd opened fire at random and screamed at his men to fire, which was obviously okay given that they were under enemy attack. But then he'd kept firing long after the fourteen miserable Iraqi prisoners had crawled out of their foxhole, arms over their heads, the rags of their once-white clothing attached to a stick to indicate surrender.

The incident would never have been reported if not for Lieutenant-Colonel Gervaise Cavendish, who claimed Fitzpatrick hadn't just responded to enemy fire: he'd been out of control, his conduct not fitting for an officer. According to Cavendish, when he arrived on the scene a couple of minutes after most of the Iraqis had been killed and the others were cowering in the shade of a rock, Fitzpatrick had shot and wounded two of the British soldiers in the colonel's ATV when they tried to prevent him finishing off the tiny group of huddled and terrified Iraqi survivors.

Fitzpatrick had never understood—still didn't—what the hell the point was of saving Iraqi soldiers, just so that they could come back and bite you on the ass a few years later. Look at what a mess America was in right now, just because the soldiers of Desert Storm hadn't been allowed to do their jobs. The top brass had balls made out of puffed cotton, and hadn't dared to head to Baghdad and take out Saddam Hussein when they had the chance. Now everyone was wondering how long it would be before Hussein aimed a nuclear rocket at New York. Wow! And the pricks in the Pentagon were surprised?

Serve them damn well right. Fitzpatrick had the satisfaction of knowing that, despite protests from the Brits, he'd at least managed to wipe out those last few Iraqi troops, cowering in front of him. Unfortunately he'd paid the price of his own bravery. The Honourable Colonel Fucking Cavendish had put him under arrest and hauled him back to camp as if he were a criminal, instead of a hero who'd slaughtered a bunch of the enemy under conditions of extreme personal danger.

Thank God, the panel of judges at his court-martial had been patriotic enough to recognize a good soldier when they saw one, and they'd refused to convict Fitzpatrick of the various crimes with which he'd been charged. They, at least, realized how much bravery was involved in fighting and killing a pocket of enemy soldiers when you were outnumbered two to one.

Despite the not guilty verdict, his career in the military was over, that much was clear. Instead of going on to win the promotion he'd deserved as a result of his outstanding Gulf War service, he'd been pushed into taking early retirement. Worse, most of his fellow officers acted toward him as if he was damned lucky not to be heading to Kansas, and the military prison in Leavenworth. Colonel Fucking Cavendish was giving interviews to his pals in the media, reminding them that Fitzpatrick hadn't just killed Iraqi soldiers, he'd fired point-blank at two British soldiers who were simply trying to enforce international rules about the surrender of prisoners.

Fitzpatrick's prosecution had caused quite a furor in the media. He understood that the *New York Times* and the rest of the baying hounds of the liberal, left-wing media would be out for his blood, but he'd expected reasonable people in places like Texas and Oklahoma to understand that he was really a hero. But, inexplicably, they hadn't, mostly because of those two damn British soldiers who'd died. Fitzpatrick had his supporters, but they were few and far between, at least in public. In private, a few more people were willing to tell him that he'd done the right thing and that the government ought to be ashamed of attempting to prosecute a soldier who'd simply done his duty.

One of Fitzpatrick's most outspoken supporters was Thomas Flannigan, who had started his own small business producing irradiation equipment for food processors back in the early eighties. By 1992, the company was growing by leaps and bounds, and Thomas offered Fitzpatrick a job as his chief operating officer.

Fitzpatrick turned out to be as good at organizing civilian factory operations as he had been at organizing military ordnance. The company experienced a spectacular growth spurt during the roaring nineties and Thomas floated shares on the NASDAQ at just the right moment to maximize profits.

Their successful share offering made millionaires of both of them. Not paper millionaires of the dot-com sort, but real ones, with a solid company and a real product. They survived the stock market crash, bloodied but not mortally wounded, and carried on generating healthy revenue right into the new millennium. When Thomas retired to his native Ireland, Fitzpatrick became president and CEO of a company with sales ranging upward of 250 million dollars a year.

Fitzpatrick's parents had both been born in Ireland, but he'd never felt much of a link to the land of his ancestors. In fact, he'd always been scornful of his grandparents' devotion to the IRA, attributing their sectarian fervor to their lack of education. Then Thomas persuaded him to stay with him in Galway for a few days, before traveling north to his parents' birthplace in Belfast—where the newly promoted Brigadier General Gervaise Cavendish was now in charge of the British troops illegally occupying the land that was Fitzpatrick's ancestral heritage.

Sitting in the cramped front parlor of one of his cousins in Belfast, a fervent, third-generation supporter of the IRA, ex-Major Brian Fitzpatrick underwent a transformation. He not only became a born-again Irish patriot, but he also saw how he could get back at the man who'd ruined his career, and simultaneously punish the idiots in the United States government who'd chosen to prosecute one of their own authentic heroes. His newfound wealth provided some consolation for having had his career as an army officer snatched away from him, but punishing Brigadier Fucking Cavendish and humiliating the U.S. government would do a hundred times more to soothe his bruised ego than accumulating additional money. Besides, the truth was that overseeing the day-to-day operations of a production line bored Fitzpatrick. He wanted back to his old glory days of combat. He set about building up the international sales of his company's products, giving him an excuse for frequent trips overseas.

For an Irish-American with money to burn and a background as a soldier, it wasn't very difficult to insinuate himself into the innermost circles of the Irish paramilitary movement. Before long, with the help of generous expenditures of cash, he'd taken over command of the Armargh Army from Colm Doherty, the previous General, a hidebound old-timer who'd smoked and plotted himself into terminal lung cancer.

Fitzpatrick's first glorious operation was the attempted assassination of Gervaise Cavendish. The Armargh Army didn't quite succeed in killing him, but they did manage to wound him so badly that he lost the use of both legs and was forced to retire from the army. All in all, Fitzpatrick decided that a crippled Brigadier Cavendish, with many years of painful life ahead of him, was almost better than having created a dead hero.

After that glowing start to his career as General of the Armargh Army, Fitzpatrick derived immense satisfaction from building his mystique as the unseen, all-powerful commander. Even the debacle at Craigavon didn't undercut his growing reputation within the movement, since the Craigavon attack had been a last fling organized by Colm Doherty, and the rank-and-file knew precisely who'd ordered the attack.

The slaughter of five long-time Armargh Army lieutenants gave Fitzpatrick the chance to move in with new men of his own choosing. With fresh personnel in place, he could impose an agenda that followed his comprehensive, cosmopolitan vision, rather than the one-eyed excuse for a game plan that had been pursued by Doherty and Doherty's chief of operations, Daniel O'Toole.

In fact, O'Toole had been a thorn in Fitzpatrick's side almost from the beginning. O'Toole had obviously expected to become General after Colm Doherty's death, and he didn't hesitate to spread the word that the new General had won his position simply by spending money to bribe supporters. Fortunately O'Toole hadn't hung around in Ireland to hammer home his slanderous message. Instead, after the debacle at Craigavon, O'Toole had taken himself off to eastern Europe and gradually built up the counterfeiting operation that had become the financial backbone of the Armargh Army. Then he'd disappeared for almost two years, and had only returned to the fold eighteen months ago.

Fitzpatrick was willing to admit that O'Toole had done a good job of training a nucleus of dedicated foot soldiers willing and able to function in the American homeland, as opposed to the familiar streets of their hometown, Belfast. Fitzpatrick also admired the painstaking way O'Toole had built a relationship with the crazy lunatic Elf. O'Toole's instant grasp of the potential of that alliance had been a breathtaking example of clever forward planning.

The trouble was, Fitzpatrick didn't trust O'Toole, not entirely, and right now he was waiting to hear that his insurance plan to insure O'Toole's unquestioning obedience had worked. Fitzpatrick paced the deck of the *Dream of Ireland,* waiting for Sean and Ryan to arrive with Charlotte Leone. Every time he felt himself get tense, he'd reflect on the irony that he'd used profits generated by O'Toole's counterfeiting operation to pay for the boat that was going to serve as a prison for O'Toole's ex-wife, and then he'd relax again.

He heard a car draw up, and he moved to the dockside, already relishing the prospect of his meeting later tonight with O'Toole. It was more than time that the cocky bastard was cut down to size, and Fitzpatrick would derive great satisfaction from doing the cutting. If there was one thing that really ticked off Fitzpatrick, it was a man with too good an opinion of himself.

Sean got out of the minivan, followed a second later by Ryan. There was no woman carried between them. Fitzpatrick saw them exchange glances. In the dim light, it wasn't possible to discern their expressions, but he was already getting an unpleasant feeling that this was an operation that hadn't worked out exactly according to plan.

He gestured for them to come on board and he sensed reluctance as they complied.

''Where's the woman?'' he asked, with no attempt at a greeting. Generals didn't indulge in idle chitchat with their foot soldiers.

"We didn't get her," Sean admitted.

Fitzpatrick held his temper in check. A disciplined military officer could always do that. "Why not?"

"I don't know." Sean was loyal, but he was also one of the stupidest men Fitzpatrick had ever had to deal with. "We arrived at the time we'd agreed, and we saw her dancing with the man you'd described. But before we could take her, somebody cut the electrical power to the whole fuckin' club. Even the parking lot was black."

"How do you know it wasn't just a regular power failure?" Fitzpatrick asked, still keeping his annoyance under tight control.

"Doesn't seem likely, General." Ryan cleared his throat. "After a few minutes in the dark, when all the screaming died down a bit, we could see there was somethin' goin' on over toward the other side of the club. We went over there, and we found this man stretched out on the floor. It was the man who'd been dancing with the Leone woman. We asked if anybody knew who he was and somebody told us that they'd found identification on him that showed he was an FBI agent. Name of John Hanseck—"

"Was he dead?" Fitzpatrick almost spat out the question.

"I dunno." Sean actually scratched his head. With the exercise of superhuman self-discipline, Fitzpatrick refrained from shooting him on the spot. Sean was a superb diver, an underwater operative to drool over, and they were going to need him.

"Did you even look for the Leone woman?" he demanded. "If she was dancing with Hanseck when the lights went out, she can't have vanished into thin air!''

"She was dancing all right. We both saw her. But we don't know what happened to her, sir. You couldn't see anything. It was pitch-black.'' Ryan sounded apologetic as well he might. "Dark as a coal mine it was in there until the generator kicked in. And then, when the lights came back on, there wasn't a sign of the woman.''

"Did you check her condo? The hospital?''

"Yes, sir. She didn't go home. She wasn't listed as injured.''

"Then where the hell is she?''

Ryan and Sean exchanged another wary glance. "We don't know, sir. She's gone.''

Eight

Charlotte was still half asleep when her stomach gave a panicked swoop, jolting her into consciousness. It took another few seconds to orient herself enough to recall precisely what she was afraid of. When she finally remembered, fear filmed her body with sweat.

For a few moments she was too scared to move, then anger came to her rescue. She'd been knocked unconscious, kidnapped and transported God knew where. She had no idea what had happened to John Hanseck. Worst case scenario, he might be dead. If he was dead, she wondered if he'd died from natural causes—or because he'd been guilty of the crime of knowing her. If John had just happened to suffer a heart attack moments before the lights went out at the nightclub, it sure stretched the long arm of coincidence mighty far. Stretched it beyond snapping point as far as Charlotte was concerned.

Her anger kicked a notch higher. Things might look pretty damn bleak right now, but no way was she going to play the role of passive victim for the entertainment of the sicko pervert who'd constructed such an elaborate plan to capture her. She'd already been well and truly victimized by Daniel O'Toole, and once in a lifetime was more than enough to play that lousy role. The rat bastard who'd abducted her was about to discover that he'd settled his psycho fantasies on the wrong woman.

She supposed that if she defied her kidnapper, he might kill her. But he might kill her, anyway, however much she tried to cooperate with his twisted plans. In fact, Charlotte doubted if her actions would have much impact on his decision, which had probably been made days ago for reasons that made sense only in his own sick mind. At least she could salvage her pride and decide that she wasn't going to cooperate in her own destruction. Sexual predators fed off their victims' fear, or so she'd heard, and she was going to deny this particular pervert the succor he craved.

Charlotte lay absolutely still, not even opening her eyes, but her paralysis was now intentional. She wanted to take stock of her surroundings before she alerted her kidnapper to the fact that she had regained consciousness. Feigning sleep wouldn't give her much of an advantage, but it at least allowed her to nurture the illusion that she was in control of what happened, if only for the next few minutes.

Eyes firmly shut, she let her other senses absorb as much information as they could. The mere fact of having an action plan turned out to be a good way to ward off fear. She was lying in a comfortable bed, she discovered, with sheets, pillows and some sort of cover in all the right places. She was wearing her bra and panties. The discovery that she was at least semi-clothed was a relief. As far as she could tell without moving, she was alone in the bed. Another major relief. Her body didn't feel sore or bruised or battered, except along her jaw, where the rat bastard had socked her one. Could she take the absence of aches and pains as a hopeful sign that he hadn't raped her? Or had she simply been unconscious, and therefore not resisting when he penetrated her? Charlotte just managed to repress a body-heaving shudder at the possibility of having been sexually abused while she was drugged into unconsciousness.

A man spoke from across the room. "If you are thirsty, you will find a glass of ice water already on the table beside the bed."

She recognized the rat bastard's voice, with its distinctive hint of a French accent. Possibly French Canadian? She wasn't good enough at accents to tell. How the hell had he known she was awake when she hadn't moved...hadn't even opened her eyes? Damn him, anyway. Charlotte's mouth was sandpaper dry and she longed for a drink, but no way was she going to sit up and reach meekly for the water he'd provided. Besides, it might be drugged. She kept her eyes closed, continuing to feign sleep while she grabbed a few more seconds to weigh her options.

"Your breathing has changed, Charlotte. I know you are awake. I know also that you must be thirsty. It is the inevitable consequence of the medication I injected into you last night. But if you wish to keep up the pretense that you are sleeping, it is okay with me. We have a little time to spare, so we can play games if you wish."

Time to spare? Before doing what? She sure as hell didn't intend to play any games with a pervert like him. Besides, there was no advantage in pretending to be asleep if she wasn't deceiving him. Charlotte didn't deign to answer, but she opened her eyes and sat up enough to take quick stock of her surroundings.

It seemed she was in a fairly standard motel room, the sort that could be found throughout the state of Florida, offering all the comforts of home and free orange juice for seventy-five bucks a night. There were two queen-size beds, a TV on top of a low dresser, and a Formica-topped table in the corner, with a chair on either side. The sole window seemed to be high, long and narrow above the bed behind her, but the curtains were drawn shut so that the only light came from a low-wattage fixture inside the bathroom. She could just make out the time on the clock radio beside the bed, which didn't have an illuminated dial: 10:31 a.m. She assumed on Saturday morning. The phone, she noticed, was unplugged and tossed onto the second bed. The cord that would have made it functional was nowhere to be seen.

Her captor stood by the table. It wasn't possible to see much more than that he was tall and lean with dark brown hair cut in a flat buzz close to his head. In the dim light, his skin appeared deeply tanned, and his eyes, as far as she could tell, were also brown. He wore cotton pants and a black T-shirt with no logo, and the short-sleeved shirt revealed arms corded with muscle.

Taking his features individually, there was nothing about his face or body that was especially remarkable, beyond an overall impression of extreme physical fitness, but Charlotte's skin broke out in goose bumps as she looked at him. Something about this man's appearance caused her to react with visceral intensity.

The thought flashed through her mind that he didn't look like a man who needed to abduct women in order to get sex. On the contrary, he looked like the sort of dominating alpha male who attracted flocks of women misguided enough to believe they alone had the power to tame him.

His handsome appearance brought no comfort. In Charlotte's opinion, the most frightening perverts of all were the ones who looked more or less normal. Her brother, Paul, always insisted that all serial killers showed physical signs of their insanity. That Jeffrey Dahmer, for instance, had the eyes of a cannibal. You could tell there was something creepy about the guy just by looking, Paul maintained. Charlotte had never been able to see the alleged creepiness. If she'd been shown Dahmer's picture and heard he was running for a seat on the school board or town council, she'd have been willing to give him her vote. She suspected her brother, for all his protestations to the contrary, would have been equally willing. The Jeffrey Dahmers of the world succeeded precisely because they didn't look like the monsters they were until it was too late.

She sneaked another quick glance at her captor and he inclined his head in mocking acknowledgment of her inspection. Charlotte pulled the covers up to her chin, hiding a shiver. Why had he brought her here? What did he want? Biggest question of all—did he have any intention of letting her get out alive?

Charlotte was about to let rip with a torrent of questions when she realized that silence might be a weapon. Puny, perhaps, but at least something to stash in her otherwise empty arsenal. From the point of view of her kidnapper, a silent victim would be very annoying. If he was looking forward to hearing her beg and plead, keeping silent might taunt him into losing his temper. And if he lost his temper, he might reveal more than he intended. By contrast, the more she pleaded, the more he was likely to derive pleasure from tormenting her with obscure, twisted answers that appealed to his sick sense of humor but provided her with little useful information.

It was a high-risk strategy, she realized, because her kidnapper was guaranteed to be mentally unstable and her silence could easily throw him over the top and precipitate precisely the violence she wanted to avoid. Still, on balance, she figured it was worth trying to step outside the boundaries of what he would expect her to do.

Keeping her gaze averted, she quickly rolled out of bed, dragging the sheet with her. Her legs were shaky—maybe from the drug he'd injected into her—but she ran into the bathroom without speaking or even glancing in his direction. Annoyed to notice that her hands were as unsteady as her legs, she slammed the door behind her, securing it with the laughably flimsy push-lock. The lock was so inadequate that her six-year-old nephew would have been able to break it open without much effort and she knew it would present no challenge at all to her captor.

She searched frantically for something to fortify the lock, expecting at any moment to hear the rat bastard running across the room to rip open the rickety door, but there was no sound of movement. It seemed her kidnapper was as capable of playing the silence game as she was.

Charlotte wasn't sure whether she'd just won or lost a psychological battle, but there wasn't time to hang around speculating about the score. She needed to find a way to break out of captivity.

The bathroom—no surprise—was windowless. No easy escape route there. Running water to hide the sound of her movements, she climbed onto the side of the tub and poked at a few ceiling tiles, expending just enough time to discover that the space above the tiles was no more than twelve inches high and was stuffed chock-a-block with pipes and conduits. Unlike all the movies she'd watched recently, there was no possible way to crawl conveniently to freedom via the ceiling.

Charlotte shrugged off her disappointment. She hadn't really expected to find an escape route in the bathroom. The man who'd captured her might be crazy, but from the brief glimpse she'd had, he didn't look as if he were stupid. She couldn't count on him making half-assed plans for her imprisonment that she could easily circumvent. Still, if she couldn't escape, she could shower and, with luck, wash away some of her lingering physical weakness so that she'd be better prepared to seize any chance for escape that came her way. At least he hadn't chained her to the bed, and right now she was willing to count her blessings.

She would have loved to stand for ten minutes or so under a pounding hot spray, but there was no way to guess how long she could trust her captor to stay on his side of the bathroom door, so she spent barely a minute under the shower before drying off with one of the cheap, thin towels. Then she stuck her head under the tap at the sink and drank copious amounts of water. Since this was July in Florida—she assumed they were still in Florida—the water was tepid and tasted unpleasantly of sulphur, but it was better than the alternative of meekly accepting the dictates of her captor and drinking the ice water he'd provided. At the moment, defiance was all she had to bolster her will to resist, so she grabbed her courage where she could find it.

There was a mirror over the sink, which wasn't a blessing. A single glance was enough to confirm Charlotte's suspicion that she looked like something horrid dragged in by one of her father's dogs during deer hunting season. A purple bruise bloomed along the line of her jaw, although her face wasn't as puffy as she would have expected, almost as if her captor had used an ice pack to keep down the swelling. Her hair hung in matted hanks around her shoulders, but since she had no brush, the best she could do was dampen her fingers and comb them through the mess. A process, she discovered, that had worked well for Jamie Lee Curtis in *True Lies,* but sure didn't work for Charlotte Leone in real life.

She scowled into the mirror, hating the fact that she looked so pathetic, so much like a battered victim, but since there was nothing more she could do to improve her appearance, she gave up and moved on. Dressing in her bra and panties, she discovered once again that there was quite a bit of psychological re-assurance to be gained from having underwear to put on. Then she wrapped the sheet tightly around her body, unlocked the bathroom door and stepped back into the gloomy bedroom.

Rat Bastard was sitting at the table, studying a map

with one of the tiny lights designed for reading in bed without disturbing your partner. He switched off the light as she came out of the bathroom, rising to his feet. She drew to a halt with the width of both beds remaining safely between them, but even that wasn't enough to stop her stomach clenching and her nipples growing taut with dread.

He looked at her in a silence that rapidly filled to bursting point with tension. Charlotte felt her skin grow hot, and she resisted the urge to pull the sheet even higher around her neck. Her body was responding to him in a way that she couldn't understand and made her very uncomfortable.

Rat Bastard apparently felt no need to speak, and the silence that had seemed such a good idea only a few minutes earlier now struck Charlotte as unbearably oppressive.

"What do you want with me?" she blurted out.

"What do I want?" He gave a small, ironic smile. "But of course I want to protect you, Charlotte."

Few answers could have scared her more. She'd read *Silence of the Lambs*. She'd watched all those TV documentaries about rapists and serial murderers. The Hannibal Lecters of the world always wanted to "protect" their victims. Unfortunately she wasn't wild about their methods of protection, which usually seemed to involve cutting their protégées into small pieces and storing them in the refrigerator.

Since she had no desire to become grilling steak, she decided this wasn't a good moment to let her fear show. "I don't need protecting," she said, trying her best to sound disdainful. From the wobble in her voice, she was pretty sure she merely sounded what she really was—terrified.

"That is true." He moved his hand in a gesture of acknowledgment. "Now that you are with me you are no longer in danger. Before, you were at great risk."

Arrogant bastard. "Of course I wasn't at risk! I was leading a life of totally boring safety."

"On the contrary. Your safety was an illusion."

"Why?" she asked angrily. "How? There's nobody who has any desire to harm me. Apart from you, that is."

"I have no desire to harm you. The opposite, in fact."

"You could sure have fooled me," she said. She deliberately touched the bruises along her jaw and saw his gaze follow the movement of her fingers. His expression didn't alter, but she could have sworn he was disturbed by the reminder of how he'd subdued her with a vicious punch.

When he answered her, however, his voice sounded dismissive rather than concerned. "I regret some of the methods I was forced to employ in order to bring you to safety, but my task was a difficult one. You are unaware of the forces in play around you."

"Then enlighten me."

He hesitated for a moment. "The danger comes from your connection to Daniel O'Toole."

If he was trying to grab her attention, he'd succeeded. A fresh spurt of outrage washed over her. She was in this rotten, miserable situation because of *O'Toole?* Was she never, ever going to be free of the man? But if this abduction was connected to O'Toole and his nefarious activities, then presumably her kidnapper wasn't planning to rape her. Was it possible that she'd misjudged his reasons for abducting her? Belatedly Charlotte realized that there wasn't a shred of evidence to support her previous assumption that her kidnapper was motivated by a need for kinky sex. In retrospect, she wasn't quite sure why she'd jumped to that conclusion. Because she'd sensed a strange undercurrent of sexual tension between the two of them?

Her nose wrinkling at the disgusting thought, Charlotte sat down on the bed for the simple reason that her legs would no longer support her. Sex and Daniel O'Toole were two subjects that she didn't like to think about, and here they were, thrust under her nose in one unappetizing package.

"What do you mean, the danger comes from my connection to Daniel O'Toole?" she asked. "I have no connection to O'Toole."

"You were married to him. Do you not consider that a connection?"

"I wasn't married to O'Toole," Charlotte snapped. How many times did she have to keep making the same elementary point, and to how many different people? "I was married to a man named Riordan Gray."

Her captor shrugged. "Some people might consider that a distinction without a difference."

"Then they would be fools," Charlotte replied tautly. "O'Toole was no more my husband than Toby Maguire is really Spiderman. Our entire life together was a lie. O'Toole is a terrorist and he used me against my will. I despise everything about the man." She stopped abruptly, getting up from the bed and turning her back on her captor. Her plan had been to provoke *him* into losing his cool and revealing more than he planned. So far, the exact opposite was happening.

By chance, she ended up facing the closed draperies and she saw a way to make her leap up from the bed appear purposeful. Why was the kidnapper keeping the room in this state of sepulchral gloom, anyway? She pulled the curtain cord and the drapes started to open.

"Don't." With disconcerting speed, her captor appeared at her side. He grabbed the cord and swiftly closed the drapes. "Do not open the drapes again," he said.

He spoke softly, but she didn't make the mistake of imagining he wouldn't enforce his order. "It is safer for both of us if the curtains remain shut," he said.

"Safer for you, maybe," she muttered. "How is it safer for me?"

"I cannot explain everything to you, Charlotte. I regret that necessity for silence more than you can imagine, but it is the case that you will be safer if nobody ever knows we have been here together."

"So you say," she said, under her breath. Of course he could hear what she'd said and she felt a sudden increase in the already sky high tension level between the two of them. Her stomach lurched sickeningly, and she wondered if she'd been stupid enough to precipitate the violent attack she'd been dreading ever since she woke up. Why did she feel this crazy impulse to needle him?

Fortunately her captor chose to move away from

her as swiftly as he'd approached. She realized, with a mixture of surprise and relief, that even though he'd come so close, no part of their bodies had come into contact. Not even his hand had brushed against hers when he tugged on the drapery cord.

She watched as he resumed his previous stance over by the table, the width of the two beds once again between them. With no more logic than her brief flare of defiance, all her previous fears of sexual attack returned at hurricane force.

"Why have you brought me here?" she burst out, even though she'd have preferred to maintain a dignified silence. "What do you want from me?"

"Your cooperation. I have an important meeting to attend in twenty-four hours from now and I would like both of us to be alive so that we can attend it together."

"Thanks for my share of the invitation, but I believe I'll give it a pass."

"Unfortunately this is an invitation you cannot afford to refuse. The alternative is not a safe return to your own home. The alternative to remaining with me is more than likely your imprisonment and eventual death at the hands of others."

She swallowed. "Nobody wants to kill me." Even to her own ears, she sounded pleading rather than dismissive.

Her captor shot her a glance that appeared almost sympathetic. "Look, why don't we sit down?" As he spoke, he sat in one of the chairs. After the briefest of delays, Charlotte resumed her perch on the edge of the bed. At this point, there seemed nothing to be gained by defying him over anything trivial like whether the drapes should be open, or whether she should stand or sit.

"I am truly sorry for what happened last night," he said. "I apologize also for any...discomfort...you are still suffering as a result of my methods. Given what had to be done, there was no way to make your abduction less traumatic, and perhaps no way to prevent misunderstandings this morning. But I have handled the situation since you woke up badly. Let's start over. My name is Richard Villier, and I am an officer with the French *Sûreté,* currently on loan to the Counter Terrorism unit of the FBI. Among my colleagues here in the States, I am known as Rick."

He paused, as if he expected her to make some acknowledgment of his introduction. She simply glowered at him in pointed silence.

"I am here with you to insure your safety, Charlotte, and for no other reason. I assure you, I am an officer of the law."

Right. She barely suppressed a snort. He was from the French police, and she was the Sugar Plum Fairy. "Show me your identification," she said curtly. "That, and a phone call to FBI headquarters, just might convince me that you're telling the truth."

He didn't look away, but his mouth twisted into a rueful grimace. "A reasonable request on your part, but I don't have any ID, either for the Bureau, or for the *Sûreté.* I am working under deep cover, for what is known as the Black Ops division."

"I'm sure you are." Charlotte didn't bother to hide her skepticism, or her anger. Which was totally not smart, she realized, but this man ruffled feathers she hadn't even known she possessed. "It seems really believable that an FBI agent would walk around without official ID.''

"I told you, I work for Black Ops. I don't carry ID because I cannot afford to be found with any law enforcement badges in my possession. You must realize that if I were not telling you the truth…that if, in fact, I were the sort of criminal you suspect…it would be very easy for me to have a set of forged ID cards to show you.''

She shook her head. "I don't realize any such thing. It's not easy to fake FBI identification.''

"It is easier than you think. Police badges and uniforms are for sale on the Internet, so if my aim is to deceive you, I don't need fake credentials. I can buy the real thing, and my purchase is quite legal. Or I could have printed some official-looking document on my computer and claimed that it was my ID card from the *Sûreté*. I am sure you have not the least idea what such an ID would look like.''

He had a point, Charlotte supposed. She might recognize official FBI identification, but she hadn't a clue what sort of cards and badges were issued by the French *Sûreté*. And her abductor certainly appeared smart enough to plan in advance to purchase a fake ID. He'd successfully neutralized John Hanseck, cut off the power supply to a large nightclub, delayed the start-up of the emergency generator and kidnapped her from a crowd of several hundred without a single person realizing she was being taken until it was too late. If he could mastermind all of that, he could surely have printed up a document that looked French enough and official enough to deceive her.

For the first time, she wondered if her captor could

possibly be telling the truth about who and what he was. Then the absurdity of that thought struck her. Was she totally insane? She was wondering if Rat Bastard was really French Agent Richard Villier *because* he hadn't provided her with any identification! Next she'd be agreeing that it had been kind of him to punch her and drug her into unconsciousness. Charlotte drew in a shaky breath. At least she now knew one thing about her kidnapper: for a man who didn't say much, he had a dangerously persuasive tongue.

Charlotte glared at him. ''How can you possibly expect me to believe such an unlikely story? Besides, even if you showed me a dozen pieces of official-looking ID, I'd still have every reason in the world to doubt what you're telling me. If the FBI believes I'm in danger, why didn't they take me into protective custody?''

''They did. Here I am. And here you are, under my protection.''

''Why send *you* to pick me up, a man I don't know? Anyone with a brain the size of a lima bean could surely see that's a no-fail recipe for misunderstandings and disaster.''

''You are self-evidently wrong. There had been no disaster—''

''If you judge last night a success, I'd hate to see your definition of a mission gone wrong. Leaving aside my personal feelings, what possible reason did you have for putting so many bystanders at risk? You knocked out the power to an entire nightclub on a busy weekend night. You drugged John Hanseck, supposedly one of your fellow agents, and kept me unconscious for almost twelve hours. It makes no sense to stage something so ridiculously over the top just to take me into protective custody. If the Bureau wanted me in a safe house, under guard, all they had to do was explain why. They know I'd agree to any reasonable request.''

''The FBI is made up of more than eleven thousand individuals. Obviously there are facts known to some agents that are not known to others. John Hanseck and his colleagues in the Tampa Bay office have no way to know of the danger you are facing.''

''But you do.'' Charlotte's voice dripped sarcasm. ''John Hanseck and the other agents officially assigned to work on the Daniel O'Toole case don't realize I'm in danger from him. But you do.''

''That is correct. The deep cover section of the Bureau for which I am currently working has access to sources of information that have not been shared with John Hanseck and Shirley Nicholson, who are regular field agents.''

''And it never occurred to you, or your boss in this deep cover section of the Bureau where you supposedly work, to ring my doorbell, and ask to speak to me directly so that you could share this important information with me in a more…normal…kind of a way?''

He shook his head. ''It's no secret that the FBI has had some problems with internal security over the past few years. Your American newspapers have been full of stories about how bureaucratic fumbling contributed to the massive intelligence failure that precipitated the disaster of 9/11. Those agents, like me, who are trying to prevent another disaster, are cautious about sharing information from sensitive sources.'' He hesitated for a moment, then added. ''Besides, your apartment building is being watched. I did not wish to be seen approaching you.''

His story was getting more ridiculous by the minute. ''Who's watching my apartment building?''

''People who would recognize me.''

His vagueness would have been laughable if it hadn't been so offensive. ''If my apartment building is being watched, what prevented you talking to me at work?''

''The same problem applies. I would have been recognized as soon I approached you. Your safety would have been put in jeopardy.''

''You expect me to believe I'm watched at work, too? Please don't insult my intelligence. There are former presidents of the United States who can't get that much attention from the FBI. There's no way the Bureau has the personnel to mount that sort of around-the-clock surveillance on me just because I once lived with a man who turned out to be a terrorist.''

''The people who are watching you are not necessarily from the FBI. I can't explain precisely why you are being watched, Charlotte, but you must trust me when I say that I would have been observed if I had approached you in a more normal fashion.''

''Have you any idea how unconvincing it sounds when somebody takes you prisoner and then urges you to trust him?''

He moved his hand, making a gesture that he cut off before he completed it. For some reason she couldn't identify, his half-finished gesture bothered her, nagging at her as if it had special significance.

"Sometimes we have to make judgment calls that are based on instinct, not entirely on objective facts," her captor said, interrupting her before the nagging worry could fully form. "For you, Charlotte, this is one of those times. I knocked you unconscious, I concede the point. I brought you here against your will, I concede the point. I deeply regret the necessity, but it was the only way to insure your safety. Other than that, have I done anything to justify your belief that I wish you harm?"

She stared at him, fingers tapping in her frustration. "Well, gee, let's run through a short list here. Apart from dragging me kicking and screaming from the Down Under club last night, you've drugged me, imprisoned me and failed to offer even a shred of proof to suggest you're working for law enforcement. You've rendered John Hanseck unconscious. For all I know, you killed him in order to abduct me. But now you're suggesting I should trust you. You've also suggested that I'm in such danger from mysterious, unnamed watchers—maybe the FBI, maybe not—that you were forced to terrify hundreds of people at a nightclub in order to abduct me...."

"Yes, that is precisely what I had to do. And John Hanseck is alive and well, by the way. I called the hospital and confirmed that he will be released before noon. Obviously I would have no wish to harm a fellow law enforcement officer."

She hoped he was telling the truth, but her skepticism remained. The fact that her captor knew enough about the local FBI office to mention Shirley Nicholson's name as well as John Hanseck's didn't mean a thing, she decided. For all she knew, he might be familiar with their names because he'd been arrested by them.

"If you're with the *Sûreté,* and seconded to the FBI as you claim, there's one very easy way to prove it, even without ID. Reconnect the phone and let me call one of the agents I know at the Bureau to check your credentials."

"I cannot do that—"

"No, I'll just bet you can't." It was beyond stupid to provoke him, but her frustration drove her to lash out.

"I cannot let you call the Bureau for an excellent reason." He spoke with careful patience. "The reason is this. I have no way of knowing whom within the FBI we can trust. It is imperative that nobody within the Bureau should learn that I have taken you into my custody. Complete secrecy is the only way to insure your safety."

She moistened lips that were suddenly painfully dry. "You mean that nobody else in the Bureau knows that you've kidnapped me? Nobody at all, not even in this supposedly Black Ops deep cover section of yours? How does that tie in with your claim that the Bureau knows I'm in danger?"

His hesitation was almost imperceptible. "*I* know you're in danger," he said. "I am part of the FBI—"

"But nobody else knows?"

"Nobody else knows," he agreed. "I would have told my director, but he is out of the country for another thirty-six hours."

Fear iced Charlotte's spine. So much for Rat Bastard's claim that he'd taken her into protective custody on behalf of the FBI. Her hope that her captor really was a French agent, and that she had been kidnapped as part of a bizarre attempt by the U.S. government to insure her safety, evaporated.

"What do you really want?" she asked. "Tell me the truth, please. In the end, that will be easier on both of us."

She was begging, damn it. Precisely what she'd sworn she wouldn't do, but she couldn't stop herself.

His voice softened slightly. "I have told you the truth, Charlotte. You were in danger. I have rescued you. Nobody at the Bureau can be allowed to learn that you are in my custody. There is a mole in the Bureau, a traitor who is passing on information to the Armargh Army. Everyone you know at the Bureau is connected to the O'Toole investigation and therefore a strong suspect for being that mole. Surely you understand why I cannot risk letting anyone at the Bureau know where you are?"

Charlotte pressed her hands to her head, which felt as if it would explode. When he gave his explanations, he sounded so rational, despite the absurdity of what he was saying. How in the world was she supposed to decide whether Rick Villier was a criminal or an officer of the law when she had access to nothing except her captor's words and her own gut instinct?

Her gut instincts were telling her that this man was lying, but that he wasn't crazy. She even had a sense that he truly believed she was in danger. However, her gut instincts had also told her that Daniel O'Toole was a fine person to marry, which didn't exactly inspire confidence in the reliability of her gut.

Still, she was almost ready to dismiss the idea that her kidnapping had been motivated by her captor's need to obtain a helpless sexual victim. If Rick Villier was a sexual deviant, he was behaving like no other predator she'd ever heard of, or read about. She was totally in his power, but he was giving no evidence of wanting to initiate any perverted sexual rituals. And if he wasn't a psychotic rapist, then it was difficult to imagine what kind of criminal he might be. A kidnapper holding her for ransom? If so, why had she been chosen as his prey? She clearly hadn't been plucked at random from the crowd of dancers at the Down Under club, but she wasn't a very desirable victim from a financial point of view. She had no money to speak of—the bank owned most of her condo and half of her car—and although her parents were heading toward a comfortable retirement, they weren't rich, and there had to be thousands of people who would be better able to pay a ransom demand than anyone in her family.

But if she accepted that Rick Villier wasn't planning to rape her, or extort money from her family, then she couldn't imagine what criminal purpose he could have in mind by kidnapping her. She circled back to the slight possibility that he was an agent from law enforcement, as he claimed. If he didn't have connections to the FBI, she had to admit it was surprising that he knew so many facts about her life.

But it was a giant leap to move from acknowledging that he knew a fair amount of confidential information to believing that he really was an agent with the French *Sûreté*. Maybe he was a criminal who'd escaped from FBI custody and had kidnapped her to use as a hostage. Perhaps he intended to use her as a bargaining chip for some deal he hoped to negotiate with the Bureau. The more she thought about it, the more that last idea made sense.

Charlotte's brief moment of faith in Villier's integrity flickered and died. "Even if there are a dozen moles operating inside the Bureau, how does that put me in danger?" she demanded. "I can see that the existence of a mole would be a problem for the FBI in its pursuit of Daniel O'Toole, but I don't see how it's dangerous for me. I have almost nothing to do with the Bureau's investigation, and less than nothing to do with O'Toole."

"You are in danger because however much you might want to claim that Riordan Gray and Daniel O'Toole aren't the same man, they are. It is an inescapable fact that you were married to him—"

"No—"

"But yes. You were married to Daniel O'Toole, despite what he chose to call himself during your marriage."

Revulsion closed her throat as it always did when she was forced to confront the fact that she had lived with a terrorist. That she had loved that same terrorist with a passion and intensity she sometimes suspected she would never be able to recapture with another man. At the speed of light, Charlotte slammed the door shut on that unbearable thought.

She should simply have changed the subject, but the fact of her marriage to O'Toole was a wound that she could never leave alone, constantly licking it into a state of festering agony. She spoke coldly, the only way she could keep her emotions at a safe distance.

"Yes, I was married to O'Toole, but that doesn't mean anything, however much you try to twist facts. O'Toole wanted to hide out for a couple of years, so he invented a character called Riordan Gray and moved to Iowa where he acted his way through a completely phony life. I was just the unlucky woman in Des Moines who got dragged into playing a supporting role in his performance."

"Your theory has some loopholes, Charlotte. Why was it easier for O'Toole to marry? Why add that complication to his life unless he cared about you? And why did he choose you out of all the women in Iowa?"

"Because my family is a pillar of the community," Charlotte said bitterly. "Everyone in West Des Moines knows who they are. What better cover could O'Toole have found for himself? He exploited my parents' years of hard work and community service to protect his own criminal behavior. Besides, there aren't many women who'd have been as conveniently naive as I was. He took advantage of the fact that I had been brought up surrounded by so much love that I automatically trusted him. But don't make the mistake of believing there was any reality to what took place between the two of us. Everything about the person I married, from his name, to the details about his family and his past career, were total fabrications. Since I knew absolutely nothing about the real man until after he left me, I can't imagine how his current activities could involve me in any way, shape, or form."

Her captor got up and rolled his shoulders as if easing tense muscles. Then he slouched against the table. He sounded slightly impatient as he said, "You may choose to maintain your distance from O'Toole. There are others anxious to force you back into his orbit."

"Why? How? Nobody can force me to offer my support to a terrorist. Especially a terrorist I despise from the bottom of my heart."

"You overestimate your powers of resistance." His voice was suddenly hard. "We are all capable of being blackmailed into acts that we would have believed utterly outside the realm of possibility. All it requires is knowledge of what buttons to push on the part of the blackmailers."

She didn't want to accept that what he said was true, although she suspected it might be. If somebody made convincing threats against the life and safety of her parents, or her little nieces and nephews, she might consider acting in ways that would otherwise be unthinkable. She did her best to conceal from her captor that his words had hit home.

"Are you just talking in the abstract, Mr. Villier, or do you have a specific point you're trying to make?"

"I have a point to make. I am telling you that you were being set up for use as a weapon against O'Toole."

She laughed without mirth. "Well, I'm a dud weapon. O'Toole has no interest in me."

"You're wrong. I have it from a reliable source that Daniel O'Toole was deeply in love with you. That he bitterly regrets leaving you."

The words hit her like a blow and she responded with ice-cold disdain. ''In case this insight hasn't occurred to you, Mr. Villier, it isn't flattering to know that a murdering son of a bitch is in love with you. Besides I'd take the information from your informer with a huge grain of salt. Who was your so-called reliable source?''

''Daniel O'Toole,'' he said.

Nine

It took Charlotte a while to recover her voice. "You've spoken to O'Toole in person?" she asked. "You mean you've met with him face-to-face?"

Rick nodded. "Briefly, yes. That is why I have been seconded to help the FBI. Not many people working in law enforcement have actually seen O'Toole."

"If you met him long enough to hold a conversation, and you're an agent of the French *Sûreté* as you claim, why didn't you arrest him?"

"Long story. Here is the short version. I work for the Counter-Terrorism Unit of the French *Sûreté* and five months ago we finally captured an Algerian terrorist named Hakim Belaziz, who had been on France's Most Wanted list since 1996. During the course of our interrogation, which extended over a period of several weeks, Belaziz informed us that he had recently sold a shipment of surplus Al Qaeda weapons to the Armargh Army—" He broke off. "You appear shocked. What have I said to alarm you?"

"Nothing." Charlotte hesitated only for a moment before telling Rick the truth. "I was surprised, but not alarmed. I'd already heard about Hakim Belaziz from the FBI. From John Hanseck himself, in fact. John was explaining to me how he'd learned that O'Toole was still alive. He told me the information came from an Algerian prisoner captured by the French government..." She stopped, not sure how much more it was wise to reveal to a man she didn't trust.

Rick gave her a penetrating look, then smiled with wry understanding. "And because I repeated secret information you had already heard from another source within the FBI, you are astonished to find yourself believing for the first time that I might truly be the person I claim to be?"

"Something like that," she acknowledged.

"Then I am grateful that John Hanseck found it necessary to explain how the FBI came by its information that O'Toole is alive. Since he has discussed this incident with you already, do you also know that Belaziz was persuaded to set up a meeting with Daniel O'Toole? Belaziz pretended that he wished to sell off a shipment of rocket launchers."

"Yes, I knew that," Charlotte said. "John also told me that the setup failed. A lot of people ended up getting shot."

"The carnage was horrible," Rick said, his French accent thickening with remembered emotion. "Two of our agents were killed, and Belaziz himself died of his wounds. The operation was a failure, a total disaster."

"Do you think Belaziz deliberately betrayed you to O'Toole?"

"How can we know?" Rick shrugged, the first really Gallic gesture Charlotte had seen him give. "At the time, my colleagues and I all believed that Belaziz was sincere in his offer to arrange a rendezvous with O'Toole. Belaziz had murdered half a dozen Trappist monks with shocking barbarity. The crimes had provoked outrage in France and Belaziz knew we had the evidence to achieve a conviction. A sentence of life in prison with no possibility of parole was staring him in the face. So it seemed reasonable that he would be willing to betray O'Toole—a man to whom he bore significant ill will—in order to obtain some privileges in regard to the conditions of his life sentence. He wanted a visa for his brother to visit him in prison, for example, despite the fact that his brother is himself suspected of having terrorist connections in Algeria. We were willing to arrange that visit—under supervision, of course.''

"I'm surprised Belaziz wasn't sentenced to death if he committed multiple murders.''

"In France, we do not employ the death penalty. In my opinion, that works in our favor when we deal with terrorists, since many of them are quite willing to go to glorious death in the name of their holy cause, but they are nowhere near as happy to find themselves serving lifetime sentences in uncomfortable prisons. In this case, we had good reason to believe that Hakim Belaziz genuinely dreaded the prospect of spending the next half century behind bars, far away from his family, and so we believed him to be sincere when he offered to arrange a meeting with O'Toole.''

"But it turned out he was anything but sincere, at least according to the story John Hanseck told me.''

Rick was silent for a moment, visibly debating his reply. ''As I said before, I am not sure that he deliberately betrayed us," he said finally. "O'Toole has on occasion demonstrated an almost supernatural ability to scent a trap. It is possible that the offer Belaziz made was genuine, but O'Toole suspected him, anyway. Alternatively, Belaziz may have given a secret signal to O'Toole—perhaps because he hoped to precipitate a gun battle and make good his escape. Since Hakim Belaziz is dead and O'Toole is burrowed deep into his protective cover, there is no way to discover the truth."

"You still haven't explained how you met O'Toole face-to-face long enough to have a conversation about his so-called marriage to me."

Rick glossed over her refusal to acknowledge that a marriage had ever existed between her and O'Toole. "That is simple," he said. "It was decided that I would accompany Hakim to the rendezvous with O'Toole. I went in the guise of Hakim Belaziz's most trusted lieutenant and translator—"

"Wasn't that incredibly dangerous?"

"Incredibly? Hmm...not quite *incredibly*." Her captor gave a wry smile. "But let's just say that I am grateful to be here talking to you today. Believe me, as a rule I try to avoid situations where a lot of nervous people are standing around with guns."

"You're a lucky man to have survived an encounter between Belaziz and a rival gang of angry terrorists."

"You are correct. Unfortunately capturing terrorists is not an objective that can be easily achieved while sitting behind a desk. Anyway, whether because O'Toole had been alerted by Belaziz, or because he had other reasons for suspecting the meeting was a trap, O'Toole managed to outmaneuver us to devastating effect. O'Toole engaged me in harmless personal conversation just long enough for his soldiers from the Armargh Army to move in and destroy the ambush we had organized. In the ensuing battle, Belaziz was killed, along with two of my colleagues at the *Sûreté*. To make matters worse, both of O'Toole's senior lieutenants escaped, along with the half dozen Armargh Army fighters who staged the ambush.''

Charlotte looked at Rick in unguarded astonishment. ''I can't have understood what you just told me!''

''About the ambush?''

Charlotte gave a bewildered shake of her head. ''Not the details of the ambush. They're terrible, but not all that surprising. With so many violent and fanatical people scheming to betray each other, a gun battle seems almost the inevitable outcome. No, I meant your conversation with O'Toole. You can't seriously expect me to believe that while you and O'Toole waited to negotiate the final stages of a dangerous deal for thousands of dollars worth of illegal armaments—''

''Half a million dollars' worth, actually.''

''And with all that at stake, the two of you sat down and discussed O'Toole's *love life?* With each of you knowing that you might be killed at any moment?''

''What else should we have discussed? The weather? In France, that is not a subject that occupies our attention.'' Rick gave another distinctly Gallic shrug, dismissing the strange American fascination with charts showing upper atmospheric air circulation.

"O'Toole believed me to be recently married, but separated from my wife, who remained in Algeria. His own marriage was a natural topic of conversation. He told me of the American woman he loved that he had been forced to leave behind for the sake of his cause—"

"His cause..." Charlotte almost choked on the words.

"Yes. Terrorists rarely believe themselves to be criminals, you know. O'Toole considers himself an avid supporter of the cause of freedom, a fighter for justice in a world ruled by oppressors."

This final perversion of the truth left Charlotte bereft of speech and Rick continued into the silence. "At the time, of course, I did not know that when he spoke of his wife, he referred to you. It is only in the past two months, since I have been here in America attempting to capture O'Toole, that I have become fully acquainted with his history. Previously my professional attention was focused on the Algerian terrorist cells operating within France. As you will realize, I am sure, my country is of little interest to Irish terrorists in the normal course of events. Naturally, therefore, the *Sûreté* is only informed about the various breakaway factions from the IRA in a very general way. In contrast, we have a large Islamic population and a devastating history in Algeria, and so France often provides a safe haven for Moslem extremists of every kind."

"What language were you speaking at your meeting with O'Toole?" Charlotte asked, suddenly wondering if among the other attributes O'Toole had hidden from her was the ability to speak foreign languages.

"English, of course." Rick gave a wry grin. "Although nobody in France cares to admit as much, English is the language of international commerce."

"Even among Arab terrorists? Even when the commerce is strictly illegal?"

He nodded. "Even among rabid, anti-American terrorists, at least when they have to negotiate a deal outside their own geographic boundaries. In this one area, at least, practicality trumps their ideology. O'Toole doesn't speak Arabic or French. Why would he?" Rick's voice acquired its first hint of anger. "His higher education is limited to multiple murder and methods of mass destruction. The fact that he speaks only English provided us with an excuse to introduce me into the meeting. I was identified to O'Toole as Belaziz's interpreter."

Rick's words were punctuated by a buzzing sound. "Excuse me," he murmured, pulling a cell phone from his pocket and glancing at the screen. "This is a call that I need to take." He opened the phone. "Hello?"

He listened, said yes twice, and then hung up. "It is as I expected," he said. "I have to leave to attend a meeting about a hundred miles from here. If you are willing to believe that I am Richard Villier, agent of the French government, it will make the next few hours easier for both of us."

"Yes, of course I believe you."

He shook his head. "Bad move, Charlotte. You answered much too fast. You merely said what you thought would be most likely to provide you with opportunities to escape my surveillance. Think again, and this time answer honestly. You should accept that I am a member of law enforcement and there is no chance that I will allow you out of my protection for the next forty-eight hours. Now, I will ask you again. Do you believe that I am working with the FBI, and that your safety and well-being are my most important concerns?''

Hearing Rick's story about Hakim Belaziz had changed her opinion about him, Charlotte realized. Her fear had abated and, for the first time since she woke up in the motel room, she felt calm enough to think about Rick's claims without adrenaline pushing her into flight-or-fight mode and blurring her capacity to reason.

''Right now, it seems a lot more likely that you're an undercover agent with the French *Sûreté* than it did an hour ago,'' she admitted. ''But answer me one question, straight up, no evasions and half-truths. What grounds do you have for believing I was in such danger that it justified the stunt you pulled last night?''

''The Armargh Army was getting ready to kidnap you within hours, perhaps within minutes, of my own attempt. There was no time to confer with my director, who is out of the country. You would have been snatched before dawn and, believe me, the conditions of your imprisonment would not have been pleasant.''

''The Armargh Army was going to snatch me before dawn? Why, for God's sake? What purpose could it serve to kidnap me?''

''I already told you. To keep O'Toole in line.''

"But he's the leader of the Armargh Army! Why does he need to be kept in line?"

"He's *one* of the leaders," Rick corrected. "The Armargh Army isn't structured like Al Qaeda, with Osama bin Laden firmly in charge, and acknowledged by everyone to be the supreme leader. The Armargh Army has a looser command structure, and O'Toole can't operate entirely according to his own wishes. According to the briefing I got from the FBI when I arrived here in the States two months ago, O'Toole has always received absolutely loyalty from his men and so the FBI tends to see him as invulnerable. I came in as an outsider, and the picture I see is a little different. I have been picking up rumors for the past four weeks that there are doubts within the Armargh Army about O'Toole's dedication to the cause. There have been some problems with their funding because of disruptions in the supply of counterfeit dollars from Eastern Europe into Northern Ireland. O'Toole was the mastermind behind the establishment of the counterfeiting operation, and some members of the Armargh Army have laid the blame for its current problems at O'Toole's door."

"And the Armargh Army considers that a sufficient reason to doubt O'Toole's loyalty?"

"So many shipments of cash have been intercepted that a few members of the army believe somebody must be reporting details of the shipping schedule to law enforcement. O'Toole is in charge of scheduling. He's an obvious suspect."

Charlotte shook her head in disbelief. "How many people does he need to kill to prove his sincerity? How can they doubt him after everything he's done for their cause, just because of a few problems with a counterfeiting operation?''

"Very easily." Rick's voice was dry. "The life of a terrorist does not lend itself to the establishment of mutual trust and harmony. The FBI has been infiltrating informants into the fringes of the organization, attempting to stir up trouble, and they seem to be having some success. The Bureau has also launched a disinformation campaign suggesting that O'Toole is considering selling out to the American government in exchange for a reduced prison sentence in a decent jail—"

"Is that a credible rumor?" Charlotte asked. "Surely the Armagh Army realizes the FBI would never negotiate a deal with a man who's killed as many people as O'Toole?"

"Your naiveté is charming, but dangerous to your well-being. The truth is, it's in the national interest of the United States to cut deals occasionally—"

"Even with terrorists like O'Toole?" Charlotte was appalled.

"And worse," Rick said curtly. "Cutting deals with criminals is often the single best method of acquiring insider information. And if that information can save hundreds of lives, maybe thousands, it's better to cut the deal. Anyway, whatever the true status of O'Toole's loyalty to the Armagh Army, his position within the group seems less than a hundred percent secure. I have been pursuing leads for over a month and two days ago I received rock-solid intelligence that you were marked for kidnapping. As far as we can tell, O'Toole is in absolute command of operational planning here in the States, but overall strategy is in the hands of the Army's General, and even O'Toole must report to him. The Armargh Army has the biggest operation in its history set to take place soon, and the General wants to be sure O'Toole puts forth his best efforts. Therefore the order was issued for your capture. It came directly from the General himself.''

''And this so-called General thinks he can use *me* to keep O'Toole in line?'' Charlotte gave an anguished laugh. ''That would be funny if it weren't so wide of the mark. Doesn't this General person realize that O'Toole walked out on me eighteen months ago?''

''I'm sure the General is fully informed. From everything we know about him, he is a smart man. Fanatical and utterly ruthless, but smart.''

''Then he must also realize that O'Toole has no interest in what happens to me, so kidnapping me would be a complete waste of time.''

''I don't agree with your assessment of how important you are to O'Toole and obviously neither does the General. You are forgetting the conversation I had with O'Toole in Paris, which gives the lie to your claim that he doesn't care about you. But we don't have time to argue and, to a certain extent, the truth of O'Toole's feelings toward you are irrelevant. For the purposes of our discussion, all that matters is that senior members of the Armargh Army believe you to be a source of vulnerability for O'Toole, which means in turn that you were seriously at risk. That is why I've taken you out of play. And if your disappearance causes O'Toole to lose concentration, or the local Armargh Army cell to fall into disarray, so much the better. Now I'll ask you one last time, Charlotte, because I need to get out of this motel. Do you trust me, or do I have to treat you as a hostile captive?''

She hesitated, not sure how she would reply until she heard herself speaking. ''I...trust you. I think.'' And she hoped to God she wouldn't live to regret those words.

''This time you sound a little more convincing. I'll accept your word.'' Rick pulled open one of the dresser drawers, tossing a plastic shopping bag onto the bed. ''Okay, Charlotte. You'll find some clothes in there, and a pair of lightweight sneakers. Also a hairbrush and a few toiletries. Basic stuff, but it's better than spending the day in the clothes you wore dancing last night. Get dressed fast, please. We've spent too long talking and we need to get out of here.''

Ten

Aside from the fact that he'd been damn near tongue-tied when Charlotte first woke up, and that his heart still leaped into his throat every time he looked at her, Rick supposed that the preceding few hours had gone as well as could be expected. He'd managed to get Charlotte to the motel and still make his 2:00 a.m. rendezvous with the General, although it had been a close call. Shortly before dawn, he'd checked in briefly with Sean and Ryan, who were pissed as hell that their plans to kidnap Charlotte hadn't worked out. Of course, they couldn't tell him why they were in such a bad mood, and their dread of explaining their failed mission to the General had kept them too much on edge to leave spare brain power for asking awkward questions.

In other circumstances, the situation would have had its comic moments. As it was, Rick could only thank God that so far he was keeping the balls he'd set in motion flying in the air. If one ever dropped and touched ground, it would be all over. Not just for him, but for Charlotte, too. And right now, with the information he was carrying in his head, he simply couldn't afford to die.

For the moment, there seemed a fair chance that

nobody from the Armargh Army would suspect him of Charlotte's abduction. There was a decent chance that they'd blame the FBI, which would suit him very well indeed. So much the better if Sean and Ryan were busy chasing their own tails instead of paying attention to business.

Now if he could just manage to refrain from throwing Charlotte on the bed and making love to her until they ached too much to move, they both might survive the next two days and emerge alive. Maybe. Possibly. Hell, it was time to look on the bright side. He could survive for thirty-six hours. Sure he could. All he needed was to keep his hands to himself and remember his French accent. He wasn't entirely sure which of those two tasks was more difficult. His hands seemed to have a life of their own, and his accent had slipped badly toward the end of his conversation with Charlotte. Let it slip too much, and his cover would be blown for sure.

Of course, even if his charade as Rick Villier worked out—a big if—there remained the problem of keeping Charlotte safe, while preventing a group of rabid Irish terrorists from joining with lunatic environmentalists to blow up the Kennedy Space Center. Then there was the concurrent problem of uncovering the identity of the traitor operating inside the FBI before the traitor managed to get him killed. But he could handle all that. Sure he could. Hell, it was all just another typical week at the office, Rick thought ruefully. And if this was a week when God chose to smile, he might be able to prevent a national disaster *and* get to keep the girl.

Yeah, right. Like that was going to happen this side of eternity.

Rick snapped his thoughts out of fantasy land and back into reality. As he knew better than most, staying alive required keeping your head down, your ass covered, and your attention focused strictly on the present moment. He unwound the phone cord from around his waist where he'd stored it to be sure Charlotte couldn't access it. He tossed it onto the bed next to the phone. Then he conducted a quick visual audit of the room, to triple check that all trace of their presence was gone.

Better give the table and door knobs another quick polish. Wiping down the surfaces to remove finger prints was as good a method as any to force his thoughts away from the bathroom, where Charlotte was putting on the clothes he'd bought from a twenty-four-hour Wal-Mart. Better if he dwelled on the risks they were facing and kept his thoughts completely away from subjects like how Charlotte looked when she was putting on clothes. Or taking them off.

He didn't trust her, of course, not for a second. Any more than she trusted him. But by choosing to take on the role of a French official involved in a case he knew she would already have heard about, he'd given her just enough cause to believe in him that he was confident—make that hopeful—that she wouldn't scream to passersby for help when they walked out into the motel parking lot. For now, that would have to be enough. In the long run, maybe it was better if she never quite learned to trust him, because that way he avoided the dangers inherent in any closer relationship. Above all, he had to avoid the temptation of trying to make her like him.

At least the pretense that they trusted each other achieved one major objective. He didn't have to devise some method of getting an uncooperative prisoner from the motel room to his truck without either tying her up or drugging her. Not that he'd have hesitated to do either or both of those things in normal circumstances. Unfortunately the circumstances were light years away from normal. He didn't intend to do a damn thing to Charlotte that required touching her if he could possibly avoid it. At least not while she was conscious, and not even when she was unconscious if he retained a single functioning cell in the spongiform mass that currently passed for his brain.

The motel room was clean, he decided, except for the inevitable stray hair or two. He didn't think even a partial fingerprint had escaped his notice. Since he'd paid cash in advance and registered under a false name, there was no reason for anyone to run a serious check on the room, so he didn't worry too much about the trace evidence of his presence that he was leaving behind. He worried more about going out into the bright sunlight in Charlotte's company. Now that was *really* hazardous.

Should he have kept her blindfolded? But that raised a whole new set of problems, including the fact that with a blindfold permanently in place, she might listen more intently to what he was saying. And on balance, he was more afraid of running into problems with his voice than with his appearance. The latter was much easier to disguise than the former, especially in view of the plastic surgery he'd had last year.

Rick made a small, impatient sound. He'd already gone over this in his mind a dozen times. Obsessive second-guessing of his own decisions wasn't the way he usually operated and it for sure wasn't going to lead to any place he wanted to go. He checked his cell phone and as an automatic precaution, wiped out the record of the originating number for his last phone call.

"I'm ready." Charlotte emerged from the bathroom, and Rick concealed a wince as he saw again the bruise darkening her jaw. Apart from the bruise, she looked lovely, with her hair sleek and shining, and her long, tanned legs inviting any available male eye to travel upward to the enticing curve of her hips. And boy, was his male eye ever available.

He switched his gaze to a safer region left of her shoulder. "You must be hungry," he said, although he knew that Charlotte rarely bothered with food until after noon. "We can stop at a drive-through to buy some lunch if you like."

He made the suggestion casually, as if stopping at a fast food restaurant wasn't going to be fraught with danger. Between the FBI and the Armargh Army he had two sets of highly competent trackers potentially on his ass, so he'd first have to make sure they weren't being followed. Even then, he'd be anticipating disaster every second of the way.

"What I want more than anything else is a cup of coffee," Charlotte said, a note of real yearning in her voice.

"I can promise you the best that McDonald's or Burger King has to offer."

"I'm desperate enough that either sounds wonderful." She actually smiled at him. Her first smile.

He felt it as a physical pain deep in his gut, and for a moment he couldn't speak. He had years of experience in concealing his feelings, but remaining impassive in Charlotte's company was the hardest task he'd ever set himself, and his skills were being tested as never before. He couldn't bring himself to return the smile, but he hoped his voice sounded somewhere between neutral and friendly when he spoke.

"If you are ready to leave, will you open the door? I will follow."

She sent him a questioning look, as if not quite believing that he was offering her that much freedom of action. If she only knew how quickly he would take her down if she tried to escape, she wouldn't appear so happy, Rick thought grimly.

"Turn right outside the door," he said. "The parking lot is twenty-five meters away. You will see the exit sign."

"Don't you have to pay the bill and turn in the room key?"

"I left the room key on the table and I paid the bill when I checked in."

She seemed mildly troubled by his answer, as if she suspected him of trying to duck out without paying, although she ought to know that payment in advance was standard procedure at motels located near an Interstate. An invaluable practice for people who were lying about their identity and didn't want anyone to remember them.

He did his best to allay her doubts by gesturing toward the table, where she could see the room key was just where he'd said it would be. "Let's go, Charlotte," he said softly. "It's been a long night and I for one could use some breakfast."

He liked the subtle suggestion that he'd been shut up in the room all the time she slept. No point in giving her any reason to wonder why he'd felt the need to drug her into unconsciousness. She was a smart woman, and if he didn't keep her moving, all sorts of questions like that were going to start to occur to her.

The corridor was lit only by two skylights, presumably in an attempt to keep out the fierce Florida sun and reduce cooling costs for the motel. The dim light suited Rick's purpose very well, since it left the hallway with barely sufficient illumination to meet fire department regulations. When they reached the exit, he put on wraparound mirrored sunglasses before they stepped outside. The glasses were a big help not only in shielding his eyes from the glaring sun, but also in keeping his eyes hidden from Charlotte.

Once outside, the Florida sun again worked to his advantage, since Charlotte was momentarily blinded by the brilliance of the light, and by the time they were in the car, he hoped she would be focused on looking for a restaurant rather than on studying his profile. Not that she would recognize his profile even if she did decide to stare. Safer living through cosmetic surgery. He was a walking poster boy for the advantages of nip and tuck.

At this hour, and at this time of year, there were only three vehicles in the parking lot apart from his own. "Mine is the gray Ford Taurus," he said. A nice, inconspicuous vehicle with a state-of-the-art

GPS navigation system, along with engine modifications that he'd made himself, so that the car could maintain speeds of over a hundred miles an hour without straining.

Fortunately he'd read Charlotte's attitude toward him correctly. She certainly wasn't entirely convinced that he was Richard Villier, law enforcement official, but she trusted him just enough that she didn't scream or draw attention to herself as they walked across the scorching hot motel forecourt. He held his breath as a maid came out of one of the units facing directly onto the parking lot, but Charlotte still didn't call out for help. However, her trust was barely skin deep, and he could sense her regret the second they were inside the stifling interior of the car. He knew she was already asking herself if she was crazy to have gotten into the vehicle so meekly without making any attempt to escape.

Rick turned on the air conditioning and clicked the latch of his seat belt. The best way to bolster her confidence in his integrity was to act as if he took her cooperation for granted. "We spent the night in Lakeland, about thirty miles east of Tampa Bay," he said. "Just so that you know where we are."

"It would be even better if I knew where we're going," Charlotte said.

"We are driving through the Orlando area to the East Coast. I must attend a meeting with some informants in Daytona Beach." He'd chosen that as an explanation that would best fit his purpose and also sound credible.

"Informants?" she asked.

"I have to find out if word of your disappearance

has filtered back to the Armargh Army," he said. It seemed as good an excuse as any. "I suspect that it has since you were being watched, but I need to be sure."

She digested that piece of information in silence. "I know they have car races at Daytona Beach," she said, latching her seat belt. "But I don't know exactly where it is. I haven't done much sightseeing since I arrived in Florida."

"It is north-east of Orlando," he said, not mentioning that it was also quite close to the Kennedy Space Center. Better if she never knew exactly what it was that O'Toole and the Elf had scheduled for destruction. That way she couldn't betray any information to the wrong people, either deliberately or under pressure. It was a measure of how weak Charlotte made him that he couldn't use the words *under torture* even in his thoughts.

He backed out of the parking space, taking the opportunity to scan the surrounding area for any possible hint of trouble. Everything looked sleepy, hot and typical Florida-summer-normal. The maid had disappeared, leaving her supply cart unattended. Standard practice at motels everywhere, and nothing to worry about, Rick concluded. There was nobody hanging around outside the office. The two other cars and the pickup truck remained parked and empty. The scraggy oleander bush at the corner of the lot wilted in the heat, and the faint smell of gasoline and overcooked hot dogs wafted through the car's air conditioner from the gas station across the way. Nothing out of place. Nothing to send his internal warning systems into high alert. His body sank back into the state of muted anticipation of disaster that in his case passed for routine.

He drove out of the lot into the side street, waited to make the turn onto the road leading to the Interstate, confident that he didn't have a tail. By the time they reached Kissimmee, just west of Orlando and the Disney theme parks, his confidence increased to the point that he swung off I.4 and drove into Wendy's.

"Would you like to eat inside, so that we can fully appreciate our fine dining experience?" he asked Charlotte.

She gave him another of the rare smiles that reduced him to mental and emotional rubble. "Have you any idea how snobbish and French you just sounded?"

In the circumstances, sounding French had to be considered a good thing, even if it meant that he sounded snobbish at the same time. He returned her smile. "I apologize. Let's not start a cultural war. Shall we eat inside or use the drive-through? There, is that question neutral enough to please you?"

"I'd like to eat inside," she said. "Do we have time before your meeting?"

"If we eat fast." He hesitated for a split second, then decided not to destroy their superficial harmony by issuing a redundant warning not to attempt an escape. He was confident that at this precise moment Charlotte didn't plan to do anything except drink coffee and eat a sandwich. If she developed other plans once they were inside the restaurant, he could circumvent them. She would betray any intention to escape by a dozen involuntary signs—tensed muscles, a narrowing of her extraordinary blue eyes, an alteration in the pitch of her voice. He could take care of any plan she might come up with before she put it into effect.

Charlotte ordered a chicken sandwich and an extra large coffee and followed him over to a corner booth. She scooted along the seat and leaned back against the padded vinyl, sighing with pleasure when she took her first sip of scalding coffee. He'd chosen the corner booth because of the view it provided of the entrance to the restaurant and outside to the parking lot. He kept a simultaneous watch on both areas, a skill that was now so ingrained that he could easily carry on a conversation and simultaneously be aware of what was going on around him in a one-hundred-and-eighty-degree arc.

Having Charlotte across the table was a distraction, though, and one he couldn't afford. He avoided looking at her as much as possible, so that he wouldn't get the weird tightening sensation in his lungs, as if a giant machine were sucking all the oxygen out of the room. It was a sensation that he hadn't felt in a while, and he'd forgotten how overwhelming it could be.

The restaurant was crowded with lunchtime customers, which was good news from his perspective. It meant that nobody in the restaurant was likely to remember them two minutes after they left. He double-checked to make sure that they weren't attracting any second glances, despite the bruise on Charlotte's jaw that he hadn't been able to banish last night with ice and medicated compresses. Nobody was giving them a first glance, let alone a second.

"Tell me about your work with the *Sûreté*," Charlotte said, taking only a couple of bites from her chicken sandwich before setting it aside. She was too thin, and she'd visibly lost weight since the last picture he'd seen of her, so he had to resist the urge to order her to eat more.

He invented a fluent string of lies about his supposed ten-year career with the *Sûreté*. His ability to lie on his feet had been considered one of his most valuable skills when he was recruited, and he'd only gotten better with practice. He followed up with a couple of stories about bumbling criminals that made her laugh. There was nothing like laughter for breaking down a person's defenses, and he knew just how to appeal to Charlotte's sense of humor.

"Do you live in Paris or in one of the suburbs?" she asked, taking another long, satisfied swallow of coffee, followed by another more enthusiastic bite of sandwich as her appetite woke up. He could see that she was moving closer and closer to forgetting that she was his prisoner.

He said that he lived in the city. Fortunately he knew Paris pretty well, so he had no problem spinning her a tale about his apartment on the Rive Gauche and his favorite haunts in Montmartre. He explained away his excellent English by claiming an aunt who'd married an Englishman, and frequent summer vacations spent in their home, as well as an exchange semester at an English university.

"You're lucky to have traveled so much," Charlotte said wistfully. "Apart from a ski trip to the Canadian Rockies, I've never been outside the States."

He resisted the temptation to explore with her the

countries she most wanted to visit, and to recommend places he thought she would especially enjoy. God forbid that any part of their conversation should be sincere, he reflected sardonically.

"France is one of the biggest countries in Europe," he said. "Even so, I can drive from my apartment in Paris and reach Germany, Switzerland, Belgium, Spain and Italy almost as quickly as you could drive to Chicago from your parents' home in Des Moines." He gave a brief grin. "No wonder we Europeans all seem to spend the summers in each other's countries, learning each other's languages. We're practically staring into each other's backyards, so we'd better know how to understand each other."

"Are you married?" she asked. "Does your wife like to travel, too?"

"I'm not married, but I see quite a lot of my parents and my sister." He didn't want to invent too many details about Rick Villier's supposed family he would then have to remember, so he switched the direction of their conversation and talked about the fishing village in Brittany where his family supposedly owned a vacation cottage. He could see Charlotte visibly relaxing the longer they chatted, and he thought ruefully how incredibly naive she remained, and how easy it was to deceive her.

It was painful to exploit her innocence, her lingering capacity to trust people despite the devastating betrayal O'Toole had inflicted on her, but Rick did it with his usual skill. Always the pro, he thought cynically. Never the slightest risk that he would put integrity or common humanity before the demands of the job.

"What's the matter?" Charlotte interrupted herself in midsentence to ask the question.

"Nothing," he said, genuinely surprised. "What do you mean?"

"You suddenly looked—regretful."

He couldn't remember a single occasion in the past two years when his face had expressed an emotion that he didn't want to reveal, but her presence vanquished his innate talents with almost as much ease as it demolished the rigor of his training. Either he was getting dangerously careless or, worse still, she was able to pick up on his emotions even when his features remained blandly polite. He had a frightening suspicion that it was the latter.

He flashed one of his false smiles, one that looked the essence of sincerity. "You are too perceptive, Charlotte. You have uncovered one of my secret vices. I have a passion for French fries, and I just finished my last one, which is always a cause for extreme regret."

He rose to his feet, cutting off the risk of more questions. "Are you ready to leave? We still have to negotiate the traffic around Disney World and downtown Orlando. That could easily add half an hour to our travel time and I have only a little time to spare before my meeting."

"Where is it exactly that we're going?" She followed him to the exit, stopping at the trash cans to clean off her tray and stash it on the pile.

"To a motel in Daytona Beach." That was true as far as it went. "Of course, nobody can see you in my company, so we have to get checked in before anyone else who is attending this meeting will arrive."

"Do you know which motel?"

"No. I'll choose one that looks pleasant when we get there. At this time of year in Florida there seemed no reason to book in advance."

She accepted that without comment. Probably it all sounded quite reasonable to her, now that she almost believed the basic premise that he'd rescued her from imminent danger. Instead of being gratified by his powers of deception, he felt sickened by them. He'd lied for so long about so many things that he wondered bleakly if he would ever be able to live an honest life again. His past was so littered with dishonesty, treachery and betrayal that he must fast be approaching the point that he wouldn't recognize truth or integrity if they walked up and hit him with a two-by-four.

Returning to the stifling heat of the car, he drove back onto the highway, maintaining a flow of meaningless chatter while really devoting most of his attention to checking that nobody followed them. He sped up, slowed down, dodged out of a downtown exit on the excuse of needing gas, circled the block, backed up, and generally screwed around to the point that even with multiple vehicles assigned to tail him, he was confident that he would have spotted at least some of them.

He hoped that his conversation about attending last year's Cannes Film Festival and seeing Woody Allen and Nicole Kidman up close and personal would be sufficient to distract Charlotte's attention from his strange driving pattern, but he should have known better. She might be naive still, but she was also observant and she realized exactly what he was doing.

"So did you decide whether we're being followed, or not?" she asked as they took the highway exit for Daytona.

He grimaced. "Not," he said. "We're clean."

"Why did you expect somebody to tail us?" she asked. "More to the point, *who* did you expect to tail us?"

"I didn't suspect anyone specific. I was probably being unnecessarily cautious. A habit which is often a waste of time, but sometimes has kept me alive."

For once his answer was entirely truthful. Neither the FBI nor the Armargh Army was likely to expend resources tailing him. If the FBI knew where he was, they'd arrest him. If the Armargh Army found him with Charlotte in his company, they'd kill him. And her, too. Ironically, the mere fact that he had Charlotte sitting beside him proved to both the FBI and the terrorists that he wasn't to be trusted.

Of all the people he had to deal with over the next twenty-four hours, only the Elf had no idea Charlotte existed and therefore would have no interest in the fact that she was with him. Fortunately, it was the Elf who Rick was scheduled to meet with this afternoon. The phone call he'd received earlier this morning had been from the Elf, who retained an amateur's delight in making covert assignations at the last minute, via untraceable cell phone accounts. For all the childish jiggery-pokery, this was a meeting that Rick couldn't afford to miss, because the Elf had finally committed to handing over a CD-rom that contained detailed construction and site plans for their target, the Vehicle Assembly Building at the Kennedy Space Center. He'd been working toward this for the past six months, exerting every skill he possessed to persuade the Elf to trust him. For this reason alone, Sean and Ryan's attempt to kidnap Charlotte couldn't have come at a worse time.

According to the Elf, it had taken him more than five years to gather all the information that he'd stored on the disk, including security apparatus, security procedures, and codes for ingress and egress. Rick believed him. If the Elf hadn't possessed the highest level security clearance, he would never have been able to accumulate what amounted to a complete and stunning blueprint for invasion and destruction.

Quite apart from its symbolic significance as a triumph of American technology, the Vehicle Assembly Building was one of the world's largest enclosed structures, and it made a perfect target for both the Earth Liberation Front and the Armargh Army. The Elf considered the entire space program a hideous perversion of how human beings ought to be spending their resources and utilizing their scientific knowledge. The Armargh Army wanted to punish the Americans for having brought the peace process in Northern Ireland to a successful point of cooperation. The Armargh Army and the Elf came from causes light years apart, but they were united in their conviction that blowing up the Kennedy Space Center would make a political statement that would be hard to beat.

When O'Toole first told Sean and Ryan, the lieutenants of his eight-man cell, exactly what their target would be, he'd explained that the Elf believed they were all environmental extremists just like him. And that since the Earth Liberation Front had a policy of never allowing one member to meet more than one or two other members face-to-face, they would be able to pull off the deception long enough to get the Space Center blown up.

His two senior lieutenants, showing rare common sense, had been rightly suspicious about cooperating with somebody as lunatic as the Elf. None of them saw anything irrational in their own fanatic beliefs, but they were all horrified by the Elf's craziness.

"Tell me again," Sean had said. "Let me be sure I've got this straight. This fuckin' Elf wants to blow up a building at the Kennedy Space Center because he doesn't approve of NASA's plans to explore the planet Mars."

"There you have it, boyo." He had allowed himself a half smile. "The Elf says we've already polluted earth almost to the point of no return. He isn't going to allow the U.S. government to pollute another planet."

"So now, accordin' to him, we have to save the fuckin' Martians? You're pullin' me leg, right?" Ryan looked as if he wasn't sure whether to laugh or cry.

"Not Martians. He wants to save the Martian ecosystem. There aren't any Martians, unless you want to be counting bacteria. And they've probably been dead for a hundred million years or so, if they ever existed in the first place."

"This Elf is after blowin' up the Space Center to save dead bugs? On another planet?" Ryan finally gave way to laughter. "He wants to save fuckin' dead bugs. Jesus, Mary and Joseph, the man needs to be locked up somewhere with padded walls where he can't do himself an injury.''

"But he works for the very space program he's planning to blow up!" Sean's bewilderment was understandable.

"Yeah, well, he says he was seduced by science until he saw the light seven years ago. He's been planning this mission for the past five years, but he needed more help than he could get until he made contact with me."

Sean and Ryan both rolled their eyes. "We're going to use our plan and our methods, right? Once he's provided the blueprints for the building, the Elf doesn't get any input into how we do the job, agreed? I don't want some fuckin' fairy planning any mission I'm takin' part in."

"It's our plan we'll be using," he assured them. "But, trust me, this Elf isn't quite as barmy as he looks. He managed to pass a security clearance only six months ago, including a lie detector test. He may be crazy, but he's no fool." He'd gone on to show them some of the preliminary information the Elf had provided, and even Sean and Ryan were impressed by its detail. Given the miles of territory covered by the Space Center, the thousands of employees, and the huge number of separate buildings, he wasn't worried that Sean and Ryan would be able to pinpoint their target, much less identify the Elf.

The Elf had designated Daytona Beach as their meeting place only when he called at eleven-thirty this morning. As a measure of protection for both of them, now that the Elf had chosen the city, Rick would be the person who selected the precise time and location of their face-to-face meeting later this afternoon. Despite these elementary precautions, neither of them had any real guarantee that they weren't being led into a trap. Off the top of his head, Rick could think of at least a half dozen ways the Elf could set him up. Only the fact that the Elf wanted the Vehicle Assembly Building blown up as soon as possible provided Rick with some minimal form of protection from betrayal.

The Elf was worrisome insofar as loony amateurs always made Rick nervous. On very rare occasions, an amateur could do something so stupid—so far outside the box—that he succeeded where a professional, following logic and accepted procedure, would fail.

On top of worrying that the Elf was suddenly going to send a warning message to a TV station, just to make the whole operation more exciting, Rick had to work out how he was going to handle his upcoming meeting with the General. Thwarting the General was an entirely different proposition from thwarting the Elf. The General was ruthless enough to give even hardened conspirators nightmares. To put it bluntly, the General made the Elf look like a toddler organizing a campaign to knock down castles in the kiddie sandbox.

One problem at a time, Rick reminded himself. First the Elf, then he'd prepare for his meeting with the General. And somehow, through it all, he'd keep Charlotte safe.

He turned off the highway, following signs indicating the famous beaches of Daytona, with their miles of packed sand, lapped by summer-warm Atlantic waters. He spotted an Embassy Suites hotel that looked suitable for his purpose, and not too far from the restaurant he'd mentally designated for his meeting with the Elf. It was large enough that there was almost no chance he would be remembered by any of the staff, and the fact that all the rooms came with an attached sitting area would help Charlotte to feel less claustrophobic—and make his own escape from the room tonight a fraction easier.

Rick drove around the entire hotel just to make sure that there would be no unpleasant surprises, and satisfied himself that there was nothing about the layout or amenities that was likely to present problems for his activities. Even though he hadn't known himself that he would choose this hotel until a couple of minutes ago, he automatically scrutinized the laundry truck delivering supplies of clean laundry and a man in overalls standing under the shade of a sea pine, smoking. Neither truck nor man set any alarm bells jangling, a fairly reliable certification that they were what they seemed.

He'd already obsessively debated the relative merits of various methods of keeping Charlotte safe while he checked into the motel and had concluded there was no perfect method. If she remained in the car, he had to trust her not to run away. If she accompanied him into the lobby, there was the danger that she might be overcome by a belated sense of self-preservation and use the opportunity to call for help. There was also the danger that an observant clerk at the registration desk might recognize her if the FBI had decided to go public with the news of her kidnapping—an event Rick was anticipating with grim resignation. Once Charlotte's photo was plastered all over the media, his life would become exponentially more difficult.

Charlotte so far hadn't given a thought to public reports of her kidnapping, but give her another couple of hours and she would. At which point, she'd insist that her parents needed to be notified that she was safe and he, of course, would refuse to let her call them. Just one more problem to add to his lengthening list of items to be coped with over the next thirty-six hours.

He'd checked the newspapers first thing this morning as he rushed around Wal-Mart buying clothes for Charlotte, and although the local press had devoted a couple of columns to the mysterious power failure at the Down Under club, there had been no mention of Charlotte's disappearance, nor had John Hanseck been mentioned by name. The *Tampa Tribune* reported merely that a woman and two men had been taken to the hospital where the woman was treated and released, while the two men had been held for further observation.

By now, though, John Hanseck would have recovered sufficiently to confer with his colleagues at the Bureau, and some sort of public announcement about Charlotte's disappearance was likely to be forthcoming soon. Hanseck and Nicholson both knew that Black Ops had a deep cover operative infiltrated into the Armargh Army, although they didn't know who it was. Right now, the powers-that-be would be going through the usual bureaucratic in-fighting about whether it compromised an ongoing undercover operation to publicize Charlotte's disappearance. He knew enough about the way the Bureau operated to be confident that it was only a matter of hours before the Black Ops division lost out and Charlotte's picture was flashing on TV screens across the country.

One forty-seven. He didn't have any more time to procrastinate. Rick parked the Taurus under the portico at the front of the motel and pocketed the keys. Fortunately the registration desk was visible through the smoked glass doors, which meant that once he was inside, he'd still be able to see Charlotte and the car.

"I am going to check us into a room," he said, getting out of the car as he spoke, deciding that it was less of a risk to leave her in the car than to take her inside. He was careful to betray no hint that he was worried she might run.

"Are we spending the night here?" she asked.

He nodded, noting her use of the word *we* with a relief he didn't reveal. "We have almost thirty-six hours before I can arrange for you to be taken into safe custody," he said. "We might as well spend it in relative comfort. Sit tight. I'll only be a couple of minutes."

He walked away without looking back, although he could feel sweat pooling at the base of his spine. As soon as he got to the registration desk inside he turned around and felt relief wash over him in a giant wave when he saw her still sitting in the car, watching him. Jesus, if only she knew how much danger she was in if she left him.

Thinking about Charlotte in danger left him weak-kneed, so he pushed the thought away. He was almost as good at not-thinking as he was at lying. He booked a room in the name of Leslie Carter and wrote down the number of his license plate without a murmur when the clerk asked him to do so. Leslie was a name used by both men and women, so the written records wouldn't reveal whether he was male or female, and the odds were good that the clerk wouldn't remember signing in a man. As for the license plate, he had half a dozen spare plates in the trunk, so it would be easy enough to change this one out as soon as Charlotte wasn't watching. Just one more set of precautions in a life made up of covering his tracks.

He paid cash so that he didn't have to show his driver's license, and accepted the key to Room 127, which faced the swimming pool. The clerk, looking excruciatingly bored, pulled out a printed diagram of the hotel layout and showed him where to park. She was answering the phone before he'd even picked the diagram off the counter. If it hadn't been so convenient, it would have been frightening to contemplate how easy it was to move about the country without ever having to provide any convincing proof of who you were.

Their room was spacious, cool, and more attractively decorated than he would have expected. Rick tossed his bag onto one of the beds, noting with relief that the headboards weren't entirely solid and had posts at each end, although he'd have used the leg of the bed if he'd had no other choice. Then he swiftly located the two phones, removing the cords. He straightened from unplugging the second phone and realized Charlotte was looking at him with a faint frown. Not anger, he thought immediately. Puzzlement. A chill iced down his spine. Movement and gesture were harder to disguise than anything else. Had he blown it?

He spoke quickly, to interrupt her focus and destroy a dangerous train of thought. "Sorry, Charlotte. I cannot risk leaving you the temptation of a functioning phone."

"It's all right." She turned away, her body stiff with hostility. "I'd forgotten for a moment that I'm your prisoner. How foolish of me."

He fought the impulse to walk over and take her into his arms. "Not my prisoner, Charlotte. You are the woman I have sworn to protect."

She looked at him with eyes so blue, so scornful, and so achingly beautiful that he had no idea how he managed to stand there without screaming out the pain of his loss.

"It's amazing how much your particular style of protection feels like imprisonment." She unzipped the cheap nylon bag in which he'd stored her clothes and toiletries and ostentatiously ignored him as she arranged the meager selection in the chest of drawers, banging each drawer shut with a crash.

His cell phone rang before he could say anything more. He cursed the interruption, which was probably all the indication he needed that he was damn lucky it had occurred.

He flipped open the phone. "Yes?"

The Elf spoke. "Are you in Daytona?"

"Yes."

"Where do you want us to meet?"

"The Publix grocery store at the corner of Tarpon and Marlin."

"Grocery stores are big places. Where will I find you?"

"By the fresh produce section. Three-thirty."

"Fresh?" The Elf's voice sharpened with bitterness. "You mean pickled in chemicals, don't you?"

Rick swallowed an expletive and made it a chuckle instead. Jesus, the guy never let up. "Be there at three-thirty. Don't be late." He shut the phone, cutting the connection. He'd checked with the GPS system in his car as he drove to the room, and the grocery store was a seven-minute drive from the motel. He planned to be there at least fifteen minutes early, which meant that he needed to leave here within the next couple of minutes.

There was no time for regret. No time to think about the problems he was laying up for the future. When he arrived at the meeting, he needed to have a hundred percent of his concentration. He needed to be secure in the knowledge that Charlotte couldn't escape, which left him with no choice about what he had to do now.

"You're meeting your informant in a grocery store?" Charlotte asked, surprised enough to put her hostility aside for a moment.

"It's as good a place as any." They were, in fact, far less likely to be noticed or remembered in a crowded supermarket than in a bar or restaurant.

"I suppose it's useless to ask you to take me with you?" Charlotte remembered that she was annoyed with him and her voice took on a renewed note of anger. In a moment, Rick thought bleakly, she wasn't going to be just mildly pissed at him. She was going to be justifiably furious.

''Yes. I'm sorry, you can't come, but with informants, you never know what might happen. You could be in danger.'' Rick reached into his own overnight bag and pulled out a pair of handcuffs that he'd connected with an extra long, steel-link chain.

Charlotte's eyes widened. ''What are those for? What are you doing?''

''Keeping you safe.'' Before she could fully comprehend the insulting notion that he actually planned to chain her up, Rick strode forward, grabbed her wrist and clicked the cuff onto her left wrist. Belatedly she started to struggle, but he was ready and simply twisted her arm behind her back, using the pain to force her to move toward the headboard so that he could clip the other cuff to the post of the bed. He did some more of his not-thinking in regard to the pain he was inflicting. Not to mention the closeness of her body to his. Oh, yeah. Not-thinking was definitely the way to go right now.

She refused to sit and he wasn't willing to force her down. ''Stand if you wish, Charlotte. It's going to be a long wait.''

She stared at him, eyes sparking, not deigning to speak. She looked magnificent. He wanted to make love to her with an intensity and longing that he was helpless to disguise.

Her expression changed from disdain to fear and he realized she was afraid he was going to rape her. ''Jesus, Charlotte...'' Fortunately he choked, because he'd totally forgotten his goddamn French accent and if he'd said anything more, he'd have blown it. He took a step toward her before sanity returned.

He swung away and headed for the door. ''I will

return.'' God Almighty, he sounded like former French president Charles de Gaulle in one of his periodic fits of megalomania. No way he could make this mess better.

Rick cut his losses and left the room. He had just enough self-discipline left not to bang the door shut behind him.

Eleven

She was going to be gone by the time Rat Bastard came back if she had to chop her hand off at the wrist to do it, Charlotte vowed. Except, of course, that she didn't have a knife to do the chopping. It infuriated her to remember that she'd been alone in the car when Rick checked into the hotel, and she'd sat there meekly waiting for him. Why the *hell* hadn't she made a run for it then? She was so angry with herself for not having escaped when she had the chance that she spent the first five minutes after Rick left literally pounding her free fist against the wall.

This would have been a more useful exercise if their room hadn't happened to be the end unit. Since it was, her banging meant that she managed to scrape her knuckles without attracting any attention from anybody. By the time she was sucking blood from her fist, wincing in pain, the red mists of anger finally cleared from her brain long enough for her to start using it.

Rage was getting her nowhere, that much was clear. What she needed to do was make a calm, rational plan for her escape. Criminals and magicians got free from handcuffs all the time, so why couldn't she?

Deliberately ignoring the fact that magicians got paid for escaping from locked handcuffs precisely because it was so difficult, and that criminals presumably spent years acquiring the skill as part of their stock-in-trade, Charlotte sat down on the edge of the bed and examined the cuffs with careful attention. Unfortunately they were securely latched. Rick hadn't been in too much of a hurry to take care of that little detail. However, the bracelet seemed quite loose on her wrist, relatively speaking. It might even be loose enough to compress her thumb against her palm and slide the cuff off, especially since she had her right hand free to help with the manipulation. Her wrists were pretty skinny, which was all to the good in this situation.

Anything was better than sitting here, meekly waiting for Rick to return, no doubt spouting a fresh crop of eminently believable lies, beguiling her afresh. How could she have been crazy enough to believe he was working with the FBI? Obviously he was a criminal and intended to use her as some sort of bargaining chip in a deal with law enforcement—or worse. And she'd been idiotic enough to cooperate in her own imprisonment!

Charlotte pushed back a fresh spurt of rage and worked diligently to free herself for almost half an hour, refusing to give way to frustration or despair, but in the end she was forced to acknowledge defeat. The cuff was too tight, and her manipulations had only succeeded in making her hand swell, so that the task was becoming more impossible the harder she tried. A bowl of ice water might reduce the swelling and do the trick, but she might as well wish for the moon as wish for ice water.

She leaned back against the headboard, letting rip with a string of blistering curses that would have horrified her parents and did little to relieve her state of simmering frustration. Staring at a crack in the ceiling, and trying to invent fresh insults to heap on the absent Rick, it dawned on Charlotte that her anger was an odd reaction to the situation she found herself in. Surely she ought to be feeling terror? She'd been kidnapped, drugged, moved from one location to another, and ended up chained to the bed. Why was she mad as fire, instead of frantic with fear?

Charlotte gnawed on that problem for a while and realized that—even now—she couldn't quite bring herself to believe that Rick intended to do her real bodily harm. Her reaction was so irrational she was hard put to account for it. She'd heard about the syndrome where kidnap victims begin to feel a slavish devotion to their kidnappers, and she'd always been smugly convinced that she could never fall into such a stupid and self-destructive attitude. Apparently she'd overestimated her powers of resistance. All Rick had needed to do was take her into a fast-food restaurant, buy her coffee, chatter about Paris and European vacations, and she'd begun to believe he had her best interests at heart. She'd been angry rather than fearful when he handcuffed her to the bed because—God help her—she'd actually felt *hurt* that he hadn't trusted her.

She was appalled at how far off-track her mixed-up feelings had managed to lead her in only a few hours. Good grief, at least most adult kidnap victims managed to hold out for a week or so before succumbing!

Charlotte gave a frustrated yank on the handcuff and the headboard rattled. Her attention caught by the rattle, she eyed the headboard speculatively. Could she pull hard enough to break the post where Rick had secured the second cuff? Years of her mother's training about respecting other people's property had her hesitating, until she realized how ridiculous she was being. The motel could replace the headboard if she succeeded in breaking it. Heck, she'd be more than happy to buy 'em a whole new bed if she could only get out of here. When she weighed the alternative costs of breaking the headboard, or remaining chained to the bed until Rick returned, it was a no-brainer to smash the bed.

Using both hands, she tugged on the chain that linked the two cuffs, exerting every atom of her strength in an effort to break off the end post from the rest of the headboard. It was a useless endeavor, she quickly realized. The bed frame was on castors, and simply slid across the carpet as she tugged.

Wiping sweat from her forehead, Charlotte plopped back onto the bed, blowing a wisp of hair off her forehead as she sat. In the confusion, she'd left her hair loose this morning. Now she wished she'd taken the time to pin it up, off her neck. Her exertions, or her temper, were making her hot and sweaty.

Charlotte sat bolt upright, feeling a piercing quiver of excitement as she suddenly thought of her missing hairpins. Of course! That was how heroes always escaped in action movies. Somehow they invariably managed to find themselves a paper clip, or a piece of thin metal, even if they were in a dungeon with dripping wet stone walls and nothing but the bare floor to sit on. Then they jiggled the lock on the hand-cuffs until it sprang open. At which point the evil captor would return, only to be hit over the head by the heroic prisoner, who would dash to freedom and save the world.

Charlotte smiled grimly. She especially liked the part where she got to hit Rick over the head. She'd bean him with a chair, or something, and when he was unconscious, she could steal his car keys and zoom into the sunset....

Abruptly she called a halt to her enticing flight of fancy. Tempting as it was to visualize Rick limp and helpless at her feet, such heroics were unnecessary. She was in a beachfront hotel in Florida, not the African jungle or the frozen wastes of Siberia. All she had to do was make it to the lobby, place a phone call to the FBI, and she was safe.

And Rick was toast.

Man, that toast part sounded good. She wanted him to be burned toast, singed to a crisp. There were only two snags in her brilliant new escape plan. First, she suspected it was harder to open the lock on handcuffs in real life than it was in the movies, and second, her hairpins weren't in her hair. They were inconveniently far away, packed inside the cheap nylon bag Rick had provided to transport the clothes he'd bought for her.

Charlotte eyed the distance separating her from the bag on the dresser and compared it with the length of handcuff chain. Clearly the chain was too short to permit her to reach the bag. She scowled, aware that a hairpin was her only serious hope of getting rid of her shackles and making good her escape. She was unwilling to abandon the idea without putting forth some serious effort, especially since the bag wasn't all that far out of reach.

Since she couldn't grab it with her hands, she'd use her feet, Charlotte decided. She lay down on the bed on her back and tried to use her feet to kick the bag off the dresser, but the angle was all wrong, and she just couldn't extend her foot far enough to reach. Frowning, she sat up and mulled over the problem with intense concentration.

The solution was so simple when it finally came to her, she couldn't understand why it had taken so long. She hadn't been able to break the headboard because the bed moved when she tugged on her handcuff chain. Which meant, presumably, that she could tug the bed far enough away from the wall to be able to reach the travel bag on the dresser.

Less than two minutes later, Charlotte had hauled the bed far enough toward the center of the room to stretch out her right hand and seize the bag. Panting but triumphant, she sank onto the bed and pulled out the plastic pouch that held her supply of toiletries. The pins were at the bottom, including a couple of the old-fashioned sort that looked as if they'd be ideal for picking locks.

She could reach the switch for the lamp on the dresser with no trouble, thank God, and she turned it on, holding the handcuff up to the light and scrutinizing the locking mechanism. Then she poked carefully at the clasp until she felt the resistance of the little tumblers. Another couple of pokes and she felt definite movement. Hey, this was going to be easier than she'd expected!

Fifteen minutes later, she was still poking at the lock, unwilling to stop long enough to acknowledge that the task seemed more hopeless the longer she persevered. The tumblers moved quite often, but they never completely yielded. Rick had been gone for over an hour. How much longer could she count on his absence? In a fit of frustration, she abandoned her careful gentleness and rammed the pin against the tumblers, all frustration and no finesse.

The lock clicked. The handcuff opened.

Charlotte stared at her hand—her free hand—momentarily too stunned to move. Then she gave a whoop of joy, and tugged her wrist out of the cuff. Barely stopping to draw breath, she flew through the sitting area, opened the door, and dashed out into the corridor.

Since they were in an end unit, she was close to an Exit sign. But that door must lead to the parking lot, Charlotte reasoned. Much better that she should avoid the slight chance of running outside just as Rick returned from whatever mischief he'd been up to. She turned swiftly in the opposite direction, heading in search of an inner door that would lead to the lobby.

It had been a rational assessment in theory. In practice, finding her way to the lobby through the maze of featureless corridors proved difficult. She finally came to another exit door, and breathed a sigh of relief. This must be the way to the lobby, since she'd run quite far. She pushed open the door, and a suffocating wave of hot, humid air invaded her lungs. To her dismay, she discovered that she'd run a significant distance, but apparently she'd traveled in a loop, because she'd simply emerged into the parking area closest to their room, albeit about twenty yards away from the original exit that she'd seen next to their room.

There wasn't any sign of Rick or his Taurus, thank God. In fact, the lot was silent and deserted under the baking-hot sun. Even the two cars and the pickup truck parked against the cement block wall looked wilted. It was good news that Rick was nowhere in sight; bad news that a friendly hotel employee didn't just happen to be strolling by. Charlotte drew in a steadying breath and decided that since she seemed to have no sense of direction when it came to the interior of the hotel, she'd find her way to the lobby by walking around the exterior perimeter of the building.

She'd barely made it to the first corner when she heard the sound of a car driving into the lot, followed by the screech of brakes and the sound of a car door slamming open. Heart pounding, she broke into a run, not even bothering to glance back over her shoulder to confirm that the car she'd heard was Rick's.

She was fast on her feet, she was fit, and she was running for her life, but she was no match for Rick. She felt his hand clamp on her shoulder within seconds. She started to scream, but his hand was over her mouth almost before she had time to draw breath, let alone produce any sound. He was wearing leather gloves again, she realized, making it useless for her to try to bite him. Why, oh why, hadn't she screamed as soon as she heard the car turn into the parking lot? It would have consumed valuable breath she needed for running, but somebody just might have heard her and come to her rescue.

Rick twisted her arm behind her back, as he had done when he handcuffed her to the bed. Her shoulder was sore from where he'd wrenched it earlier, and she would have cried out with pain if she'd been able to make any sound.

He spoke softly into her ear. "I have a gun, Charlotte. I beg that you will not compel me to use it. Now we shall walk back to the room, quietly, as if we are good friends."

Charlotte wasn't sure how Rick could expect to get away with shooting her in broad daylight, in the middle of a parking lot. But there was nobody in the immediate vicinity, the gun might have a silencer, and she discovered she wasn't ready to test his willingness to use it. If only somebody would come! Even a hotel employee who spoke no English would be fine, since it required no language to understand what Rick was doing.

Nobody came, however, and Rick continued to frog-march her around the hotel exterior, with his hand pressed so tightly across her mouth that she could hardly breathe, let alone scream. Since this was Florida in the middle of a late June afternoon, most people had enough sense to be at the beach, or sitting on a park bench, or shut up inside some facility where the air-conditioning blasted full force. The parking lot remained deserted for the minute it took for them to cross it.

Despite her despairing conclusions about the likelihood of rescue, Charlotte fought with fierce determination, trying to at least slow down their progress back to the hotel building, but the outcome was a foregone conclusion, just as it had been when Rick kidnapped her from the nightclub. This time he didn't even have the inconvenience of hiding her struggles from a crowd of people.

He was incredibly strong, as she already knew. His body was so densely muscled that it felt like a single block of hardwood pressed against her spine. Charlotte became aware of a sudden wild yearning to have him totally in her power, lying beneath her, bound hand and foot, begging for mercy. She wanted him naked, she thought. Naked, helpless, and totally vulnerable—with her holding the gun and making the threats.

She recognized the sexual undertones to her wish, and she recoiled from them, horrified. A few days ago she'd been kissed by John Hanseck, a charming, upright citizen with impeccable credentials, and she had felt nothing more than polite boredom. But a criminal lowlife like Rick abused her and she felt sexually attracted to him. It wasn't an insight to improve her self-esteem.

The door to their room was locked, but Rick barely slowed down. He held her pinned to the wall with half his body weight, his left hand gripping her mouth, while he swiped the key card through the lock. It worked the first time—what else? Charlotte thought in frustration—and he pushed her inside, finally relaxing his hold over her mouth as he turned to bolt the door and slide the chain into place. She realized he wasn't holding a gun and started to scream, more in defiance than because she expected to summon rescuers.

"Don't, Charlotte." He sounded almost pleading, but he put that damned gloved hand over her mouth again and propelled her out of the sitting area into the bedroom. He pushed her against the wall with a swift economy of movement that suggested he was accustomed to physically forcing people to obey his will. He held her lower body still with the pressure of his knee against her groin. She shivered, despite the fact that she was sweating.

"Don't make me gag you, Charlotte. Nod your head if you'll agree not to scream when I release my hand."

She stared at him, hypnotized by his mirror-image sunglasses that reflected back her own image, keeping his eyes hidden. Except for this morning, when the drapes had been drawn, she'd never seen him without his sunglasses, Charlotte realized.

"Charlotte?" Something about the way he said her name made fresh chills run down her spine. "I asked if you will promise not to scream."

She nodded, having not the slightest intention of keeping her promise. She expected him to lift his hand tentatively, testing the reliability of her word, but he looked at her intently for a moment, then moved away with such abruptness that she almost lost her balance.

Oddly, she didn't scream once she was free. She was too angry at being a prisoner again to waste her breath on an action that clearly wasn't going to produce any worthwhile results. With her luck, any neighboring hotel guests who heard her scream would think she was enjoying some late-afternoon sex.

"You don't have a gun," she said. She sounded

accusing, but the person she was accusing was herself for having been so credulous.

One second she was looking at his empty hands. The next second she was staring into the barrel of a Sig 9 mm revolver. "I have a gun," he said neutrally. "As I informed you."

She gulped, swallowing hard as she watched Rick return the gun to a belt holster that nestled the gun in the small of his back. He pulled his T-shirt down to cover it, leaving no sign from the front that he carried a weapon. It brought no comfort to realize that in this, at least, he'd been telling the truth. It brought even less comfort to realize how quickly he could remove the Sig from its holster and have it ready to fire.

With the gun stashed to his satisfaction, his gaze flicked briefly toward the bed, where the handcuffs still dangled from the bedpost. He shoved the bed back into place and unlocked the cuffs, tossing them into his bag. His expression didn't visibly change, and yet Charlotte sensed a welter of emotions building inside him to a level of explosive intensity.

When he spoke, his voice betrayed none of the tension she was convinced he was feeling. "Will you come into the sitting area, where there are chairs and we can be comfortable?"

"I can't be comfortable when you're around. Your presence and comfort are a contradiction in terms."

"Then will you sit for a moment and listen to me, despite your discomfort?"

She went into the sitting room, flouncing like a pissed-off teen, and sat down on one of the chairs. Her obedience wasn't entirely because the knowledge that he had a gun made obedience the sensible choice.

When she was actually in his presence, she had this insane urge to cooperate with him.

Rick spoke flatly. "Nothing has changed since I explained the situation this morning, Charlotte. I handcuffed you to the bed because I wanted to prevent you running away, and thus ensure your safety. If you leave my protection, you not only endanger yourself, you put the entire United States at risk."

"Oh, please!" Charlotte felt a fortifying burst of anger. "For God's sake, credit me with a grain of sense! Do I look like the sort of woman who's going to believe that the safety of the nation hinges on whether you keep me prisoner or not?"

"Unfortunately, no. You look like a woman who has zero confidence in my integrity."

"Bingo! Give the man a prize!" Charlotte sprang up from the chair and paced the small room, feeling more of a prisoner now than she had when she was chained to the bed. Rick's presence filled the room, suffocating her, making it impossible to think clearly.

Rick had his expressionless face on again, but she wasn't deceived. She could feel the tension bubbling and seething beneath his supposedly calm exterior. He spoke with a flatness that Charlotte interpreted as rigid control rather than absence of emotion. "Why do you always wear your sunglasses?" she asked, the question springing from nowhere.

"No special reason. I had simply forgotten that I was wearing them." Rick removed his sunglasses, and hooked them into the neck of his T-shirt. Charlotte wondered if she imagined a split second of hesitation before he took them off. His eyes, she noticed, were dark brown, exactly as she'd assumed first thing this morning. O'Toole's eyes had been a wonderful deep shade of blue.

And she had absolutely no clue why that irrelevant fact had drifted into her mind.

"Since the handcuffs didn't work as a safety device, that leaves me with only two choices where you are concerned," Rick said. "I can drug you into unconsciousness, and keep you that way for the next twenty-four hours. Or I can attempt yet again to win your trust." His hesitation was barely perceptible. "I know which of those two options I ought to choose."

"You want to drug me."

"No. I feel obligated to drug you. I *want* you to trust me."

Damn it, she detected a note of what sounded like genuine yearning in his voice. To her dismay, Charlotte felt herself weakening. If there were a mole in the FBI and Rick didn't know who he or she was…if he really did have to complete some undercover assignment related to O'Toole's activities under a tight schedule…if she really had been targeted for kidnapping by O'Toole's associates and the head of Rick's covert operations department was out of the country—

Charlotte stopped her train of thought before she sank even deeper into the swamp of mindless credulity. "You can't be telling me the truth," she said. "Even if there's a mole at work in the FBI, you could easily make an end-run around him. Or her. If you have to stay here in Florida for some mysterious reason, why don't you buy me a plane ticket to Washington, D.C., and give me a note to hand-carry to the director of the FBI? Or are you suggesting that the director himself could be the mole?''

"No, I'm one hundred percent sure that he is not."

"Then escort me to Orlando airport and put me on a flight to D.C. I promise to report to the director as soon as I can catch a cab to transport me from Dulles airport to the J. Edgar Hoover building.''

"It's Saturday, tomorrow's Sunday. The director won't be at the office for another thirty-six hours at least."

She scratched her head, feigning deep thought. "Well, let's see… I heard a while back about this great invention called the telephone. I'll take a wild guess that the FBI director has one, or even three or four, wherever he goes. In fact, I'll go way out on a limb and suggest that someone at the Bureau probably knows how he can be reached. What do you think? Am I being too far out there?"

"I think you are conveniently ignoring the fact that you would have to tell your story to a minimum of twenty or thirty people before anyone would place that call to the director, much less let you anywhere near him. Which means twenty or thirty opportunities for the wrong person to hear what you have to say. Since you have been interviewed by the FBI on several previous occasions, one of the agents who knows you would be called in to debrief you and make certain that you are who you claim to be. That is precisely the meeting I am desperate to avoid. If he or she is the mole, I am left totally exposed.''

When she was face-to-face with him as she was now, she couldn't seem to find fault with Rick's logic. "Then let me fly home to my parents' house. You pretend you're so anxious about my safety. Well, I have three brothers, and twenty-four first cousins who all live in the greater Des Moines area, not to mention uncles, aunts, and sisters-in-law. If I asked them to keep me safe, it would take nuclear war to get me away from their protection.''

An utter stillness descended over him and several seconds ticked by in silence. Finally he turned and looked straight at her. ''What if I told you that a nuclear detonation is precisely what I'm trying to prevent?''

Twelve

Rick could barely credit what he'd just allowed to escape from his mouth. But he'd tried everything else, he thought despairingly. Now he seemed to have no choice left but to tell her some of the truth. Unfortunately the General had been correct to instruct his lieutenants to kidnap Charlotte. She was the one point of vulnerability where he was concerned, and the General had exploited that weakness with his usual brilliant insight.

Rick had bought himself time by kidnapping Charlotte first, before Sean and Ryan could get to her. Unfortunately the fact that she was sitting six feet away from him didn't mean his ability to make rational assessments had been restored. Worry about keeping his actions hidden from the General, not to mention Sean and Ryan, was compounded with worry about keeping the FBI off his ass so that he could insure her safety. The plain truth was that having Charlotte around compromised his judgment. He was wasting far too much effort keeping his feelings hidden as opposed to concentrating on the myriad other problems at hand.

Keep your eye on the prize, boyo. And while you're

at it, keep your hands off Charlotte's body and quit thinking with your dick.

She was staring at him with an expression of mingled doubt, indecision and horror that he should have been able to view with indifference, and couldn't. At this point, with all that was at stake, what the hell did it matter if she didn't like him much, and trusted him even less? What he needed right now was a vigorous kick in the butt to restore his sense of perspective and reorder his priorities.

"What are you talking about?" Charlotte perched on the edge of her chair, her body stiff and awkward with tension. "Wh-what do you mean, you're trying to prevent a nuclear explosion?"

"Just that," he said curtly. "Perhaps you've already heard about the would-be nuclear terrorist the FBI arrested last spring? He was a petty criminal who'd converted to Islam and decided he could find salvation by offering his services to Al Qaeda. He'd made it his mission in life to get the radioactive material necessary to produce a dirty bomb. He was halfway toward succeeding when agents moved in and arrested him."

She nodded. "Yes, I read about that. According to the papers, he seemed to believe he could bomb the United States into accepting Islam."

"If not that, he hoped at least to inflict a crippling blow on America, so that Muslim countries would be in a better position to take what he considered their proper place as leaders of the world."

Charlotte pushed impatiently at her hair, which had fallen in a seductive sweep across her eyes. "Somebody should have pointed out to him that being the only superpower isn't all it's cracked up to be. It's no fun being the target of every loony-toons this side of the planet Jupiter.''

Rick shrugged in rueful agreement, keeping his attention focused rigidly on what they were discussing, rather than his overwhelming urge to take Charlotte to bed. ''Unfortunately it's not only Al Qaeda operatives who want to teach the U.S. a nuclear lesson. The Armargh Army is another group that's been identified by the FBI as actively in the market for radioactive material, and they have serious money to spend because of the profits from their counterfeiting operations. A year ago there were rumors that they were attempting to buy a bomb from the stockpile of nuclear weapons that haven't yet been decommissioned by the successor states to the former Soviet Union. O'Toole is known to have made at least two trips to Kazakhstan, which is a prime source of supply for black market weapons.''

She turned pale. ''Oh my God!'' She pressed her hand to her chest. ''Are you saying… Does O'Toole have a…nuclear *bomb?*''

She'd leaped right to the heart of the matter. The fact that he'd told her this much of the truth left Rick hollow with fear, but he'd gone too far now to back down. ''O'Toole doesn't have a nuclear weapon— yet. And with the failure of his buying trips to Kazakhstan, it's unlikely that the Armargh Army would be able to acquire a full-scale nuclear weapon in the near future. But he's going to have all the necessary components to manufacture a dirty bomb very soon. According to the intel I've been receiving, at some point within the next thirty-six hours O'Toole will take possession of processed nuclear waste and an explosive device to deliver it. We're talking about a bomb that would be capable of scattering radioactive material over an area the size of a small town.''

Charlotte looked as if she was about to be sick, and Rick grimly pressed his advantage. ''Can you imagine what would happen to Florida's tourist industry after an explosion like that? The state would be bankrupt within the year, which would throw the entire country into serious trouble, given the precarious state of today's economy. And that's quite apart from the loss of life in the actual bomb blast. Not to mention the cancers and the birth defects likely to result a few years down the road.''

Charlotte had been pale before, but now she turned so white that Rick was afraid she would pass out. She held out her hand, as if to push his words away. ''Don't say any more. I don't think I can bear to hear any more.''

She got up from the chair, almost losing her balance. He ached to comfort her, but he couldn't, of course. He watched, helpless, as she steadied herself against the wall and went into the bathroom. She splashed water on her face, then poured herself a glass of water that she barely sipped. She didn't shut the door, so he could see her standing with her hands braced on either side of the sink. Her stomach was visibly heaving, but she held herself rigidly still and managed not to throw up.

She came out of the bathroom at last. She leaned in the doorway, wrapping her arms around her body as if she felt chilled to her innermost core, although the air-conditioning was barely sufficient to keep the room cool.

"I guess I need to know the rest," she said. "I can't hide from the truth, so it's better to hear the facts rather than let my imagination run riot. Tell me what O'Toole is planning to do once he gets this bomb."

"It's a long story."

She gave a laugh that hovered dangerously close to tears. "I guess I can spare the time to listen. I have nothing more urgent to take care of right now. There's nothing like hearing O'Toole is threatening a nuclear explosion to catch my attention."

Rick drew out a small computer disk from his T-shirt pocket and laid it flat on the palm of his hand. "This is what I picked up from the man I went to meet this afternoon."

"From your informant?"

Rick nodded. "Although it would be more accurate to call him a conspirator, rather than an informant. He is a physicist who is employed by NASA. He has no idea I am working with the FBI, of course. This disk contains maps and detailed blueprints of both the Kennedy Space Center itself and the Merritt Island National Wildlife Refuge, which is where the Space Center is located."

"But if he doesn't know you work for the FBI, who does he think you are? Why would a NASA physicist give you a disk containing that sort of information? It must be confidential, so where would he get blueprints, anyway?"

"He stole them," Rick replied, with perfect truth. "I told you I have been working on a deep cover assignment. Now you know what that assignment is, and why I can't afford to carry any ID that reveals my employment by the *Sûreté*. The physicist gave me this disk because he believes I am a fellow conspirator—his ally in an effort to blow up the Space Center.''

Charlotte lost what little color she retained. ''He can't possibly succeed, can he?''

''On his own, no, he cannot succeed. But the Armargh Army has the power to make his dreams come true.''

''Is that what O'Toole and his gang have been working on since they arrived in the States?'' Charlotte asked, her voice scratchy with horror. ''They're planning to help this physicist blow up the Kennedy Space Center?''

''Yes.'' The truth seemed worse to Rick when spoken out loud. ''In normal circumstances, the Armargh Army could never hope to pull off such an enormous feat. But with the assistance of this NASA insider, they very well might succeed, because access is the key to a successful attack and my informant is obsessed. He's spent the past five years accumulating all the information that any group of saboteurs might need and he's done a great job. But he doesn't have the manpower or the physical skills to carry out the actual attack. So the alliance between him and the Armargh Army is truly a match made in hell.''

Charlotte rocked back and forth in the chair, her arms wrapped hard around her waist. ''The Space Center must have really tight security. Insider help or not, the chances of success ought to be close to zero.''

''Nowhere near as close to zero as you would

think,'' Rick said grimly. "The wildlife refuge covers a big area, roughly a fifth of the size of the state of Rhode Island, although the Space Center only occupies six thousand acres of the total. This disk provides top-secret details of the entire security system for the Space Center, right along with military satellite data showing the topography of every inch of the wildlife refuge at maximum resolution. If you want to know the best way to access the Center from the ocean, or if you want to know when the security guards make their rounds of the Vehicle Assembly Building, this disk tells you. Or any other similar question somebody planting a bomb might want answered. It also provides the access codes for virtually every ingress and egress point in the entire Space Center Complex.''

"You sound as if you believe O'Toole and the Armargh Army can pull this off.''

"I believe they can. Especially if O'Toole has men trained as deep sea divers among his soldiers, and we believe he has.''

There, he'd told her the stark truth, so he might as well give her some more of the frightening details. "With the help of my NASA physicist, the Armargh Army plans to hide their bomb in a limited-access area of the Vehicle Assembly Building, which happens to be one of the largest structures by volume in the world. The bomb will operate on a timer, of course, so the Armargh Army soldiers will be miles away—probably on a plane to South America—before the bomb explodes and radiation starts mushrooming over the area.''

"Why did they choose the Vehicle Assembly Building, do you know?"

"It's big, so it's suitably symbolic as a target for the Armargh Army, and the NASA physicist cares only that the U.S. space exploration program should be set back for as many years as possible. So all parties are happy, even though you would never expect Irish nationalists and an environmental freak to find any way to work together."

"But I still don't understand why a NASA scientist would want to blow up the Kennedy Space Center." Charlotte's expression was one of acute distress and her voice shook occasionally as she asked a question, but she was doing an amazing job of retaining control while she forced herself to understand what was at stake. "What bug is chewing on his toes that he would do something that's not only immoral and illegal but flat-out nuts?"

Rick shrugged. "It's hard for us to grasp his reasoning, but he has what seem to him compelling reasons."

"Share them."

"A few years ago, he became disillusioned with NASA when he was passed over for a promotion. He was already a pretty senior guy, but he believes he should have been put in charge of an entire division. Then he happened to meet and fall in love with a woman who was an active member of a radical environmental group called the Earth Liberation Front—"

"The Earth Liberation Front?" Charlotte said, startled. "Does that mean she was an elf?"

"Yes." Rick was surprised by her knowledge.

"Not many people have heard of the elves, despite the amount of damage they've done, one way and another. How does it happen that you know about them?"

She hesitated for a moment. "John Hanseck asked me to listen to a clandestine recording the FBI had made to see if I could identify O'Toole's voice. As far as I know, the voice wasn't O'Toole's, but the recording was definitely of a member of the Armargh Army, and he was talking to somebody about his meeting with an elf. Since the speakers on the tape kept talking about elves, Hanseck and his partner, Shirley Nicholson, explained all about the Earth Liberation Front and what their aims were."

Jesus H. Christ. Rick absorbed the information in silence. Obviously when Padraig was arrested in Miami for passing counterfeit currency, he had rolled over on his fellow conspirators and helped law enforcement to plant a bug in their apartment rented by the Armargh Army. Thank God they'd walked out on their lease the moment they discovered Padraig was in custody. They'd lived in motels ever since, changing locations often enough that bugging would be virtually impossible.

Still, it wasn't good news to know the folks at the Bureau had been able to get that close to O'Toole. And if some over-eager federal agent arrested the General within the next couple of days, it would spell disaster for Rick. The government lawyers wouldn't have a hope in hell of winning a conviction against the General, but O'Toole's cover would inevitably be blown. Worse, the Armargh Army would lie low for a few months, and then reform as soon as the investigative heat was turned down, leaving O'Toole once again acutely vulnerable to blackmail. Except that this time around, O'Toole would be even more at risk, because every single Armargh Army soldier would be gunning for him. And for Charlotte.

Rick thrust aside a bone-deep shudder of fear. There was nothing for him to do right now except watch his ass with increased vigilance, if that were humanly possible. He thought back to this afternoon's meeting with the Elf, mentally checking to make sure there wasn't some new area of danger to be covered in light of Charlotte's information.

He decided there wasn't. He was willing to stake his life on the fact—he *was* staking his life on the fact—that the Elf wasn't planning a double cross. He wanted the Space Center blown up too badly to have turned state's evidence.

Charlotte spoke again, reminding Rick he'd been silent too long. "You started to explain why this NASA scientist became so disillusioned that he decided to blow up the entire Space Center," she said. "Was it something to do with the woman he fell in love with?"

"Yes, but not because she converted him into an environmental radical," Rick said, pulling his attention back on track. "In fact, she more or less dropped out of the Earth Liberation Front when she married the physicist. It seems as if they both fell so deeply in love that she forgot about saving the planet and he forgot about problems at work, and how mad he was at his bosses. They bought a house, they talked about having kids. I really believe they were blissfully happy together. Then his wife was diagnosed with pancreatic cancer, and six months later she was dead. He convinced himself the disease had been caused by the toxic wastes being dumped into the river near her family's home in upstate New York.''

"He could be right about that,'' Charlotte said. "It's a sad story, anyway.''

"Yes, it is,'' Rick acknowledged. "But everybody who loses their spouse in tragic circumstances does not go around making plans to blow up government buildings. Even if the physicist is correct about the cause of his wife's cancer, the logical course of action would have been for him to start a campaign to clean up the river and get legislation passed that would prevent companies from dumping their waste into the nearest handy pool of water.''

Charlotte looked dubious. "That sounds good in theory, but people have tried going the legislative route for years. There must be hundreds of environmental protection laws on the books. The problem is, companies don't obey them.''

"In that case, the physicist could have chosen the all-American way to deal with a problem and sued the hell out of the company dumping the toxic waste. Look at what Erin Brockovich managed to do—in real life, not just in the movie—and she had nothing like the education and resources of a NASA scientist. Anyway, bottom line, after his wife died, the physicist had the equivalent of a religious conversion. According to him, all human beings have an obligation to live in harmony with nature and we need to stop being obsessed with progress and material possessions. We need to get back to our primitive roots and restore our planet to health.''

"Has he noticed that there are about a billion people in the world who aren't even willing to give up their TV sets, let alone go back to living in mud huts and catching dinner with spears?"

Rick turned his hands palm up. "He truly can not seem to grasp that our lifestyle in America and Europe is the result of millions and millions of personal, individual choices, not the result of government edicts. He is convinced the United States government is the enemy. He believes there is an all-powerful military-industrial complex that secretly controls Congress and manipulates the judicial system, so there is no way for ordinary citizens to get their voices heard above the clink of money changing hands."

Charlotte shook her head. "I agree with him that there are some sleazy politicians out there, and that big money has too much influence on politics. But that's a far cry from saying the whole U.S. government is corrupt."

"You are right, but it is most amazing how many different people manage to hate the government of your country, and for such a bizarre variety of reasons." Rick gave a rueful smile. "My own countrymen are not famous for their admiration of the U.S."

"Well, you French are just annoyed that the rest of the world prefers to speak English." Charlotte smiled to take away the sting of her words.

"Which shows appalling bad taste by the rest of the world," he responded, without missing a beat. "Try making love in English and then try again in French, and you'll see what I mean."

Charlotte realized she was blushing and decided

she absolutely wasn't going to get sidetracked down that particular byway. "I wonder why none of these fanatics ever notices that the U.S. government is made up of a few dedicated public servants and a whole bunch of bungling bureaucrats who spend a fair portion of each day groping their way from one major screw-up to the next."

"I wish I could answer that," Rick said wryly. "All I know is that my informant sees different things when he looks at the government from what you and I see. In his opinion, he's fighting a deadly foe, and right is on his side, so the end justifies the means."

"He truly believes he's one of the world's good guys?"

"Absolutely. He is one hundred percent sincere. Soon after he buried his wife, he joined the Earth Liberation Front, but he kept his membership secret so that he could continue with his job at NASA. Since the government uses science and technology to pursue unworthy aims, he was determined to undercut the government from within. He is clever as well as crazy, and he has been cunning about maintaining the facade of dedicated space program scientist. Despite outward appearances, though, over the past half dozen years, his opinion of the government has sunk even further, and he's become especially disapproving of the program to explore Mars."

Charlotte looked startled. "You've lost me again. What's the Mars exploration program got to do with his wife's illness and dumping toxic waste here on earth?"

"He claims that NASA is lying about the purposes of the Mars exploration program. It is not about pure science, and the search for extraterrestrial life. He claims the U.S. government is planning to establish a mining colony on Mars to exploit the natural resources of the planet.''

"He might even be right. It's always easier to get Congress to vote funds if there's a chance of making a profit.''

Rick grimaced. "Could be, I guess, but do you care? We're talking about a planet that consists of barren rock, with—maybe—a few fossilized bacteria to break up the monotony. It's difficult to see what a mining operation could destroy.''

"Evidence of alien life, maybe? However primitive the lifeforms, that would be an amazing discovery.''

"No NASA scientist is going to allow alien lifeforms to be destroyed. Never. And even if the goal is to make a profit one day in the future, nobody is going to be mining anything on Mars for at least another generation. With current technology, the transportation costs would be so high that whatever we mined would cost millions of dollars per kilo by the time we got it back to earth.''

"Have you tried pointing that out to the Elf?''

Rick smiled tightly. "Of course not. He believes I'm a fellow elf, so I spend a lot of time talking about the beauty of preserving the integrity of a virgin planet. I've agreed with him on several occasions that we human beings polluted the whole world with our first industrial revolution, and now we plan to pollute our neighboring planet in the course of our second industrial revolution. The Elf believes we're a two-man crusade, united to save the planet Mars.''

Charlotte shot him a curious glance. "Don't you

find it difficult to keep a straight face when you have to spout stuff like that?''

"Not at all," he said coolly. "When I'm with him, I believe what I'm saying. That's how a good undercover operative stays alive. If I ever accidentally betrayed my true opinions, the Elf would not pat me on the shoulder, and agree that we should part friends. He is a dangerous fanatic who believes he is at one with the Founding Spirit of the Universe. Trust me, if he discovered that I'm an agent of the *Sûreté,* working with the FBI, he would kill me."

Charlotte shuddered. "His views seem so far out, it's hard to take them seriously, but I guess not doing so would be a bad mistake."

"Yes, a very bad mistake."

Her forehead wrinkled in puzzlement. "But even if he's right and Mars needs saving from the greedy industrialists, how does it help the problem to explode a dirty bomb here on earth, and make the pollution in the world a dozen times worse with radiation? Polluting earth to save Mars makes absolutely no sense, even by his logic."

"Well, destroying the Vehicle Assembly Building would certainly delay all of NASA's space exploration programs by at least a decade, and that's what he cares about at this moment." Rick hesitated for a second, then told her the truth. "Besides, he does not realize that his fellow conspirators plan to use a dirty bomb. He knows he is involved in a plot to blow up the Kennedy Space Center. But he does not know that his fellow conspirators plan to use a dirty bomb to do it. The Armargh Army have been careful to hide that choice detail from him."

Charlotte mulled over his response for a moment. "Now that this physicist has given you the disk, you have objective proof of what he's involved with, right? Evidence that doesn't depend on your word against his."

Rick nodded. "That is true."

"Then why don't you just report him to his bosses? Given that he doesn't really know the full extent of what's going on, he might even be grateful in the long run that he was stopped before his fellow conspirators could set off a radioactive explosion. Surely to god, an environmental fanatic can't want to leave the east coast of Florida contaminated with radiation for the next hundred years or so?"

"Probably not, but I can not turn him in just yet. It would be disastrous if the physicist were arrested, because it would scare off the Armargh Army."

"But the tradeoff is that you'd save the Space Center and prevent a nuclear disaster! Who cares if the Armargh Army is scared off? Obviously, they're bad guys, but they can be arrested any time!"

Rick shook his head. "You are only half right. True, we could prevent the attack on the Space Center if I reported the physicist to his bosses right now, or even if I called in a secret tip to the FBI, provided I gave them names and enough details to be convincing."

"Exactly! You'd prevent a nuclear explosion. Why are we even sitting here talking? We should tell somebody now, this minute—"

She half rose from her chair, and he waved her back again. "No, we absolutely should not. The Armargh Army would disappear at the first hint that their inside contact at the Space Center was in trouble—''

"Good!"

"Bad. Very bad. They'd take their dirty bomb with them. Then we would never find them again, or their weapon."

"How can you know that?"

"Easily. They've been avoiding the British police and Interpol for over a decade. Not to mention their success in keeping clear of their deadly rivals, the Red Hand Protestant paramilitary fanatics, who are every bit as ruthless as they are."

"But the FBI managed to record some of the Armagh Army's conversations! They must know where they can be found."

"I very much doubt it. You can take it from me that the so-called soldiers who are going to plant this bomb are scattered all over south Florida at this point, and there's not a chance in hell that the FBI could pick them all up. Believe me, Charlotte, if the Armagh Army disappears now, the next time we hear from them will be when their dirty bomb is detonated in some totally unexpected place. Probably the basement of a crowded apartment building in Manhattan or Washington, D.C. Or how about Disney World, since they're already in the neighborhood and they might want to get rid of the bomb in a hurry? At least as things stand now, we have a fairly precise idea about what is going to happen."

"Yes, we know that there's going to be a disaster!" Charlotte sounded despairing.

"No," he said. "If I can just keep all the balls up in the air for another twenty-four hours or so, it means we can prevent the Space Center being blown up. We can arrest the leader of the Armargh Army and his most important lieutenants, plus we shall be taking at least one dirty bomb out of circulation for ever. Those seem to me to be goals worth striving for.''

Charlotte wasn't reassured. On the contrary, she seemed to shrink inwardly as he watched. ''You keep talking about the Armargh Army as if it were an abstraction. But what you really mean is that you're going after O'Toole. You're waiting for Daniel O'Toole to take possession of the dirty bomb, and then you're going to arrest him.''

''That's more or less the plan.'' Somewhat less than more, but there were limits to Rick's sharing of the truth.

''This whole plot to blow up the Kennedy Space Center is O'Toole's work, isn't it? This is what he's been scheming to achieve for the past eighteen months since he left me. I'll bet he's been working on your informant to make sure that he doesn't have second thoughts and decide the government isn't so bad after all. God forbid that the Elf should see reason and undercut O'Toole's schemes.''

Rick felt the muscles in his stomach clench into a tight, hard knot, but he managed to keep all trace of emotion out of his voice when he spoke. ''Even if that is true, why do you sound so upset? Earlier today, you told me that you know nothing about the real O'Toole, so his life and activities can't touch you in any way.''

''I lied.'' She spoke so softly he had to strain to hear her words. Her eyes were dark with anguish and she flinched as she met his gaze. ''O'Toole was my husband,'' she said, her voice cracking on the admission. "However much I want to pretend otherwise, the bottom line is I was in love with a man who's trying to buy a nuclear bomb for the purpose of killing and injuring thousands of people. I slept with him. We held hands in the movies and laughed at the same jokes. He was godfather to one of my nieces, and I was the person who brought that monster into the heart of my family.''

"You didn't know the truth. You can't blame yourself.''

"I should have seen the truth, and I do blame myself.'' She swung away, but not in time to hide the tears that spilled out of the corners of her eyes. She dashed them angrily away. "I *hate* that I never sensed the core of darkness inside him. How could I have been so blind?''

If there was any comfort to offer her, Rick sure as hell couldn't think what it might be. Anything he said at this point was likely to compromise him irretrievably. The muscles in his arms ached from the stress of not going to Charlotte's side, of not holding her, of not gathering her against his body and smothering her pain by sheer force of his will.

He had thought that not seeing Charlotte was the worst punishment that could ever be inflicted on him. Now he knew that there were levels of hell that made the simple fact of not seeing Charlotte seem relatively painless. He took a pleading step toward her that she fortunately didn't see.

He tried to turn away so that at least he wouldn't be condemned to watch her weep, but he didn't seem to be capable of making any movement that didn't bring him closer to Charlotte's side.

His cell phone rang as he stood helplessly by. Rick had never imagined he could be so grateful for an interruption. He didn't recognize the number the call was coming from, but that didn't mean much. Most of his incoming calls originated from public phones. He pressed the talk button as he walked into the bedroom, where he hoped Charlotte wouldn't be able to overhear what he said. Not that he would be saying anything very revealing, but she wouldn't be able to avoid noticing his abrupt change of accent if he said more than a couple of words. "Yes?"

As he'd half-anticipated, it was the General. "Was your meeting this afternoon a success? Did you receive the information we've been waiting for?"

The General spoke with the crispness of a military officer, which is what he'd been for twelve years, Rick had discovered recently, after months of painstaking research. Fitzpatrick had been court-martialed for the death of three Iraqi prisoners during the Gulf War. The prosecution had lost their case, and the General hadn't served a day of time, but Rick was never quite sure how much the General truly cared about the cause of a united, Catholic Ireland and how much he simply enjoyed the feeling that he was pissing on the British officer who'd acted as chief witness for the prosecution. Not to mention working off some of his rage against the American government for daring to question his conduct under fire. Both his parents had been born and raised in Belfast, but until the time of his court martial, Rick had the impression that the General had been bored by Irish politics and considered himself a one hundred percent American.

Rick responded to the General's question about his meeting with the Elf. "Yes, the meeting was successful. He finally trusted me enough to give me all the data we need to complete the job." To Rick's relief, he heard Charlotte going into the bathroom and shutting the door behind her.

"Good." The General permitted himself a small sigh of satisfaction. "Now that you have the data, has your supplier been paid?"

Translation: he wanted to know if Rick had killed the Elf. "No. We need him for admission purposes. Retinal scan."

"Unfortunate."

"Not entirely. We don't want to precipitate a premature investigation. He'll be paid later. I'll meet you tonight at the agreed place and time and explain further."

"Very well. If the data are as complete as you claim, I'll make the delivery twelve hours later."

"Assembly and other last minute preparations shouldn't take us more than twenty-four hours after delivery. We'll be ready for the targeted date."

"I should bloody well hope so." The General's almost imperceptible Irish accent was suddenly thicker. "You've been practicing for two months. I need a July Fourth performance." He cut the connection.

Rick allowed himself the childish luxury of making a rude face at the phone before erasing the record of the call and walking back into the sitting room. He really disliked the General, and he was determined to bring him to justice. The fact that the General was in reality ex-army Colonel Brian Fitzpatrick, currently president and CEO of a major international corporation, wasn't going to protect the bastard if Rick could just get him to actually hand over the makings of a dirty bomb.

As things currently stood, a conviction was more problematic. The General could be charged with conspiracy, and the prosecution might even manage to wheedle a guilty verdict from a jury, but the General had enough money to buy himself the best lawyers in the country, not to mention the fact that he had friends in very high places. Without actual evidence of handing over the bomb, Rick wouldn't like to lay odds on the chances of the General actually copping serious prison time.

Charlotte came out of the bathroom a couple of minutes later. She'd washed her face, and combed her hair, but the evidence of her tears remained visible. ''I'm sorry to be reacting so emotionally,'' she said. ''I got through the last eighteen months pretending that O'Toole's activities had nothing to do with me, and that defense doesn't seem to be working anymore. I'm not sure if that's good or bad.''

She looked wretched, although she was trying valiantly to present a brave facade. At that moment, Rick despised the choices he'd made in his life, hated everything he'd done in the name of O'Toole, and cursed the injustice of fate. Since the lives and safety of thousands of people were held within his grasp, all he could do was force his mouth into some expression that he hoped approximated a smile.

''It is good,'' he said. ''It is always better to shed

illusions and face the truth." He was in no mood for analyzing the ironies of that particular statement, so he moved on quickly. "The day has been difficult," he said. "You ate almost nothing at lunch, and you must be hungry. Why don't we find a Chinese restaurant that does takeout and bring back some food to the room? There is nothing like dim-sum and moo-shu pork for taking your mind off your problems."

"Thanks, but I'm not sure I could eat right now."

"Charlotte—" He broke off, appalled. Holy shit, he'd almost said *Charlotte, honey.* He forced himself back into his role as French special agent Richard Villier. "You do not have to eat now, but at least let us go and buy the food so that we have something available if you decide later that you are hungry." He gestured to the tiny fridge and the microwave. "You see the hotel has provided us with all we need to eat like kings."

She gave him a smile at last, albeit a rather fragile one. "I thought the French despised food heated in microwaves."

He grinned. "I am a desperate foreigner, plunged into the American gastronomic wilderness, so I have learned to adapt. Where are the Yellow Pages? Probably in the desk drawer. Let us find a restaurant and call in our order so that we do not have to wait too long for it to be ready."

They picked the closest Chinese restaurant, and Rick was relieved to see that Charlotte's appetite perked up enough for her to at least contribute that she would like noodles rather than rice with the cashew chicken and moo-shu pork.

Their order placed, Rick took his car keys and held

them up. "Okay. Are you ready to come food-hunting with me?"

She nodded and followed him out of the door without making any attempt to run away, or to scream, or to draw attention to herself as they walked to the car. He'd done a really great job of beating down her resistance, Rick thought. One more jewel to add to his glittering crown of achievements where his relationship with Charlotte was concerned.

Thirteen

They drove past the famous Daytona beaches, the sands shimmering in the haze of early evening heat. Charlotte pushed away images of purple nuclear clouds rising above the ocean and tried to convince herself that Rick would manage to arrest O'Toole and prevent the Armargh Army from carrying out its horrendous plans.

Her mind recoiled from visualizing the harm that her ex-husband would inflict on thousands of people if he succeeded in detonating a radioactive explosive device in the heart of the Kennedy Space Center. If the bomb went off, she wondered if she would ever again be at peace. How could she be, with the deaths and financial ruin of so many innocent people on her conscience? Rather than wallowing in the horror of what might happen, she decided it was better to concentrate on the more pleasant vision of O'Toole, captured and defeated, incarcerated in a dark, maximum security prison, subjected to the careless brutality of unsympathetic guards.

Once, in another lifetime, Charlotte had been accused by her favorite sister-in-law of being so annoyingly cheerful that she ought to come packaged with a warning label, so that normal people could avoid her in the morning before they'd had an inoculating shot of caffeine. Even now, despite her experiences over the past eighteen months, it seemed that she couldn't stay mired in the pits of depression for long. After a few minutes of silent gloom, her inborn optimism pushed her inexorably toward hope.

The situation wasn't entirely desperate, she reflected. Rick seemed confident that he could avert disaster, and she was beginning to trust his judgment. For her part, she would do everything in her power to help him. With a little luck, and a lot of hard work on Rick's part, Daniel O'Toole was going to discover that he'd schemed and plotted his last.

Despite her renewed flicker of optimism, Charlotte felt unbearably restless. She returned desultory replies to Rick's attempts at conversation, and squirmed behind her seat belt, unable to get comfortable, even though she recognized that her restlessness was mental rather than physical. She wanted O'Toole captured. She wanted him tried. She wanted him convicted and imprisoned. Most of all, she wanted him to suffer, as he had caused her to suffer. Vengeance might not be a pretty emotion, but Charlotte decided that it beat the hell out of mooning around feeling guilty.

Being kidnapped by Rick had jolted her out of her eighteen-month long state of emotional paralysis, she realized. She'd been shaken so far out of her routine that the log-jam of self-blame and victimhood had broken at last, and she had turned the corner in her attitude toward Daniel O'Toole.

From her new perspective, she could see that she'd reacted to her ex-husband's disappearance with too much guilt, too much repressed anger, and nowhere near enough honest rage. She'd run away from Des Moines and cut herself off from her family to punish herself for the crime of having been married to O'Toole. She'd shut down her emotions, buried herself in work, denied herself the pleasure of new friendships, all because she couldn't forgive herself for not having penetrated the disguise of a master deceiver.

There was an element of excessive pride buried somewhere within all that sackcloth and ashes, and Charlotte was tired both of the pride and the repentance. It was past time to move out of her state of mourning and rejoin the land of the living. And one of the quickest and most certain ways of liberating herself from the shadows of the past was to do everything in her power to frustrate O'Toole's plans to blow up the Space Center. With her ex-husband arrested and imprisoned, her life could turn to a fresh, clean page. It was no surprise to discover that the idea of a genuinely new beginning had enormous appeal.

What part could she play in making sure that O'Toole was captured and imprisoned? Charlotte trusted Rick to know what he was doing. Everything she'd seen suggested he was a competent professional who was accustomed to working in dangerous situations. Now that she'd put aside the haunting fear that he was trying to deceive her, she felt confident of his abilities. And the best way for her to help Rick was to cooperate instead of constantly trying to escape. She needed to stop viewing herself as the victim of a kidnapping and accept that Rick had taken her into protective custody, just as he had claimed all along.

Rick had turned inland while she was occupied
with satisfying images of O'Toole locked in a small
prison cell, surrounded by hostile guards. A couple of
minutes later, he drew up at a strip mall where the
Chinese restaurant they were looking for turned out
to be located between a hardware store and a shop
selling light fixtures. Two gold-painted lions sat on
pedestals on either side of the entrance to the restaurant, and Charlotte gave their heads an absentminded
pat as they passed. The heads were on springs and
they nodded at her in stately greeting, surprising a
laugh out of her.

Rick turned, his mirrored sunglasses reflecting the
setting sun. "You are beautiful when you laugh," he
said softly.

Heat flared in her cheeks and she quickly covered
the last few steps to the restaurant. "This looks like
a pretty fancy place," she said.

"Yes, it does. Let us hope the food is as good as
the decor." Rick pushed open the smoked glass doors
and they were greeted by a smiling young Chinese
woman, wearing a traditional embroidered silk cos-
tume, with a mandarin collar and above-the-knee slit
in the long, tight skirt.

"Good evening," she said, bowing. "Welcome to
Shanghai Palace."

"We called in an order from your takeout menu,"
Rick said. "We are here to pick it up."

"Of course. Your name, sir?"

"Rick. Villier. We ordered spicy cashew chicken,
moo-shu pork, noodles, and grilled vegetables."

Bowing again, the hostess gestured to a pair of
high-backed, carved chairs that flanked the entrance,

their appearance more elegant than comfortable. "I will check to see if your order is ready, sir. Do you wish for a drink from the bar while you wait?"

"Not for me, thanks." Rick turned. "Charlotte?"

She shook her head. "No, not right now, thanks."

Rick ordered two bottles of chilled Chinese beer to add to their takeout order, and they sat down to wait for their food. The hostess disappeared into the back of the restaurant, then returned to escort another couple to a table in the dining room. As the trio passed by, Charlotte had the odd impression that the hostess was sneaking covert glances at her. Charlotte stared back at the woman, tilting her head in pointed inquiry.

The hostess gave a flustered smile, accompanied by a half-bow, but she didn't say anything. Then she vanished once again in the direction of the kitchens and came back a few minutes later, carrying two glasses of scented iced tea on a lacquered tray.

"We are most sorry for inconvenience," she said. "Please accept tea while you wait. I regret, cashew chicken is not yet ready." She held up her hand. "Five minutes only."

Maybe the hostess was upset at keeping them waiting, Charlotte thought. That might explain why she had such an agitated manner beneath her scrupulous veneer of courtesy.

Rick gave a relaxed smile as he reached for the glasses of iced tea, dismissing the hostess's concerns with a friendly gesture. "Thanks for the drinks," he said, keeping one and handing the second glass to Charlotte. "Don't worry about the chicken. We're in no great rush, are we, chérie?"

"Er...no. We can wait." Charlotte was thrown off

by Rick's laid-back attitude and even more surprised by the unexpected endearment, although she recognized that it was strictly for the benefit of the hostess. Rick had struck her as the sort of man who would actively dislike hanging out in the lobby of a Chinese restaurant, waiting to pick up an order of takeout food. Still, she couldn't really know him after mere hours in his company, despite a sense of familiarity created by their enforced intimacy. In truth, she had virtually no basis for making judgments about his habits and characteristics.

She took a sip of the tea, and then another. ''It's very refreshing,'' she said to the hostess, who was still hovering at their side. ''Thank you.''

''You are welcome.'' The woman backed away, smiling and bowing. The moment she'd vanished around the screen that separated the entrance from the main body of the dining room, Rick leaned close to Charlotte's ear and spoke in a low voice. ''Put your glass down on the seat of the chair. Then stand up, and walk out of here. Do not run, do not speak and try not to draw any attention to what we are doing.''

''But why—''

''Do not ask questions. Just follow me.''

Rick got up, the movement fluid and seemingly casual. When she didn't immediately follow suit, he shot her a glance that was as much silent appeal as a command, and Charlotte found herself meekly trailing him out of the restaurant.

The second they were outside the smoked glass doors, he clicked the electronic opener on his key chain, and the lights of the Taurus flashed on, indicating the doors had opened. He grabbed her hand

and ran the few remaining yards to where they'd parked the car.

"Get in," he said, dropping her hand to run around to the driver's side of the car. He opened the door and slid behind the wheel in a single swift movement. "Charlotte, get in the damn car!"

He didn't yell, but the low-pitched urgency of his voice was more commanding than any shouted order could have been. As soon as she was inside, and long before she could latch her seat belt, he pushed the gear into Reverse and backed out of their parking spot. As the car swung around, facing forward, Charlotte saw a police cruiser turn into the strip mall, its emergency lights flashing, but its sirens muted, as if to avoid giving warning of its arrival.

"There's a police car!" she said to Rick, as if he could possibly have failed to notice it.

He didn't break his concentration to answer. Instead of taking one of the side exits, he drove directly toward the police cruiser, swung alongside it at a leisurely pace, then made a right-hand turn out of the parking lot and onto the road.

Rick's level of tension was high enough to be contagious and Charlotte fully expected the police car to give chase, but looking back over her shoulder, she saw that the cruiser had carried on in its original direction and come to a halt directly outside the Shanghai Palace.

Rick's slow drive toward the cruiser had probably been crucial to their getaway, she realized. If he'd turned and driven fast in the opposite direction—which would have been her immediate reaction—the police would have pursued them.

She had no chance to see how many cops entered the restaurant because Rick accelerated away from the strip mall as soon as he was sure he and Charlotte weren't attracting their attention. He raced the Taurus down a side street and cut across the road that led back toward the beach. Instead of heading toward their motel, he drove onto the highway.

"Where are we going? Why are we taking the interstate?" Charlotte asked.

"We are making sure we lose the cops before we attempt to go back to the motel. We do not want to lead them right to us."

"But we've already lost them. Even if they were really coming after us."

"They could easily radio for backup, and probably identify the color, make and model of the car we are driving. We were the only car moving when they turned into the strip mall."

Charlotte cast a nervous glance over her shoulder, relieved to see that the highway appeared blessedly free of marauding cops. "How did you know the police were coming?" she demanded. "What happened back there, Rick? Why did you suddenly tell me we had to leave the restaurant as if you anticipated trouble?"

"The hostess. She was not a good liar. Her eyes kept sliding sideways to sneak another glance at you and her neck flushed bright red when she told us the cashew chicken wasn't ready. I realized she was inventing an excuse to keep us there long enough for the cops to arrive."

Since Charlotte had herself noticed that the hostess was on edge, she couldn't dispute Rick's opinion, but she'd assumed the woman was worried because the takeout meal wasn't ready within the twenty minutes promised in the restaurant's Yellow Pages ad. It was a revealing window into Rick's lifestyle that he interpreted every twinge of tension in another person as being a direct personal threat.

"How can you be sure the cops came to the restaurant looking for us? Maybe one of the cooks went after another cook with a knife. Maybe one of the waiters was caught stealing from the cash register—"

"It is quite possible. There are a thousand possible explanations for the hostess's behavior. I wasn't prepared to wait around to find out which one was correct."

And Charlotte wasn't yet prepared to enter Rick's paranoid world, even if the hostess had behaved strangely. Maybe the woman had been so tense because she expected the chefs to spill out of the kitchen at any moment, bringing their fight into the dining room and alarming the patrons.

The more Charlotte thought about it, the more unlikely it seemed that the hostess had been suspicious of her and Rick. Why would she be, for heaven's sake? There was absolutely nothing about the two of them to arouse anyone's suspicions. Their appearance could hardly be more ordinary for Florida in midsummer.

Rick was sticking to the center lane, driving at a constant four miles over the speed limit. Just slow enough to avoid attracting attention from a traffic cop, fast enough to move them away from the Chinese restaurant at a rapid clip.

"*Why* would the cops be coming after us?" she

asked him. "They don't know you're an undercover agent, working against a deadline and skirting the edges of the law. What did we do to make the hostess suspicious? There's no reason on earth for her to have called the cops to come and pick us up."

"I said your name," Rick said. He made it sound as if uttering her name in public was an obscene act. "Christ almighty, I said your name."

"And so?" Charlotte stared at him. "Is saying my name an indictable offense?"

"If they handed out indictments for stupidity it would be." Rick sounded furious with himself.

"Drop a few more cryptic clues," Charlotte said with heavy sarcasm. "Then in a couple of weeks' time I might work out what the hell was going on back there at the good ol' Shanghai Palace. Or you could just tell me what happened and save us both a whole heap of aggravation."

She could see that Rick really didn't want to say anything more. His gaze was still fixed alternately on the road ahead and the rearview mirror, creating the impression of intense concentration, but she would have bet large sums of money that more than half his attention was devoted to the problem of what he was going to say to her. If he could have dreamed up a convincing lie, she was pretty sure he would have used it. In the end, though, he opted for the truth. Undoubtedly because he saw no alternative, she reflected wryly.

"It was you who attracted the attention of the hostess," he said. "She wasn't paying much attention to me, but she recognized you. When I said your name, it must have confirmed her suspicions about your identity to the point that she called the police."

For a moment, Charlotte didn't grasp the significance of what Rick was saying. Why would the hostess recognize her? She wasn't a celebrity. She'd never set foot in Daytona Beach until today. Then she understood.

"Oh my God! The hostess knew I'd been kidnapped! The FBI must have gone public about my disappearance."

"Yes, I think they have," Rick acknowledged. "I hoped we might have another few hours before they broadcast the news. But I should have checked the reports on television before I took you out of the motel room. A bad mistake on my part, compounded by saying your name. I'm guessing the FBI has released your picture to the media. It's probably being flashed nationwide on a regular basis."

Charlotte was silent for a moment, reflecting on the implications of being publicly identified as a kidnap victim. The realization hit her that if the FBI wasn't keeping her abduction under wraps, then her parents must have been told that she was missing—that she'd been snatched from the Down Under dance floor and hadn't been seen since. Her family would have no way of knowing that she wasn't lying decapitated in a ditch, or bound hand and foot, locked in the basement of some sexual pervert with murder on his mind.

In other words, they would be frantic.

"We have to call my parents," she said. "Right now. My God, Rick, they'll be worried out of their minds. And it's not only my parents who'll be worried. All my family will be going crazy, wondering what's happened to me. We have to let them know I'm okay.''

He didn't answer immediately, concentrating instead on changing lanes so that he could take the upcoming highway exit. Charlotte suppressed a moment of panic. ''Rick, don't be difficult about this. Surely you can see why I have to get in touch with my parents? They need to know I'm alive. It's…vicious…to leave them wondering.''

''Vicious, perhaps, but necessary.'' He spoke in a cool, remote voice that hit her with the force of a lash. ''Their suffering will be of limited duration. In twenty-four hours, they will know you are safe.''

''Twenty-four hours!'' Her stomach churned sickly. ''Have you any idea how long twenty-four hours will seem to my family? They'll be going through hell, imagining the very worst.''

''I regret their suffering,'' he said.

''That's it? That's all you have to say? You *regret* their suffering? Gee, thanks a lot for your wild outburst of sympathy!''

''What else do you want from me?'' He swung the car under an overpass and waited at a stop light so that he could get back on the Interstate in the direction they'd just come from. ''Unfortunately, there is no way you can call them. It would put my entire mission in jeopardy. No, that's an understatement. The moment you speak to your parents, my current assignment is over. The dirty bomb is as good as exploded.''

She didn't want to hear that because she was afraid it might be true. ''I'll make Mom and Dad promise not to call the FBI—''

He shot her an incredulous glance. "But of course. That will work well."

"Why wouldn't it? They're honorable people—"

"They're your parents and they love you," he said flatly. "Even if they agreed, would you trust their word? You should not. You could not. It would be their duty as citizens to inform the authorities that you had phoned them—"

"I can swear to them that I'm okay. I'll tell them there's been a misunderstanding. That I left to spend the weekend with my boyfriend...."

"Then how do you explain why you don't turn yourself in to the FBI now you know that concerns have been raised about your well-being? If you are with a lover, why did you disappear from a nightclub where you were dancing with John Hanseck? That's rather an odd way to start a weekend assignation, don't you think? And why didn't you call the hospital to check on Hanseck's status? I think your parents might find your story of a weekend with your lover a little unconvincing."

"Then work on a better story! You're accustomed to inventing lies. I'm not."

"There is no lie that would satisfy them, Charlotte. We already found out between the two of us that lies simply don't work. In the end, I had to tell you the truth about what was at stake or you would have been justified in constantly trying to thwart my plans and escape. Even so, you have spent hours in my company, and you still aren't quite sure that you trust me."

"That's not true. Not anymore."

"Good. I am most happy to hear that. Now trust

me on this. Your parents would have to be fools to remain silent about receiving a phone call from their supposedly missing daughter. How could they possibly believe that you are not in danger, whatever you might say? Besides, even if by some miracle they believed you were safe, and not speaking to them under duress, their phone is certainly tapped, and a trace would start running automatically on your call the second the connection was made—''

''You can't tap people's phones without a court order.''

''Not true.'' Rick gave an impatient shake of his head. ''That only applies if the law enforcement agency is requesting a secret wiretap. Your parents would willingly agree to have their phone tapped, so the Bureau wouldn't need to get a court order. I'm sorry, but it's too risky for you to phone them, Charlotte. I cannot permit it.''

She begged, pleaded, cajoled and threatened. She had about as much impact on his decision as a toothpick scratching on granite. As they took the exit ramp off the interstate, Rick finally turned to her and met her gaze.

''Charlotte, shut up.''

She blinked. ''What?''

''You're a smart woman. You know as well as I do that we cannot call your parents. The equation is twenty-four hours of worry for them, or a dirty bomb exploding at some unknown location in the very near future. It isn't a choice. You know that as well as I do. Therefore, it is time for this discussion to end.''

''We haven't discussed.'' Charlotte repressed a

crazy desire to throw a punch at him. "You've laid down the law, just like you always do."

"If it makes you feel better, I acknowledge that what you say is true. I have laid down the law. That admission doesn't change my decision. There will be no calls to your family."

"You like to give orders, don't you?"

"Not particularly, but sometimes it is necessary to take charge of a situation."

"To you it's a *situation*. To me, it's my family." She turned to look out of the window to hide the fact that she was having a hard time fighting back tears. She knew he was right, dammit. So what was with the crying, anyway? She'd barely cried since she'd first learned the truth about her ex-husband eighteen months ago. Now she seemed to have turned into a soggy sponge that only had to be touched in the wrong emotional spot and tears started to leak out.

"God, Charlotte, don't cry. I can't bear it when you cry." Unlike his previous cool tones, Rick's voice had suddenly become low and harsh with tension. Charlotte was obscurely pleased to realize that she'd gotten to him.

She sniffed, patting the pocket of her shorts in search of a tissue. "I'm not crying. Not really." She drew in a deep breath. "I guess I'm hungry after all. I'm beginning to regret the loss of our infamous cashew chicken."

"I do not think we can risk another Chinese restaurant, or anywhere that we have to show our faces, but here is a sign promising us Burger King and McDonalds at the very next exit." Rick drove off the highway. "Obviously we cannot go inside, but at least we can stave off starvation. When we are at the pickup window, can you please screen your face with your hair, and avoid looking directly at the person handing out the food? I really would like to get something to eat without attracting the attention of the police this time.''

Fourteen

Perhaps she really had been hungry, Charlotte thought, munching on a French fry a few minutes later, and simultaneously squirting extra ketchup onto her burger. At least her mysterious tendency to cry seemed to have been vanquished by the infusion of a generous dose of grease and carbohydrates.

Rick took a circuitous route back to the motel, but eventually he seemed satisfied that they weren't being followed and he turned into the motel parking lot, leaving the car under the dubious shade of a scraggy sea pine. The sun was lower in the sky at this hour and the shadows were getting longer, but the heat was still intense and Charlotte found the tranquil coolness of the room welcoming by contrast.

"We need to find out if the media really is reporting you as the victim of a kidnapping," Rick said, switching on CNN's Headline News, and dispelling her brief but odd sensation of coming home.

"If they're not, I don't know how else to explain what happened back at the Shanghai Palace," Charlotte said.

Rick was tactful enough not to remind her of her earlier reluctance to believe that she was the target of the hostess's suspicions. They sat through fifteen minutes of general news programming before the segment they were waiting for came on. The newscaster read her piece, staring wide-eyed and incongruously smiling into the camera.

"And now the latest in the hunt for missing Tampa Bay architect, Charlotte Leone. The FBI is following up on almost two hundred separate leads in their efforts to trace the whereabouts of the thirty-two-year-old Ms. Leone, who also uses the name Charlotte Gray. Ms. Leone is wanted for questioning in the attempted murder of FBI agent John Hanseck—"

Charlotte shot off the bed. "What's she talking about? Attempted *murder?* They can't possibly be suggesting that I tried to kill John Hanseck? Are they nuts?"

Rick pulled her back down onto the bed. "Shush. Listen. We need to hear what they are reporting."

"Tampa General Hospital is refusing to comment on reports that FBI Special Agent John Hanseck is in critical condition following surgery to remove a bullet fired at close range into his chest. At the request of Hanseck's family, the hospital is issuing no bulletins regarding his progress and all inquiries are being referred to the Tampa office of the FBI. Agent Shirley Nicholson spoke with our reporter earlier and confirmed that Charlotte Leone is officially a suspect. It's believed that she worked with an accomplice who timed the power failure at the Down Under nightclub to coincide with her attack on Agent Hanseck. The motive for Ms. Leone's attack is believed to be tied in with an antiterrorism investigation that was being conducted by Agent Hanseck prior to his injury. Ms.

Nicholson refused to provide any details as to the nature and scope of this antiterrorism investigation.

"The FBI has released additional photos of Ms. Leone during the past hour, and we are showing these on your screens now. Charlotte Leone is known to be armed and should be considered dangerous. Anyone who can give the FBI information about her whereabouts should contact their local police station, or call the Tampa Bay office of the FBI at the special 800 number they've established for leads on this case."

A wedding picture flashed onto the screen, showing Charlotte laughing into the camera, a cloud of puffy white veil framing her softly curling hair. An 800 number for the FBI trailed across the bottom of the screen.

The wedding picture jarred Charlotte, but only for a moment. The naively smiling woman in bridal lace was so far removed from the woman she had become today that it was like viewing another person. The wedding picture changed to a publicity photo she'd had taken at work six months ago, and the newscaster's voice could be heard telling viewers to stay tuned to CNN for all the latest developments in the hunt for Charlotte Leone.

The Hunt for Charlotte Leone. Charlotte shook her head, feeling disoriented. Good grief, it sounded like the title of one of Hollywood's less inspired movies. How could the FBI suspect her of shooting John Hanseck? The idea that they could believe she was armed and dangerous—a would-be murderer—was simply too crazy for her to register as a serious problem. And they thought she'd shot John Hanseck, of all people!

Didn't they know she'd been at the Down Under club because the two of them were on a *date?*

Her disorientation was quickly replaced by the painful realization that, even though she hadn't done the shooting, John was apparently lying near death in Tampa General Hospital. A hot flood of anger swept over her as she realized the truth about the way John must have been injured. She knew for sure she hadn't hurt him, which left only one person as a possible culprit.

Rick Villier.

If Hanseck had been shot, then Rick must be the shooter. There was no other explanation. Rick had obviously lied to her about what happened last night, and—gullible idiot that she was—she'd fallen for his lies. What was it with her that she could never manage to penetrate the smooth-talking facade of criminal lowlifes? Why did she believe con men that smarter women would see through in a flash? She wasn't a stupid woman, so what was her problem?

Rick muted the sound on the TV as the pictures of her faded to a commercial break. She swung around to confront him, rage building to fever pitch inside her. ''Did you hear what they're saying about John Hanseck? He's in the hospital, fighting for his life!''

''I heard, of course—''

''You lied to me from the beginning. You told me John was fine, that you'd just made him unconscious for an hour or two. But the truth is you *shot* him! You shot him in the chest, and now he may die! How could you?''

Tears streamed down her cheeks, as much from fury over Rick's betrayal as from sorrow for John

Hanseck. In a burst of outrage, she clenched her fists and started pummeling Rick with all the pent-up force of a year and a half of repression. She wasn't going to take on the burden of guilt for John Hanseck's death, she simply couldn't bear it. She would force Rick to admit what he'd done. She'd damn well *beat* him into telling her the truth and then she'd turn him into the police.

Rick didn't react to her attack. His face impassive, he just stood in front of her, letting her hit him. She might as well have been batting him with a powder puff for all the damage she seemed to be inflicting. With a hiss of frustration, Charlotte redoubled her efforts.

After a couple of minutes, he grabbed her wrists and returned them to her side. "Okay, enough already. Are you prepared to listen now?"

"No!" She pounded him some more. "I never want to listen to you again! You're a liar and a murderer! You're a toad. You're a disgusting piece of rotting pond scum. I despise you and everything you stand for."

Rick turned and started toward the bathroom and she stormed after him. "Don't you walk away from me! We're not done. You have a load of explaining to do before we're through."

He poured water into a plastic cup. "You are hysterical, Charlotte. You can drink this, or I can try something more drastic to make you calm again."

She took the cup, drank a single sip, then flung the rest of the water into Rick's face. "Something drastic like that, you mean?"

His face betrayed zero reaction to what she'd done.

He wiped away the water with a towel. "Feel better now?" he asked, tossing the towel into the sink. "Are you ready to stop behaving like a spoiled child and listen to me?"

Like a child? He thought she was behaving like a spoiled child? Death was too kind a punishment for him. Charlotte drew in a long, shuddering breath, forcing her rage back inside. She could only defeat him by guile, not by strength, where she was clearly outclassed.

"I'm ready to listen to you." She kept her gaze downcast, and let her shoulders slump as they walked back into the bedroom. Rick seemed to accept that she was calm again. Who was being a fool now? Did he really think that her distress at John Hanseck's fatal injury was going to vanish simply because she'd thrown some cold water at him? She clamped her jaw shut, the only way she could prevent herself yelling more insults.

"I told you the truth about what happened at the Down Under club, Charlotte. I injected Hanseck with a fast-acting drug that causes unconsciousness. When I checked with a nurse at the hospital early this morning, before you were awake, I was told that he would be released before noon—"

Rick had on his sincere expression, but Charlotte couldn't bear to hear any more of his lies. The rat bastard obviously had an endless supply of them, available for any and every occasion. She brought her clenched fists up in a swift, punishing arc and, because Rick wasn't expecting her to do anything except listen meekly, she managed to deliver a hefty uppercut to his jaw.

She saw his eyes glaze—probably in astonishment that she hadn't tamely swallowed his latest false-hoods—and he slumped forward onto the bed, landing in a sagging heap.

Shaking with a potent mixture of triumph and anger, not to mention a pinch of dismay at having actually slugged a fellow human being hard enough to knock him out, she leaned over Rick's limp body to remove his gun before he could regain consciousness and use it against her.

She realized her mistake only when it was too late. Rick obviously had a cast-iron jaw, or at least a cast-iron brain, and he'd already come to. He arched under her, tipping her off his back and using her own weight to topple her over so that she ended up lying underneath him. He leaned over her, his eyes glittering, holding her hands above her head, his body sprawled across hers.

"Okay, Charlotte, enough with the fun and games. I'm through. Are you ready to listen to me now?"

"Get off me." Her breath came in short, hard pants. The realization that he was aroused, that she could feel his erection pressing against her belly, made her want to scream. Or something. "Get off me right now."

He moved as fast as she could have wished, but when she sat up, she saw that he was standing only a couple of feet away, and he was aiming his gun straight at her. "Just so that you don't decide to take another swing at me," he said. "I think it's a good idea to maintain a little distance between the two of us, no?"

If he was going to get sexually aroused if he came

near her, she hoped he'd stay a thousand miles away. Maybe a million. Perhaps his precious elf could arrange for him to be put in the cargo hold of a rocket to Mars. She'd press the launch button herself.

"Why did you shoot John Hanseck?" she asked, then dropped her head into her hands, the anger seeping out of her as fast as it had come, to be replaced by a feeling of bitter, cynical despair. "No, don't even bother to answer that. You'll only feed me another of your stupid, slimeball lies."

"I can see that your trust in me is profound. Has it not occurred to you that I might have told you the truth, and the FBI might have chosen to lie to the public? I assure you, I did not shoot John Hanseck, any more than you did. In fact, I very much doubt if he's injured. This is a ruse. A ploy to make sure both citizens and local law enforcement are on the lookout for you without forcing the Bureau to reveal any accurate details about your disappearance."

She laughed without mirth. "That's a good one, Rick. Okay, let me see. We know somebody's lying here. On one side, we have the FBI. On the other side, we have you. All I know about you is that you kidnapped me from a nightclub, and that you've kept me prisoner ever since. Gee, what a dilemma! I wonder who I should trust. Who should I believe? Gosh, it's so hard to make up my tiny little feminine mind."

"You should believe me," he said quietly. "I didn't shoot Agent Hanseck. I swear it."

"Oh for God's sake." Her frustration level skyrocketed again and she sprang off the bed, completely ignoring the gun Rick still had pointed straight at her. She knocked his hand sideways, and he allowed his arm to drop to his side, although she didn't kid herself that she'd forced him into making the concession. For whatever reason, he'd chosen to lower his weapon.

"Charlotte…" His voice was strained, barely audible. "Charlotte, don't come near me. Move away."

"Why should I?" She tipped her head back and stared into his dark brown eyes, searching for some reaction from him although she wasn't sure what. His eyes bothered her. There was something about them that wasn't *right*. "If I don't move away, are you going to shoot me?"

His voice became very dry. "Believe me, I'm seriously tempted.…"

"Then go ahead. What's stopping you? You like shooting people, don't you? Why make an exception for me?" She didn't understand why she felt such an overpowering need to taunt him. He had a weapon and she had no reason to suppose he wouldn't use it, even though he still held the gun loosely at his side, making no attempt to aim it. After all, she was angry with him precisely because she believed he'd shot John Hanseck in cold blood. That *was* what she believed, wasn't it?

She wasn't sure how her anger at Rick's lies had morphed into this overwhelming desire to break his self-control, and her own feelings were too tumultuous to be understood. But she was absolutely sure of at least one thing: that she wasn't in the mood for self-analysis right now. She wanted action, and she wanted it now, although she refused to define to herself what, precisely, she meant by action.

She moved toward him, deliberately provocative.

"Why mustn't I come near you, Rick? What are you afraid of if I touch you?"

His gaze rested on her mouth for a moment, then slid sideways and became fixed on the wall. "Stay away from me, Charlotte. I'm...begging you."

"I don't see you begging, Rick. I think I'd like to see you beg."

"You would? Then how's this?" His hand shot out, faster than sight. He let the gun drop onto the floor and he wrapped his arms around her, pulling her to him. "You win, Charlie. I'm begging. I can't keep this up anymore."

His mouth came down on hers, voracious with demand. She opened her mouth to flay him with self-righteous protests, and his tongue shot inside, probing, thrusting, forcing a response. She fought him for no more than a few seconds before her desire burst into flame, consuming her ability to resist. She returned his kiss with a wildfire, out-of-control passion that would have shocked her if she'd been capable of coherent thought.

His hands moved aggressively over her hips, holding her rammed against his lower body, making sure that she felt the full impact of his erection. A few minutes ago, she'd been offended by evidence that he was aroused. Now she unzipped her shorts and tossed them aside, frantic for the sensation of his flesh naked against hers. He trailed kisses down her neck as she rocked against him, but she grabbed his hair and pulled him back up to her mouth, ravenous for the taste of him. Her need was so intense that her breath came in short, sharp gasps, as if her body couldn't waste the energy to fulfill any basic function beyond the primal necessity to mate.

She tugged at his T-shirt, placing her palms flat against his back. She heard herself give a soft moan of pleasure when he tugged off her T-shirt and his hands closed, hot and yet oddly tender, over her breasts.

She had never experienced desire like this, desire that was overwhelming in its power, frantic in its pace, and brutal in its urgency. There was no time for foreplay. She wanted to be naked on the bed, with him inside her, taking her back to a place that had been lost to her since Dan walked out of her life.

He unbuckled the holster from around his waist and ripped off his T-shirt. She felt his muscles ripple beneath her fingertips as he lifted her up and carried her to the bed. She was burning up with heat and longing, feverish with the need to be possessed. He laid her down against the pillows, then tumbled on top of her, reaching down to part her legs.

Her body was hit with the first tremors of orgasm as soon as he touched her. She arched off the bed and he slid into her, murmuring her name.

"Charlie...I love you so much."

It was the first time either of them had spoken since he took her in his arms, and her whole body resonated to the familiar vibrations of his voice. Her throat ached with unshed tears, closing up so that she couldn't speak, but she kissed him again and he thrust hard and deep, reaching that magical place tucked far away inside her that had been frozen since the night of Dan's disappearance. Within seconds, she felt him come, and her body responded instantly, soaring high and fast before shattering into a second orgasm that left her exhausted, limp, trembling—and yearning for more.

Fifteen

Even when she'd climbed down from her incredible high, Charlotte lay beneath him for a minute or two, struggling to orient herself in a world turned upside down. She thought back over everything he'd told her and realized she had a surprisingly clear picture of what was going to happen over the next few hours. All she had to do was make a very minor adjustment: rename the man lying beside her as Daniel O'Toole, ex-husband and terrorist, instead of Richard Villier, government agent, and she could see exactly how events would unravel.

She supposed he was going to kill her, or he would never have had sex with her. He must have known she would guess his true identity if they ended up in bed. With the crystal clear vision bestowed by her new awareness of his identity, she realized he would never have revealed the fact that he was scheduled to take delivery of a radioactive bomb if he'd thought she would live to tell the tale.

Bad enough that she herself should die, but it was a thousand times worse to contemplate his plans for the destruction of the Kennedy Space Center. Charlotte shrank from visualizing the disaster that loomed ahead unless she could kill him first. But how could she possibly kill him, when he was a professional assassin, with reflexes supercharged by years of intensive training? Then she remembered that his gun was on the floor.

Quick as thought, she pushed him aside, leaped out of bed, grabbed the gun, and pointed it at him as he slowly sat up, untangling himself from the covers. How could she have failed to recognize him? Now that she knew the truth, his every movement looked achingly familiar, despite the drastic changes in his appearance.

Fury at how she'd been deceived overcame her fear. "You son of a bitch! You lying, deceptive bastard! How could you do this to me? Were you having fun with your crazy masquerade?" She meant to sound cool, controlled and disdainful, but her words tumbled out feverish and incoherent, loaded with anguish and self-reproach.

He didn't look guilty. Why would he? Obviously the man had no shred of conscience. He was even smiling, as if he had every right to feel happy about what had just happened between them.

"How could I do it?" He repeated her question. "With very few regrets and a hell of a lot of pleasure. For both of us, in case you think I didn't notice."

"Don't say that! If I'd known who you were, I'd never have had sex with you. I hadn't the remotest clue who you were...."

"Yes, you did, Charlie. Admit it. At some level, you've known for several hours, I think."

"No!" Her finger itched on the trigger of the gun. Anything to make him shut up. Anything to avoid admitting the truth of what he'd just said. "I want you gone. I want you dead. God, how I loathe you! I'm going to shoot you!''

Her hand shook as she tried to work up the gumption to squeeze the damn trigger. He got up from the bed, infuriatingly unconcerned about her threats, and took the gun from her with casual efficiency. "If you're going to threaten murder, Charlie, you need to make sure the safety catch is off on your weapon."

"Don't call me Charlie! Jesus, don't call me that!"

"Why not?" he asked softly. "I always did. You told me once that the way I said your name made you feel sexy."

His words pierced the protective bubble of her anger, leaving her stripped bare, her darkest emotions exposed. She hated him for destroying the illusion that her feelings for him were dead, and she injected that hate into her voice. "Your eyes used to be blue, and you're not wearing contacts but now they're brown. Your nose is different. The whole shape of your face has changed. And you're taller. How is that possible? People can't add inches to their height just because they need to evade the law."

"I'm not taller. I'm thinner, and that creates the illusion of height." He sounded as if the subject of his radically altered appearance bored him. "Plastic surgery changed the shape of my face, specifically my nose and the line of my jaw. I have colored lenses surgically implanted in my eyes. I used to wear my hair long. Now it's short. You'd be surprised how much difference that makes."

"Who are you trying to deceive with all these changes? Presumably not me."

"Not you," he agreed. "I wasn't sure I'd ever see

you again, although I never gave up hope. But there were a lot of other people to throw off the trail. Law enforcement of all kinds. The FBI. Interpol. The CIA. The British military. The Protestant paramilitary groups, especially the Red Hand Faction, which has Daniel O'Toole at the top of their kill-list. A few really nasty crooks in Eastern Europe who didn't like the fact that I'd double-crossed them with my counterfeiting operation.''

''Whatever happened to honor among thieves?'' she asked bitterly, her stomach churning at the litany of people he'd deceived and/or betrayed.

''It's an overrated notion,'' he said neutrally. ''Personally, I try hard to make sure that the bad guys don't make a profit from my activities and it tends to piss them off when they realize they've been screwed.''

It was agony to listen to him. Agony to wonder how much blood there was on the hands that had just seduced her with such speed and tender passion. Not looking at him, she picked up her clothes from the floor and started to put them on.

''I'm leaving,'' she said, fumbling with the metal button at the waist of her shorts. Her fingers were shaking so badly that she couldn't get it closed. ''I have no idea what this masquerade is all about, and no idea why you kidnapped me yesterday, but you'll have to kill me to stop me leaving. Since you're planning to kill me, anyway, I guess it doesn't make much difference if you do it now rather than later.''

''For God's sake, Charlotte, I love you more than anything or anybody in the entire world. How could you possibly believe I'm planning to kill you? I'm trying to protect you, for Christ's sake. Haven't you realized that yet?''

''Don't.'' She closed her eyes, shutting out the unsettling image of Dan's familiar voice speaking out of Rick Villier's mouth. She turned away to tuck her shirt into her shorts. ''It doesn't make me feel good to know that you love me, Dan. If you want the truth, it makes me sick to my stomach. You're a terrorist, which means you're filled to the brim with irrational hatreds. What can it possibly mean when you claim to love me? Nothing flattering to me, that's for sure.''

''You should have more faith in your own judgment, Charlie. Do you really believe you're capable of loving a man…a terrorist…who murders innocent people in pursuit of some dubious political goal?''

''It seems that I am,'' she said bleakly, and she could hear that her voice was as ravaged as her feelings. ''If you want me to say the words, then I will. I loved you once, a long time ago. But don't count on that old love to make me stupid, Dan. Believe me, now that I know who and what you really are, I despise you and everything you stand for.''

Dan's face was suddenly clouded with regret. ''When I walked away from our marriage, I wanted you to despise me,'' he said. ''I wanted you to despise the fact that you'd married me because I knew that was the only way you'd ever be able to move on with your life after I'd betrayed you so badly.''

''Then you succeeded beyond your wildest dreams.'' Charlotte was washed by a tidal wave of regret and she scrambled to restoke her anger. Stoking her rage was a much better option than giving way to the grief that threatened to overwhelm her. ''I've wasted a lot of time over the past eighteen months regretting the day we met.''

Dan's expression didn't alter, but a muscle ticked just once in his jaw. ''I had to leave you, Charlie, I had no choice. The Armargh Army discovered where I was living, and they threatened to kill you unless I straightened out the mess they'd made of the counterfeiting operation I'd set up in Eastern Europe. It was a devil's bargain: I could rejoin them, and you would be safe. Or I could refuse, and you would have died. Because I never doubted for a second that the Armargh Army would carry out their threats. Their vengeance would have been swift and brutal.''

''If you're expecting me to thank you for being noble, don't hold your breath. It's not comforting to know that my life was basically nothing more than a bargaining chip for terrorists. You should never have married me, Dan, although I guess it's crazy to complain about such a minor sin in comparison to all the others you've committed. But you had no right to drag me into the middle of your messed up life.''

''I know that now, but only in retrospect. We'd all be really smart if we lived our lives with the advantage of hindsight, Charlie. But as it is, I have to stumble through blindfolded, just like everyone else.'' He wrapped a sheet around her shoulders, and she realized she was shivering. She moved away, not because his touch repelled her, but because it felt too good. Dammit, after everything that had happened, after all that she knew, how could his touch still have the power to set her on fire?

Dan spoke to her back. ''When we met in Des

Moines at your cousin's party, I thought my past was entirely behind me—''

''You'd retired from terrorism?'' she asked with heavy sarcasm. ''Gee, and I thought that was one of those careers people pursued to the death.''

''In a way, that's what I'd done. I'd faked Daniel O'Toole's death in Albania—those years of civil war in the Balkans were really convenient for people who wanted to disappear—and I managed to make it home to the United States without anyone in the Armargh Army being the wiser. I'd handed in my resignation to the Bureau—''

''What did the Bureau have to do with any of this?''

''I'd been working for them all along, Charlie.''

She dampened the inevitable flare of hope. After everything that had happened, it seemed she was still trying to find a way to believe that Daniel O'Toole was a good person. ''You're claiming you were a secret agent? That you work for the government?''

''Secret agent makes my profession sound more glamorous than it is. Operational asset is how the Bureau referred to me.'' She didn't respond and a harsh note crept into his voice when he spoke again. ''Tell me, Charlie, why is it any more difficult to believe that I'm an FBI undercover operative than it is to believe I'm a fanatic blowing up buildings and killing people in the name of a united Ireland?''

She couldn't meet his eyes, but she told him the truth. ''Because I'm afraid to let myself be sucked in by your lies again....''

''I didn't lie to you about anything important, Charlie—''

She laughed. "No, nothing at all. Just your name, your education, your life history, your entire family background." She broke off in an effort to regain some mastery of her runaway emotions, but the accusations bubbled up again, refusing to be controlled.

"Have you any idea how stupid I felt when I realized that I couldn't even tell the police who your mother was, or where she lived? That I'd bought into your whole ridiculous fabrication about a woman living on a sheep farm in New Zealand? That I couldn't name one friend of yours that I'd ever met? Or give them a single clue about where they might start looking for you...?"

"Those are just details. I never lied about anything important—"

She stared at him, incredulous. "I guess we have different ideas about what's important—"

"Lies are only a betrayal if they're intended to deceive. I lied to keep you safe, Charlie."

"Thanks," she said bitterly. "But I'd have traded safety for the sake of knowing a couple of real facts about the man I married."

"Then here are some real facts about me. I was sent by the Counter Terrorism Center to infiltrate the Armargh Army and neutralize its power to harm the United States. In order to do that, I took on the persona of Daniel O'Toole. After two years undercover, I was so burned out that I killed off O'Toole in Albania, and the government agreed to help me start a new life as a civilian, although they weren't happy about my decision to resign from the Bureau. Still, I convinced them that I was totally finished with black ops and infiltrating organizations where killing was the chief recreational activity for the membership. I wanted off the reservation and I was leaving with or without their permission. In the end, they figured I was sufficiently burned out that it was less dangerous to set me free than to keep me in the pen. They let me choose a new name, and then they gave me documentation that authenticated Riordan Gray's existence all the way back to his birth, complete with fake college records, and a Social Security number that would withstand any and all scrutiny. When I became Riordan Gray, I was supposed to be completely insulated from discovery—''

"That worked well," she said with biting sarcasm.

"Obviously it didn't work at all well. But I would never have married you if I'd realized there was any chance the Armargh Army could find me again."

"So how did they find you, according to you? Out of all the 270 million people in the States, how did the Armargh Army ever find out that Riordan Gray was really Daniel O'Toole?"

"Easily." Dan's expression hardened into a mask of such icy cold cynicism that Charlotte shivered. "My boss, my good ole buddy Tremayne Washington, betrayed me. All in the name of national security, of course. Not to mention service to a higher cause."

"What higher cause?"

Dan's expression became a shade more cynical. "Tremayne Washington's promotion to the position of deputy director."

There couldn't be all that many FBI agents with a name like Tremayne Washington, but Charlotte checked just to be sure. "You're talking about the man who came to my house after you disappeared?"

"That's the guy. A couple of weeks after 9/11, he contacted me, asking me to return to active duty at the Counter Terrorism Center. I told him I couldn't. That I was sorry for the national tragedy, but I was married, happier than I'd ever been in my life, and totally out of shape, mentally and physically. I not only didn't want to return to my old life, I wasn't in any condition to do it. Tremayne seemed to accept my decision without too much fuss, which ought to have warned me to watch out for the knife aimed at my back."

"You weren't all that out of shape," Charlotte said, feeling an odd need to defend the man she'd been married to. "You jogged two or three times a week and you watched your diet."

"Yeah, I jogged. Sort of. And I watched my diet. Kind of." Dan gave a smile that contained a hint of sadness mixed in with nostalgia. "You've no idea how much I enjoyed being just a little bit out of shape, Charlie. Those extra ten pounds I carried around were my way of reassuring myself that I didn't need to be honed to perfect fitness anymore. That my life wasn't going to be on the line if it took me a couple of seconds to react to an unidentified sound, or the arrival of a stranger in the room."

Charlotte experienced an absurd longing to wrap her arms around him and comfort him. She steeled herself to stay right where she was, a safe couple of feet away from him and his insidious appeal.

She glared at him, because that seemed smarter than giving in to her urge to melt into his arms. "It's going to take a lot more than slick story-telling to convince me that you work for the FBI. I stopped being a naive idiot eighteen months ago. It was one of the few valuable lessons to come out of our marriage.''

"I'm not giving you slick explanations. I'm telling you the truth."

"Yeah, right. Which truth would that be, Dan? My sort, or your sort?"

"Your sort," he said tightly. "I served six years in the Marine Corps after I finished college. My mother died a few weeks later of a brain aneurysm, and I was recruited straight into the black ops division of the Counter Terrorism Center. I stayed with the Bureau for seven years, working various undercover assignments, the last being with the Armargh Army. At which point I was totally burned out. I was done with death and betrayal and double-crosses that worked the ends against the middle and then twisted the middle one more time, just to make absolutely sure nobody could emerge from the mess with clean hands.''

"So you'd resigned from the Bureau before we were married?"

"More than six months before we even met. Like I told you, I was taken into a special branch of the Witness Protection Program, designed for ex-government agents, and I moved to Des Moines. I wanted to settle down in the American heartland and never think about espionage, and military coups, and national security ever again. By the time we met, I was having a ball running my coffee shops, not reading the newspapers, and making sure I knew as little as possible about the politics of Northern Ireland. When I asked you to marry me, my only ambitions were to be a loving husband to you and a doting father to our kids. Period.''

He sounded almost as defeated and weary as she felt but Charlotte was afraid to soften. She'd watched him in action as Richard Villier so she knew exactly how skilled he was at spinning a web of lies that skirted the truth, but seemed entirely credible.

''You're forgetting that I know the details of Daniel O'Toole's past,'' she said. ''There's no way to convince me you were working for the FBI when you attacked the Craigavon Hotel. You and the other members of the Armargh Army were trying to kill the political leaders who had the most hope of bringing peace to Northern Ireland. The U.S. Government would never have agreed to let one of its agents participate in that sort of vicious, mindless slaughter.''

''When the Armargh Army attacked the Craigavon Hotel, I hadn't become Daniel O'Toole.''

''For heaven's sake, stop acting as if I'm mentally defective!'' Charlotte paced the small sitting area, her skin feeling too tight to contain her simmering emotions. ''Of course you were part of that attack. Tremayne Washington told me exactly what happened there and he specifically said Daniel O'Toole was wounded, captured, and taken into custody by the Brits.''

''Tremayne Washington gave you the official FBI version of events—''

''But he made a mistake over the little matter of whether the British military picked you up half dead from the battlefield? That's believable.''

''Tremayne Washington told you the truth about Daniel O'Toole's participation in the Craigavon attack up to a point. But he couldn't tell you the most important fact, because that would have blown my cover. O'Toole didn't miraculously survive the gun battle at Craigavon. He died.''

"What do you mean, he died? You're here. You're not dead.…''

"No, but that's because I'm not really Daniel O'Toole—''

She let out a yell of sheer frustration. "Stop it, Dan! For God's sake, stop it!''

"Listen to me.'' He visibly gritted his teeth. "Daniel O'Toole died five years ago at Craigavon, and that's when I was sent in to take his place. Tremayne Washington saw O'Toole's death as a unique opportunity to infiltrate an undercover operative into the Armargh Army. Not just at the foot soldier level, but in a leadership capacity. The FBI had been trying to insert an agent into the Armargh Army for over a year, but it's not easy to infiltrate operatives into a tightly knit terrorist organization where all the members of any individual cell have known each other since they were kids in kindergarten.''

Against her will, Charlotte found her attention riveted by what Dan was saying. He might be spinning her a yarn, but it was a compelling one. "How could you possibly have taken O'Toole's place? There must have been dozens of people who'd witnessed his death.''

Dan shook his head. "In fact nobody knew for sure what had happened to him in the heat of the battle with the Red Hand Faction. Remember, the Armargh Army had expected to attack harmless politicians. Instead, they found themselves fighting the fiercest and most ruthless Protestant paramilitary organization in the country. After the initial hail of gunfire, there was total chaos. When the bullets stopped flying, there were bodies sprawled everywhere with varying degrees of gunshot wounds, and the five men who knew O'Toole best had all died in the fight. The British soldiers rushed O'Toole's body away to a military medical facility where he died without ever regaining consciousness.''

''So how do you come into the picture? The Armargh Army was fighting the Red Hand Faction, and the Brits were cleaning up the mess. The Americans don't seem to have had anything to do with what was going on.''

''They had more of an interest than you might expect. Tremayne Washington was in Ireland right when O'Toole died. As it happened, he was conferring with his counterpart in British intelligence about the chances of infiltrating an operative into the Armargh Army. The Brits agreed with Tremayne's assessment that O'Toole's death, and the loss of his five senior lieutenants, provided a unique opportunity to insert an operative into their ranks.''

''But why would the FBI be the law enforcement agency to send in a ringer for O'Toole? Why didn't the British want to be in charge of the infiltration? They must have had many more suitable candidates than the Bureau, and they have much more of an interest in what's going on in Northern Ireland.''

''The Brits didn't think there was any chance the infiltrated agent would survive, so they took a pass on the suggested operation. I guess Tremayne Washington was more optimistic than his counterpart in

MI5." Dan's mouth twisted into a self-mocking smile. "Besides, I volunteered. I had more balls than brains in those days, and I seemed the obvious candidate to send in. I had all the necessary training, and I'd already completed a couple of missions, so the FBI brass knew I could survive the mental pressure. More important, I'm the exact same height as the real O'Toole. Plus I have a similar basic body build, and my hair is about the same texture as his. And the final fact that cinched the deal—the computer said my ears were a surprisingly close match to O'Toole's."

Charlotte's head jerked up. "Your ears matched O'Toole's? Who cares if your ears matched?"

"Hair texture and the shape of your ears are the most difficult characteristics to change," Dan said. "So on two important issues, I was good to go. Then in addition to all that, my mother was born and raised in Belfast. After my father died in Vietnam, she tried to settle down in the States, but she had a really hard time of it. Eventually she returned to Belfast to live with her parents. I was ten when she moved back, and I stayed there with her until I was eighteen, which meant I had a lot of the cultural and lifestyle details about life in Belfast already at my fingertips."

"Even so, I'm having a hard time believing that you could be substituted for the real Daniel O'Toole and nobody found you out."

He shot her a look that was mostly apologetic, but tinged with just enough arrogance to annoy her. "Yeah, well, I'm very good at what I do."

"Good at killing people, you mean," she said tartly, although she knew quite well that he hadn't meant any such thing.

"Good at impersonating people," he said quietly. "You were married to me, Charlie, and even so you didn't realize who Rick Villier was for quite a few hours. If I could deceive you, of all people, why do you doubt that I could deceive members of the Armargh Army? Besides, there was less risk of discovery than you might expect. Remember, O'Toole was already known to have had plastic surgery at least once to change his appearance. It was agreed that if the FBI sent in an agent who was about the right height and body build, we could explain away any differences in appearance by saying that O'Toole had undergone a second round of plastic surgery while he was in the hospital, supposedly recovering from the injuries he'd received at Craigavon. I've always had a knack for imitating voices and accents, so there seemed to be a good chance that I could pull off the impersonation."

He made it sound as if it had been nothing more than a parlor trick to duplicate O'Toole's speech patterns. She would have said that changing your voice sufficiently to deceive old friends was impossible, if not for the fact that Dan had, as he'd just reminded her, tricked her for several hours into believing that he was actually Richard Villier.

She looked up at him, torn between disbelief, confusion and an incongruous desire to laugh. "Have you any idea how crazy it sounds to say that you were picked for this assignment because a computer program liked the shape of your ears?"

"Hey, don't forget that I'd been to school in Belfast so I had lots of good background." Dan's eyes gleamed with silent amusement and she had to fight not to smile back at him. He shrugged. "Like I said, I was young and aggressive back then, with no ties or responsibilities to hold me in check. I'd been training intensively to penetrate the Armargh Army, and there was never going to be a better moment. Bottom line. We took a risk, and it paid off."

When he smiled, it was all too easy to forget about bombs and terrorists, and remember instead Sunday mornings on the back porch, doing the crossword puzzle with her feet tucked into his lap, and his eyes making love to her every time their glances met. Charlotte swallowed over the sudden lump in her throat, forcing herself back into the present.

"I don't understand why the FBI would risk an American citizen's life to get information about an organization whose mission was to throw the Brits out of Northern Ireland. To be brutally frank, if the Brits thought it was too risky to send in an operative, why would the FBI do their dirty work for them?"

"The FBI wouldn't have stepped in under normal circumstances. But the Armargh Army was a special case. It had been identified as the organization that attempted to blow up the American Embassy in London back in 1995 and damn near succeeded—"

"I never heard about any attacks on the embassy in London," Charlotte protested.

"Well, no, you wouldn't have. We managed to prevent that particular attack before it happened. It's our failures that capture the headlines, Charlie. Our successes get buried in files marked Top Secret."

"Okay, but if the attack on the embassy in London didn't happen, why did the FBI still care about the

Armargh Army? And why wasn't the CIA running this operation? Why was the FBI even involved?''

"The Counter Terrorism Center is a joint operation of the CIA and the FBI. The FBI took the lead on this particular case because we had reliable intelligence that suggested the Armargh Army was changing its tactics and bringing their grievances to the American homeland. A few weeks before the attack on Craigavon, the leadership of the Armargh Army had passed into the hands of a man known as the General. There was a definite power struggle between O'Toole and the General, which was settled more by the mass slaughter at Craigavon than anything else. The real Daniel O'Toole was very strongly focused on Ireland, and he looked inward to solve Ireland's problems. The General, on the other hand, is more cosmopolitan and he has a very different set of interests. Instead of blowing up people in Belfast, or even London, he wanted to blow up people in American cities. He figured that was the way to get the most bang for his buck.''

"Obviously we're here because the General won the argument."

Dan lifted his shoulders in a dismissive gesture. "He won because he was right, of course, and after the disaster at Craigavon, his point of view prevailed among the rank and file of the Armargh Army. Meanwhile, as soon as I'd been accepted by everyone as Daniel O'Toole, I volunteered to take myself off to Eastern Europe for a couple of months. I promised to set up a counterfeiting operation that would provide the funds the Army needed to mount a serious, large-scale operation in the United States. For a while there, while I was churning out thousands of fake fifty-dollar bills, I was everyone's golden boy. Even the General overlooked our past disagreements in light of the profits I was making.''

"Let me get this straight." Charlotte sent him a smile that was razor sharp. "You did such a brilliant job of setting up your counterfeiting operation that the Armargh Army has enough money to buy a dirty bomb and launch an attack on the Kennedy Space Center. Wow! That's what I call a really successful undercover operation. Wait until my fellow citizens hear about this one. Thanks to you, the lucky American taxpayer is going to get a sabotaged space program and a hundred years of radioactive contamination along the east coast of Florida—and all we had to pay was a few million counterfeit dollars. Now there's a deal that can't be beat.''

Dan actually laughed. "Trust you to put everything in a different perspective, Charlie. But the operation isn't over yet. In case you haven't noticed, I'm working my ass off to *prevent* the Armargh Army from blowing up the Space Center, or any other target.''

"Would you say you've cut your margins for success pretty damn fine? Or is that just the impression I get because I'm a naive, ignorant civilian?''

Dan's laughter faded. "The margins for success have been cut pretty damn fine," he agreed. "But that's unavoidable, given what I'm trying to achieve." He glanced at his watch. "It's eight o'clock. In two hours from now I have to meet with the General so that he can examine the information on the disk the Elf has given me. If the General's satisfied that we have sufficient data to guarantee a successful penetration of Space Center security, he's going to set the time and place for our next meeting. At that meeting, he's going to deliver the radioactive bomb we've all been waiting for. And, as I've already told you, I'm going to take possession of that bomb and deliver it straight to the nearest FBI office. Hopefully twenty-four hours from now, the General will be cooling his heels in a prison cell, with his lawyers fighting unsuccessfully to get him out on bail.''

He sounded entirely sincere about what he planned to do. Charlotte was tired of the roller coaster of belief and disbelief, exhausted by the constant seesawing of her emotions. It was clear to her now, as it never had been in the past, that in the subterranean world of terrorism and counter-terrorism, the players moved in a tightly choreographed dance that outsiders penetrated at high risk. In a world made up of illusion, held together by betrayal and double-cross, how could she possibly expect to identify the good guys? In such an environment, was there even such a thing as a good guy?

Dan reached out his hand and tucked a loose strand of her hair behind her ear. ''Don't sweat it, honey. Sometimes you just have to trust your gut, and to hell with the logic.''

''Suppose my gut is telling me you're not to be trusted?''

''I'm pretty sure it isn't. At gut level, you've been convinced for a while that I'm telling you the truth. You're just afraid to trust your instincts.''

Dan moved close—really close—to her for the first time since he'd wrapped the sheet around her shoulders. He folded her into his arms, and she resisted for no more than a second or two before letting her head fall onto his chest. She breathed in the familiar smell of Dan's skin, overwhelmed by a sense of homecoming. It might be dangerous to give way to her feelings, but she felt more at peace in Dan's arms than she'd felt at any time for the past eighteen months.

He crooked his index finger under her chin and tipped her face up so that she was looking straight into his eyes. Alien brown eyes, that nevertheless gleamed with a mixture of love and desire that struck a reminiscent chord deep within her, igniting old passions and inflaming new ones.

"It feels damn good to have you back in my arms, Charlie." She didn't move away as his head slowly bent toward her, and her lips parted without protest as he covered her mouth in a kiss that tasted of sweetness and tender devotion, warmed by a hint of passion.

The last time he'd kissed her she had at least been able to pretend that she didn't know the truth about the man she was making love to with such urgency and voracious hunger. This time, she had no convenient mental barrier to hide behind. The truth was exposed, laid bare for her to deal with. If she had sex with Dan again, it would be in full, conscious knowledge of what she was doing.

Dan brushed his thumbs gently across her mouth and kissed her slowly. "Don't think, Charlie. Thinking only gets in the way of things. I love you. You love me. Right now, that's all that matters."

"Yes." She let the word escape on a soft sigh, although she knew that love wasn't always enough, and that it could never be an excuse for condoning evil. But she could no longer keep up the pretense that she seriously believed Dan was evil. She didn't. Far from sensing a core of darkness in him, she sensed a rock-solid core of integrity.

The truth was that she loved him to distraction, and it was useless to pretend otherwise. She ran her hands over his chest, marveling at how familiar his body felt, despite the new muscles and the hardened frame.

"You're more beautiful than ever," he said, tugging her T-shirt over her head and cupping his hands around her breasts. "God, Charlie, I've missed you so much. Not just the lovemaking, but all the little, unimportant things that we did together."

"I missed you, too." The admission hung in the air between them, and he pulled her tightly against his body, as if trying to offer comfort and protection in compensation for the long, empty months when they'd been apart. They clung to each other as they walked back into the bedroom, and sank onto the tangled sheets of the bed.

Last time, it had been all hot passion and stark sexual need. This time the hunger was still there, but softened to the point that Charlotte was able to luxuriate in the pleasure of lovemaking that climbed gradually through all the stages of arousal to ultimate release. Afterwards, she lay in Dan's arms, drowsy and not really thinking of anything at all.

Suddenly, a little gurgle of laughter erupted from somewhere deep inside.

"What is it?" Dan rolled over, propping himself on his elbow so that he could look at her.

"I don't know your real name," she said. Her laughter tailed away, and her voice thickened with tears. "We were married but I don't even know your real name."

There was a noticeable silence. "Elliott Danforth Hargreaves the Fourth," Dan said finally.

She gaped at him, tears vanishing. "Elliott Danforth Hargreaves the *Fourth?*"

"Yeah, well, my dad came from a very proper New England family that was big on tradition and names with Roman numerals at the end of them. And if you laugh, Charlie, I'm going to consider that grounds for divorce."

"We're already divorced, so that's not much of a threat." Charlotte couldn't help it. She laughed.

Sixteen

Shirley Nicholson came into the windowless, inner office where John Hanseck had been keeping out of public view since his release from hospital shortly after eleven that morning. Designed to accommodate agents working around the clock on urgent or secret investigations, the office had an attached bathroom with a shower, and a sofa that doubled as a makeshift bed. There were also two TVs, which John currently had tuned to two separate cable news channels, with no sound playing on either.

He gave a click of his mouse when he noticed his partner's arrival, and his computer screen dissolved into a picture of snowflakes falling on a mountainside, a wistful contrast to the muggy heat outside. He gave her a tired smile. "Hey, Shirl. You're a welcome interruption. I was just running another check on all previous targets of the Armargh Army and the Earth Liberation Front to see if there was any tourist attraction in Florida that stood out as being especially appealing to both groups."

"Didn't we do that already?" she asked wryly. "Twice, in fact."

"Yeah, maybe even three times." John sighed and leaned back in his chair, hands linked behind his head, the tension of his body belying the relaxed pose. ''But why are you still here? It's almost ten o'clock. You should go home and get some rest. At least one of us might as well be comfortable, and I'm too wired to sleep.''

''I can't sleep either,'' Shirley confessed. ''It's getting too close to July Fourth.'' She flashed a smile. ''Besides, we just got a hot lead and I'm feeling re-energized. We had a phone call from the duty sergeant in Daytona Beach in regard to Charlotte Leone. That's what I came in to tell you.''

John leaned forward so fast his chair skidded sideways. ''We've gotten a solid lead about Charlotte's location?''

''Better than that. Way better. The cops in Daytona have her in custody.''

''All right!'' John gave the thumbs-up sign with both hands and returned her smile. ''Hey, I feel more cheerful already.''

''I thought you would. They're holding her as a material witness, and they're arranging to transport her back to Tampa as we speak. Another couple of hours and we should be getting some answers as to what happened last night at the club.''

John grimaced. ''We're placing a hell of a lot of hope in the possibility that Charlotte's disappearance is connected to the Armargh Army's plans.''

''With good reason. I don't know exactly how, but I'm willing to bet my next paycheck that Charlotte's disappearance is connected in some way to Daniel O'Toole.''

John gave a nod of agreement. ''You'll get no arguments from me. How did Charlotte end up in custody? Did she finally catch some of the media coverage, and turn herself in?''

In Shirley's professional opinion, there had been about as much chance of the Leone woman turning herself in as there was of the FBI director announcing that all agents should take a week's vacation in the Bahamas at government expense. If John was still clinging to the hope that Charlotte Leone wanted to help them out with their investigation of O'Toole and the Armargh Army, his judgment was more screwed up than she'd guessed.

''No, Charlotte didn't turn herself in,'' she said, paying her partner the courtesy of keeping her voice neutral. Now that she was forty, she'd given up expecting men to think with their heads instead of their dumbsticks, even normally smart ones like John Hanseck. ''She seems to have been hiding out in a motel in Daytona.''

John frowned. ''So how did the police find her?''

''We caught a lucky break.'' Shirley grinned. ''That's not just a figure of speech, either. There was a massive water leak in the pipe leading to the end block of units in the motel where she was staying, and she was forcibly evacuated just before nine o'clock tonight. There were a bunch of people hanging out in the corridor when she emerged by herself from her motel room, of course, and she was recognized by several different people.''

''So whaddya know? We finally got lucky,'' John said. ''God knows, it was about time. What happened when the cops went to pick up Charlotte? Did she resist? Try to make a run for it?''

''Not as far as I know.'' Shirley shook her head.

"It sounds as if the arrest was very low key. The assistant manager escorted her to a room that wasn't affected by the floods, and a couple of staff members sat with her until the cops arrived. The duty sergeant was too harassed to give a real good account of exactly what happened, but I gather there were three or four maintenance people working right outside her room, trying to fix the leak, not to mention the assistant manager and all the displaced guests milling around. If she'd tried to run, it would simply have provided the hotel manager and guests with an excuse to rough her up."

"Has Charlotte given any explanation as to why she took off from the Down Under club last night?" John asked. "She must have known I was unconscious. In fact, I have a distinct memory of her leaning over me right before I finally passed out. I can't understand how she could just have left me lying there in the pitch-black...."

He must have realized he was sounding hurt, and much too personally involved. He quickly snapped back into professional mode. "What story did she come up with for the cops to account for her disappearance?"

"Nothing very credible." Shirley yawned and walked around the desk to stretch out on the sofa, putting her feet up on the arm, and shoving a cushion behind her head. "Jeez, that feels good. I guess it's been a longer day than I realized. Anyway, Charlotte insists she didn't shoot you—"

John rocked back on his chair so that he could see his partner in her new resting place. "Well, we both know she's right about that! But somebody sure as hell injected me with enough methohexital to knock out a horse.''

''Yeah, well according to Charlotte, she wasn't the person who injected you.'' Shirley rolled her eyes. ''She admits she knew you were unconscious when the lights went out last night, but she also insists there wasn't a thing she could do about it.''

''Why not?''

Shirley's voice became very dry. ''She claims she was kidnapped from the Down Under club by a Frenchman—''

''What?'' John's chair crashed back onto all four legs. He swiveled around to face her, his questions coming out so fast Shirley could hardly disentangle them.

''Wait,'' she said. ''You haven't heard the best bit yet. According to Charlotte, the guy who kidnapped her was an undercover agent for the French *Sûreté,* currently working as a liaison with the FBI.''

Shirley was relieved to see that her partner retained some sense of perspective where the Leone woman was concerned. He stared at her bug-eyed with astonishment for a few moments, then laughed with real amusement. ''What the hell reason did she give for any law enforcement official doing something that crazy?''

''He apparently had orders to rescue her from imminent danger.'' Shirley sucked in her cheeks in an effort not to giggle. ''According to Charlotte, when he grabbed her from the dance floor, he was actually taking her into protective custody—''

John gave another crack of disbelieving laughter. ''Yeah, that's exactly the sort of operation us law enforcement types put into effect when we're planning to take someone into protective custody.''

Shirley finally allowed herself a giggle. "Hey, you're forgetting the guy who supposedly grabbed her was French. Maybe they work differently over in Gay Paree.''

John's only response was a snort. Then he rubbed his forehead. "Why would she make up an idiotic story like that? And why a Frenchman, for Christ's sake?''

"You're asking me?'' Shirley stretched and sat back up again. "Anyway, in a little while, you can ask her yourself. The cops in Daytona took her back to the station and arranged for transportation here as fast as they could push through the paperwork. They've worked amazingly fast. Probably because they want her out of their jurisdiction and into our hands before a hotshot lawyer turns up demanding to know what the grounds are for holding her. Which I don't have to tell you are flimsy, to say the least.''

"Did the cops at least point out to Charlotte that she was alone in the hotel room and free to leave at any time she wanted?'' John asked. "That makes it impossible to believe she was being held against her will.''

"Yeah, they pointed that out and her response was that she'd been kidnapped without any prior knowledge of what was planned, but that the agent from the *Sûreté* eventually left, after persuading her to stay hidden for her own good. At which point the cops expressed polite disbelief, asked her if she cared to change her story, and she clammed up. Said she wasn't going to talk anymore until she'd seen a law-yer.''

John winced. "Damn. That's not good news."

"No, it's not. We'd better hope we can persuade her to hold off on calling her attorney once she gets here, because he'll have her sprung so fast the exit door will hit us in the face as it swings shut behind her. Meanwhile, it's getting closer to July Fourth by the second and I sure as heck don't see any other leads rushing down the pike toward us.''

John's face looked pinched with worry. Shirley could see that this case was taking as much of a toll on her partner as it was on her, even though he'd only been assigned to it four months ago. Still, his rapid plunge into deep personal involvement wasn't sur-prising, given what was at stake. The nation's atten-tion might be focused on the Middle East and Islamic terrorists, but in Shirley's opinion, the Armargh Army posed a more immediate threat to public safety than anything the remnants of Al Qaeda could mount. Un-fortunately the big brass at Bureau headquarters weren't giving them either the personnel or the re-sources that they needed to neutralize the threat.

"I called Tremayne Washington last week and tried to squeeze some more information out of him," John said. "It was like squeezing a stone. He says his informant has been incommunicado for a month and he has nothing to give us."

"I wonder who the hell his source is?" Shirley asked the question as if she and John hadn't discussed the same subject a hundred times before.

John shook his head. "From something Washing-ton let slip to me during that last conversation we had,

I think it might be somebody with the Earth Liberation Movement, not with the Armargh Army at all. But that's just my guess.''

"Every damn thing about this case seems to be guesswork, held together with speculation, sewn up with coincidence." Shirley felt frustration welling up again, after a few minutes respite following the good news of Charlotte's apprehension. "We keep getting all these solid-seeming leads and then they just evaporate into nothing right in front of our eyes."

"Yeah, I'd noticed." John sent a rueful glance toward his partner. "I don't know about you, Shirl, but my ass is feeling mighty bare right about now. What happens if we don't manage to get a noose around O'Toole's neck before he puts his plan into action? Whatever the hell his plan might be.''

"We will." Shirley hoped her voice didn't shake when she made her prediction.

"You're more confident than I am." John played anxiously with a couple of intertwined paper clips, but looked thoroughly disgruntled. "Honest to Pete, O'Toole sometimes seems to have a guardian angel standing right at his shoulders.''

"More likely a guardian devil," Shirley said morosely.

John ran his hands through his hair, leaving it sticking up in spikes. "We should have worked harder on our interrogation of Padraig.''

"How?" Shirley demanded. "There are still rules against torture, and nothing else would have loosened his tongue. Those Armargh Army boys learn to resist police interrogation while they're still in diapers. I'm amazed Padraig even gave up the fact that O'Toole was in Florida.''

She prowled the perimeter of the room, tension once again consuming her. ''Besides, I'm not sure Padraig knew all that much about O'Toole's future plans. We can take it as a given that O'Toole and the General are the only two people fully aware of what the target will be.''

''The Elf must know,'' John pointed out. ''The only reason for O'Toole to use him is if he's providing vital insider information regarding the target.''

''Yeah, the Elf must know. But the poor schmuck probably doesn't realize he's going to be offed the moment he isn't needed anymore.''

''Obviously not,'' John said, his voice dry.

Shirley made a frustrated sound. John had managed to reactivate all her self-doubt and she could feel herself starting to rake over the still-glowing embers of past decisions. ''I suppose we could have arrested O'Toole and the other members of his cell on immigration charges last month, but then where would we have gone with the rest of the investigation?''

John shrugged. ''It's too late for second guesses now. I was as firm as anyone else that we needed to give him more time and space so that we could identify the Elf and the General. Not to mention the target.''

''I guess.'' Shirley sighed. ''The hard truth is that since we know zero about the real world identity of the Elf, and ditto for the General of the Armargh Army, putting O'Toole behind bars gives us virtually no guarantee that we've headed off disaster.''

They'd had variations of this same discussion a

dozen times already. John made an exasperated noise and flung his paper clips into the trash can. They missed. With a disgusted mutter, he bent down and picked them up.

"Did you know that when I sent out a warning of possible impending terrorist activity to likely targets in Central Florida, I estimated that there were at least twenty-three major tourist attractions in this area that would be internationally recognized? In other words, twenty-three prime choices for O'Toole and his boys."

"I know. I counted, too." Shirley forced herself to stop pacing. "If we were in St. Louis, we could guess O'Toole would have his sights set on the arch. In South Dakota, we figure he's going after Mount Rushmore. In San Francisco, the Golden Gate Bridge. But here—who can guess?"

John, not usually prone to swearing, let rip with a string of curses that singed Shirley's ears.

"You can't blame yourself for not arresting O'Toole last month," she said when he finally calmed down. "We had a lot of good reasons for deciding to give them a little more rope to hang themselves with."

"I just didn't expect to lose track of them completely within less than forty-eight hours. Dammit, we had surveillance on their Miami apartment from the moment Padraig gave us the address. How the hell did they manage to slip away? I was watching the place myself when they must have left." John brought himself up short, obviously not wanting to start on the treadmill of that discussion again. He made another attempt to toss the paper clips into the trash can, this time successfully.

"How's that for hitting the target?" he said, giving Shirley a smile that made even her middle-aged heart beat a little faster.

"You're a real hotshot. If you ever leave the Bureau, I'm sure there'll be a home for you in the NBA."

"It's good to know I have a range of other career options if this one doesn't pan out." Instead of sinking back into depression, John suddenly seemed to cheer up. His smile deepened. "Listen to us! We're a fine pair. We're forgetting we've just had a piece of really good news. Charlotte's on her way to Tampa. That's cause for celebration, right?"

"Right."

"And we still have another six whole days before it's July Fourth."

"Right."

"Okay, I'm tucking my exposed ass back in my pants, and from now on, I'll try to keep my neuroses decently covered. I've spent too long in this room, I guess, and much too long working exclusively on the O'Toole case. I'm not only chasing my own tail, I'm starting to eat it. Hell, let's be optimistic and believe that once Charlotte gets here, she's going to give up some information that will help to develop a few hot new leads."

"I'll drink to that." Shirley saluted him with a mug of pencils. "You know, I'm getting more suspicious of sweet little Charlotte by the minute. I mean, why else did she leave Iowa and come to Tampa if not because she knew O'Toole was planning to return here? She isn't just the injured and abandoned wife, you mark my words. She's a coconspirator, or at the very least a silent accomplice.''

It wasn't a new thought, and John for once didn't rush to protest her innocence. ''Let's hope you're right, and she gives up something really useful.''

''We just have to ask the right questions. Let's work on how we're going to handle the interrogation while we wait for her to arrive in Tampa. You know, I'm getting more and more certain that Charlotte could lead us straight to Daniel O'Toole if she only had a mind to do it.''

''Hold that thought. It's worthy of a real toast.'' John bent down and opened the cooler stashed beside his desk, popping the flip tops and straightening with a can of diet soda held in each hand. He handed one of the cans to Shirley. ''Here's to the swift arrival of Charlotte Leone in Tampa—''

''And lots of great leads as a result of our brilliant questions,'' Shirley finished for him. She raised the can. ''Thanks for the soda.''

''You're very welcome.'' John popped the top on his own can, and smiled as he watched Shirley drink.

Seventeen

Dan parked his car in one of the several outdoor lots
scattered around the Arnold Palmer Hospital for
Women and Children in Orlando. Visiting hours
might be over for the day but the lot remained more
than half full, and nobody seemed likely to pay the
slightest attention to him. He put the car into park and
reached for his cell phone to call the General. A picture of Charlie curled up in bed, trying not to giggle
when he told her his real name, sprang unbidden into
his mind.

He felt his entire body soften as he thought of her,
his focus melting away like a candle in the afternoon
sun. He allowed himself a couple of seconds to indulge in the captivating knowledge that Charlotte
would be waiting for him when this meeting with
Fitzpatrick was finally over. For the first time in way
too long, he was going to be able to get five or six
hours sleep with the woman he loved lying beside
him, his arms wrapped around her waist, holding her
close beside him.

The images were too tempting, and much too dis-
tracting. He threw a mental switch, shutting them
down with ruthless efficiency. He once again became
Daniel O'Toole, dedicated commander of the Ar-

margh Army, intent only on getting his hands on the radioactive bomb and securing his position as the General's most efficient lieutenant.

He used his cell phone to call Fitzpatrick. Since cell phone conversations were difficult to monitor specifically, but easy to overhear by accident, he kept his comments brief and cryptic. "I'm here, as we agreed."

"I'm in Aisle 3. Section J," the General replied. "I'm in a midnight blue Expedition. Dade County license plates."

Aisle 3 was two aisles over. The rules were that Dan had to approach the General's vehicle on foot, so that Fitzpatrick could verify he had arrived alone. For security reasons, the parking lot was reasonably well lit, so despite the late hour, it wasn't difficult to spot his quarry. Dan locked his car, tucked the keys and cellphone into the pouch of his briefcase, and slipped through the ranks of parked cars until he reached the blue SUV under the Section J marker post.

He never made any protest about complying with Fitzpatrick's various security rituals, although he and Fitzpatrick both knew that if either one of them wanted to set the other up, there were dozens of ways to do it, and having Dan approach the Expedition on foot sure as hell wasn't going to guard against betrayal. On either side. In any terrorist network, the only real protection the members had was the loyalty of all the other members.

Of course, Fitzpatrick believed that he was guarding his true identity by never meeting anywhere that required the revelation of his name and, in fact, Dan had been surprised by how long and hard he'd been compelled to work in order to uncover the General's name and occupation. His task would have been easier if he'd simply been able to hand over a picture, taken with a hidden camera, and ask Tremayne Washington to run an ID match through one of the Bureau's super-powered computer programs. Ex-Major Brian Fitzpatrick would have been thrown up as a match for any number of news stories at the time of his court martial.

Unfortunately that simple move hadn't been possible, since there was no way for Tremayne to run such a wide-ranging check without other people inside the Bureau becoming aware of the result, and the last thing Dan wanted to do was tip off the mole operating inside the Bureau that the General's identity had been unmasked. Dan's life already hung by a thread that was too slender for comfort, and although he trusted Tremayne Washington up to a point, that point didn't extend very far. Dan was where he was right now because—when pushed to the wall—Tremayne had valued national security above personal friendship.

That was undoubtedly a good fault in somebody holding the rank of deputy director at the FBI. It sucked from the point of view of Dan putting his personal life and his marriage back together again and looking for help from Tremayne to do it. It wasn't enough for Dan to prevent the Armargh Army carrying out this specific operation. The leaders of the army had to be rounded up, killed, or incarcerated without Dan's treachery to their cause ever being revealed. If anyone in the Armargh Army ever learned that Dan was an undercover agent, not a true believer, his life expectancy—and Charlotte's—would be counted in days.

The door to the SUV opened and Fitzpatrick beckoned Dan inside. Dan climbed into the van, nodding his head in salutation. "Evenin', General. It's a fine night, to be sure."

Fitzpatrick responded with a warmer greeting than usual, obviously relieved that the Elf had finally come through with the disk after a week of broken promises. "In more ways than one, Danny-boy. You've done well."

Dan gave a brief nod, accepting his due. Fitzpatrick only called him Danny-boy in moments of rare excitement. He lifted the flap on his briefcase and took out a tiny data disk in a transparent case, holding it flat on the palm of his hand. "I believe this is what you've been waitin' for, General. The password you'll be needing to run the program is *Dublin*."

Fitzpatrick took the disk with no more than a grunt of acknowledgment and slipped it into the laptop perched on the armrests between the two of them, his fingers fumbling a bit in his eagerness. Dan listened to the soft whir of the program loading and kept his mind blank, waiting for Fitzpatrick's reaction.

It came with a predictable string of obscenities. "There are black patches in the middle of each screen." Fitzpatrick swung the laptop around and showed Dan a colored map with the crucial center obliterated. He flicked to the next screen, where a diagram of the security wiring in the Vehicle Assembly Building showed a similar gaping hole. And so on through twenty more screens until Dan reached out his hand and stopped Fitzpatrick's increasingly frantic clicking from screen to screen.

"No need to be wastin' your time, General. They all look the same."

"Why did you tell me you'd gotten the information we need? I'm a busy man, and I can't afford to keep making trips to Florida while you try to get your crazy Elf to deliver what he's been promising to deliver for the past month." Fitzpatrick jabbed an angry finger at the screen. "If this is what we've been waiting for the Elf to give us then you know as well as I do that it's fucking goddamn useless."

"That disk you're lookin' at isn't exactly what the Elf delivered to me," Dan said, his calm all the more noticeable in contrast to Fitzpatrick's spluttering rage. "That disk you're lookin' at is merely what I'm willin' to deliver to you of the information I received from the Elf this afternoon. An overview, so to speak, of the information the Elf has given me."

Fitzpatrick stared at him from eyes that were near boiling with fury. "And what the *hell* does that mean?"

Dan gave a small laugh. "Come along now, General. You must be thinkin' I'm a very foolish man if you believe that I would spend the past five months makin' a close friend out of my contact inside the Space Center, only to hand over the fruits of my labors without so much as a single attempt to protect my own interests."

"Are you telling me that *you've* blacked out the center of each screen like this? *You* did it? Deliberately?" Fitzpatrick took the disk out of the drive and threw it at Dan.

Dan caught the disk and tucked it into his shirt pocket. The program for obscuring crucial text and images was one of the few really useful aids he'd received recently from Tremayne Washington. He'd been able to copy the Elf's original CD and then burn holes in the resulting data, all with a few simple commands on his laptop. The work of a few minutes after he and Charlotte had made love. "Sure, and isn't it good to know that all those months I spent learnin' the latest computer techniques to help with our counterfeiting operation in Albania have paid off in another field entirely?"

Fitzpatrick took a visibly deep breath, and then another, smart enough to realize that losing his temper was no way to win this argument. "Dan, we've been working together now for more than five years." The conciliatory tone made his face flush with the effort at restraint. "Money that came out of my own pocket—lots of my money—kept the Armargh Army afloat after the disaster at Craigavon—"

"Ah yes, Craigavon," Dan said. "I'm glad you mentioned that sad affair. Let's talk a little bit about what happened at Craigavon, shall we, General? Because, you see, the battle at Craigavon is one of the reasons why you're sittin' here lookin' at black holes in the middle of your computer screen. You may have been able to fool the rest of the boys into believin' that we were just unlucky that night, but I'm not so easy to deceive."

"Who deceived you? I've no idea what you're talking about." Fitzpatrick managed to sound genuinely puzzled, but Dan could see that he was rattled. The General was no actor, except insofar as he had mastered the art of playing the role of conservative, right-wing patriot while secretly plotting revenge against the government that he believed had prosecuted him unjustly.

"*You* deceived us," Dan said. "You wanted to be rid of me and some of my very best friends, and so you delivered us straight into the murderin' hands of our bitterest enemies—"

"What nonsense are you spouting now?" Fitzpatrick's neck flushed dark red. "Of course I did no such thing—"

"You can be splutterin' and denyin' all you want, General, but I know the facts of the situation, and bein' an Irishman, and loyal to my friends, I've never forgotten your treachery to the men who fought and died alongside of me that night at Craigavon."

"Your friends were slaughtered by the Red Hand Faction. The same enemies we've always had—"

"It's true enough that the Red Hand Faction did the actual killings," Dan conceded. "But only because you told them where to wait for us. And then, to guarantee their success, you betrayed our battle plan to them so that they could slaughter us."

"I'm the leader of the Armargh Army, for Christ's sake! There's no reason why I would want my own troops killed. None."

"You had the title of leader, but you weren't sure that you had the loyalty of your men. That's why you orchestrated the massacre at Craigavon—to secure your position."

"I never had the slightest doubt about my leadership role! I was appointed by Colm Doherty as his successor. I'm the General of the Armargh Army—"

"True enough, you have the title. But to your way of thinkin', the men have always paid too much attention to me and nowhere near enough attention to you and your grand schemes for takin' our struggle across the Atlantic to America. You decided to get rid of me and as many of my loyal followers as the Red Hand boys could slaughter. Then you would be free promote your own cronies to positions of power and remake the Armargh Army in your own image."

"The fact that you're here, sitting beside me, proves you're not talking sense."

"No, General. The fact that I'm here proves only that I'm a lot harder to kill than you ever expected. I survived Craigavon, though too many of my friends died. Which brings us right back to the fact that you were lookin' at a computer screen with black holes in the middle of your data."

"I see no connection."

"It's simple. I have no reason to trust you, and many a good reason not to. As it happens, in terms of overall strategy for the Armargh Army, I've come around to your way of thinking. I agree with your opinion that we need to bring our cause to the attention of the Americans, and that continuing our fight in Ireland and Britain isn't going to get us anywhere now that the IRA and Sinn Fein have betrayed our cause and started to negotiate with the very people who are our oppressors."

"Then since we're in agreement, I don't understand why you won't give me the information from the Elf that we need to complete the mission."

"Sure you understand, General. You're a smart man, but you need to remember I'm a smart man, too.

We both know that once I give you the computer disk
with all the information from the Elf, you don't need
me anymore. You're thinkin' you can get rid of me
and give your orders direct to Sean and Ryan, with
no risk that either one of them is ever goin' to challenge your leadership. They're followers, not leaders.
Whereas, with me around, you're never quite certain
who's actually in charge of the Armargh Army. And
a lot of the time, you're thinking to yourself that
maybe it isn't really you who is in charge.''

Dan knew right away that he'd hit the nail squarely
on the head. Fitzpatrick had never been trained as a
conspirator and he was hopeless at concealing his
body language. The General protested vehemently,
but all the bluster merely confirmed Dan's conviction
that he'd been slated for death, although probably not
until after the Vehicle Assembly Building had actually been blown up. Sean and Ryan would have been
given instructions on getting rid of both the Elf and
Dan before flying off to freedom in Central America.

Dan let Fitzpatrick rant for a while, until his lies
became annoying as well as boring. ''General, you're
not convincing me, so save your breath for fightin'
the enemy. Let's get down to brass tacks, shall we?
You have a bomb that I need. I have the disk that
tells you how the bomb can be planted in the heart
of the Vehicle Assembly Building without any of our
team being detected. The fact is, like it or not, we
need each other.''

''I don't need your fucking disk.'' Fitzpatrick
sounded petulant. ''I can take my bomb to a shopping
mall in Orlando and there'll be radiation spread over

Florida's tourist attractions just the same as if I planted the bomb in the Space Center.''

"Sure you can do that," Dan agreed mildly. "Although it isn't just a question of planting the bomb and pulling the trigger as you walk away. You have to place it where it won't be found for long enough that you can be hundreds of miles away when the device detonates. We're talking hours, not minutes."

"That's hardly a major obstacle for me to overcome. You seem to forget that I'm a man with extensive military training in weapons deployment."

"Your military training might help you to set the bomb so that it doesn't explode too soon, but will it help you to place it somewhere so that it won't be found? These days, a stall in the men's room at the mall isn't going to cut it."

"You're not the only man in the world with battle experience, you know, O'Toole."

"Formal pitched battles and guerilla operations are two very different things, General. And I'm suspecting you don't have much practical experience in planning an operation against civilians. But this argument is irrelevant, anyway. We both know that you want the symbolism of blowing up the Space Center. If you'd wanted to blow up a shopping mall, you could have done that six months ago. You didn't do that because you want to prove to the United States government that even their most high-tech installations aren't safe from your reach—"

"Because that's the only way we're going to force them to take action to save Ireland."

"I agree. And I admit I want the same thing."

"Then why are we sitting here arguing?" Fitzpatrick demanded irritably.

"Because I want to be sure you understand the dynamics of this mission, General. I can't get my hands on a dirty bomb, that's true. But I've spent a lot of time in the Balkans dealing with men who'd sell their grandmother's heart for the right sum of money. We both know I have the contacts to purchase enough Semtex to blow the Vehicle Assembly Building all the way to Mars. Face facts. You need me a lot more than I need you."

"You couldn't get enough explosive by July Fourth." The General must have realized he sounded cranky rather than scathing, because he closed his laptop with a decisive snap. "All right. Bottom line, we need each other."

"Bottom line, we don't trust each other," Dan corrected.

"And what's your solution to that dilemma?"

"We both want the Space Center blown up," Dan said. "We both want the Americans to pressure the British to get their troops out of Northern Ireland and hand over control of Northern Ireland to the legitimate government in Dublin. I'm tellin' you I have all the information I need to place your dirty bomb in a snug little nest right in the heart of the Vehicle Assembly Building. I'm tellin' you that my men are trained and ready to carry out their mission. All I need is the bomb. Give it to me."

"Give it to you," the General murmured. "Just like that, I'm supposed to hand it over to you."

Please God, let him agree. "Like you said yourself, we've been workin' together for more than five years.

You don't have to like me, General. You just have to accept that I'm the only man you know who can bring your grand scheme to the glorious finale it deserves.''

Fitzpatrick stared straight ahead into the glare of a street light at the boundary of the parking lot. Tension wrapped the interior of the car in a smothering blanket of silence that was finally broken not by either of the men speaking, but by the electronic buzz of a cell phone.

The General removed his phone from a built-in receptacle and opened it. ''Yes?'' He listened without saying another word, the phone held to his ear farthest away from Dan, making it impossible to overhear what was being said. ''Where is she right now?'' the General asked then listened again. ''Well done,'' he said at last, his mouth curving into a gratified smile. ''As soon as you have her in custody, take her to the boat. Call me when you have her situated.''

A chill raced down Dan's spine as Fitzpatrick turned to him, his smile becoming triumphant as he shut the phone. ''Well now,'' the General said. ''Let's start our little bargaining session over again, shall we?''

''Why would we do that?'' Dan asked, although the cold knot of dread forming in the pit of his stomach made a mockery of his response.

''Because your ex-wife—the lovely Charlotte Leone—is in the custody of a good friend of mine.'' Fitzpatrick's eyes gleamed with cruel pleasure. ''When you've given me the Elf's disk, I'll give you back your woman.''

And if he believed that, Dan thought despairingly, the General undoubtedly had a piece of St. Patrick's jeweled crown that he'd be happy to sell him. He had rarely been more grateful that he'd mastered the skill of keeping his face expressionless.

"What are you proposin'?" he asked. "And keep in mind, General, that I'm a patriot, a true son of Ireland. I want my bomb a hell of a lot more than I want my woman."

Eighteen

Charlotte had plenty of time during the drive from the Daytona police station to the FBI offices in Tampa Bay to calm down from the adrenaline rush that had left her reacting to one crisis after another with no time to analyze rationally what she ought to be doing. Ever since the nightmare moment when the hotel manager pounded on her door and informed her that she needed to evacuate the room due to a burst water pipe, she'd been reacting out of sheer gut instinct, with scarcely a glimmer of reasoned thought intruding.

The hotel room had no closets she could hide in, only a metal pole with a few coat hangers, so she'd run to the bathroom and tried to conceal herself behind the shower curtain, hoping against hope the manager would poke his head around the door, assume the room was empty, and go away.

Unfortunately the manager was too conscientious for such a sloppy procedure. When she didn't respond to his second volley of knocks, he'd used a master key to unlock the door and come inside to conduct a thorough search.

The closed bathroom door didn't stop his search for more than a few seconds. When his knocking once again produced no results, he simply walked in. Charlotte was caught standing in the tub fully clothed, with no idea how she was supposed to explain her refusal to answer his repeated requests for her to exit the room. Inventing credible lies, she discovered, was an art form she definitely hadn't mastered. Somehow she was quite sure that if Dan were here, neither one of them would have been caught cowering in the bathtub.

The manager eyed her sternly as she babbled incoherent excuses about a leaking shower. He glanced up at the bone-dry shower head and down at the equally dry tub. Then his gaze circled the bathroom, probably in search of drug paraphernalia. Detecting no trace of drugs or booze, his usual explanation for irrational behavior on the part of motel guests, he ordered her with barely concealed irritation to leave the room.

The poor guy undoubtedly thought he was having a hard day, Charlotte reflected with an edge of hysteria. He should try coping with hers and his burst pipe would seem trivial by comparison.

''I've already explained there's water still gushing from the main water line,'' the manager said. ''The maintenance folk are trying to plug the leak and they haven't been able to isolate all the electrical cables. There's a risk of electrical shock and your carpet's going to be soaking wet any moment now. For health and safety reasons, you need to leave this room.'' `

''I don't mind damp carpet.'' Even Charlotte winced at how lame that sounded. ''I'd prefer to stay put in this room. My friend's expecting to find me here.''

"I'm sure your friend will notice that there's been a little problem. The workmen tearing up carpeting in the corridor will be his first clue." The manager made no attempt to hide his sarcasm. "We'll pin a note on the door to say that there's been a room change and to ask at the front desk for your new room number. I'm sorry for the inconvenience, but we'll deduct fifty percent from your bill for your trouble. Please collect your things as quickly as possible."

The manager ushered her out of the bathroom, his expression implacable. If she protested anymore, he would probably call the police to get her evicted. She could either risk being seen by the people congregated in the corridor, or face the greater risk of confronting a cop. Faced with a lose-lose situation, Charlotte shoved her few belongings into her bag and followed the manager out into the corridor, trying to appear casually unconcerned.

As soon as she exited the room, she realized she was doomed. She heard a gasp of indrawn breath from a woman standing across the hall. The gasp was quickly stifled, but then the whispers began, confirming that she'd been recognized even more quickly than she feared. She debated making a run for it, but the corridor was already crowded with displaced guests, and a trio of extra plumbers arrived while she watched, wrenches clasped at the ready. She calculated her chances of escape at somewhere between zero and minus-ten.

People in motel rooms must spend a heck of a lot of time watching the news, Charlotte concluded gloomily, because it seemed as if every one of her fellow guests had seen her photos flashing across their

TV screens. Within seconds, an informal posse of hotel staff and guests had her corraled, and although she tried to deny her identity, nobody believed her. If the media had shown only her wedding picture, she might have passed unrecognized, but the photograph she'd had taken for PR purposes at work was both recent and a very good likeness.

"I'd like to see your driver's license," the manager said, beginning to sound rather pleased with himself as he realized that he hadn't just flushed out another druggie or run-of-the-mill weirdo, but perhaps a criminal who rated air time on national TV.

"Why?" Charlotte asked, too distraught to be subtle.

"You're registered here under the name of Leslie Carter," the manager said, checking his clipboard for the name. "I have a right to see that you are, in fact, Leslie Carter."

"But I'm not her. I mean him."

The manager raised an exasperated eyebrow.

"Because I'm not the person who registered!" Charlotte scrambled to recover. "That's my friend's name and he's not here right now."

"Then who are you? I need to see some ID, please."

Charlotte's mind went totally blank. Who would ever have guessed that it was so difficult to think of a fake name? Jane Doe. Mary Smith. Blankety Blank. She finally managed to blurt out that she was Ruth Nowaski—the name of the receptionist at her office.

"Fine, Ms. Nowaski. Could you show me some identification, please?"

She stubbornly insisted that she didn't have any ID

with her, which achieved nothing much except to make her look foolish when the police later searched her belongings and found her Florida driver's license tucked into the flap of her evening purse, proclaiming her to be Charlotte Leone for everyone to see. Vivid proof of Dan's earlier statement that it was never safe to carry identification when you were working under-cover—or had something to hide.

Fortunately, there was nothing for the police to find that identified Dan in any of his incarnations. He'd left little behind when he departed for his meeting, only a disposable razor, a toothbrush, and a few items of clean clothing. He'd even taken the infamous hand-cuffs out to his car, Charlotte reflected wryly. Not that the police would have believed that she'd been held captive if they had found the cuffs. They'd probably have assumed the cuffs were a kinky sex toy and Charlotte an aggressive dominatrix given to cowing her helpless partners into sexual submission.

By the time she arrived at the police station, a ten-minute drive from the motel, the local twenty-four-hour news TV crew was already scrambling to get its camera gear operational, no doubt summoned by a cop eager to broadcast the triumph of Daytona law enforcement in capturing a nationally wanted criminal suspect. The cops obligingly delayed her exit from the squad car long enough for the cameraman to get his equipment up and running, thus insuring that her picture would be flashed nationwide.

She might even rate a cameo appearance on *Good Morning, America* doing the perp walk, Charlotte thought, repressing a shudder that threatened to turn into a giggle. The events of the past twenty-four hours had taken on a surreal glow that produced a compelling urge to laugh. Or cry. She recognized that her reactions were out of whack, but her ability to adjust her behavior to suit the situation seemed to have been consumed by fatigue, worry, and general emotional overload.

Walking past the camera, she seesawed between delight that her family in Iowa would soon know she wasn't dead, and humiliation because they would see her being marched into the police station, handcuffed and surrounded by cops. On balance, she decided that she felt more relief than chagrin. Especially since it meant that Dan wouldn't have to wonder what had happened to her. Just like her parents, he'd be able to watch the nearest available TV screen and see exactly what had transpired. *Please God,* his meeting with the General would have been successful and her arrest would have no impact on his ability to recover the dirty bomb and thwart the deadly plans of the Armagh Army.

When the cops started to question her about the events at the Down Under club, Charlotte instinctively fell back on the cover story Dan had invented. She told the detectives that she'd been taken into protective custody by Richard Villier, a French government agent working in alliance with the FBI. The hotel room, she explained, had been her safe haven. The detectives didn't even pretend to believe her, but she didn't much care. When she got tired and their questions got tougher, she simply clammed up and demanded to see her lawyer. They immediately stopped their interrogation and told her she could arrange for legal representation as soon as she arrived at the FBI offices in Tampa.

The three-hour journey to Tampa was mind-numbing in its tedium, and yet too short to decide on the best way to avert disaster. If it had been easy for her to lie to the Daytona cops, it was a different matter to consider defying the FBI. Driving through the darkness, handcuffed, shackled with chains, and miserably uncomfortable, Charlotte had plenty of time to consider the wider ramifications of her situation.

The tiny glow of happiness that had been rekindled when she made love to Dan didn't disappear—that flame seemed unquenchable—but she was painfully aware that the chance she and Dan had been given to reclaim their life together was fragile in the extreme. She had an uneasy suspicion that Dan's fate lay in her hands right now, which meant, incredibly, that the safety of the entire Kennedy Space Center was also her responsibility. If Dan died as a result of what she did or didn't do over the next few hours, she couldn't bear to contemplate the national disaster that would result from her failure, or the desolation she would feel at losing her husband for the second time.

Should she tell the FBI what she knew? At heart, despite all that had happened over the past couple of years, she was still a small-town, law-abiding Midwesterner, and the impulse to tell the truth was very strong. In her world, if an FBI agent asked you a question, you answered honestly. Except she was no longer operating within the parameters of her familiar world, and in Dan's world, she was beginning to realize that telling the truth could have devastating consequences.

For what seemed like the hundredth time, Charlotte mentally reviewed the reasons Dan felt it was imperative to go it alone in his mission to save the Space Center. A few hours earlier, those reasons had seemed compelling, but she suspected the complex calculations about how best to defeat the Armargh Army had changed the moment she was taken into custody. Last night Dan had kidnapped her because he was afraid she was about to be abducted and used as a hostage. But surely kidnapping wasn't a concern now that she was in police custody, en route to an interrogation room at the FBI? Whatever else you could say about her current situation, at least she was safe from being seized by terrorists.

Given the changed circumstances, wouldn't it be better for everyone if she took the easy way out and told the truth? The FBI had thousands of employees, and vast resources. Was it realistic to believe that Dan, working alone, stood a better chance of averting disaster than the entire FBI with all its technological assets and its wealth of highly-trained personnel?

The answer ought to have been simple, and totally in favor of telling the FBI what was going on. But her impulse to confide the truth kept shattering against the rock of Dan's months of determined silence. He strongly believed there was a mole working inside the FBI and that revealing the Armargh Army's plans would have terrible consequences for the nation. He was an expert and she was a complete novice. How could she set aside his judgment?

She couldn't, Charlotte decided as they drove through the outskirts of Tampa. She had no choice other than to trust Dan's judgment and keep silent. If

John Hanseck was in the hospital, then Shirley Nicholson would most likely be the agent who interrogated her. Shirley's questions might be tough, but she couldn't force Charlotte to answer. No FBI agent was going to pull out Charlotte's fingernails, or starve her into confessing that she'd shot John Hanseck.

Even if she ended up in jail, so what? She'd just have to suck it up, Charlotte decided. Besides, jail might be the safest place for her right now. If she was behind bars, at least she'd be securely out of reach of the Armargh Army's kidnappers. She could survive being locked away for a few days, and her stay wasn't likely to be much more than that. Once Dan got possession of the dirty bomb, he would spring her by revealing the truth.

Unless he failed in his mission and the bomb went off. Charlotte shuddered at the thought. If the bomb exploded, it would mean Dan was dead and Cape Canaveral contaminated with lethal radiation. She fought against a flash of sheer terror. Scaring herself into a panic was the last thing she needed to do right now. Of course Dan wouldn't die. Think positively, she lectured herself. Visualize Dan in his Superman cape, single-handedly saving the Kennedy Space Center.

She drew in a shaky breath, quelling the niggling thought that Superman capes were in short supply in the real world. Her husband was a man of extraordinary talents and dedication. He would succeed, and she would help him by saying nothing that might reveal his clandestine role to the wrong people.

By the time the Daytona cops escorted her inside the FBI's Tampa Bay offices, Charlotte's confidence was slightly bolstered by the mere fact of having an action plan, even if the proposed action was nothing more dramatic than remaining silent. But it was only minutes short of two in the morning and she stumbled from a fatigue she hadn't been fully aware of feeling as they approached the desk where the night guard was keeping an eye on a bank of security monitors. She could only hope that her brain was more alert than her body and that she hadn't made a dangerous choice in deciding not to cooperate.

The FBI security guard examined the police IDs carefully, then gave the two uniformed officers a friendly smile. "We've been waiting for you," he said. "Ms. Nicholson, the agent in charge of the case, will be relieved to know you're finally here."

"We made pretty good time on the way over," the sergeant who'd done the driving said. "Agent Nicholson couldn't have expected us to arrive any quicker than this."

"I'll call her now to let her know you're here." The security guard checked a number from a list beside the phone and punched it into the console on his desk. "Ms. Nicholson, the police from Daytona have arrived with the suspect."

He listened for a moment, then responded. "Yes, sir. We'll wait right here for you to come and pick her up."

The security guard hung up the phone. "Agent Nicholson is on a call to headquarters right now, so Agent Hanseck is going to come downstairs and escort Ms. Leone to the interrogation area."

The Daytona cops both looked startled at the news that John Hanseck was out of the hospital and fit enough to be working at this late hour of the night.

Charlotte gave a silent nod of acknowledgment to Dan. It seemed he'd been right all along, and that the FBI had been lying, at least about the gravity of John's injuries.

"I thought John Hanseck had been shot and seriously wounded," the sergeant said, echoing her thoughts. "The bulletin said Ms. Leone here was wanted for questioning in the attempted murder of FBI Agent Hanseck."

"Agent Hanseck was injured, but he was released from the hospital earlier today," the night guard explained. "He's been in the office for a while now, but I guess that piece of information hasn't been made public as yet."

The elevator doors opened and John Hanseck stepped out into the lobby before the two cops could ask any more questions. John's left arm was in a sling, and his shirt sleeve had been cut away almost at the shoulder, exposing a bulky bandage that stretched from his upper arm to below the elbow. He looked tired and grim, but his step as he crossed the lobby was firm and purposeful.

"Thanks for bringing in Ms. Leone," he said, extending his right hand first to the sergeant and then to the other cop, and shaking warmly. "I appreciate the prompt actions by your department. It's a big step forward for our office to have Ms. Leone in custody."

"We weren't expecting to find you here," the sergeant said, with a definite note of accusation in his voice. "From the bulletin your office issued, we understood you were just about on death's door."

"Fortunately not. As you've probably guessed already, there's more to this situation than we've released to the media.'' John's hushed and grave tone suggested he was revealing a huge secret instead of a snippet of self-evident information. ''The Daytona police department has made a major contribution to national security. I can't say any more right now, but we're grateful. Very grateful. I'm sure your captain will be hearing from the Deputy Director with more details within the next couple of days. But for now, the less information that gets leaked to the media the better. You understand how it is with these top-secret national security cases.'' His voice lowered another note, adding extra solemnity. ''I'm relying on your absolute discretion to see that the media doesn't get any information beyond the fact that Ms. Leone has been transferred to the custody of the FBI's Tampa office.''

The cops appeared mollified by John's confirmation that they were involved in a big-time case, and his bandages seemed to reassure them that they hadn't arrested an innocent woman. They swore the media would get no leaks from them. A promise they probably intended to keep as long as Larry King didn't come calling, Charlotte thought cynically.

Far from being impressed by John's sling, she wondered whether there was any wound at all beneath the bulky medical dressings. When she'd first heard the TV newscaster announce that Agent Hanseck had been shot, she'd assumed the wound was in his back, where she might not have noticed the blood. If he had been shot in the left upper arm, however, the wound must have been inflicted after Dan abducted her, otherwise she would have seen the injury the moment it happened. In fact, she and John had been dancing closely enough that she would have been sprayed with his blood the minute the bullet hit him, which made her even more dubious about the reality of his injury.

The cops were sufficiently anxious to start the drive back to the east coast that they didn't seem to notice the haste with which John Hanseck signed off on the paperwork concerning Charlotte's transfer. The two of them hadn't even reached the exit when John spoke crisply, without looking at her.

"Follow me, Ms. Leone. We're going to conduct our initial conversation in Agent Nicholson's office."

His formal manner, the implicit pretense that he'd didn't know her, jolted Charlotte into speech. "Look, I understand you have to obey certain rules, John, but don't act as if you've never seen me before. That's silly." If the security guard hadn't been listening, she'd have reminded John that he not only knew her, a few nights earlier he'd been kissing her with every appearance of pleasure.

"I'm sorry for your injuries," she said. "But you must know they have nothing to do with me. When I last saw you, you were unconscious, but there was no blood, and no sign that you'd been shot."

John's expression froze from formality into icy remoteness, and he made no direct acknowledgment of her claim of innocence. "Please come with me, Ms. Leone. If you wish to make a statement, I'll be happy to take it from you when we're in Agent Nicholson's office." He nodded to the security guard, his expression thawing just a little. "Good night, George. See you later."

He put his hand under Charlotte's elbow and pushed her in the direction of the elevators, using a

key to unlock the doors. She shuffled in, depressed
by his coldness. The handcuffs and the chains around
her waist and feet had been chafing painfully for the
last two hours, and she felt distinctly sorry for herself.
Far from being the ally she'd hoped for, John was
acting as if he really believed she'd set him up to be
shot. She leaned against the side of the elevator, tired
to the bone. Jail almost seemed like a good place to
be right now, provided they'd give her a bed and a
cell with nobody else in it.

John ushered her off the elevator on the third floor.
At this hour of the morning, the corridor was deserted
and the lights were dimmed from their daytime glare.
John hadn't spoken since they got into the elevator,
and Charlotte was in no mood to make chitchat, so
she stumbled along the corridor in his wake, chains
clanking like a cartoon ghost. She was tired and worried enough that when John suddenly shot out his arm
and pulled her into a shallow alcove, she simply
lurched in the direction he indicated, staring at him
in mute stupefaction.

He brought his finger to his lips, indicating that she
was to remain silent. She obeyed because she was too
bemused to do otherwise. John craned his neck
around the corner of the alcove and she saw that his
gaze seemed to be fixed on a point close to the ceiling
on the opposite wall. Her shock-numbed brain took
several seconds to register that he was watching the
movement of a security camera that swept the corridor in a constant slow arc. After about thirty seconds,
he grabbed her arm and hustled her toward a door
that she only now noticed was marked Fire Exit in
giant neon letters.

He punched in a code on the keypad fixed to the wall next to the double doors. "To stop the alarm sounding," he whispered.

She nodded, as if his explanation made perfect sense, and followed him through the heavy metal doors to the concrete stairwell outside. "Hurry," he said as soon as they were through the doors. "I'll explain later."

"Where are we going? Why were you trying to avoid being seen by the security camera? Why aren't you taking me to Shirley Nicholson's office?"

"No time to talk." John took his bandaged arm out of the sling and grabbed her hand. "Come on, Charlotte, honey. We need to haul ass."

He set a punishing pace down the stairs. Impeded by the chains around her waist and feet, she would never have kept up if he hadn't put his arm around her and more or less carried her down the stairs.

They ended up in the parking garage under the building. John half ran, half dragged her across the almost-empty lot. She recognized his car from their two dates and felt a brief flash of relief that at least something was as she expected. In a world taking yet another tilt sideways, even a familiar car was welcome.

John opened the rear door. "Get in. Pull the blanket over you, and don't lift up your head. There's a security checkpoint at the exit. Fortunately the guard only searches incoming vehicles, so if you keep your head down we won't have any problems."

She finally gathered her wits sufficiently to speak but he ignored her rapid-fire questions, pushing her into a reclining position on the back seat. "For God's sake, Charlotte, this isn't the time to play Twenty Questions. You're in real danger. You're being set up to take the fall and I have to get you out of here.''

To take what fall? Charlotte tried to ask, but John shot out another instruction to keep her head down. Then he flung the blanket over her, shoving her feet under the cover, and slamming the door. He hurriedly got into the driver's seat and turned on the ignition. She listened to the sounds of him backing out of the parking place, then heard the engine revving as the car climbed a ramp out onto the street at what sounded like high speed. They'd been driving for at least three or four minutes before John told her they were clear of the garage, that nobody seemed to be following them, and she could sit up.

She pulled herself upright, her movements awkward because of the cuffs and chains. ''Okay, John, enough. You need to explain what's going on. Where are you taking me? More to the point, why have you taken me? You must have put your entire career at risk when you smuggled me out of the FBI offices.''

''I'll answer the easy question first,'' he said. ''I'm taking you to my boat. We'll be able to talk there without the risk of people finding you.''

''Why don't you want anyone to find me?''

''Well, I don't like to sound too dramatic, but you're in a hell of a bad situation, Charlotte. There's a faction inside the FBI that I believe is trying to set you up, and I'm doing my damnedest to save you.''

It was late, she was exhausted, and the past twenty-four hours had been crammed to bursting with shocks and surprises. Charlotte discovered that she was having a really hard time processing what she heard.

"Somebody is trying to set me up for what?" she asked. "Attempting to murder you? But we both know you weren't even shot!"

She began to feel distinct regret that he'd rushed her out of the FBI building so quickly. "Maybe you should take me back, John. I can call my lawyer, and he'll subpoena the hospital records—"

John shook his head. "Your lawyer won't be able to help you. The attempted murder charge was just a ruse to make sure you'd be found and brought in as quickly as possible without the Bureau being forced to reveal its hand."

"Then if I'm not accused of trying to kill you, what are the charges against me?"

"We have orders to hold you as a material witness, accused of conspiracy to commit acts of terrorism."

"What?" Charlotte closed her eyes until the darkness stopped spinning. "The FBI believes I'm a terrorist? Me, personally? Not just the wife of a terrorist?"

"Yes." John nodded. "Shirley Nicholson has built a pretty compelling case that you're an active accomplice to Daniel O'Toole and the Armagh Army, rather than a victim."

"What possible grounds does she have for believing something so crazy?"

"Multiple reasons, starting with the fact that you were married to O'Toole."

"That's not even a statistical reason to suspect me. Most terrorists have wives and mothers and girlfriends who are paralyzed with shock when they discover the truth about the man they love. I was one of those women. I had no clue what kind of a man I'd married. None." And that, God knew, was still the truth. She'd married Mr. Middle America, and woken up six months later in an alternate reality.

"I believe you, Charlotte." John hesitated for a moment. "Shirley Nicholson doesn't."

"Then give me a better reason why she suspects me than the fact that O'Toole tricked me into marriage."

"Your move to Tampa Bay—"

"My move?" Charlotte pressed her hands to her head and the manacles bumped against her nose. She dropped her hands back into her lap. "You're joking, right? Tell me when we get to the punch line so I can laugh."

"It's no joke, Charlotte. You transferred from Iowa to Florida, although you have no connections here, and you quit a well-paying job in your family's company in the process. And then O'Toole suddenly left Eastern Europe and moved the most important part of his operation not just to America, but to the same state where you were living—"

"I wanted to move somewhere warm! O'Toole wants to blow up tourist attractions and there are lots of them in Florida, in case you didn't notice! Hasn't anyone in your office heard of coincidence?"

"The Bureau doesn't like coincidences. Besides, the Bureau believes you've met with O'Toole on several occasions. We have you tracked to the same location as Daniel O'Toole on at least five occasions over the past five months."

"That's not possible. I scarcely ever leave home—"

"On the contrary, you and O'Toole both made trips

to Boca Raton as recently as May 6. That's when I was assigned to watch you—"

"I went to Boca Raton to attend a seminar on designing energy-efficient buildings for semitropical climates," she snapped. "If O'Toole happened to be in Boca Raton at the same time, I didn't know and I sure as *hell* didn't meet with him."

"I believe you," John said again. "But then there was your trip to Naples in April, and one to Miami in June—"

"Yes, to study the layout of the Emergency Room at Saint Luke's hospital! I was the project manager on my firm's bid for an important hospital extension here in Tampa—"

"Your trip coincided precisely with the period when we believe O'Toole was preparing to move from Miami."

"Okay, my trip coincided. As in *coincidence*—"

"Unfortunately, there have been way too many coincidences like that over the past few months, not to mention various activities on the part of O'Toole that suggest your involvement."

"Suggest my involvement how? Good grief, John, I was putting in sixty-hour work weeks for most of the past year! My life consisted of going to the office and going home. With a few sidetrips on the weekend to the grocery store. Not forgetting the occasional wild outing to the dry cleaners."

"I'm merely the messenger, Charlotte. Don't shoot me." John glanced into the rearview mirror and gave her a wry grin. "Sorry, that was just a figure of speech. Anyway, those tapes we asked you to audit were the clincher as far as Shirley was concerned."

"The tapes? Are you talking about the recordings you asked me to listen to a couple of weeks ago?" Charlotte felt as if she'd fallen down the rabbit hole and emerged in a land even more lunatic than Wonderland.

"They were a test," John explained. "If you were innocent, Shirley was convinced you'd identify your ex-husband as one of the speakers. We were all satisfied that his voice was unmistakable, you know. If you were guilty, Shirley insisted that you would pretend you didn't recognize him, and then it would only be a matter of days before you disappeared." He paused for a beat. "You didn't identify him, and then you disappeared, leaving me unconscious on the dance floor in the process."

"But I didn't make you unconscious and I didn't plan to disappear!" Charlotte protested, feeling more and more lost in the Mad Hatter's garden. "I was kidnapped, for God's sake."

Half of her was terrified, the other half was fighting an insane desire to laugh at the absurdity of her situation. For a woman who'd been living a hermitlike existence, she'd certainly managed to attract a heck of a lot of attention from people she had not the faintest idea were interested in her. While she'd been locked in an Arctic wasteland of emotional repression, hot currents of violence had apparently been swirling all around her.

John drove in silence for several blocks. "The truth is, I'm not sure Shirley believes the case she's built herself," he said finally.

"What does that mean?"

Once again, John took a few moments to reply.

"There's something going on with this investigation that I don't understand. We keep getting leads that turn to nothing in our hands. We track the location of O'Toole and then, before we can move in and make an arrest, he vanishes."

"That might just be your bad luck. The members of the Armargh Army have been evading capture for almost twenty years. They're masters at the game."

"It could be chance, I guess." John's voice took on a sudden harshness. "No, dammit! I don't believe that. I think our investigation is being sabotaged from within. Somebody in the Bureau is tipping off O'Toole so that we never manage to close in and prevent him pursuing whatever nightmare scenario he has planned for the Fourth."

"And you suspect Shirley Nicholson of being the source of the leaks?" Charlotte asked. "Do you think that her attempts to set me up are somehow connected to the fact that the Bureau's investigation of the Armargh Army isn't getting anywhere?"

"I think the fact that she's pushing you as a suspect is connected to the core problems we're having with the investigation," John said. "But I'm not sure if she's the direct source of the leaks to O'Toole." He shook his head. "No, I don't really suspect her of sabotaging the investigation, except in my most paranoid moments. She's African-American. Her parents still live in rural Alabama. What possible interest would she have in betraying the United States in order to help O'Toole and the cause of Irish freedom?"

Having heard Dan's explanation of why the Elf wanted to blow up the Space Center, Charlotte could imagine several twisted scenarios whereby a mentally disturbed African-American could manage to convince herself that blowing up American landmarks on behalf of the oppressed Catholic minority in Northern Ireland was somehow just retribution for the evils of slavery and the continuing racial intolerance on the part of some Americans. However, that was in the abstract. In reality, it was impossible for her to visualize smart, good-humored, down-to-earth Shirley Nicholson as mentally disturbed enough to aid and abet any form of terrorism.

"If Shirley isn't the source of the leaks, then who do you suspect?" she asked.

"There are dozens of people working on the investigation back at headquarters," John said. "I've been doing some off-the-record research into their backgrounds, but I haven't come up with any really compelling leads."

"How about agents and analysts with Irish ancestry?"

John pulled a face. "A third of the American population has at least one grandparent with connections to Ireland, so that's not exactly a flaming arrow pointing to guilt. And all the time I'm screwing around on background checks that don't take me anywhere, the sand in the hourglass is running out. Jesus, every time I think about how close we are to the Fourth, I get chills."

He had managed to reawaken every fear of her own. Charlotte was still trying to decide what to say when he pulled the car to the side of the road and turned to look at her.

"Will you tell me what really happened at the club?" he asked. "Will you trust me, Charlotte? I sure as hell need all the help I can get to track down O'Toole, and you could use some friendly insider help right about now. Tremayne Washington is a heartbeat away from signing off on the paperwork to have you tossed in jail as a material witness.''

She had already reconciled herself to the possibility of being jailed, so the threat didn't totally throw her. But she was shocked to hear that Tremayne Washington was ready to sign off on her imprisonment. Since Tremayne was the agent running Dan, he of all people must know that she was an innocent victim, a person who had absolutely no reason to feel any sympathy for the plans and terrorist methods of the Armargh Army.

Unless Dan had lied to her, and he wasn't a covert agent for the FBI but a genuine, hardcore member of the Armargh Army.

The thought had barely formed before Charlotte dismissed it. She had spent the eighteen months after Dan left burying the gut instinct that told her he was a good and honorable man. She wasn't going to slide back down that nightmare road. Everything she'd learned from Dan over the past twenty-four hours suggested there could be a dozen reasons why Tremayne Washington would pretend to suspect her of crimes he knew she had no motive or capacity to commit. Besides, for all that he sounded so sincere and anxious to help, John himself could have an agenda that she knew nothing about.

She reminded herself of her earlier decision. Since it was impossible for her to separate truth from lies, friend from foe, there was no way for her to reveal what Dan had told her without running terrible risks.

Risks, moreover, that she wouldn't even know she was running until it was too late and the damage was done. Bottom line, she couldn't risk dropping even the slightest hint that it was Dan who had kidnapped her.

Her decision to lie to John was taken so firmly and swiftly that she was answering before she'd consciously decided how to reply. He wanted to know what had happened at the club, so she gave him a vivid, detailed account of how scared she'd been when he passed out at the club, and how relieved she'd been when the manager had arrived on the scene, followed by a doctor who happened to be at hand.

"It couldn't have been more than a couple of seconds after the lights went out that I felt this man come up behind me," she elaborated. "He clamped one arm around my waist and put his other hand over my mouth. Then he told me to start walking toward the door. At first, I assumed he was some sort of sexual pervert taking advantage of the unexpected darkness. I screamed, I struggled, I even tried to bite his hand, but he was wearing gloves, and he was exceptionally strong. I had no impact on him at all."

"Didn't anyone try to help you?" John asked.

"Nobody saw what was happening," she said. "It was pitch-black inside the club. Even the emergency generator had been put out of action, so there wasn't a glimmer of light. Before too long, I realized this wasn't a random attack. The kidnapper knew me, and he had me specifically targeted. That just made me struggle all the harder, but the kidnapper got tired of my struggles. He said something about needing to be outside the club before the lights came on again. He punched me on the jaw—''

''The bastard hit you?''

''He did apologize later.''

''Well, that makes it all okay,'' John said with heavy sarcasm.

''No, of course it doesn't. But he had to subdue me in a hurry, and I guess he didn't have much choice.'' Charlotte realized that it was dangerous to sound too defensive of a kidnapper who'd used brute force to capture her. ''Anyway, I passed out and that was the last I knew until I woke up hours later in a motel bed. Alone.''

''I'm sorry, but I have to ask. Did the bastard rape you?''

''No.''

''That's at least something. You're sure? This isn't any time for false modesty, Charlotte.''

''I'm sure. He didn't rape me.''

''Thank God for that.'' John reached back over the seat and put his hand over hers. ''The Daytona police said you told them the man who abducted you identified himself as an agent of the French *Sûreté,* working as a liaison with the FBI.'' The careful neutrality of John's voice was almost more damning than if he'd come right out and said that he didn't believe her.

''Yes, that's what he told me.''

''And you believed him?''

''Yes, I did. He was very convincing. I assume that's because he was telling me the truth.'' Charlotte was determined to protect her husband's identity as the kidnapper with every ruse and subterfuge at her command. In the last resort, she couldn't help thinking that if she had to rely on either John Hanseck or Elliott Danforth Hargreaves IV to single-handedly save the United States from disaster, her money was definitely on Dan.

"Did this supposed French agent give you a name?" John asked, his thumb scraping over her knuckles in a gentle caress. She wished she could tell him to stop, but that didn't seem like a good idea.

"Yes, of course he told me his name. It was…is…Richard Villier."

"Richard Villier!" John's hand moved, jerking hers sideways. She'd finally said something that surprised him, Charlotte realized, relieved that he'd stopped caressing her. "Did Villier give you some reason to explain how he came to be over here in the States?"

Charlotte nodded. "He told me that he had been one of the French agents involved in the Hakkim Belaziz case—the one you told me about. The Algerian terrorist who'd murdered French priests and nuns. Villier said after Belaziz was killed and O'Toole escaped, the FBI had requested his assistance in tracking down O'Toole over here."

"And you believed that unlikely story?" John asked. "Surely you must have recognized that the FBI would never need assistance from one of the very people who screwed up the Belaziz operation?"

"How do you know Villier screwed it up? He said the FBI requested his transfer to the States because he was one of the few law. enforcement officials who'd ever spoken to O'Toole face-to-face. His input was considered valuable given that O'Toole is known to change his appearance so frequently. The top brass at FBI headquarters hoped that Villier would be able to give them some fresh insights in a difficult case. That seemed like a reasonable explanation to me. Besides, all the details Villier gave tied in with the information you'd already shared with me. I had no reason to doubt him—''

"Except that he'd kidnapped you from a nightclub and—for all you knew to the contrary—killed me in the process!"

"He gave a perfectly logical explanation of why he needed to kidnap me."

"Which was?"

"That the Armargh Army was getting ready to kidnap me. He claimed they planned to use me as a hostage, so he took me into protective custody before they could."

"Why did he leave you alone in the hotel room if he was supposed to be keeping you in protective custody?"

"Villier told me he had to meet with an informant. That it was really urgent for him to go, or he would never have left me alone. He told me not to open the door to anyone. Unfortunately, the water pipe burst." She gave a slight shrug. "You know the rest."

"And you still believe his story, even though he's made no attempt to contact either the police or the FBI and confirm what you're telling us?"

"Well, he's working undercover, so he can't exactly march into the Daytona police station, can he?" She was getting pretty good at this lying thing, Charlotte decided. Her powers of invention seemed to be expanding exponentially. "And we don't know that he hasn't contacted the FBI. Maybe he's already

called headquarters, or even Shirley Nicholson. I have
no way to contact him to find out, but you could call
Shirley and ask her, couldn't you? Or maybe one of
the deputy directors in Washington?''

Charlotte wasn't entirely blowing hot air. Dan must
know by now that she'd been taken to the FBI's
Tampa offices. She didn't put it beyond the bounds
of possibility for Dan to have a contact at FBI headquarters who would be willing to ''verify'' that
French *Sûreté* agent Richard Villier was currently
working with the Bureau as a top-secret consultant on
the O'Toole case.

''John, can't you get these damned cuffs off me,
for heaven's sake?''

''I have nothing with me. I was in too much of a
hurry to get you out of there. As soon as we get on
the boat, I'll find something to get them off you.''

John turned around and put the car back into drive,
moving out into the center of the almost deserted
road. It was several seconds before he spoke again,
and then he didn't address her suggestion that he
should call Shirley Nicholson. ''How the hell could
Villier know that the Armargh Army was planning to
abduct you?'' he asked finally. ''Did he explain that
to you?''

''No, he didn't share that sort of information with
me.''

''And how did he explain his attack on me at the
nightclub? How did he even know we were going to
be there in time to make all those elaborate preparations?''

''I've no idea. But he swore that you weren't seriously injured and I had no cause to be alarmed on

your behalf. He claimed he'd merely administered a quick-acting sedative, one of the drugs that's sometimes used before surgery and is perfectly safe. And that part of his story is true, isn't it? You were just sedated, nothing worse.''

"Yes, that is true." John shook his head and sighed deeply. "I'm sure you believe what you're telling me, Charlotte, but I don't know how you expect your story to hold water with anyone else.''

"Villier told me he reported to Tremayne Washington. Presumably he will have to contact FBI headquarters quite soon, even if he hasn't done so already. Then everyone will know I'm telling the truth.''

"Charlotte, honey, that's only going to work out for you if this Villier person is who and what he claimed to be. Which I very much doubt.''

"Well, who else could he be? And why would he invent such a crazy story if he was really kidnapping me for a ransom, or something?''

Not surprisingly, John had no answer for that. He turned into a side street leading over a narrow causeway to a series of docks where a dozen boats floated at anchor.

A little late, Charlotte realized that none of the reasons John had given her so far came close to explaining why he'd put his career on the line in order to remove her from FBI custody. "However much trouble I'm in, you have to be in more. There must be massive penalties for an agent who disappears with a material witness in tow.''

"Yes, there are," he acknowledged, slowing to a crawl on the narrow street. "Although no final charges have been laid against you as yet, which helps a bit...."

Charlotte wasn't sure how. "Whatever excuses you make, your actions tonight aren't exactly career-enhancing, to say the least. I don't understand why you've risked so much to help me. If everyone else at the Bureau thinks I'm guilty of conspiring with O'Toole to commit treason, why don't you? Why do you keep saying that you believe me, even though other people don't?"

John drew the car to a halt alongside the dock. He put the car into park and applied the brakes before turning around to look at her, his gaze earnest and even a little pleading in the dim lighting of the quay.

"I thought you knew," he said, his voice not quite steady. "I fell in love with you the first time I saw you, Charlotte. How could I stand by and watch Tremayne Washington and the other by-the-book morons in headquarters ruin your life?"

Nineteen

"Here's the deal," Fitzpatrick said, fingering his phone with a touch that was almost caressing. "You hand over the disk, and I'll give you back your wife."

Dan laughed, a camouflage for the cold fury that threatened to consume him. "Here's the deal, General. You give me back the woman, and show me the bomb you claim to have waitin' for me and my boys. Then I'll *consider* handing over the disk."

"It's dangerous to make threats when your adversary holds all the aces." Fitzpatrick shut the lid on his laptop with a snap that sounded ominously triumphant. "And before you spout any more lies about your beloved Ireland being more important to you than your wife, allow me to point out that you faked your own death so that you could abandon the Armagh Army and take up residence in America. If you were willing to quit Ireland forever, just so that you could marry her and live the good life in the suburbs, don't try to pretend you're indifferent about whether she lives or dies."

Dan's gaze narrowed. "I care about Charlotte." He had to admit that much, or Fitzpatrick might give orders to have her killed as a useless encumbrance. "I just don't love her enough to throw away everything

that I've spent my whole life workin' for. If Charlotte
was as important to me as you seem to think, I could
have gone to her any time this past five months. It
was no big secret where she was livin'."

Fitzpatrick, thank God, had no way of knowing
how many nights Dan had lain awake fighting the
urge to visit Charlotte's condo so that he could beg
her forgiveness and plead for just one more night in
her bed. Only the danger to Charlotte herself had
given him the strength to keep away from a lure of
almost irresistible potency.

"Last I saw on the telly, the police were claiming
that my wife had tried to kill an FBI agent," Dan
continued, expressing no particular emotion in regard
to Charlotte's alleged crime. "How did it happen that
you got to her before the Feds did? And where was
she hidin' when you found her?"

"She was hunkered down in a motel near Daytona.
She claims she's innocent, of course."

"Then why was she hidin' out in a motel hours
away from her condo?" *What the hell story had she
told that didn't have Fitzpatrick ready to rip Dan's
throat out—as a first step on the way to killing him.*

Fitzpatrick gave a snort of laughter. "She claims
to have been taken into protective custody by a
Frenchman, an agent from the *Sûreté,* who was working as a liaison with the FBI."

Good move, Charlie, babe. Smart. Dan mentally
kissed Charlotte's elegant feet. "She might even be
tellin' the truth," he said laconically. "Only a government agent would take my wife into protective
custody and then be careless enough to lose her." He
gave a seemingly casual shrug that cost him at least

a month off his life. "How did you manage to find her? You didn't say."

"Sheer goddamn luck," Fitzpatrick admitted with surprising candor. "Apparently there was some sort of major sewage leak at the motel where she was staying. She was recognized when she was evacuated from the room. The police picked her up and charged her with attempting to murder an FBI agent. They're transferring her to the FBI offices in Tampa Bay as we speak."

Dan's gaze narrowed. "Then you don't actually have Charlotte in your own custody right now? You're countin' your chickens quite a bit before they're hatched, aren't you, General?"

"I'll have her shortly. No fuss, no muss. Guaranteed."

"You're dreamin'. How in hell are you plannin' to get her away from the FBI? They aren't goin' to be foolish enough to stash her in a motel and leave her alone." As he had done, Dan thought with biting self-reproach.

Fitzpatrick smiled. "I've told you before, O'Toole, I'm connected. I have friends in high places. Including inside help at the Bureau."

Dan didn't let his fear show. "Even if you have the Director himself in your hip pocket, beggin' permission to lick your ass, I don't see how he could spring somebody accused of attemptin' to murder one of his own agents."

"Trust me, Danny-boy, it's a done deal." Fitzpatrick spoke with none of his usual bluster, which was worrying in itself. He obviously had complete confidence that Charlotte would shortly be in his custody, which meant Dan had to work on the assumption that Charlotte was, for all intents and purposes, already in the General's grasp.

"We've wasted enough time discussing your wife," Fitzpatrick said. "I have her, and if you want her, I need to see some cooperation from you. Let's get back to the important discussion we started a few minutes ago. Where's the Elf's disk, Dan? The one with all the real information about the Kennedy Space Center security provisions."

"In a safe place not far from here."

"What does that mean? Ten minutes away? Two hours?"

"Closer than that." Dan reached into his pocket and pulled out the disk he'd already shown to Fitzpatrick earlier. "This is the disk the Elf gave me—"

Fitzpatrick swore long and hard. "We've already had this fucking stupid conversation once tonight. I'm goddamn losing patience, O'Toole."

"You didn't let me finish what I was saying. All the information is right here, on this disk. I can restore those blocks of missing data whenever I choose—"

"How?"

"By insertin' the disk into my own laptop and typin' in a certain code at the same time as the computer performs a retinal scan." Dan looked straight at Fitzpatrick. "Trust me, General, like I'm trustin' you when you say you have Charlotte, although you've given me no shred of proof beyond your own words. There's absolutely no way to access this data without my agreement. You're only going to see this information when I choose to show you."

Fitzpatrick was silent for a while. "Here's what

we're going to do," he said finally. "We're going to
drive in my car to Flamingo Key, where a colleague
of mine keeps his boat docked. Charlotte will already
be there, waiting for our arrival, along with Sean and
Ryan. You'll restore the missing data, and I'll give
you your woman. The two of you can have free run
of the boat from now until the third. You can lock
yourselves in the master cabin and fuck your brains
out, for all I care."

"Sounds encitin'," Dan said, his voice deceptively
quiet. "And then what will happen to Charlotte?"

"My colleague will sail the boat down to Key West
when you and the other boys leave for Cape Canaveral. He'll go from there to Jamaica. You can meet
up with Charlotte in Kingston when you've completed our mission. It's where you planned to go, anyway, so that should suit you fine. And if she's accused
of shooting an FBI agent, she should be delighted to
leave the country."

It sounded almost too good to be true, but Fitzpatrick might be making a sincere offer, Dan reflected.
The General had serious leadership issues with
O'Toole, but at bottom he had no reason to doubt
O'Toole's willingness to blow up the Space Center.
Fitzpatrick had ordered Charlotte's kidnapping because he wanted to be sure Dan understood who was
in charge of the Armargh Army. He hadn't kidnapped
her because he suspected Dan would try to sabotage
the mission without the added inducement of a hostage wife. Such a thought hadn't crossed the General's mind, Dan was a hundred percent sure. If Fitzpatrick had suspected him of true disloyalty to the
cause, he'd be dead.

"Just so long as your *colleague* remembers to keep his hands off of my wife while he's sailin' his yacht in the Gulf of Mexico and I'm crawlin' on my belly through the goddamn swamps with pieces of a radiation bomb strapped to my back."

"I'll tell him," Fitzpatrick said mildly. "We're in agreement, then?"

"Not so fast, General. You're forgettin', aren't you, that there's still the little matter of the bomb. I'm not willin' to be shown the bomb a few hours before I have to lead my men on the most dangerous and important mission of their lives. I need to be sure that I understand every last detail of how it's put together. My men and I need to assemble and disassemble it at least three times. We're comin' in underwater, and I have to decide who's goin' to carry what part, and precisely how it's going to be packaged. I need to know exactly how the bomb looks, how it feels, and what precautions I have to take if I don't want my testicles crawlin' with cancerous tumors six months from now. I need to be given access to that bomb within the next twelve hours, or I'm tellin' you, our mission can't be accomplished by the Fourth."

Fitzpatrick stared straight ahead, his fingers drumming on the steering column. The man was so bitter and so prejudiced that he could no longer be called intelligent or clever, but he was cunning. He was also an officer who'd been trained well by the U.S. army. He'd planned military operations and he knew Dan was right. This wasn't a mission where they could pack explosives into the back of a truck, crash into a big building and—at the cheap cost of the driver's life—create another Oklahoma City. This was a high tech operation where everything had to be practiced and tested, or they were likely to arrive at the Vehicle Assembly Building and not be able to reconstruct the bomb in the limited time available to them.

"I guess you're in luck, O'Toole." Fitzpatrick finally broke the lengthening silence. "I agree you need access to the bomb, and it so happens that your woman and the bomb are in the same place."

Dan's heart skipped a beat. From the point of view of national security, this was the best news he'd heard in the past five months. From the point of view of Charlotte's safety, the news was terrifying. "That's very convenient," he said. "I'll look forward to examining the bomb after I've had some sleep."

Fitzpatrick laughed, a note of anticipation in his voice, as if his decision to finally reveal the location of the bomb brought home the exciting imminence of their attack on the Space Center. "After you've shown me the full data from the Elf, you mean."

"That, too," Dan said. He paused, then added as if it were an afterthought, "I want to drive my own car to Flamingo Key."

Fitzpatrick's lingering smile turned to a frown. "No. You're driving with me. I want to keep an eye on you until I've seen every last bit of data on that goddamn disk.

Dan shook his head. "Doesn't make sense, General. We don't want anyone to notice my car sitting in the parking lot here for the next few days. Besides, I'll need it to drive to my final meeting with the Elf."

"I didn't know you had another meeting scheduled. Why do you need to see him again?" Fitzpatrick's voice was sharp.

"Because I need to make sure he hasn't done anything fuckin' crazy like phoning the media. Because he's under stress and I need to calm him down. Because I have to be absolutely one hundred percent sure that he knows what he has to do. We can't get into the restricted area of the Vehicle Assembly Building where I plan to locate the bomb without him. They have sophisticated retinal scanning equipment that operates in combination with a voice recognition program and a new password every day, so that you can't hold up a dead eyeball and gain access, despite what they show you in the movies." It wasn't true that the password changed every day, but Dan had to come up with some iron-clad excuse for not having killed the Elf.

"Ah. So that's why you needed him alive."

"Yeah, that's why."

"I guess you do need your own car, then." Fitzpatrick gave the address of the boat dock and added a few directions on how to reach it. "The boat is called the *Dream of Ireland*. I'll see you at the dockside. Don't try to board until I get there. My colleague is a high-strung kind of a guy. If he sees you trying to get on board, he's likely to shoot first and ask questions afterwards."

"I'll keep that in mind," Dan said dryly. "See you at the boat dock, General."

Twenty

John was lying, Charlotte thought with sudden conviction. His expression was perfectly calibrated to express a mixture of desire, uncertainty, and longing, but she didn't sense any trace of those emotions coming from him. He was no more in love with her than she was with him. She would bet her life on it.

Then why the hell was he pretending to be in love with her? Maybe he'd discovered that declaring his love was an easy way to get women into bed and she shouldn't look for any more profound explanation. The hours she'd spent with Dan were making her paranoid, causing her to assume that every unexpected event was somehow tied back to the Armargh Army. Maybe she should quit looking for complex explanations where a basic one would do.

"I didn't realize how you felt," she said, leaning forward as if she wanted to be closer to him. Presumably the best way to find out what he wanted was to pretend to feel the same way.

"I'm really attracted to you." She hoped her voice didn't sound as flat as she felt. "But we'd only just met.... We only had two dates...."

"It took me about twenty seconds after we met to decide I wanted to take you to bed." John smiled, confident that his charm would erase the brashness of his remark. "After that, it took about another two hours to realize that I wanted something much more from you than a quick tumble in the sack."

He was very good, Charlotte thought, alarmed to discover that her own newborn capacity to lie seemed to be shriveling in the face of his deceit. She tried for a casual smile, rattling her chains to emphasize her point. "This is a crazy time and place to be discussing our feelings for each other."

"We can soon fix that." John reached into the back of the car, swiveling around so that he could take her hands. He lifted them up and kissed her knuckles. She stiffened, the reaction involuntary, and he looked at her questioningly.

Charlotte smiled weakly. "The cuffs have made my wrists sore," she said, with perfect honesty.

He insinuated his fingers between the handcuffs and her wrists, rubbing the chafed flesh. She winced. If he intended to ease the discomfort, he definitely wasn't succeeding.

"Did that hurt?" he asked, and murmured an apology when she nodded.

She was definitely paranoid, Charlotte decided. Why else did she have this squirmy feeling that he'd taken pleasure in hurting her?

"I have a key onboard that should unlock these darn things," he said, giving a final tug on the handcuffs. "Let's get onto the boat and I can soon make you more comfortable." He took the keys from the ignition, and got out of the car. "Here, hang on to my arm." He put his hand under her elbow and helped her out of the back seat, all friendly consideration.

All fake, all the time.

Charlotte was suddenly furious with herself for having been so quiescent for so long. Fatigue and bewilderment were pathetic excuses for having reacted so passively to John's dominating behavior. She wished there were some brilliant way to leap into the driver's seat and make off with the car, leaving John stranded on the quayside. Unfortunately she could barely hobble across the uneven paving of the quayside to the boat slip, much less dodge around him, filch the car keys from his pants pocket, and make a daring escape.

Arm solicitously around her waist, John propelled her toward the ramp leading to a yacht of impressive size with a fiberglass hull that gleamed fluorescent white in the moonlight. The boat had to be more than fifty feet long, Charlotte calculated, and definitely powerful enough to be ocean-going. Growing up in Iowa, boating had never been her thing, but a year in Florida was more than long enough for her to be quite sure that nothing this big and sleek could be bought for much less than half a million. Where in the world did John get the money to buy a boat this fancy? Unless he'd inherited family money, of course, which he might easily have done for all she knew to the contrary.

The idea of getting onto the boat with him began to seem more ominous the closer they got to the ramp, but at this hour of the night, the dock was deserted so she had no hope of outside rescue and, shackled as she was, no way of escaping by means of her own ingenuity. Trying frantically to think of some way to avoid going on board, she won a few extra seconds' respite by exclaiming over the wonders of his boat.

"My boss has a fifty-five-foot Sunseeker that looks a lot like this one," she said, pausing on the dockside, as if lost in admiration of its beauty. "He always claims that it's the biggest pleasure in his life, and the biggest aggravation as well."

"I know exactly what he means." John smiled. "You must have heard the old joke. What's the second happiest day of a deep sea fisherman's life? The day he buys his own boat. What's the happiest day of a deep sea fisherman's life? The day he sells his own boat."

She laughed, scanning the dock one final time in desperate hope of seeing someone—anyone—who might offer a hope of rescue. "How did you choose the name?" she asked. "The *Dream of Ireland*. I thought your family background was Italian, like mine."

"It is," he said. "I just never got around to changing the name of the boat after I bought it. I kind of like it, anyway. It's unusual in amongst all the corny choices people seem to make."

A perfectly logical explanation, Charlotte supposed, except that the hairs on the back of her neck were pricking.

John smiled at her, extending his hand. "Come on. I'll help you up the step onto the ramp."

She took his hand because she could see no way to refuse, although she felt like a medieval prisoner lighting the bonfire that was going to burn her to death. Looking back over everything that had happened since she arrived at FBI headquarters in Tampa Bay, she recognized that it wasn't only John's declaration of love that was carefully calculated. Hindsight, that amazing aid to clear vision, enabled her to see that every action he'd taken had been designed to get her out of the FBI offices without attracting any attention, or doing anything that would cause her to protest what amounted to his virtual kidnapping of her from under the very noses of law enforcement.

He'd kidnapped her. Charlotte froze midway across the gangplank, unwilling to cooperate a moment longer in her own doom. Just because John had been kind and solicitous and sworn that he was helping her didn't change the facts. John had kidnapped her, and now he was forcing her onto an ocean-going yacht. She recalled thinking while the police drove her to Tampa that at least when she was in the custody of the FBI, the Armargh Army couldn't kidnap her. No, they couldn't. But apparently John had been just as anxious to get her away from the official protection of the FBI's Tampa offices as the terrorists. Why?

Her exhausted brain provided no answer. She only knew that she would be crazy to go onto the boat with him. He could zoom down the coast, heading toward the islands of the Caribbean, and toss her overboard the moment he found a nice empty stretch of ocean. He might eventually be caught, she supposed, although that was slim consolation. Even if he spent the rest of his life in prison, that would hardly make her feel better when the sharks were munching on her for their dinner.

Escape seemed like a better idea by the moment, but the dockside was still deserted and she was still

chained. If she jumped into the water she'd either
drown, or be fished out by John. If she screamed,
she'd betray the fact that she didn't trust him. Screaming would be worth attempting if there was a reasonable chance of rescue. It would be a very bad move
if there wasn't.

"What's the matter, honey?" John paused, and
turned around to see why she wasn't following.

"I lost my balance," she said quickly. "These stupid ankle bracelets make it really difficult to walk up
a ramp."

"I'll help you onto the boat," John said, with a
reassurance that struck her as so false she wondered
how she hadn't picked up on it long before they left
the FBI offices. He jumped onto the deck of the yacht
and held out his hands. "Come on, honey."

She heard the sound of an approaching car with a
relief that escalated to euphoria when she realized the
car was slowing and stopping almost opposite John's
boat. She rejected John's outstretched hands and tot-
tered back down the ramp as fast as she could, lurch-
ing terrifyingly from side to side. She ignored John's
shouted demand for her to return.

"Help!" she called, as two men got out of the car.
She held up her manacled wrists. "Help, I'm being
kidnapped!"

She made it onto the quayside before John caught
up with her. "That wasn't a smart decision, Charlotte." He grabbed her around the waist and neck
with a force so punishing it made her realize how
reluctant Dan had been to hurt her when he took her
from the Down Under club.

"Help!" she screamed again, although not very

loudly, because John's arm was pressing hard against her windpipe. He'd dragged her around facing the boat again, so she was unable to see what the two new arrivals were doing, but she at least hoped they'd call the police, even if they didn't want to risk intervening personally.

"Hel—" Her scream was cut off by a hand clamped over her mouth. John still had her grasped around the waist and neck, so it couldn't be his hand.

"Jesus, she has a fine pair of lungs on her. Why didn't you tape her mouth shut hours ago?" The speaker had an Irish accent thick enough to cut with a knife.

"Because I wanted to convince her to trust me. Because I wanted to hear what she had to say for herself about the events of last night, since the pair of you fucked up and let her get away." John sounded seriously pissed and coldly furious. "Carry her onto the boat before she wakes up the entire fucking neighborhood."

"At this hour of night, there's nobody to wake up." Another Irish voice made the comment as he slapped a piece of duct tape over Charlotte's mouth.

If she wasn't mistaken, she was listening to two of the voices she'd last heard discussing meat pies and boinking on the FBI tapes. She could probably conclude that she'd made a seriously bad decision when she called for help, Charlotte thought despairingly.

John marched ahead, leaving the two newcomers to carry her up the gangplank. They didn't bother to be gentle, and when they arrived at the boat, they simply tossed her over the side. She landed on the deck with a crash that was hard enough to wind her and tear flesh from her elbow. She thought she might have lost consciousness, but it couldn't have been for longer than a moment or two, because the second man was just clambering on board when she came to.

Wasting no time in abandoning his pretense of being in love, John hauled her to her feet, unlocked the entryway, and dragged her into the main cabin, flicking on a light switch to reveal a saloon with polished wooden floors and built-in, leather-cushioned seating that curved around a drop-leaf center table. Behind one section of seating, two elegantly-paneled doors stood half open, revealing sleeping quarters, one with a queen-sized bed, the other with tiered bunks. A galley, equipped with gleaming, scaled-down appliances, was divided from the main saloon only by a bar, fitted with glasses, clamped into place with fancy chrome holders.

She was making an inventory of her surroundings in an effort to control her panic, Charlotte realized, but that was probably better than giving way to hysteria. She didn't resist when John pushed her onto the section of seating that formed the bend of the U. She wished she could pretend that there was even a glimmer of hope that she might escape at some point, but if there was a way for her to get rid of her shackles and overcome three men—two of whom were visibly armed—she sure as hell couldn't think what that might be.

"I'm Sean. This is Ryan," one of the men said to John. "The General told us you'd be here with the woman, but he didn't tell us your name."

John hesitated for a moment. "Since this is my boat, I guess you can call me Captain," he said.

If her mouth hadn't been taped shut, Charlotte would have been delighted to inform Sean and Ryan that the "Captain" was in reality a double-dealing piece of slime called John Hanseck. As it was, she could only seethe in silent impotence, although she probably wouldn't have been able to sow dissension among the conspirators even if she'd been able to speak. She assumed Sean and Ryan already knew the Armargh Army had inside help from an FBI agent, even if they didn't know John's name.

Now that it was way too late to be wise, it was painfully clear to her that Hanseck must be the mole inside the Bureau who was sabotaging the Armargh Army investigation. Yeah, she was a woman with razor-sharp intelligence and superb powers of judging character, all right. She only needed to be chained, kidnapped, brutalized, and imprisoned and she realized she was dealing with a trio of bad guys. What insight! What fabulous powers of deduction!

How the hell had she been stupid enough not to realize that any car stopping right opposite John's boat was likely to contain people with no interest in rescuing her?

"There's beer in the fridge," John said to the two men. "Help yourself."

"Thanks, but we don't drink when we're on the job," Ryan said primly. He turned to his companion. "I'll wait for the General on deck. How about you?"

"I'm going to make some tea, if I can find any. You know what O'Toole's like. He always wants a mug of strong tea in his hands when he's going over plans for a mission."

For a second or two, Charlotte was almost grateful

for the tape across her mouth that prevented her from speaking. In all the time she'd spent with Dan, she'd never known him to drink tea, which he cordially disliked. Presumably the original Daniel O'Toole had been a tea drinker, as most Irish people were, and her husband had been forced to carry on the habit of the man he was impersonating.

Of all the sacrifices her husband had been required to make, the minor penance of regularly drinking something he didn't enjoy brought home to Charlotte just how close to unbearable Dan's life must have been for the past eighteen months. She felt tears form at the corner of her eyes, and blinked them away. She didn't have time for sentiment. If Dan really was scheduled to arrive here some time soon, it was the best news she'd heard in the past several hours and she needed to work out what it meant. God forbid that when he arrived she said or did the wrong thing.

John leaned over her, jerking her head up so that he was staring straight into her eyes. "I hope you're feeling in the mood to put out, sugar, because you're being provided as O'Toole's reward for good behavior."

Charlotte let her gaze lock with John's. Then she closed her eyes and slowly turned her head sideways, the only method available to her to show her contempt.

Twenty-One

Fitzpatrick's eyes were boring into Dan's back, watching to make sure that he went straight to his car. Dan disciplined himself not to run as he crossed the hospital parking lot, although he was itching to fling himself behind the wheel of his Taurus and floor the accelerator. The primitive urge to rush to Charlotte's rescue gnawed at his gut, all the more powerful because it was heavily tinged with guilt. He'd left her alone, dammit. Alone, unprotected and vulnerable— and now her life was being held hostage to his actions. Dan fought against a consuming anger that he knew would achieve nothing except to cloud his judgment.

He managed to hold his stride to a moderate pace, but his mind was racing, calculating distances and weighing options. It was barely ninety miles from here to downtown Tampa, plus another ten miles north to Flamingo Key. The GPS system in his car would pinpoint the exact distance and give him various alternate directions to Flamingo Key, while the engine modifications to his nondescript-looking car would provide him with enough power and handling stability to sustain speeds of over a hundred miles an hour on the highway. Still, he had city traffic and city streets to navigate going through Orlando and again approaching Flamingo Key. Speed killers both.

If everything broke his way, it was still going to be difficult to gain much time on Fitzpatrick. Dan had state-of-the-art radar detection equipment so he could risk driving at high speed when he was on the interstate, especially since the road would be relatively free of traffic at this hour of the night. As a bonus, the General's cumbersome SUV was designed to deliver hauling power, not speed. Even so, there was no reason why Fitzpatrick couldn't average sixty miles an hour over the entire journey.

Driving flat-out, with no traffic cops forcing him to slow down, Dan might gain, at best, a twenty minute window to access the *Dream of Ireland,* search the boat, and find the bomb. Always assuming Fitzpatrick was telling the truth and the bomb truly was on board. And even that tiny window would only be his if Charlotte wasn't already on the boat, guarded by Sean, Ryan and whichever FBI agent Fitzpatrick had in his pocket.

Hang in there, Charlie, babe. Dan allowed himself fifteen seconds of intense longing, then blacked out all thoughts of his wife. He clicked open the door to the Taurus, shutting down his emotions and locking them away where they could offer no distractions. As always when he was under the intense pressure of an active mission, his brain worked at an accelerated pace, analyzing what he needed to do and assessing risks while his body switched to automatic pilot as it went through the necessary motions to complete the physical aspects of his task.

He drove the Taurus out of the parking lot, making

no effort to lose Fitzpatrick. Traffic was much too sparse to make such a maneuver appear accidental. With luck, he might be able to get away at a stoplight, but Dan was resigned to waiting for the interstate where he would be able to weave in and out of a few giant trucks and break away without being too obvious about it.

A cop cruiser turned out of a strip mall and cut in front of Dan's car. He used the enforced slow place to program his GPS system, and to key in a request for a printout of a detailed map of Flamingo Key. He'd driven barely three blocks, one eye on the cop, the other studying the computer screen, when a glance into his rearview mirror showed him that Fitzpatrick was turning off the road into a twenty-four-hour gas station and pulling up at the pump to refuel. At almost the same moment, the cop turned right into another strip mall.

Dan felt a flash of profound gratitude, then accepted his good fortune with the same controlled calm that he'd have expended for an unexpected setback. The SUV had a monster gas tank, and he figured that losing the cop at the same time as the General stopped to refuel had gained him at least another five minutes. And those were five minutes he could really use. He cruised to the end of the street, rounded the corner, and raced like hell for the interstate.

He covered the seventy-eight miles to the outskirts of Tampa in forty-eight minutes. He reached Flamingo Key seventeen minutes later. Counting the time before he shook Fitzpatrick from his tail, one hour and eighteen minutes had elapsed since he'd gotten out of the General's SUV in the hospital parking lot. Three minutes faster than his most optimistic calculation. He estimated that, barring something totally unexpected, he was now thirty-minutes ahead of Fitzpatrick.

Dan slowed to a crawl as he passed the small marina where the *Dream of Ireland* was docked. The area was well-lit and he discovered that he could pick the boat out from its neighbors without actually turning onto the causeway. He confirmed what he had anticipated: that there was nowhere to park on the dockside without his car being visible to Fitzpatrick and anyone else who happened to drive up.

Even though he'd identified the boat, at this distance there was no way to know if anyone was already on board. The *Dream of Ireland* was dark, as were all its neighbors, but Dan wasn't reckless enough to believe that the absence of visible lighting guaranteed that the boat was empty.

He accelerated again, driving past the marina and following the shore road for half a mile before coming to a halt at a second promontory of land that served as a docking bay for another twenty boats or so. The coastline of Flamingo Key curved at this point in a natural semicircle, which meant that although by road the two marinas were separated by half a mile and three sprawling developments of beachfront condos, for a boat—or a swimmer in the water—the tips of each promontory were barely a hundred yards apart.

About one and a half minutes of swim time for Dan.

He parked his car in a space designed to accommodate visitors to the condos, adding his vehicle to the two already there. The landscaped surrounds of the complex were brightly lit, which meant that he might be noticed if he attempted to change his clothes inside the car. However, the parking space was screened on one side by a clump of tall, dense ole-ander bushes that would provide adequate cover for his activities. Dan spared a moment of gratitude for the landscape architect who had allowed aesthetics to win out over security concerns. Wedged between the stucco perimeter fence and the bushes, he could make his preparations with little risk of being observed by any insomniacs or night security patrols.

The plan for blowing up the Vehicle Assembly Building required that the bomb squad should ap-proach the Kennedy Space Center by sea. Along with his men, Dan had spent hundreds of hours since he arrived in Florida perfecting his scuba-diving skills. He had a complete wet suit stored in the trunk of his car, as well as air tanks, filled and ready to go. At this time of year, the waters of the Gulf of Mexico hovered around eighty-two degrees Farenheit, and they would be even warmer this close to shore, so he wouldn't need the wet suit, but the air tanks and spe-cially designed face masks were going to come in useful.

He heard a car cruise by on the other side of the stucco fence, but nobody came out onto the road, so he risked ignoring the sounds, guessing they'd been made by a security patrol making its regular rounds. Dan disliked guesswork, but he didn't have time to take as many precautions as he would normally con-sider essential.

In less than two minutes, he'd removed his shirt, chinos and leather belt and put on a body-hugging black swimsuit with a micromesh vest. He stowed his street clothes in the trunk before strapping on the air tanks and buckling his Glock into a waterproof pouch at his waist. He donned the vinyl headgear, designed to decrease the likelihood of being spotted in the waters around Cape Canaveral—pale skin tended to gleam in the moonlight—and added a set of lock picks and a high-intensity, slender flashlight to the pouch where he'd packed his gun. He decided against taking flippers, since the distance he needed to swim was short and the cumbersome flippers would seriously impede his mobility on land.

Shutting the trunk with a muted thud, Dan made one final sweeping check of his surroundings to make sure there were no unexpected bystanders or security guards in the vicinity before crossing the road to the narrow strip of beach. He stood at the edge of the lapping water to take off his sneakers, then zipped the shoes into another waterproof pouch designed to fit on his back, directly beneath the tanks. Carrying shoes was a nuisance, but marinas tended to be landscaped with scrimshaw, and walking barefoot on pathways made out of crushed shells would create the far greater hazard of badly cut feet.

Twenty-three minutes remained before he could expect the General to arrive.

Dan waded into the water, his mouthpiece and goggles already in place. He didn't even have to cope with the complications of nighttime underwater navigation since he could swim close to the surface until he was within a dozen feet of the *Dream of Ireland.*

The beach fell off abruptly when he was only six feet from the shore. The waters of the Gulf closed around him, welcoming him into their silky embrace. He swam silently, as he'd practiced for weeks, without creating any wake, gliding just beneath the surface of the water and diving deeper only when the hull was a body-length away.

He checked the entire perimeter of the boat underwater, detecting no hint of anyone on board. He surfaced at the prow, ready to dive at the first hint of trouble, but nothing disturbed the nighttime tranquility. Both the dockside and the *Dream of Ireland* still appeared deserted.

Dan inched along the side farthest away from the dock until he came to the first porthole. Even if the shutters on the inside of the portholes were all closed, he would be able to see at least a peripheral glow if any interior lights were in use.

He saw only darkness, unrelieved and opaque. He pressed his ear against the keel, above the water line, listening not just for voices, but for any vibration that would suggest people moving about inside the boat. He heard the slap of water against the hull, and the whisper of his own breathing, but no other sounds.

He didn't have time to debate the odds any longer. Unless it was a very well-planned trap, the boat was empty. Sean and Ryan hadn't arrived, and Charlotte was still en route with her kidnapper.

Dan pulled himself onto the deck in a single, swift motion, and immediately took off his air tanks before they could pool water on the deck. He was sacrificing speed if he needed to make a quick getaway, but gaining agility as he moved around the boat. Tanks disposed of, he stood stock still, only his eyes moving as he raked the boat in search of any hint of somebody moving. Nothing. He rubbed the soles of his feet on a rolled-up deck awning in order to avoid leaving a trail of damp prints. There wouldn't be time for the wet patches to dry out before the others arrived, a dead giveaway that the boat had been boarded.

He walked across the deck, his bare feet soundless, and halted in front of the locked door that led to the cabin. He not only had to get the lock unfastened in the shortest time possible, he had to do it without damaging the tumblers. The lock needed to be functional, so that he could shut the door after him when he left.

Eighteen minutes before he could expect the General to arrive.

Having acknowledged the time pressure, Dan let it go. With his back to the quayside so that his body shielded the light from any passing vehicles, he held the flashlight between his teeth, directed at the lock.

Three minutes and forty-five seconds later, the door was open. Dan stepped inside and latched the door behind him.

Fourteen minutes left.

He moved forward, gun in his right hand, flashlight in his left, with the flashlight pointed toward the ground, where its narrow beam would be invisible from the outside.

The yacht's living quarters were compact enough that he could stand in the main living area and scope out the entire interior. Galley. Two staterooms. Two heads. Both bathrooms were tiny, and neither had any windows, so he could switch on the overhead lighting to search. It took him only one minute per head to determine that neither room contained anything ex-

cept a shower, a toilet, a sink, and a mirrored medi-
cine cabinet stocked with toilet articles. There wasn't
even a cupboard for towels, which hung from racks
attached to the back of each door.

Eleven minutes to go.

The smaller state room had two sets of bunk beds
screwed and bracketed into the walls, providing sleeping accommodation for four in a claustrophobically
tight space. There was no closet, only a chest with
four drawers. Presumably guests were warned to pack
light, because apart from the chest of drawers, there
was nowhere to store their belongings except in their
beds.

At least it made for easy searching.

The galley was equally compact, and jam-packed
with utensils, dishes, and groceries, mostly canned
goods. The tiny fridge held beer and white wine, but
no fresh food. The drawer to the left of the two-burner
electric stove held cutlery. The drawer to the right of
the stove held a Smith & Wesson revolver. Dan
opened the chamber and took out the bullets. You
never knew when it might come in handy for your
opponents to discover they'd fired an empty gun.

Only seven minutes left.

Dan ignored the fact that he was starting to sweat
and crossed the salon into the master stateroom.
Queen-size bed covered with a neat, navy-blue
spread. Two small nightstands with drawers. Drawers
built into the underside of the bed contained blankets,
spare pillows and striped blue and white sheets with
embroidered anchors decorating the hem. Masculine
underwear in the left-hand nightstand. Condoms and

a fancy Smith & Wesson .357 magnum in the right. Dan removed the bullet clip and left the condoms.

This room was large enough to boast a small closet, which contained an assortment of slacks, shirts, sweaters, and zippered waterproof jackets in various weights. And on the top shelf, in plain sight, was a small hard-sided suitcase, of the sort that used to be advertised with a gorilla dancing on top of it to demonstrate its superior strength.

Five minutes.

His hands were shaking as he lifted the suitcase down from the shelf, keeping it rigidly horizontal. The suitcase was certainly heavy enough to contain a bomb, but not heavy enough to be lead-shielded. Obviously the radioactive material hadn't been set in place yet, or it wouldn't be stashed in a clothes closet. The absence of radiological material didn't bother him too much, since he already had a pretty good idea where the General planned to get it.

Dan scrutinized the suitcase locks, which included a combination dial currently set to triple zero. Even if he'd had hours of time at his disposal, no way would he have attempted to open the case. If the locks weren't booby-trapped, then the General was a fool as well as a fanatic.

Three minutes.

Definitely time to get the hell out of here. Dan placed the suitcase on the bed and shut the closet doors. Another minute was consumed putting on his sneakers and tying the laces.

If he hadn't found the bomb, he'd have been able to dive back into the water and make an easy escape. As it was, he had no choice but to walk out onto the deck and strap on his air tanks again, making sure that the door's self-locking mechanism worked when he closed it behind him.

Still no sign of the General's SUV. Dan walked down the ramp, aware that it was in the final moments when victory seems certain that plenty of battles were lost. He stepped out onto the quay, turned right and walked farther down the causeway, putting a safe distance of two boats between him and the *Dream of Ireland.*

He'd just made it on board the third boat down, and was lying flat on the deck in the shadow of the canopy, when a car turned onto the causeway and drew to a halt on the patch of scrimshaw directly opposite the *Dream of Ireland.*

Dan waited, so still that even a close observer might have believed him to be dead.

A man got out of the car. He recognized John Hanseck with almost no shock of surprise. He'd suspected John Hanseck of being the FBI mole ever since he rescued Charlotte from the Down Under club. Sean and Ryan had known in advance that she was going to be there. It had always seemed likely, therefore, that the man escorting her would have been responsible for setting her up and making sure that she was in the right place at the right time.

He was watching the FBI mole at work.

Twenty-Two

Sean was still waiting for the kettle to boil so that he could brew some tea, and John Hanseck was brooding over a beer, when Charlotte heard the sounds of a newcomer arriving on board.

"Put out the damn cigarette, Ryan," a man's voice said. "Filthy habit. I thought you'd given it up."

"Yes, sir. I have given it up, mostly. Except now and again when I'm under stress."

"You have no reason to be stressed. Everything's under control. The mission is going to be a grand success."

"Yes, sir."

"Come on inside. That way you won't be tempted to smoke again. You don't want to ruin your lungs when you have lots of swimming ahead of you."

The door opened with a bang and Sean shot out of the galley. Even John rose to his feet as a man in his fifties, slightly above average height and with a stocky build, strode into the saloon, trailed by Ryan. The newcomer's gaze scanned the room, his presence undeniably commanding.

"Where's O'Toole? Not here yet?" His questions held no overtones beyond a simple desire for information.

John Hanseck stepped forward. "He hasn't arrived yet, Br—" A glare from the newcomer stopped him in midword and midstep. "Er...good to see you, General," he finished.

"And you, my boy." The General's gaze settled on Charlotte. "I take it this is O'Toole's wife. Why is she trussed up like a Thanksgiving turkey?"

"She was handcuffed by the Daytona police," John explained. "She wasn't very cooperative, so I decided it would be better to keep the restraints on her."

"Bad decision." The General shook his head. "You're lucky I got here before O'Toole. What are you trying to do? Completely piss him off?"

"No." John's voice was stiff. "I'm merely trying to prevent her causing us unnecessary problems. She's not exactly docile, you know."

The General raised an eyebrow. "Hmm...let me see. We're four highly-trained military men and she's one woman. Rather a slender woman, at that. Sean and Ryan are both carrying guns. Exactly what sort of problem are you expecting her to create?"

"She tried to escape when we were on the dockside." John sounded sulky. "If a passer-by had heard her screaming, we'd have been in big trouble...."

"I'm sure she's learned her lesson. She realizes now that if she tries to leave this cabin, she's going to be shot." The General directed a kindly smile toward Charlotte, as if he'd just promised her a treat, instead of threatening to kill her.

"You're going to be sensible and not cause any more problems for us, aren't you, my dear? I'm sure you're looking forward to seeing your husband again

after so many months of separation. You wouldn't
want to do anything that might jeopardize that, would
you?''

His words confirmed Charlotte's suspicion that nobody on the boat had any clue that she and Dan had
spent the last twenty-four hours together, and she certainly wasn't going to correct their misapprehension.
It cost her, but she managed to respond to the General's threats with a meek nod of her head.

''Very good.'' The General delivered an avuncular
pat on her arm, looking and sounding like a genial
host at a party. With the exercise of a lot of will-
power, Charlotte managed not to cringe away from
his touch.

''Give me the keys for the cuffs, John, and let's
get the little lady some wriggle room.''

''I suggested that Sean and Ryan should call me
the Captain,'' John said pointedly.

''Whatever.'' The General seemed a lot less anxious about preserving John's anonymity than he was
about his own. He took the key that John, with a
barely disguised smirk directed at his captive, retrieved from his hip pocket, and gave Charlotte another friendly smile.

''We've never met in person, my dear, but I've
heard a lot about you. Your husband is my very good
friend and lieutenant. My right-hand man, in fact.''

There were reasons to be grateful for the tape covering her mouth, Charlotte decided. It prevented her
from speaking before she considered her words. She
looked up at the General, trying to mold her expression into something between scared and pleading,
which is what she thought he would like to see. One

valuable lesson she'd learned from her escape attempt on the dockside was not to attempt resistance until you had at least a better-than-even chance of winning.

In the interests of being free to speak and move around the cabin when Dan finally arrived—if he arrived?—Charlotte was prepared to put up with a lot. She didn't flinch when the General bent much too close under the pretext of unlocking her restraints. He took what seemed an excessively long time, with a lot of groping, then extended his hand to help her stand up when the cuffs and ankle bracelets were at last unlocked.

"Much better," he said, as the chains clinked onto the floor. "Ryan, see if there's some baby oil in one of the bathroom cabinets, will you? We need to get this tape off the young lady's mouth."

The young lady, with considerable effort, refrained from rewarding him with a sock in the jaw, and made a show of rubbing her ankles and wrists instead.

The General went into the galley and took a beer from the fridge. "What's the situation at your office?" he asked John, sitting down and stretching his arm along the upholstered back of the banquette.

"Everything's under control," John said, as Sean plugged in the kettle again, and Ryan set about the task of loosening the duct tape on Charlotte's mouth.

The General tugged at his lower lip. "How long before your colleagues realize that Charlotte's gone missing, do you think?"

"I'd say we have at least until eight. That's when the clerical workers start to arrive."

"What about your partner? I take it that she's been successfully neutralized?"

"I doped her can of soda," John said. "Popped the top and dropped in a couple of Roofies. She's out for the count."

"There's no danger that a guard will find her?"

John shook his head. "She's in the shower stall of a bathroom attached to an office that's rarely used. It'll be another four or five hours at least before she wakes up, and nobody's going to find her."

"But she'll be able to identify you as the person who doped her, won't she?"

"Probably, depending on how much she remembers. Roofies can wipe out quite a lot."

"Even so, I'd say your career as an FBI agent is definitely over, my boy. You might be able to blame somebody else for your partner's situation, but you can't explain away the fact that you whipped Charlotte away, right from under their noses."

"It doesn't matter." John shrugged. "The Bureau was only a means to an end, and you don't need me there anymore. They have to catch me if they want to prosecute, and I'll be out of the country way before the morons in headquarters take their heads out of their asses long enough to realize they need to find me."

"You've done well." The General saluted him with the beer bottle. "Your grandmother would be proud of you."

"Thanks, but I'm holding off on my celebrations until we pull everything off on the Fourth. I'll only be completely happy when I turn on the TV and see the newsreaders' faces when they report that the bomb has gone off."

"And that they've received a warning that similar

radiological bombs will go off on a regular schedule until they negotiate a new deal for the suffering people of Northern Ireland,'' the General murmured.

Charlotte managed to turn her snort of disgust into a cry of pain, which was entirely genuine as Ryan gave up on the baby oil and ripped the tape from her mouth.

"Sorry," he muttered.

"That's okay." Her voice was husky from the pressure of the tape, which had the fortunate effect of making her sound suitably humble. She massaged her sore lips and accepted Sean's offer of a cup of tea, asking him to dilute it with plenty of boiling water.

The General glanced at his watch. "Where's O'Toole?" This time there was a note or urgency in his voice. "I got here fifteen minutes ago. What's keeping him? Where the hell is he?"

"Maybe he got lost," John suggested. "This marina is tricky to find."

Sean and Ryan both laughed. "O'Toole doesn't get lost," Sean said, as if the suggestion were completely ridiculous.

"Listen," Ryan said. "Isn't that a car comin' right now?"

"Open the door," the General said.

Sean opened the door and stuck his head out. "It's O'Toole's car," he reported. "Yep, here he comes."

At almost the same moment, Charlotte heard the sound of feet scrunching over scrimshaw and then boarding the boat.

"I've got your cuppa waitin'," Sean said, as O'Toole bent down to step through the doorway.

"That's my man," Dan said, giving Sean a friendly

thump on the shoulder. He walked into the saloon, a briefcase in his left hand. "Ryan, how are you this fine night?" He nodded toward the General. "Sorry I'm a bit late, but I was starvin' hungry and stopped for a bite to eat."

His gaze swept over John Hanseck and came to rest on Charlotte. His mouth twisted into an impudent, sexy grin. "Well, now, my sweet. As I live and breathe, aren't you just a sight for sore eyes?" He set his briefcase on the table and walked toward her, sweeping her into his arms and giving her a passionate kiss.

He smelled of the salt and the sea, Charlotte thought. She allowed herself a few seconds of reassuring contact, blotting out the memory of the General's groping hands, before she pulled herself away. Glaring at him, she swung her arm back and slapped his face.

"Who are you?" she demanded. "What the hell do you think you're doing? Get your hands off me!"

Dan laughed, and she saw a gleam of approval in his eyes, directed just at her. "What? And you didn't recognize me the moment your lips touched mine? You're breakin' my heart, Charlie. Can't you see beyond a little bit of plastic surgery?"

"Stop trying to trick me! You don't look or sound anything like Dan." God knew, that was the truth. She turned to John Hanseck. "If this man is really Daniel O'Toole, then there's been a terrible mistake. I swear to you he isn't the man I knew as Riordan Gray."

"Well now, darlin', you don't want to be committin' perjury, do you?" Dan tipped up her chin and spoke softly, as if fully prepared to seduce her in front of the four other men. "If seein' isn't believin', Charlie, I'll just have to take you into that nice bedroom right behind us and find another way to convince you of my identity."

"Later, O'Toole." The General got up, chuckling. "Entertaining as it is to watch your reunion with your loving wife, I need to remind you that we have business to discuss before you can move on to enjoying the pleasures of her company. I've kept my part of the bargain. She's here, and as you can see she's not been harmed in any way. Now it's time for you to fulfill your part of our agreement."

"I'm more than ready to do business, General. But first I need an introduction to the stranger in our midst." Dan positioned himself in front of John Hanseck.

"This is my cousin and colleague," the General said, startling Charlotte, if nobody else. Hanseck and the General were *cousins?*

"He served in the military with me years ago," the General continued. "He's been a great deal of help in making sure that the FBI investigations into the activities of the Armargh Army never actually got anywhere dangerous. He was especially helpful after Padraig was arrested. He made sure that the FBI decided to plant bugs instead of moving in to arrest you and the members of your team. And then, of course, he had to make sure that the bugs didn't work properly."

"It's a pleasure to meet you," Dan said, shaking Hanseck's hand with every appearance of goodwill. "Do you have a name I can use?"

"You can call me Captain, since this is my boat," Hanseck said.

"My men and I are grateful for your help, Captain. You've proved yourself a true friend of Ireland."

John Hanseck merely nodded before turning away to finish his final swig of beer. He's jealous of Dan's charisma, Charlotte realized. He hates the way that Dan—and even the General—dominate the room while he just seems to fade into the woodwork.

Dan leaned forward and unzipped the briefcase on the coffee table, revealing a sleek charcoal gray laptop. He opened the lid and started the booting-up process.

"Okay, I'm all set, and I have the Elf's disk safe in my pocket." He drew it out to prove his point, then tucked it away again. "In fact, I'm rarin' to go, General. Show me our bomb, and I'll be happy to key in the commands that will demonstrate to everyone here exactly how we're goin' to be able to access our target. I can promise you all that the Elf may be more than a bit crazy, but he's given us some very fine directions."

Charlotte watched the General and John Hanseck exchange glances. The fact that this discussion was taking place in front of her suggested that Dan had huge bargaining powers with the General. Or, more likely, that the General and Hanseck didn't care what she heard because they had every intention of killing her sometime very soon. Of those two options, she had a gloomy suspicion that killing her was the way they would choose to go.

"Get the bomb," the General said to Hanseck, with

sudden decisiveness. "It's time for O'Toole and the men to see exactly what it is they're dealing with."

Sean and Ryan came and stood next to Dan, their bodies tense, their expressions eager as their gazes followed Hanseck's passage into the main stateroom. From where she was standing, Charlotte could see him open the doors to the room's only closet.

Immediately the doors were open, he stepped back, his fists clenching. He stood stock still for a moment, staring into the closet. Then he gave a strangled cry and rushed forward, frantically sweeping shirts and shorts and socks off the shelves, letting them drop unheeded on the floor.

"What is it?" The General followed him into the stateroom. "What's the problem, John? For Christ's sake, what are you doing?"

"It's not here! The bomb is gone!"

The General turned visibly paler. "Nonsense. It can't be gone. What are you talking about?"

Hanseck grabbed an armful of slacks and jackets that had been hanging up, and flung them onto the bed. Nothing was left in the closet but a rackful of shoes. "Now do you believe me?" he yelled. "There's nothing in here. The bomb has disappeared! It's been stolen."

The General, for once, appeared to be speechless.

Dan followed the General into the stateroom. "You must think I'm a blitherin' idiot, General. You don't expect me to believe this piece of playactin', do you?"

"It's not an act," the General said. "I fully intended to show you and your men the bomb." He turned to his "cousin and colleague" with an expression of bitter fury. "Goddammit, John, all you had to do was take care of the bomb for a week. Was that too much to ask? Where the hell is it?"

"I don't know." John sat down on the bed, indifferent to the piles of clothing that surrounded him.

"There's no way we can get all the replacement parts we need to rebuild that bomb by the Fourth," the General said. "My God, this is a disaster."

"For me and my men it's worse than a disaster," Dan said coldly. "I've had six men intensively training for three months. During that time, I've personally developed and cultivated the Elf to the point that he's trusted me with complete directions on how to access the Kennedy Space Center. I've made arrangements for renting the boat that's supposed to drop us offshore and pick us up again after the bomb has been infiltrated into the Vehicle Assembly Building. I've organized documentation to get me and my men out of Orlando Airport and on planes to South America, en route home to Ireland."

He swung around, grabbing Hanseck by the throat, lifting him bodily off the bed. "All you had to do was provide me with a bomb, and you've fucked up. Give me a reason—any reason—why I shouldn't kill you."

The General spoke quickly. "Let's be reasonable, O'Toole. Let's talk about this. As you can plainly see, John here is as upset as you are—"

"I can guarantee he isn't as upset as I am." Dan released his grip around John's neck and flung him back onto the bed. John leaned up against the headboard, gasping for air.

"I'm not a bomb-maker," Dan said to the General,

his back turned toward John, deliberately ignoring the man's labored breathing. "You are. That's supposed to be your field of expertise. Why can't you get busy and make us another bomb? We still have five days."

"It's not possible," the General said. He rubbed his hand across his eyes. "Give me a minute. Let me think what some of our alternatives might be."

"I think one of the alternatives you need to consider is that your fine cousin with the FBI has been sellin' us out, General. You can't just lose a bomb unless that's what you planned to do all along."

"I've known him since he was a boy. I can't believe he'd betray me—"

"Either he removed the bomb, General, or you did. Or you're in this together—"

"Liar, liar, *liar!*" Hanseck yelled from the bed. "You have the bomb, O'Toole! You stole it. You!"

Sean suddenly yelled out. "Watch your back, Dan! He has a gun!"

Charlotte screamed, a reflex reaction that she couldn't control. Dan ducked and dodged to the side, but Hanseck was already squeezing the trigger. He squeezed again, and again, and again, before giving a howl of fury and throwing the gun onto the floor.

"The bullets are gone! There aren't any bullets in my gun!" Hanseck stared at his useless weapon as if it had turned into an alien creature with poisoned fangs. Then he jumped up from the bed, so angry and frustrated that he was literally hopping with rage. He rushed toward Dan, arms outstretched and hands curved into claws, but Sean and Ryan got there first. They dragged Hanseck out into the saloon where they proceeded to beat him into unconsciousness with quiet, brutal efficiency.

Charlotte knew that Hanseck would have killed Dan in a heartbeat if his gun had functioned. Not to mention the fact that he'd been willing to explode a dirty bomb in the center of Florida. Still, she had to turn away so that she wouldn't be forced to watch what Ryan and Sean were doing. Just listening to Hanseck's moans and the repeated dull, soft thumps of fists hitting into flesh was almost more than she could stomach. A horrible reminder that Hanseck, Sean and Ryan were all three men for whom violence was always the answer.

"Don't kill him." The General came out of the stateroom into the saloon.

"Why not?" Sean gave Hanseck's limp body a scornful kick. Hanseck didn't so much as whimper, and Charlotte wondered sickly if he were already dead.

"You and your fine cousin between you have ruined Ireland's best hope of freedom," Sean said. "Losin' the bloody bomb! I can't believe it."

"I *won't* believe it," Ryan said. He confronted the General, his previous deference entirely gone. "Let's try this one more time. Do you have a bomb to give us in time for our mission on the Fourth?"

Reluctantly, the General shook his head. "No."

"That's it, then," Ryan said. "Seems to me there are two choices here. Either you never had a bomb and you've been stringin' us along. Or you had a bomb and you've lost it. Doesn't make much difference to me which one of those two is the truth. Either you're a bunglin' fool, or you're a traitor. However you look at it, you've betrayed us, and betrayed our cause.''

The General stared at his accusers, drawing himself up with unexpected dignity. ''Go ahead, shoot me and make O'Toole your leader. You've always preferred him over me, anyway. But I'll die knowing that I dedicated my life to our sacred cause. My innocent blood will be on your hands.''

''Very dramatic, General, but you have a lot more explaining to do before I can allow you to die.'' Dan moved with deceptive casualness, interposing himself between the General and Sean and Ryan, who both had their weapons drawn and cocked. Because of the way Dan had positioned himself, only Charlotte, who was standing off to the side, saw the swift, covert movement with which he plunged a needle into the General's midriff, slipping the empty syringe back into the pocket of his chinos.

The drug was almost instantaneous in its action. The General gasped as the needle went in, then tried to speak, but within seconds his eyes began to roll upward, and he clutched his throat, struggling for air. If Charlotte hadn't already observed John Hanseck exhibit similar symptoms on the Down Under dance floor, she'd certainly have believed the General was having a heart attack.

''Mother of God! What's the matter with him?'' Sean demanded.

''Looks like he's having a heart attack,'' Dan said laconically, his arm around the General's waist, preventing him crashing to the floor. ''He must have frightened himself damn near to death.''

''Move aside, boss,'' Ryan said, pointing his gun.

"I'll put a bullet in him. Put the stupid bugger out of his misery."

"No need," Dan said, hauling the General into the stateroom. Away from Sean and Ryan's itchy trigger fingers, Charlotte didn't doubt.

"I have a better plan," he said, returning to the saloon. "We don't want to leave behind dead bodies with bullets in 'em for the police to investigate. Bullets mean murder, and our prints must be all over the boat. We'd be identified in no time and there's no need to have half the cops in Florida chasing after us with murder warrants. We have enough warrants out against us already."

"We can't leave the General alive," Sean protested. "Nor his cousin, either. They know too much about us." He glanced back to where Hanseck's body lay on the saloon floor. "And I sure as breathin' don't want that measly excuse for a human bein' to survive long enough to rat on us."

"I said there wouldn't be any bodies," Dan murmured. "I didn't say the General and his cousin wouldn't die."

"Then how are you plannin' to off 'em so's the police don't realize it's murder?" Ryan demanded.

Dan smiled. "Have you forgotten we're on a boat? A bloody great ocean-going yacht, in fact. We can take the bodies out to sea and dump them in the middle of the Gulf of Mexico where they'll never be found." He flapped his hand up and down in a mocking wave. "Good-bye, General and Captain. Hello, sharks—enjoy your dinner."

Sean and Ryan both laughed, delighted with Dan's ingenuity. Charlotte could practically see a new layer of luster being added to O'Toole's legend before her eyes.

"That's brilliant," Ryan said. "We'd better set sail right away. I'll uncouple the moorings. It's going to be light in another couple of hours and we don't want anyone to see us dumping the bodies."

"There's no need for all of us to go cruisin'," Dan said. "I'll take care of these two lyin' bags of shit, and then I'll head for the airport. You should leave right now, and get a head start on your getaway. You have your passports and your tickets, right?"

Sean, who didn't appear to be encumbered with an excess of brainpower, rubbed his forehead. "The tickets are dated for the Fourth," he said.

"You can change them at the airport," Dan said. "Go back to your motel, warn the other members of our team what's happened, then pack up and make for the airport. All of you. You two can fly out to Buenos Aires, and the others to Rio de Janeiro and Caracas, just like we always planned. But leave Florida as soon as you possibly can. There's no point in any of us hanging around here now that the General and his sidekick have buggered up our mission. I'll meet you in Belfast, on the first of September, and we'll start working on our next operation. And you can be sure that we'll come up with a blueprint for the mission that doesn't depend on outsiders for delivery of the bomb."

As a final shot, Dan looked over his shoulder to where the General lay on the bed and gave a scornful snort. "Bloody Americans."

"What about the Elf?" Ryan asked. "Don't we need to take care of him before we leave?"

"Nothin' to take care of," Dan said. He walked into the kitchen and poured himself another mug of tea. "The Elf has no way to trace me, and he's never so much as heard the name of the Armargh Army, much less your names. The Feds could arrest him tomorrow and there's not a damn thing he could give up that would hurt us." He gave a bitter smile. "*My* part of the operation was taken care of properly."

"What about her?" Sean asked, jerking his head toward Charlotte. Ryan nudged him and he amended his question. "What about your wife?"

"She's comin' with me," Dan said smoothly. "I already organized the paperwork."

"But her picture's been all over the telly," Sean protested. "Takin' her with you to South America increases the risks for you. And that means increased risk for us as well."

Dan laughed, and put his arm around Sean's shoulders. "You're talkin' to the master of disguises here. Do you think I can't show Charlotte how to change her appearance so as her own mother would pass her on the street and not know her?"

"I guess so." Sean cast another unfriendly glance in Charlotte's direction. "Makes me nervous that she's seen our faces and knows our names."

"She's my wife," Dan said, his voice hardening. "I think you can rely on me to take care of her. Besides, once I take this boat out and dump the bodies, there's been no crime and nobody's goin' to be on the lookout for us. You've got no worries."

"Except that the Space Center hasn't been blown up," Ryan said glumly.

"We'll turn that around soon," Dan said, giving

him a friendly punch with his empty mug. "I'm thinkin' we could do a lot of good for our cause if we planted a nice bomb in the middle of the Channel Tunnel. And I've already got a good idea how we could do it, too."

Ryan and Sean looked cheered by this new prospect of massive destruction. "See you in Belfast at the usual place, then," Ryan said, saluting Dan by touching his gun to his forehead. "September 1."

"Seven o'clock," Sean confirmed. "We'll have breakfast. With proper Irish sausages."

"I'm already tastin' them," Dan said. "Now go. I need to be takin' this boat out for a little spin."

He left with the two men, and Charlotte occupied herself putting a pillow under Hanseck's head and covering him with a blanket. His pulse was thready, but it was there, although she worried about internal bleeding. She really wanted him to survive long enough to stand trial and spend the next fifty years in a very uncomfortable prison.

"Sean and Ryan have gone back to their motel," Dan said, returning to the saloon. "And without a suspicion in the world that they've been conned."

"Are you going to call the police to pick them up?"

He took her into his arms, holding her head against his chest and gently stroking her hair. "I'll call a little later, when they've had time to warn the other members of my cell. I want them all taken into custody at the airport, so that they never suspect me of betraying them. Otherwise my future is likely to be short, and my end unpleasant."

She looked up at him, light-headed with a mixture

388   *Jasmine Cresswell*

of relief and foreboding. "Aren't they likely to suspect you, anyway?"

Dan shook his head. "I don't believe so. I can arrange it so that they're picked up on charges of using
fake passports. They should attribute that to nothing
more than sheer bad luck. The final disaster in a
doomed mission."

"We need an ambulance for Hanseck," she said.
"And maybe for the General, too?"

"Not yet. We still have some work to do. Stay
here, and I'll be right back."

Dan returned carrying a small suitcase that he held
balanced horizontally. "What's that?" Charlotte
asked, although she had a horrifying suspicion that
she knew the answer.

"It's the General's bomb," Dan said, grinning. He
walked into the stateroom. "I'm going to put it back
in the closet where it belongs."

Charlotte followed him, wide-eyed. "You were the
person who stole it? You knew all along where it
was? How in the world did you make that happen?"

"Long story. I'll tell you later when we have more
time. Here, help me press the General's hands onto
the side of the case. I want to make sure he leaves a
fingerprint or two on the surface."

Charlotte picked up the General's limp hand and
pressed his fingers against the sides. "Isn't your word
enough to convict him?"

"Possibly. But let's not take any chances. The
General is really Brian Fitzpatrick, the CEO of a corporation that manufacturers equipment for irradiating
foodstuffs. Which is how he had access to radioactive
material, by the way, and a place to store the materia

until he was ready to put it inside the bomb. He's contributed a ton of money to both major political parties and he has a lot of friends in high places. I need to be sure there's no room for him to plead not guilty and hire a lawyer clever enough to sow seeds of reasonable doubt.''

Dan eased the bomb back onto the shelf and started to hang the scattered clothes in the closet. Charlotte followed suit, folding shirts and returning them to the shelves.

"Why are we doing this?" she asked.

"Because when the Feds present their case in court, I don't want the defense suggesting that the bomb was ever missing from its hiding place. Sean and Ryan will never talk, so I can claim the argument that caused Hanseck to get beaten up was about anything that sounds believable other than the absence of the bomb.''

Dan shut the doors on the now-tidy closet. "Fitzpatrick and Hanseck are both really rotten human beings, Charlie. Sometimes you have to take your convictions any way you can get 'em.''

Reaction was beginning to set in for Charlotte. The knowledge that the dirty bomb intended to blow up the Kennedy Space Center was lying on a shelf only a couple of feet from her head made her legs wobble at the knees. She couldn't bear the idea of sitting on the bed near Fitzpatrick, so she walked hurriedly into the saloon, and collapsed on the section of seating farthest away from Hanseck's limp body.

"What are we going to do now?" she asked. She was so exhausted that it was an effort to ask the question, let alone think of a sensible answer.

Dan smiled as he drew her gently to her feet and pointed her toward the main cabin door. "We're going to get the hell out of here and then call the cops. I think an anonymous tip that there are two injured men and a bomb on board the *Dream of Ireland* should get a couple of squad cars out here pretty fast."

"That should work," Charlotte acknowledged. "Then what are we going to do?"

He bent down and kissed her softly on the lips. "Then we're going home," he said.

As far as she knew, Dan had been living in motels for weeks now. "Where is your home these days?" she asked.

He smiled, and kissed her again. "Wherever you are," he said.

Epilogue

Christmas 2003

At 10:30 p.m., two days after Christmas, Charlotte and her husband, Elliott Danforth Hargreaves IV, arrived back in their brand-new villa in Tampa Bay, after flying home to Florida from her parents' house in West Des Moines. They'd celebrated the holiday with a somewhat subdued crowd of Leone relatives, who were still more than a little wary of Dan's reappearance in their midst.

Charlotte's three older brothers had all been at her parents' home, along with her sisters-in-law and a cluster of young nieces and nephews. Miscellaneous cousins, part of the sprawling Leone clan, had dropped in to check out the returning Prodigal Son, and to sample Eleanor Leone's famous cookies. As with many family holidays, what remained unspoken was probably more important than anything that was actually said.

Months earlier, Tremayne Washington had paid a personal visit to Charlotte's parents to explain Dan's disappearance. Dan, he said, had been an undercover narcotics agent and he'd spent those missing eighteen months on a highly dangerous assignment in Central

America. Washington assured the worried Leones that Dan had now retired, and there was no danger of him ever being recalled to active duty.

Charlotte was resigned to the fact that it was going to take a few years before her parents would fully trust her husband, but she was willing to wait. In the meantime, she and Dan were rebuilding their lives in Florida, away from the pressure cooker of her family's expectations. Dan had started a new chain of coffee shops, using the hazardous-duty bonus paid to him by the FBI as start-up capital, and Charlotte had just been made a junior partner in Scott & Stravinsky, a reward for submitting the winning design for the new Tampa Bay hospital extension.

Despite the fact that she and Dan now lived in Tampa, their holiday celebrations in Des Moines had followed the family's traditional pattern. The two of them had overdosed on eggnog, played with her nephew Billy's cool new construction set, and threatened to murder the cousin who had given preschool Emma a bongo drum with attached cymbals.

Her parents tactfully made no mention of the fact that Dan had arrived in Des Moines only on Christmas Eve, having been detained, so he claimed, by a protracted negotiation with a Costa Rican coffee grower. In reality, he had been delivering secret testimony at ex-Major Brian Fitzpatrick's trial in Washington, D.C., and he brought to Charlotte the welcome news that a conviction had been won and a sentence of life imprisonment imposed. The Elf, otherwise known as Maurice Breton, Ph.D., had shot himself when the police came to arrest him. John Hansec had plea-bargained himself down to a mere twenty years in prison in exchange for testifying against his cousin and former commanding officer, Brian Fitzpatrick. Sean and Ryan, along with the four other men actively involved in the plot to blow up the Kennedy Space Center, were isolated from each other in various federal prisons, after having been arrested at Orlando airport as they tried to make their escape.

Shirley Nicholson, having been found in a bathroom off a rarely-used office at Tampa headquarters, unconscious but alive, had finally recovered somewhat from the shock of being betrayed by her own partner. She had recently accepted a transfer to FBI headquarters, where she was relieved to have a job at the academy training new recruits, since the idea of active fieldwork still left her a little queasy. And Tremayne Washington, unrepentant for having dragged Dan back into covert activity, and indifferent to the fact that he'd inflicted eighteen months of torment on Charlotte, had just received a commendation from the president for his work in destroying the operational effectiveness of the Armargh Army.

It bothered Charlotte that Tremayne Washington hadn't suffered at all for betraying Dan's identity to the Irish terrorists. But Dan had pointed out that their payoff for eighteen months of misery was the knowledge that they had almost certainly prevented the detonation of a dirty bomb in the heart of the Kennedy Space Center. All in all, Charlotte thought, an acceptable reward. But only because everything had turned out okay. For a month after his return, she suffered from health-destroying insomnia, worrying about what would have happened if Dan had been killed. Eventually Dan managed to convince her that there were some might-have-beens that it just wasn't smart to dwell on. And now, after five months of re-building their lives, she felt almost secure again.

At ten-thirty-three—it took them only a couple of minutes to race upstairs and tear each other's clothes off—Charlotte and Dan tumbled on top of their new, king-size bed and made passionate love. Then, for good measure, they started over more slowly and made love again. They had been remarried in a quiet ceremony in early August, and they were both still hungry for each other's bodies. Even so, their love-making on this special night seemed extraordinary to Charlotte in its tenderness and intensity.

Afterwards, she would always claim that their son had been conceived that wonderful first night in their new Tampa Bay home.

Shortly after midnight, Dan remembered that gar-bage pick-up was scheduled for the early hours of the next morning. He leaned over, tickled Charlotte under the chin, and suggested that maybe he ought to take care of it.

She sat up in bed, glaring at him. "Don't even think of it," she said.

Dan laughed, and snuggled up against her, his arms warm and strong. "Okay," he agreed. "No big deal. We'll let it go until next week."

Helen R. Myers

No Sanctuary

Where do you go when there's no place to hide?

Metal sculptor Bay Butler spent six years in a Texas prison for a crime she did not commit—until the efforts of a powerful client get her conviction overturned. Suddenly Bay is free, but she is still plagued with questions. Why was she imprisoned based on circumstantial evidence? And what really happened the night her business partner was found brutally murdered in their studio?

Her quest for the truth brings her face-to-face with Jack Burke, the cop who arrested her for the murder. Bay Butler's case has haunted him for six years—and so has the woman herself. Together they embark on a trail of deadly secrets that threaten the foundation of a small Texas town...a town where power and money have exacted a price in blood.

Available the first week of May 2003, wherever paperbacks are sold!

MIRA®

ROMANTIC SUSPENSE

JASMINE CRESSWELL

66931	THE THIRD WIFE	___ $6.50 U.S.	___ $7.99 CAN.
66838	THE CONSPIRACY	___ $6.50 U.S.	___ $7.99 CAN.
66608	THE REFUGE	___ $6.50 U.S.	___ $7.99 CAN.
66511	THE INHERITANCE	___ $5.99 U.S.	___ $6.99 CAN.
66486	THE DISAPPEARANCE	___ $5.99 U.S.	___ $6.99 CAN.
66425	THE DAUGHTER	___ $5.99 U.S.	___ $6.99 CAN.
66261	SECRET SINS	___ $5.99 U.S.	___ $6.99 CAN.
66154	CHARADES	___ $5.50 U.S.	___ $6.50 CAN.
66147	NO SIN TOO GREAT	___ $5.99 U.S.	___ $6.99 CAN.

(limited quantities available)

TOTAL AMOUNT $_____
POSTAGE & HANDLING $_____
($1.00 for one book; 50¢ for each additional)
APPLICABLE TAXES* $_____
<u>TOTAL PAYABLE</u> $_____
(check or money order—please do not send cash)

To order, complete this form and send it, along with a check or money order for the total above, payable to MIRA® Books to: **In the U.S.:** 3010 Walden Avenue, P.O. Box 9077, Buffalo NY 14269-9077; **In Canada:** P.O. Box 636, Fort Erie, Ontario L2A 5X3.

Name:_____
Address:_____ City:_____
State/Prov.:_____ Zip/Postal Code:_____
Account Number (if applicable):_____
075 CSAS

*New York residents remit applicable sales taxes.
Canadian residents remit applicable
GST and provincial taxes.

MIRA

Visit us at www.mirabooks.com   MJC0503B